TRANZLATY

Language is for everyone

اللغة للجميع

Folk Tales of Bengal

حكايات شعبية من البنغال

Part One
الجزء الأول

1 / 2

Lal Behari Day

English / العربية

Life's Secret
سر الحياة

Once upon a time there was a king.

ذات مرة كان هناك ملك.

This King had married two Queens.

كان هذا الملك متزوجا من ملكتين.

The two queens were called Duo and Suo.

وكان اسم الملكتين ديو وسو.

Both of the queens were childless.

وكانت كلتا الملكتين بلا أطفال.

One day a Faquir came to the palace gate.

في أحد الأيام جاء فقير إلى بوابة القصر.

The Faquir had come to ask for alms.

لقد جاء الفقير ليطلب الصدقات.

Queen Suo went to the door.

ذهبت الملكة سوو إلى الباب.

And she gave him a handful of rice.

وأعطته حفنة من الأرز.

The mendicant asked her a question.

سألها المتسول سؤالا.

"Do you have any children?"

هل لديك أطفال؟

The queen had no children.

ولم يكن للملكة أطفال.

"I wish had children, but I have none"

أتمنى أن يكون لدي أطفال، ولكن ليس لدي أي أطفال

The holy man refused to take alms from her.

رفض الرجل المقدس أن يأخذ منها الصدقات.

In these times there were different traditions.

وفي تلك الأوقات كانت هناك تقاليد مختلفة.

And the people believed many different things.

وكان الناس يعتقدون أشياء كثيرة مختلفة.

Don't take charity from the hands of a childless woman.

لا تأخذ الصدقة من يد امرأة ليس لها ولد.

Such hands were ceremonially unclean.

وكانت هذه الأيدي نجسة من الناحية الطقسية.

The mendicant offered her a drug.

عرض عليها المتسول دواء.

This drug was to remove her barrenness.

وكان هذا الدواء لإزالة عقمها.

She expressed her willingness to take the drug.

أعربت عن استعدادها لتناول الدواء.

The mendicant told her how to take the drug.

أخبرها المتسول كيف تتناول الدواء.

"This is the potion you must swallow"

هذه هي الجرعة التي يجب أن تبتلعها

"Prepare the juice of a pomegranate flower"

تحضير عصير زهرة الرمان

"Swallow the drug with the juice"

ابتلع الدواء مع العصير

"If you do this, you will soon have a son"

إذا فعلت هذا، فسوف يكون لديك ابنًا قريبًا

"Your son will be exceedingly handsome"

ابنك سيكون وسيمًا جدًا

"His complexion will be beautiful"

سوف يكون وجهه جميلا

"He will have the colour of pomegranate flowers"

سيكون لونه مثل لون زهرة الرمان

"And you shall call him Dalim Kumar"

وتسميه داليم كومار

"But he will also have enemies"

ولكن سيكون له أعداء أيضًا

"They will try to take your son's life"

سيحاولون أن يأخذوا حياة ابنك

"But there is a secret to his life"

ولكن هناك سر في حياته

"And I will tell you this secret"

وسأخبرك بهذا السر

"In front of your palace is a pond"

أمام قصرك بركة

"In that pond there is a big Boal fish"

في تلك البركة يوجد سمكة بوال كبيرة

"Your son's life is connected to that fish"

حياة ابنك مرتبطة بهذه السمكة

"In the heart of the fish is a small box"

في قلب السمكة صندوق صغير

"This small box is made of wood"

هذا الصندوق الصغير مصنوع من الخشب

"In the box of wood is a necklace of gold"

في صندوق الخشب يوجد عقد من الذهب

"That necklace is the life of your son"

هذه القلادة هي حياة ابنك

The mendicant gave her the drugs.

لقد أعطاها المتسول المخدرات.

And they said their farewells.

وقالوا وداعا.

Soon all in the palace whispered of an heir.

وبعد قليل همس الجميع في القصر عن وريث.

Great was the joy of the King.

وكان فرح الملك عظيما.

He had visions of an heir to the throne.

لقد كانت لديه رؤى حول وريث العرش.

A never-ending succession of powerful monarchs.

سلسلة لا تنتهي من الملوك الأقوياء.

He dreamt of how they perpetuated his dynasty.

كان يحلم بكيفية استمرار سلالته.

These ideas floated before his mind.

كانت هذه الأفكار تطفو أمام ذهنه.

It made him the happiest he had ever been.

لقد جعله أسعد من أي وقت مضى.

Many ceremonies were performed for the occasion.

وقد أقيمت العديد من الاحتفالات بهذه المناسبة.

The people of the kingdom played loud music.

كان شعب المملكة يعزف الموسيقى بصوت عالٍ.

The birth of a prince was a truly special event.

لقد كان ميلاد الأمير حدثًا مميزًا حقًا.

Soon queen Suo gave birth to a son.

وبعد قليل أنجبت الملكة سوو ابنًا.

He was more beautiful than anyone had imagined.

لقد كان أكثر جمالا مما كان يتصوره أي شخص.

The King saw his son's face.

ورأى الملك وجه ابنه.

And his heart leaped with joy.

وقفز قلبه فرحا.

Soon the child ate his first rice.

وبعد قليل أكل الطفل أرزته الأولى.

Mukhe bhaat was celebrated with great joy.

تم الاحتفال بموكي بهات بفرح عظيم.

And the whole kingdom was filled with gladness.

وامتلأت المملكة كلها فرحاً.

Dalim Kumar grew up to be a fine boy.

لقد نشأ داليم كومار ليصبح صبيًا رائعًا.

There was one activity he particularly liked.

كان هناك نشاط واحد أحبه بشكل خاص.

He loved playing with the pigeons.

كان يحب اللعب مع الحمام.

However, the pigeons often flew to Queen Duo.

ومع ذلك، فإن الحمام كان يطير في كثير من الأحيان إلى الملكة ديو.

Nobody knows why they did this.

لا أحد يعرف لماذا فعلوا هذا.

And they flew into her apartment.

وطاروا إلى شقتها.

So Dalim Kumar often met Queen Duo.

لذلك التقى دليم كومار في كثير من الأحيان بالملكة ديو.

At first, she happily gave the pigeons back.

في البداية، أعادت الحمام بكل سرور.

But later she wasn't as willing to return the pigeons.

لكنها في وقت لاحق لم تعد راغبة في إرجاع الحمام.

She gave the pigeons up with some reluctance.

لقد تخلت عن الحمام مع بعض التردد.

She felt she could use this to her advantage.

شعرت أنها يمكن أن تستخدم هذا لصالحها۔

She naturally hated the child.

لقد كرهت الطفل بطبيعة الحال۔

Since Dalim's birth the king had neglected her.

منذ ولادة داليم، أهملها الملك۔

And the King idolized the mother of Dalim.

وكان الملك يعبد أم داليم۔

Somehow, she had heard of the mendicant.

بطريقة ما، كانت قد سمعت عن المتسول۔

She heard he had given queen Suo a medicine.

سمعت أنه أعطى الملكة سو دواء۔

She had also heard about what he had said.

لقد سمعت أيضًا عما قاله۔

There was a secret to the prince's life.

كان هناك سر في حياة الأمير۔

She had heard his life was bound to something.

لقد سمعت أن حياته مرتبطة بشيء ما۔

But she did not know what his life was bound to.

لكنها لم تكن تعلم ما هي علاقته بحياته۔

She was determined to get the secret.

لقد كانت مصممة على الحصول على السر۔

Of course, the pigeons came back to her.

وبطبيعة الحال، عادت الحمام إليها۔

And the pigeons flew into her room again.

وعادت الحمامة إلى غرفتها مرة أخرى۔

This time she refused to give the pigeons back.

هذه المرة رفضت إرجاع الحمام۔

"I won't just give you your pigeon back"

لن أعيد لك حمامتك فحسب

"First, you have to tell me something"

أولا، عليك أن تخبرني بشيء

"What do you want, aunty?" the boy asked.

ماذا تريدين يا عمتي؟ سأل الصبي۔

"Oh, my darling, do not worry"

يا حبيبتي لا تقلقي

"It's just a small thing I want"

إنه مجرد شيء صغير أريده

"I want to know where your life is hidden"

أريد أن أعرف أين تختبئ حياتك

The boy was very confused by this.

لقد كان الصبي مرتبكًا جدًا بسبب هذا.

"What is that, aunty?"

ما هذا يا عمتي؟

"Where can my life be, except in me?"

أين يمكن أن تكون حياتي إلا فيّ؟

"No, child, that is not what I meant"

لا يا صغيرتي، هذا ليس ما قصدته

"A holy mendicant told your mother a secret"

قال متسول مقدس لوالدتك سرًّا

"Your life is bound up with something"

حياتك مرتبطة بشيء ما

"I wish to know what that thing is"

أريد أن أعرف ما هو هذا الشيء

The boy was confused by what she said.

لقد ارتبك الصبي بسبب ما قالته.

"I never heard of any such thing"

لم أسمع بمثل هذا الشيء من قبل

But Queen Duo insisted it was true.

لكن الملكة ديو أصرت على أن هذا صحيح.

"Promise to find out from your mother"

أعدك أن أعرف ذلك من والدتك

"Ask her where your life is hidden"

اسألها أين تختبئ حياتك

"Then I will let you have the pigeons"

ثم سأسمح لك بالحصول على الحمام

"Otherwise, I will keep the pigeons"

وإلا سأحتفظ بالحمام

The boy wanted his pigeons back.

أراد الصبي استعادة حمامه.

So he agreed to get the information.

فوافق على الحصول على المعلومات.

But first she made him promise.

لكنها في البداية جعلته يعدها.

"Promise me you won't tell your mother"

أوعدني أنك لن تخبر والدتك

And the boy promised not to tell her.

ووعدها الصبي بأنه لن يخبرها.

"I promise I won't tell my mum"

أعدك أنني لن أخبر أمي

Queen Duo freed the prince's pigeons.

حررت الملكة ديو حمام الأمير.

Dalim was overjoyed to have his birds again.

كان داليم سعيدًا جدًا بحصوله على طيوره مرة أخرى.

And he forgot the entire conversation.

ونسي المحادثة بأكملها.

The next day Dalim was playing again.

وفي اليوم التالي كان داليم يلعب مرة أخرى.

You can imagine what happened again.

يمكنك أن تتخيل ما حدث مرة أخرى.

The pigeons flew to Queen Duo's apartment.

طارت الحمامة إلى شقة الملكة ديو.

And they flew into her room again.

وطاروا إلى غرفتها مرة أخرى.

Dalim went in to his stepmother's apartment.

ذهب داليم إلى شقة زوجة أبيه.

And he asked her for the pigeons.

وطلب منها الحمام.

Of course she asked him for the information.

بالطبع سألته عن المعلومات.

Dalim could not tell her where his life was hidden.

لم يتمكن داليم من إخبارها أين كانت حياته مخفية.

"I promise I will ask her today"

أعدك بأنني سأسألها اليوم

"But please can I have my pigeons"

لكن من فضلك هل يمكنني الحصول على حمامي؟

She didn't give the pigeons back so quickly.

ولم تعيد الحمام بسرعة.

But, in the end, he got his pigeons again.

ولكن في النهاية، حصل على حمامه مرة أخرى.

After playing, Dalim went to his mother.

بعد اللعب ذهب داليم إلى أمه.

"Mamma, please tell me where my life is hidden"

ماما، من فضلك أخبريني أين حياتي مخفية

"What do you mean, child?" asked the mother.

ماذا تقصد يا طفلي؟ سألت الأم.

She was astonished at the question.

لقد دهشت من السؤال.

Why would her child ask her this?

لماذا يسألها طفلها هذا السؤال؟

"Yes, mamma," replied the child.

نعم يا أمي أجاب الطفل.

"I have heard of a holy mendicant"

لقد سمعت عن متسول مقدس

"He told you something about my life"

لقد أخبرك شيئًا عن حياتي

"He said my life is hidden in something"

قال إن حياتي مخفية في شيء ما

"Tell me what that thing is"

أخبرني ما هو هذا الشيء

"My child, my darling, my treasure"

طفلي، حبيبتي، كنزي

"My golden moon," his mother pleaded.

قمري الذهبي توسلت أمه.

"Do not ask such a question"

لا تسأل مثل هذا السؤال

"Cover my enemies' mouths with ashes"

غطِّ أفواه أعدائي بالرماد

"Let my Dalim live forever," she begged.

دع داليم الخاص بي يعيش إلى الأبد، توسلت.

But the child insisted knowing the secret.

لكن الطفل أصر على معرفة السر.

He refused to eat or drink until he knew.

رفض أن يأكل أو يشرب حتى علم.

Queen Suo had no choice but to tell him.

ولم يكن أمام الملكة سو خيار سوى أن تخبره.

Eventually she told him the secret of his life.

وأخيراً أخبرته بسر حياته.

The next day Dalim was playing again.

وفي اليوم التالي كان داليم يلعب مرة أخرى.

You can imagine where the pigeons flew.

يمكنك أن تتخيل أين طار الحمام.

Dalim chased after the birds into the apartment.

طارد داليم الطيور إلى داخل الشقة.

His stepmother told him many sweet words.

قالت له زوجة أبيه الكثير من الكلمات الحلوة.

And finally, she got his secret from him.

وأخيراً حصلت على سره منه.

She wasted no time to start her wicked plan.

ولم تضيع أي وقت لبدء خطتها الشريرة.

And she gave orders to her servants.

وأصدرت أوامرها إلى عبيدها.

"Get some dried stalk from the hemp plant"

احصل على بعض السيقان المجففة من نبات القنب

"Make sure the stalks are very brittle"

تأكد من أن السيقان هشة للغاية

Brittle hemp stalks make a cracking sound.

سيقان القنب الهشة تصدر صوت طقطقة.

The sound is similar to the cracking of joints.

الصوت يشبه صوت طقطقة المفاصل.

And it sounds like the bones of old people.

ويبدو مثل عظام كبار السن.

She put the brittle hemp stalks under her bed.

وضعت سيقان القنب الهشة تحت سريرها.

And then she lied on her bed.

ثم استلقت على سريرها.

She wanted to test the hemp stalks.

أرادت اختبار سيقان القنب.

The stalks cracked just as much as she wanted.

تشققت السيقان تمامًا كما أرادت.

She was satisfied with how her plan was going.

لقد كانت راضية عن كيفية سير خطتها.

She gave more orders to her servants.

وأعطت المزيد من الأوامر لخدمها.

"Tell the King I am very ill"

أخبر الملك أنني مريض جدًا

"He must come to see me immediately"

يجب أن يأتي لرؤيتي على الفور

The king did not love this queen.

ولم يحب الملك هذه الملكة.

But he still had a duty to care for her.

لكن ما زال لديه واجب رعايتها.

If she was ill, he had to look after her.

إذا كانت مريضة، كان عليه أن يعتني بها.

The King came to her bedroom.

جاء الملك إلى غرفة نومها.

She rolled on the bed in pain.

لقد تدحرجت على السرير من الألم.

The King heard the cracking of her bones.

سمع الملك صوت طقطقة عظامها.

He ordered his best physician to attend her.

وأمر أفضل طبيب لديه بمعالجتها.

But the queen had thought of this.

ولكن الملكة فكرت في هذا.

She had already spoken with the physician.

لقد تحدثت بالفعل مع الطبيب.

"There is only one remedy," he told the king.

ليس هناك سوى علاج واحد، قال للملك.

"There's a pond in front of the palace"

هناك بركة أمام القصر

"In the pond there's a large Boal fish"

في البركة يوجد سمكة بوال كبيرة

"The remedy is in that fish"

العلاج موجود في تلك السمكة

So the king let the physician catch the fish.

فـسمح الملك للطبيب أن يصطاد السمكة.

Meanwhile Dalim was busy playing.

وفي هذه الأثناء كان داليم مشغولاً باللعب.

He knew nothing of his aunt's illness.

لم يكن يعلم شيئًا عن مرض عمته.

The fish was taken out the water.

تم إخراج السمكة من الماء.

Dalim fell to the ground immediately.

سقط داليم على الأرض فورًا.

He flopped around on the floor.

لقد سقط على الأرض.

And he could not breathe.

ولم يكن يستطيع التنفس.

The guards immediately noticed.

لاحظ الحراس ذلك على الفور.

Dalim was taken to his mother's room.

تم اصطحاب داليم إلى غرفة والدته.

And the King was informed of his son.

وأُخبِر الملك بابنه.

He couldn't believe his son's illness.

لم يستطع أن يصدق مرض ابنه.

The fish was taken to Queen Duo.

تم أخذ السمكة إلى الملكة ديو.

Queen Duo was being saved.

تم إنقاذ الملكة ديو.

At the same time Dalim was dying.

وفي نفس الوقت كان داليم يموت.

The fish was cut open.

تم قطع السمكة.

And they found the wooden box.

ووجدوا الصندوق الخشبي.

In the box lay a necklace of gold.

كان في الصندوق قلادة من الذهب.

Queen Duo put on the necklace.

الملكة ديو تضع القلادة.

And Dalim died at the very same moment.

ومات داليم في نفس اللحظة.

News of the tragedy reached the king.

وصل خبر المأساة إلى الملك.

He was plunged into an ocean of grief.

لقد غرق في محيط من الحزن.

News of Queen Duo's recovery did not help.

لم تساعد أخبار تعافي الملكة ديو.

He wept painful and bitter tears.

لقد بكى دموعًا مؤلمة ومرة.

No one thought he would recover.

لم يعتقد أحد أنه سيتعافى.

He could not bear to bury his son.

لم يستطع أن يتحمل دفن ابنه.

Nor did he allow his body to be burned.

ولم يسمح بحرق جسده.

He could not accept that his son had died.

لم يستطع أن يتقبل فكرة أن ابنه قد مات.

His death was so sudden and senseless.

لقد كان موته مفاجئا وبلا معنى.

He had the dead body moved to a garden-houses.

قام بنقل الجثة إلى حديقة المنزل.

This garden-house was in the suburbs.

كان هذا المنزل ذو الحديقة يقع في الضواحي.

Here his son was laid in state.

هنا تم دفن ابنه.

All sorts of provisions were put there.

وقد تم وضع كل أنواع الأحكام هناك.

Although everyone knew it was unnecessary.

على الرغم من أن الجميع يعلمون أنه ليس ضروريا.

The young boy did not need food anymore.

لم يعد الصبي بحاجة إلى الطعام بعد الآن.

The house was kept locked day and night.

كان المنزل مغلقا طوال النهار والليل.

Dalim had had one very close friend.

وكان لدى داليم صديقًا مقربًا جدًا.

Only this friend was allowed to visit.

كان هذا الصديق فقط هو المسموح له بالزيارة.

He was the son of the prime minister.

كان ابن رئيس الوزراء.

He was entrusted with the key of the house.

لقد أوكِلَ إليه مفتاح البيت.

Once a day he could visit his dead friend.

كان بإمكانه زيارة صديقه المتوفى مرة واحدة في اليوم.

Queen Suo retired after the loss of her son.

تقاعدت الملكة سو بعد فقدان ابنها.

Now the King spent the nights with Queen Duo.

والآن أمضى الملك الليل مع الملكة ديو.

The Queen wanted to avoid suspicion.

أرادت الملكة تجنب الشكوك.

So she took the necklace off at night.

لذلك خلعت القلادة في الليل.

But Dalim's life was tied to the necklace.

لكن حياة داليم كانت مرتبطة بالقلادة.

And his death was not so simple.

ولم يكن موته بهذه البساطة.

He was dead when the queen wore the necklace.

لقد مات عندما ارتدت الملكة القلادة.

But when she took the necklace off, he returned to life.

ولكن عندما خلعت القلادة، عاد إلى الحياة.

And so he returned to life every night.

وهكذا عاد إلى الحياة كل ليلة.

Every morning she put the necklace on again.

كل صباح كانت تضع القلادة مرة أخرى.

And so, he died again every morning.

وهكذا مات مرة أخرى كل صباح.

At night he ate whatever food he liked.

وفي الليل كان يأكل أي طعام يحبه.

Because there was plenty of food for him.

لأنه كان هناك الكثير من الطعام له.

He walked around in the premises.

كان يتجول في المبنى.

And he meditated on the strangeness of his life.

وتأمل في غرابة حياته.

Dalim's friend only visited him during the day.

صديق دليم كان يزوره خلال النهار فقط

So he always saw him as a lifeless corpse.

لذلك كان يراه دائمًا جثة هامدة.

But his body never seemed to change.

لكن جسده لم يبدو وكأنه يتغير أبدًا.

There was no sign of putrefaction.

ولم تظهر أي علامة على التعفن.

The body was lifeless and pale.

وكان الجسد بلا حياة وشاحبًا.

But there were no symptoms of death.

ولكن لم تكن هناك أي أعراض للوفاة.

It all seemed too strange for him.

لقد بدا الأمر غريبًا جدًا بالنسبة له.

So he decided to watch the corpse more closely.

فقرر أن يراقب الجثة عن كثب.

And he visited his friend at night.

وذهب إلى صديقه ليلاً.

He was astonished at what he saw that night.

لقد اندهش مما رأى تلك الليلة.

His dead friend was walking about in the garden.

وكان صديقه الميت يتجول في الحديقة.

At first he thought Dalim might a ghost.

في البداية ظن أن داليم ربما يكون شبحًا.

So he went to see if he could touch him.

فذهب ليرى هل يستطيع أن يلمسه.

And then he saw it was really his friend.

ثم رأى أنه كان صديقه حقًا.

Dalim told his friend everything that had happened.

أخبر داليم صديقه بكل ما حدث.

He told him all the circumstances of his death.

وأخبره بكل ملابسات وفاته.

And soon they solved the mystery.

وسرعان ما تمكنوا من حل اللغز.

They understood why he revived only at night.

لقد فهموا لماذا كان يستيقظ في الليل فقط

Every night the king came to see Queen Duo.

كل ليلة كان الملك يأتي لرؤية الملكة ديو.

When the King visited, she took off her necklace.

عندما زارها الملك، خلعت قلادتها.

The life of the prince depended on the necklace.

كانت حياة الأمير تعتمد على القلادة.

So the two friends worked on a plan.

لذلك عمل الصديقان على خطة.

Night after night they consulted together.

ليلة بعد ليلة كانوا يتشاورون مع بعضهم البعض.

But they could not think of any feasible scheme.

لكنهم لم يتمكنوا من التفكير في أي خطة ممكنة.

Eventually the Gods must have taken pity.

في نهاية المطاف لا بد أن الآلهة قد شفقت علينا.

And they decided to free Dalim.

وقرروا تحرير داليم.

But we must understand how the Gods work.

ولكن يجب علينا أن نفهم كيف تعمل الآلهة.

These things are planned long before.

تم التخطيط لهذه الأمور منذ وقت طويل.

The sister of Bidhata-Purusha had had a daughter.

كان لأخت بيدهاتا بوروشا ابنة.

Bidhata-Purusha was a great fortune teller.

كان بيدهاتا بوروشا عرافًا عظيمًا.

He had written something on the child's forehead.

لقد كتب شيئًا على جبين الطفل.

"This child will marry the dead bridegroom"

هذه الطفلة ستتزوج العريس الميت

Her mother was very saddened by this.

لقد حزنت والدتها كثيرًا بسبب هذا.

She did not want this destiny for her daughter.

لم تكن تريد هذا المصير لابنتها.

But she could not argue with him.

لكنها لم تستطع الجدال معه.

He never changed what he had written.

لم يغير ما كتبه أبدًا.

The child became exceedingly beautiful.

وأصبح الطفل جميلاً للغاية.

But the mother could not take any pleasure in this.

ولكن الأم لم تستطع أن تجد أي متعة في هذا.

Because she knew the destiny of her child.

لأنها عرفت مصير طفلها.

Eventually the girl came to marriageable age.

وفي نهاية المطاف وصلت الفتاة إلى سن الزواج.

She had to find a way to avoid her fate.

كان عليها أن تجد طريقة لتجنب مصيرها.

So the mother fled the country with her child.

لذلك هربت الأم من البلاد مع طفلها.

Perhaps she could avoid her dreadful destiny.

ربما استطاعت أن تتجنب مصيرها الرهيب.

But what was written was written.

ولكن ما كتب قد كتب.

And fate cannot be overruled like this.

ولا يمكن أن يتغلب القدر على هذا النحو.

Together they journeyed through the land.

لقد سافروا معًا عبر الأرض.

You can imagine how fate was working.

يمكنك أن تتخيل كيف كان القدر يعمل.

They wandered past Dalim's resting place.

لقد تجولوا بالقرب من مكان استراحة داليم.

The shade of the evening was approaching.

كان ظل المساء يقترب.

"Mother, I am thirsty," said her child.

أمي، أنا عطشان، قال طفلها.

"Sit at this gate," replied her mother.

اجلسي عند هذه البوابة أجابت أمها.

"I will search for water in the village"

سأبحث عن الماء في القرية

The girl was curious about the garden.

كانت الفتاة فضولية بشأن الحديقة.

And in the garden she saw strange house.

وفي الحديقة رأت بيتًا غريبًا.

She pushed the gate, which opened itself.

دفعت الباب، الذي انفتح من تلقاء نفسه.

When she went in, she saw a beautiful palace.

وعندما دخلت رأت قصرًا جميلًا.

But she had an uneasy feeling about the palace.

لكنها كانت تشعر بعدم الارتياح تجاه القصر.

However, the door had shut itself.

لكن الباب كان قد أغلق نفسه.

So she had no way of getting out.

لذلك لم يكن لديها أي وسيلة للخروج.

When night came the prince revived.

عندما جاء الليل عاد الأمير إلى الحياة.

As usual, he walked around in the garden.

كما جرت العادة، كان يتجول في الحديقة.

But this time he saw a female figure.

لكن هذه المرة رأى شخصية أنثوية.

The figure was standing near the gate.

وكان هذا الشخص واقفًا بالقرب من البوابة.

Soon he saw that it was a girl.

وسرعان ما رأى أنها كانت فتاة.

And he saw she was of unsurpassed beauty.

ورأى أنها كانت ذات جمال لا مثيل له.

"Who are you?" he asked her.

من أنت؟ سألها.

She told Dalim everything that had happened.

لقد أخبرت داليم بكل ما حدث.

All the details of her little history.

كل تفاصيل تاريخها الصغير.

"My uncle is the divine Bidhata-Purusha"

عمي هو بيدهاتا بوروشا الإلهي

"He wrote on my forehead at birth"

كتب على جبهتي عند ولادتي

"This child will marry the dead bridegroom"

هذه الطفلة ستتزوج العريس الميت

"My mother did not want that life for me"

لم ترغب أمي في أن أعيش تلك الحياة

"So we left our house and city"

فتركنا منزلنا ومدينتنا

"And we wandered through the country"

وتجولنا في البلاد

"We had come to the gate of your palace"

لقد وصلنا إلى بوابة قصرك

"After our journey I was thirsty"

بعد رحلتنا كنت عطشانًا

"So my mother went to look for water"

فذهبت أمي للبحث عن الماء

"And now I am standing here before you"

والآن أنا واقف هنا أمامك

Dalim Kumar knew the meaning of the story.

عرف داليم كومار معنى القصة.

"I am the dead bridegroom," he told the girl.

أنا العريس الميت، قال للفتاة.

"It is me who you will marry"

أنا من ستتزوجينه

"Come with me to the house," he asked of her.

تعالي معي إلى المنزل طلب منها.

But the girl wasn't so easily persuaded.

ولكن لم يكن من السهل إقناع الفتاة.

"You are standing and speaking to me"

أنت تقف وتتحدث معي

"How can you be the dead bridegroom?"

كيف يمكنك أن تكون العريس الميت؟

The prince understood her objection.

لقد فهم الأمير اعتراضها.

"You will understand it afterwards"

سوف تفهم ذلك لاحقًا

The girl followed the prince into the house.

وتبعت الفتاة الأمير إلى داخل المنزل.

She had been fasting the whole day.

لقد كانت صائمة طوال اليوم.

So the prince gave her wonderful food.

فأعطاها الأمير طعامًا رائعًا.

Meanwhile, the girl's mother had come back.

وفي هذه الأثناء، عادت والدة الفتاة.

She was standing at the gates of the garden.

كانت واقفة عند أبواب الحديقة.

But her daughter was not there anymore.

ولكن ابنتها لم تعد موجودة.

She cried out for her daughter.

لقد صرخت من أجل ابنتها.

But she got no reply from her daughter.

ولكنها لم تتلق أي رد من ابنتها.

So she went looking for her in the village.

فذهبت للبحث عنها في القرية.

As usual, Dalim's friend came that night.

كما جرت العادة، جاء صديق داليم في تلك الليلة.

Dalim was still entertaining his guest.

كان داليم لا يزال يستضيف ضيفه.

He was not expecting to see a stranger.

لم يكن يتوقع رؤية شخص غريب.

And the girl retold him her story.

وأعادت الفتاة إخباره بقصتها.

You can imagine his surprise when she told him.

يمكنك أن تتخيل دهشته عندما أخبرته.

He was able to confirm Dalim's story.

وتمكن من تأكيد قصة داليم.

Soon they had all accepted destiny.

وبعد فترة قصيرة، تقبلوا جميعًا القدر.

That night they fulfilled their fates.

وفي تلك الليلة حققوا مصيرهم.

They decided to unite the couple in matrimony.

قرروا توحيد الزوجين بالزواج.

It was going to be impossible to get a priest.

لقد كان من المستحيل الحصول على كاهن.

So Dalim's friend performed the hymeneal rites.

فقام صديق داليم بأداء طقوس غشاء البكارة.

The friend of the bridegroom left the palace.

صديق العريس غادر القصر.

The newly-weds had the palace to themselves.

كان القصر ملكًا للزوجين حديثًا.

The happy couple did not sleep much that night.

لم ينم الزوجان السعيدان كثيرًا في تلك الليلة.

So it was long after sunrise that they woke up.

لقد كان الأمر كذلك بعد وقت طويل من شروق الشمس عندما استيقظوا.

Of course it was only the young wife that woke up.

وبطبيعة الحال كانت الزوجة الشابة فقط هي التي استيقظت.

The prince had become a cold corpse again.

وأصبح الأمير جثة باردة مرة أخرى.

The queen had put on her necklace.

لقد وضعت الملكة قلادتها.

And life had departed from him again.

وفارقته الحياة مرة أخرى.

You can imagine how the young wife felt.

يمكنك أن تتخيل كيف شعرت الزوجة الشابة.

She shook her husband to try and wake him.

لقد هزت زوجها محاولة إيقاظه.

She kissed him on his cold lips.

قبلته على شفتيه الباردة.

But all her efforts were in vain.

ولكن كل جهودها كانت بلا جدوى.

He was as lifeless as a marble statue.

لقد كان بلا حياة مثل تمثال الرخام.

The young wife was stricken with horror.

لقد أصيبت الزوجة الشابة بالرعب.

She smote her breast with her fists.

ضربت صدرها بقبضتيها.

She struck her forehead with her palms.

ضربت جبهتها بكفيها.

And she tore her hair from her head.

وانتزعت شعرها من رأسها.

She ran through the garden like a mad woman.

لقد ركضت في الحديقة مثل امرأة مجنونة.

Dalim's friend did not come during the day.

صديق دليم لم يأتي خلال النهار.

He did not want to see his friend this way.

لم يكن يريد أن يرى صديقه بهذه الطريقة.

The poor girl did not know what to do.

لم تعرف الفتاة المسكينة ماذا تفعل.

Time could not pass quickly enough.

لم يكن الوقت ليمر بسرعة كافية.

The day seemed as long as a year.

لقد بدا اليوم وكأنه طول العام.

But the even longest day has its end.

ولكن أطول يوم له نهايته.

The shades of evening were descending.

كانت ظلال المساء تنزل.

Her dead husband was awakened into consciousness.

لقد استيقظ زوجها المتوفى إلى وعيه.

He rose up from his bed again.

وقام من سريره مرة أخرى.

And he embraced his new wife.

واحتضن زوجته الجديدة.

Again they ate, drank, and became merry.

ثم أكلوا وشربوا وفرحوا.

His friend made his usual appearance.

لقد ظهر صديقه كعادته.

And the whole night was spent celebrating.

وقضينا الليل كله في الاحتفال.

They spent the next seven years this way.

لقد أمضوا السنوات السبع التالية بهذه الطريقة.

During the day Dalim was lifeless.

خلال النهار كان داليم بلا حياة.

But at night he came to life.

ولكن في الليل عاد إلى الحياة.

And their life was quite usual.

وكانت حياتهم عادية جدًا.

The princess gave her husband two lovely boys.

أعطت الأميرة لزوجها ولدين جميلين.

They were the exact image of their father.

لقد كانوا صورة طبق الأصل من والدهم.

Of course the king and Queens did not know.

وبطبيعة الحال فإن الملك والملكات لم يكونوا على علم بذلك.

They did not know they were grandparents.

لم يعرفوا أنهم أجداد.

And they did not know Dalim was alive.

ولم يعلموا أن داليم كان على قيد الحياة.

To be precise I should say he was alive at night.

ولكي أكون دقيقًا، يجب أن أقول إنه كان على قيد الحياة في الليل.

They all thought he had long been dead.

اعتقد الجميع أنه مات منذ زمن طويل.

They assumed his corpse would now be gone.

افترضوا أن جثته قد اختفت الآن.

But the heart of Dalim s wife was yearning.

لكن قلب زوجة داليم كان يتوق.

She wanted nothing more than her mother-in-law.

لم تكن تريد شيئا أكثر من حماتها.

Over the years she had come up with a plan.

لقد توصلت إلى خطة على مر السنين.

Perhaps she could see her mother-in-law.

ربما استطاعت رؤية حماتها.

Maybe they could get hold of the necklace.

ربما يمكنهم الحصول على القلادة.

She asked for the consent of her husband.

طلبت موافقة زوجها.

And he allowed her to disguise herself.

وسمح لها بإخفاء نفسها.

She took on the appearance of a female barber.

لقد اتخذت مظهر حلاق أنثى.

Like every female barber, she needed equipment.

مثل كل حلاق أنثى، كانت بحاجة إلى معدات.

She took the following tools;

أخذت الأدوات التالية؛

An iron instrument for preparing finger nails.

أداة حديدية لتحضير الأظافر.

Another iron instrument for scraping the feet.

أداة أخرى من الحديد لكشط الأقدام.

A piece of burnt jhama brick.

قطعة من الطوب الجهاما المحروق.

For rubbing the soles of the feet.

لفرك باطن القدمين.

And paint for the edges of the feet.

ورسم حواف القدمين.

She took all her tools with her.

لقد أخذت جميع أدواتها معها.

And she stood at the gate of the King's palace.

ووقفت على باب قصر الملك.

I forgot something else she brought.

لقد نسيت شيئا آخر أحضرته.

She had come with her two sons.

لقد جاءت مع ابنيها.

She spoke with the guards.

تحدثت مع الحراس.

"I work as a barber"

أنا أعمل حلاقًا

"I have come to offer my services"

لقد جئت لتقديم خدماتي

"I desire to see Queen Suo"

أرغب في رؤية الملكة سو

Queen Suo quickly gave her an interview.

وأجرت الملكة سو مقابلة معها بسرعة.

The queen was quite fond of the two little boys.

لقد كانت الملكة تحب الصبيين الصغيرين كثيرًا.

They strangely reminded her of her own son.

لقد ذكّروها بشكل غريب بابنها۔

And she remembered her lost treasure.

وتذكرت كنزها المفقود۔

Tears fell profusely from her eyes.

سقطت الدموع بغزارة من عينيها۔

She had not the remotest idea who they were.

لم تكن لديها أدنى فكرة عمن كانوا۔

Of course we know who they are.

بالطبع نحن نعلم من هم۔

The two little boys are her grandsons.

والولدان الصغيران هما حفيداها۔

She spoke to the barber.

تحدثت مع الحلاق۔

"My son died when he was young"

لقد مات ابني عندما كان صغيرًا

"I have given up these vanities"

لقد تخليت عن هذه الغرور

"I stopped having my feet ceremoniously dyed"

لقد توقفت عن صبغ قدمي احتفاليًا

"But I would be glad to see your two fine boys"

لكنني سأكون سعيدًا برؤية ولديك الجميلين

The barber agreed to let Queen Suo see her boys.

وافق الحلاق على السماح للملكة سو برؤية أولادها۔

But she had one question before she went.

ولكن كان لديها سؤال واحد قبل أن تذهب۔

"Are there other ladies in the palace?

هل هناك سيدات أخريات في القصر؟

"Someone else I could provide my service to"

شخص آخر يمكنني تقديم خدمتي له

She was told there was another queen.

قيل لها أن هناك ملكة أخرى۔

And she was also allowed to go to that queen.

وقد سُمح لها أيضًا بالذهاب إلى تلك الملكة۔

Queen Duo allowed her to prepare her nails.

سمحت لها الملكة ديو بتحضير أظافرها۔

And she was allowed to scrape her feet.

وقد سُمح لها بخدش قدميها.

She painted her feet with alakta.

لـقد رسمت قدميها بالالاكتا.

And the queen was very pleased with her skill.

وكانت الملكة سعيدة جدًا بمهارتها.

She also enjoyed the sweetness of her disposition.

كما أنها استمتعت بحلاوة تصرفها.

So she booked to have more of her services.

لذلك حجزت للحصول على المزيد من خدماتها.

The female barber had come for something else.

لـقد جاءت الحلاقه لشيء آخر.

And she quickly noticed the necklace.

وسرعان ما لاحظت القلادة.

The necklace was around the Queen's neck.

وكان العقد حول عنق الملكة.

The day of her second visit had come.

لـقد جاء يوم زيارتها الثانية.

She gave her eldest son the instructions.

أعطت ابنها الأكبر التعليمات.

"We are going into the palace again"

نحن ذاهبون إلى القصر مرة أخرى

"When in the palace you have to cry"

عندما تكون في القصر عليك أن تبكي

"Say you would like the queen's necklace"

قل أنك تريد قلادة الملكة

"Don't stop crying until you have her necklace"

لا تتوقف عن البكاء حتى تحصل على قلادتها

The female barber went to queen Duo's apartment.

ذهبت الحلاقه إلى شقة الملكة دوو.

Soon the elder boy started to cry.

وبعد قليل بدأ الصبي الأكبر بالبكاء.

The boy acted his role well.

لـقد قام الصبي بدوره بشكل جيد.

Nothing would console the boy.

لـا شيء يمكن أن يواسي الصبي.

"What is wrong?" Queen Duo asked.

ما الخطب ؟ سألت الملكة ديو.

They boy could hardly speak.

كان الصبي بالكاد يستطيع التحدث.

"Your necklace is so beautiful"

قلادتك جميلة جدًا

And he continued to sob.

واستمر في البكاء.

"Can I please hold the necklace?"

هل يمكنني أن أمسك القلادة من فضلك؟

Queen Duo did not want to let him.

الملكة ديو لم ترغب في السماح له بذلك.

"I cannot part with my necklace"

لا أستطيع أن أتخلى عن قلادتي

"It is my most valuable jewel"

إنها جوهرتي الأكثر قيمة

But the boy did not stop crying.

ولكن الصبي لم يتوقف عن البكاء.

So she took the necklace off her neck.

فخلعت القلادة من رقبتها.

And she put the necklace into the boy's hand.

ووضعت القلادة في يد الصبي.

The boy quickly stopped crying.

توقف الصبي عن البكاء بسرعة.

And he held the necklace in his hand.

وكان يحمل القلادة في يده.

The female barber had finished her work.

انتهت الحلاقه من عملها.

She was packing up her tools.

كانت تحزم أدواتها.

And she was about to leave the palace.

وكانت على وشك مغادرة القصر.

So the queen wanted the necklace back.

لذلك أرادت الملكة استعادة القلادة.

But the boy would not let her have the necklace.

ولكن الصبي لم يسمح لها بالحصول على القلادة.

His mother attempted to snatch the necklace from him.

حاولت والدته انتزاع القلادة منه.

But he wept bitterly when she tried.

ولكنه بكى بشدة عندما حاولت.

And he cried as if his heart would break.

وبكى وكأن قلبه سينكسر.

The female barber politely asked the queen;

س:ألت الحلاقه الملكة بأدب

"Please let the boy take the necklace home"

من فضلك دع الصبي يأخذ القلادة إلى المنزل

"He will fall asleep after drinking his milk"

سوف ينام بعد شرب حليبه

"And then I will bring your necklace back"

وبعد ذلك سأعيد لك قلادتك

She could see she had no choice.

استطاعت أن ترى أنه ليس لديها خيار.

The boy would not allow her to take the necklace.

ل.م يسمح لها الصبي بأخذ القلادة.

So she agreed to the proposal.

فوافقت على العرض.

"Dalim must now be long dead," she thought.

لا بد أن داليم قد مات منذ زمن طويل، فكرت.

And she had nothing to worry about.

ولم يكن لديها ما يدعو للقلق.

The princess had the prized necklace.

كانت الأميرة تمتلك القلادة الثمينة.

The treasure bound to her husband's life.

الكنز المرتبط بحياة زوجها.

She rushed back to the garden-house.

هرعت عائدة إلى منزل الحديقة.

And she gave the necklace to Dalim.

وأعطت القلادة لداليم.

Dalim had been alive all morning.

لقد كان داليم على قيد الحياة طوال الصباح.

It was the first time he saw the sun again.

لقد كانت المرة الأولى التي يرى فيها الشمس مرة أخرى.

Their joy of his life knew no bounds.

فـرحتهم في حياته لم تكن لها حدود.

Their friend advised them to go to the palace.

نصـحهم صديقهم بالذهاب إلى القصر.

"Go to the palace tomorrow"

اذهب إلى القصر غدًا

"Present yourselves to the King and Queen"

قدموا أنفسكم للملك والملكة

"Let them know you're alive and well"

أعلمـهم أنك على قيد الحياة وبصحة جيدة

The couple accepted their friend's advice.

وقد قبل الزوجان نصيحة صديقهما.

And they prepared everything for their arrival.

وأعدوا كل شيء لاستقبالهم.

An elephant was brought for the prince.

لـقد تم إحضار الفيل للأمير.

A pair of ponies were brought for the boys.

تـم إحضار زوج من المهور للأولاد.

And there was a grand chaturdala.

وكانت هناك شاتوردالا عظيمة.

It was furnished with curtains of gold lace.

وقد تم تجهيزها بستائر من الدانتيل الذهبي.

Word was sent to the king and the Queen Suo.

أرسلت الكلمة إلى الملك والملكة سوُّ.

"Prince Dalim Kumar is alive and well"

الأمير دليم كومار على قيد الحياة وبصحة جيدة

"And he is coming to visit you"

وهو قادم لزيارتك

"Now he has a wife and two sons"

الآن لديه زوجة وولدين

The King and Queen Suo could hardly believe it.

لـم يتمكن الملك والملكة سوو من تصديق ذلك.

But they were assured that it was all true.

لـكنهم أكدوا أن كل هذا كان صحيحا.

Queen Duo quickly realized her predicament.

أدركت الملكة ديو بسرعة مأزقها.

And she became overwhelmed with grief.

فأصابها الحزن الشديد.

A band of musicians followed the prince.

وتبع الأمير فرقة من الموسيقيين.

Prince Dalim Kumar approached the palace-gate.

اقترب الأمير داليم كومار من بوابة القصر.

The King and Queen Suo went to the gates.

ذهب الملك والملكة سوو إلى البوابة.

And they welcomed their long-lost son.

ورحبوا بابنهم المفقود منذ زمن طويل.

You can imagine how happy they were.

يمكنك أن تتخيل مدى سعادتهم.

Dalim told his parents of his death.

أخبر دليم والديه بوفاته.

He told them of the pond by the palace.

وأخبرهم عن البركة التي بجانب القصر.

And he told them of the fish in the pond.

وأخبرهم عن السمك الذي في البركة.

He told them of the wooden box in the fish.

أخبرهم عن الصندوق الخشبي الموجود في السمكة.

He told them of the necklace in the wooden box.

أخبرهم عن القلادة الموجودة في الصندوق الخشبي.

And he told them the secret of his life.

وأخبرهم بسر حياته.

He told them how he died each night.

وأخبرهم كيف مات كل ليلة.

Of course he also mentioned his new wife.

وبطبيعة الحال ذكر أيضًا زوجته الجديدة.

The king was inflamed with rage at the news.

لقد غضب الملك بشدة عند سماع هذا الخبر.

He ordered Queen Duo into his presence.

أمر الملكة ديو بالحضور إلى حضوره.

A large hole was dug in the ground.

تم حفر حفرة كبيرة في الأرض.

The hole was as deep as the height of a man.

وكان الحفرة عميقة بقدر طول الرجل.

Queen Duo was made to stand in the hole.

تـم جعل الملكة ديو تقف في الحفرة.

Prickly thorns were heaped around her.

كـانت الأشواك الشائكة متراكمة حولها.

The thorns went up to the crown of her head.

وصل الشوك إلى قمة رأسها.

And in this manner she was buried alive.

وبهذه الطريقة تم دفنها حية.

Phakir Chand
فاكير تشاند

There was once a king, who had a son.

كان هناك ملك، وكان له ابن.

The king's minister also had a son.

وكان لوزير الملك ابن أيضًا.

The two sons loved each other dearly.

لقد أحب الابنان بعضهما البعض بشدة.

And they did everything together.

وفعلوا كل شيء معًا.

The two sons sat and stood up together.

جلس الابنان ووقفا معًا.

They walked together to the same places.

لقد مشيا معًا إلى نفس الأماكن.

They ate their meals together.

لقد تناولوا وجباتهم معًا.

They slept and got up together.

لقد ناموا واستيقظوا معًا.

They spent years in each other's company.

لقد أمضوا سنوات في صحبة بعضهم البعض.

One day they both felt a new desire.

ذات يوم شعر كلاهما برغبة جديدة.

They wanted to see foreign lands.

أرادوا رؤية الأراضي الأجنبية.

And so they set out on their journey.

وهكذا انطلقوا في رحلتهم.

One of them was the son of a king.

وكان أحدهم ابنًا للملك.

One of them was the son of his chief minister.

وكان أحدهم ابن رئيس وزرائه.

So of course they were both quite rich.

وبطبيعة الحال كان كلاهما غنيين جدًا.

But they did not take any servants with them.

ولكنهم لم يأخذوا معهم أي خادم.

They went by themselves, on horseback.

لقد ذهبوا بمفردهم، على ظهور الخيل.

The horses were beautiful to look at.

كانت الخيول جميلة المظهر.

They were Pakshirajes horses.

لقد كانت خيول باكشيراج.

Such horses are known as the kings of birds.

وتُعرف هذه الخيول باسم ملوك الطيور.

The two sons rode together for many days.

كان الابنان يركبان معًا لعدة أيام.

They passed through extensive plains.

لقد مروا عبر سهول واسعة.

And the plains were covered with paddy.

وكانت السهول مغطاة بالأرز.

And they passed through strange cities.

ومرّوا بمدنٍ غريبة.

And they passed through towns, and villages.

وعبروا المدن والقرى.

They passed through treeless deserts.

لقد مروا عبر صحاري خالية من الأشجار.

And they passed through forests.

ومروا عبر الغابات.

And the forests were dense with trees.

وكانت الغابات كثيفة بالأشجار.

These forests were the abode of the tiger.

كانت هذه الغابات مسكن النمر.

And the bear also lived in these forests.

وكان الدب يعيش أيضًا في هذه الغابات.

One evening they were overtaken by the night.

وفي أحد الأمسيات، فاجأهم الليل.

They had not seen any human habitations.

ولم يروا أي مساكن بشرية.

But it was getting darker and darker.

لكن الأمر كان يصبح أكثر وأكثر ظلامًا.

So they dismounted beneath a lofty tree.

فنزلوا تحت شجرة عالية.

They tied their horses to the tree.

ربطوا خيولهم بالشجرة.

And then they climbed up the tree.

وبعد ذلك تسلقوا الشجرة.

They covered the branches with thick foliage.

قاموا بتغطية الفروع بأوراق الشجر السميكة.

So that they could sit on the branches.

لكي يتمكنوا من الجلوس على الأغصان.

The tree had grown near a large body of water.

كانت الشجرة تنمو بالقرب من مساحة كبيرة من المياه.

The water was as clear as the eye of a crow.

وكان الماء صافيا مثل عين الغراب.

The two friends made themselves comfortable.

جعل الصديقان أنفسهم مرتاحين.

Of course it wasn't very comfortable in a tree.

بالطبع لم يكن الأمر مريحًا جدًا في الشجرة.

But it wasn't uncomfortable in the tree either.

ولكن لم يكن الأمر غير مريح في الشجرة أيضًا.

They had decided to spend the night there.

لقد قرروا قضاء الليل هناك.

They sometimes chatted together in whispers.

وكانوا يتحدثون مع بعضهم البعض همسًا في بعض الأحيان.

They felt whispering was better than talking.

لقد شعروا أن الهمس أفضل من الكلام.

Because the region seemed very strange to them.

لأن المنطقة بدت لهم غريبة جدًا.

And soon they were falling into a doze.

وسرعان ما سقطوا في النعاس.

But their attention was suddenly jolted.

ولكن انتباههم لفت فجأة.

From the water they heard a noise.

سمعوا صوتا من الماء.

It sounded like the rushing of water.

لقد بدا الأمر مثل صوت اندفاع الماء.

In front of them was a terrible sight!

وكان أمامهم مشهد رهيب

A huge serpent came from under the water.

وخرج ثعبان ضخم من تحت الماء.
The snake swam ashore and slithered around.
سبح الثعبان إلى الشاطئ وانزلق حوله.
But something else attracted their attention.
لكن هناك شيء آخر لفت انتباههم.
The crested hood of the serpent was shining.
كان غطاء الرأس المتوج للثعبان لامعًا.
The snake had a brilliant manikya embedded.
كان الثعبان يحتوي على مانيكيا رائعة مدمجة.
The jewel shone like a thousand diamonds.
كانت الجوهرة تلمع مثل ألف ماسة.
The crystal lit up the water in the tank.
أضاءت البلورة الماء في الخزان.
The embankments and trees were irradiated.
تم إشعاع الجسور والأشجار.
The serpent doffed the jewel from its crest.
خلع الثعبان الجوهرة من قمته.
And the serpent threw the jewel on the ground.
وألقى الثعبان الجوهرة على الأرض.
And then the serpent went in search of food.
وبعد ذلك ذهب الثعبان للبحث عن الطعام.
They could not believe what they had seen.
لم يتمكنوا من تصديق ما رأوه.
They stayed in the safety of the tree.
لقد بقوا في أمان الشجرة.
But they greatly admired the jewel.
لكنهم أعجبوا بالجوهرة كثيرا.
The ruby shed an ineffable luster.
ألقى الياقوت بريقًا لا يوصف.
Everything had a magical glow around it.
كان كل شيء يتوهج سحريًا حوله.
They had never seen anything like it.
لم يروا شيئا مثله من قبل.
Although, they had heard of this treasure.
على الرغم من أنهم سمعوا عن هذا الكنز.
The jewel equaled the treasures of seven kings.

كانت الجوهرة تعادل كنوز سبعة ملوك.

But their admiration soon changed to fear.

ولكن سرعان ما تحول إعجابهم إلى خوف.

The serpent came to the foot of their tree.

وجاء الثعبان إلى أسفل شجرتهم.

The serpent had found their horses!

لقد وجد الثعبان خيولهم

The poor horses had been tied to the tree.

لقد تم ربط الخيول المسكينة بالشجرة.

The animals had no way of escaping.

ولم يكن لدى الحيوانات أي وسيلة للهروب.

One by one the serpent ate their horses.

واحدا تلو الآخر أكل الثعبان خيولهم.

But the serpent's appetite did not seem satisfied.

ولكن يبدو أن شهية الثعبان لم تكن قد اشبعت.

They feared they would be the next victims.

لقد خافوا من أن يكونوا الضحايا التاليين.

But their fears were soon relieved.

ولكن مخاوفهم سرعان ما تبددت.

The gigantic cobra had not seen them.

ولم يكن الكوبرا العملاق قد رآهم.

And eventually the snake left again.

وفي النهاية غادر الثعبان مرة أخرى.

The minister's son saw an opportunity.

رأى ابن الوزير فرصة.

This was his chance to take the gem.

لقد كانت هذه فرصته للحصول على الجوهرة.

But there was one problem they had.

ولكن كانت هناك مشكلة واحدة واجهتهم.

The jewel shone incredibly bright.

لقد أشرقت الجوهرة بشكل لا يصدق.

The serpent would know what had happened.

فالثعبان سوف يعرف ما حدث.

But there was a way to overcome this problem.

ولكن كان هناك طريقة للتغلب على هذه المشكلة.

And the minister's son knew the solution.

وابن الوزير عرف الحل.

He had to cover the stone with horse-dung.

كان عليه أن يغطي الحجر بروث الخيل.

And there was some horse-dung by the tree.

وكان هناك بعض روث الخيل بالقرب من الشجرة.

He quietly came down from the tree.

نزل من الشجرة بهدوء.

He picked up the horse-dung off the floor.

التقط روث الخيل من على الأرض.

And he threw the dung upon the precious stone.

وألقى الروث على الحجر الكريم.

And then he climbed up into the tree again.

ثم صعد إلى الشجرة مرة أخرى.

The serpent noticed something had happened.

لقد لاحظ الثعبان أن شيئاً ما قد حدث.

The light of the jewel had vanished.

لقد اختفى ضوء الجوهرة.

The serpent rushed back with great fury.

اندفع الثعبان مرة أخرى بغضب عظيم.

The serpent returned to where it had left the stone.

عادت الحية إلى المكان الذي تركت فيه الحجر.

The serpent let out a frightful hiss at the night.

أطلق الثعبان هسهسة مخيفة في الليل.

The snake's groans and convulsions were terrible.

كانت أنين الثعبان وتشنجاته رهيبة.

The snake went round and round the jewel.

دارت الأفعى حول الجوهرة مرارا وتكرارا.

But the stone was covered with horse-dung.

ولكن الحجر كان مغطى بروث الخيل.

This way the serpent could not see its treasure.

بهذه الطريقة لم يتمكن الثعبان من رؤية كنزه.

Finally, the serpent breathed its last breath.

وأخيراً لفظ الثعبان أنفاسه الأخيرة.

The two friends did not sleep much that night.

لم ينم الصديقان كثيرا تلك الليلة.

In the morning they came down from the tree.

وفي الصباح نزلوا من الشجرة.

They went to where the crest-jewel was.

ذهبوا إلى حيث كان يوجد جوهرة الشعار.

The mighty serpent was still laying there.

وكان الثعبان العظيم لا يزال مستلقيا هناك.

But now the snake's body was perfectly lifeless.

ولكن الآن أصبح جسد الثعبان خاليا تماما من الحياة.

The friend of the prince stepped over the dead snake.

صديق الأمير خطا فوق الثعبان الميت.

And he picked up the dung covered jewel.

والتقط الجوهرة المغطاة بالروث.

Both of them went to the bank of the water.

ذهب كلاهما إلى ضفة الماء.

And they washed the precious stone.

وغسلوا الحجر الكريم.

Finally, all the dung had been washed off.

وأخيرا تم غسل كل الروث.

And the jewel shone as brilliantly as before.

وأشرقت الجوهرة بنفس التألق كما في السابق.

The jewel lit up the entire bed of the tank of water.

أضاءت الجوهرة فراش خزان الماء بأكمله.

Now they could see the innumerable fishes.

والآن أصبح بإمكانهم رؤية الأسماك التي لا تعد ولا تحصى.

But the light also revealed something else.

لكن النور كشف أيضًا عن شيء آخر.

This astonished them more than all the fishes.

فأذهلهم هذا أكثر من جميع الأسماك.

In the bottom of the water there was something.

في قاع الماء كان هناك شيئًا.

They could see there were lofty walls.

لقد استطاعوا أن يروا أن هناك جدران عالية.

The walls were from a magnificent palace.

وكانت الجدران من قصر رائع.

The prince's friend was feeling venturesome.

كان صديق الأمير يشعر بالمغامرة.

He convinced the king's son to follow him.

أقنع ابن الملك باتباعه.

And then they wanted to swim to the palace below.

وبعد ذلك أرادوا السباحة إلى القصر أدناه.

The prince's friend took the jewel in his hand.

أخذ صديق الأمير الجوهرة في يده.

And they both dived into the waters.

وغاص كلاهما في المياه.

Soon they stood at the gate of the palace.

وسرعان ما وقفوا عند بوابة القصر.

To their surprise the gate was open.

لقد فوجئوا عندما وجدوا البوابة مفتوحة.

They saw no being, human or superhuman.

ولم يروا أي كائن، إنساني أو خارق للطبيعة.

So they decided to venture inside the gate.

لذلك قرروا المغامرة بالدخول إلى البوابة.

Inside the walls there was a beautiful garden.

وكان داخل الأسوار حديقة جميلة.

In the middle of the garden was a house.

وفي وسط الحديقة كان هناك منزل.

No one had ever seen so many flowers.

لم يسبق لأحد أن رأى هذا العدد الكبير من الزهور.

There were roses of all imaginable varieties.

كانت هناك ورود من جميع الأنواع التي يمكن تخيلها.

There were endless numbers of yellow jessamine.

كان هناك عدد لا حصر له من الياسمين الأصفر.

And there were numerous white bell flowers.

وكانت هناك العديد من أزهار الجرس البيضاء.

These flowers were the king of smells.

كانت هذه الزهور ملك الروائح.

The most scented lily of the valley.

زنبق الوادي الأكثر عطراً.

There were the flowers from the champaka tree.

كانت هناك أزهار من شجرة الشامباكا.

And a thousand other sweet-scented flowers.

وألف زهرة أخرى ذات رائحة عطرة.

Acres covered with the delicious jessamine.

فدان مغطاة بالياسمين اللذيذ.

All the plants were gemmed with flowers.

كانت جميع النباتات مزينة بالزهور.

And all the flowers were in full bloom.

وكانت كل الزهور متفتحة بالكامل.

So the air was loaded with rich perfume.

فكان الهواء محملاً بالعطر الغني.

A wilderness of sweet scents everywhere.

برية من الروائح الحلوة في كل مكان.

They went through this paradise of perfumery.

لقد مروا عبر هذه الجنة من العطور.

And eventually they reached the house.

وأخيرًا وصلوا إلى المنزل.

The house was surrounded by lofty trees.

وكان المنزل محاطًا بأشجار عالية.

Soon they stood at the door of the house.

وسرعان ما وقفوا عند باب المنزل.

Now they could see it was a fairy palace.

والآن استطاعوا أن يروا أنه كان قصرًا جنيًا.

The walls were of burnished gold.

وكانت الجدران مصنوعة من الذهب المصقول.

Here and there shone diamonds of dazzling hue.

هنا وهناك، أشرقت الماسات ذات اللون المبهر.

But they did not see any beings.

ولكنهم لم يروا أي كائنات.

So they went inside the palace.

فدخلوا إلى القصر.

The palace was richly furnished.

وكان القصر مؤثثاً بشكل غني.

They went from room to room.

لقد انتقلوا من غرفة إلى غرفة.

But they did not see anyone.

ولكنهم لم يروا أحدا.

It seemed to be a deserted house.

لقد بدا وكأنه منزل مهجور.

At last, however, they found a special room.

وأخيرًا، وجدوا غرفة خاصة.

In this room there was a young lady.

كانت هناك سيدة شابة في هذه الغرفة.

She was sleeping on a golden bed.

كانت نائمة على سرير ذهبي.

The young lady was of exquisite beauty.

وكانت الشابة ذات جمال رائع.

Her complexion was a mixture of red and white.

كان لون بشرتها مزيجًا من الأحمر والأبيض.

She seemed to be about sixteen years of age.

يبدو أنها كانت في السادسة عشر من عمرها تقريباً.

The two friends gazed upon her.

كان الصديقان ينظران إليها.

They were enchanted by her beauty.

لقد سحرهم جمالها.

But they could not admire her for long.

لكنهم لم يتمكنوا من الإعجاب بها لفترة طويلة.

Because the young lady opened her eyes.

لأن الشابة فتحت عينيها.

Her eyes seemed like the eyes of a gazelle.

بدت عيناها كعيني غزال.

On seeing the strangers she said;

و: عندما رأت الغرباء قالت

"How have you come here, ye unfortunate men?"

كيف وصلتم إلى هنا أيها الرجال التعساء؟

"Be gone, be gone! I beg of you two"

اذهبا، اذهبا أتوسل إليكما

"This is the abode of a mighty serpent"

هذا مسكن ثعبان عظيم

"The serpent which has devoured my parents"

الثعبان الذي التهم والديّ

"And my brothers, and all my relatives"

وإخوتي وجميع أقاربي

"I am the only one that he has spared"

أنا الوحيد الذي نجا

"Flee for your lives while you still can"

اهربوا لإنقاذ حياتكم بينما لا يزال بإمكانكم ذلك

"Or else the serpent will eat you both"

وإلا فإن الحية ستأكلكما

The prince's friend told her what had happened.

أخبرها صديق الأمير بما حدث.

"The serpent has breathed his last breath"

لقد لفظ الثعبان أنفاسه الأخيرة

"The snake's body lies lifeless on the floor"

جسد الثعبان يرقد بلا حياة على الأرض

"We took the head-jewel of the serpent"

لقد أخذنا جوهرة رأس الثعبان

"The jewel's light showed us to the palace.

أرشدنا ضوء الجوهرة إلى القصر.

She thanked the strangers for their bravery.

وشكرت الغرباء على شجاعتهم.

"You have freed me from the infernal serpent"

لقد حررتني من الثعبان الجهنمي

"Please live with me in my palace"

من فضلك عش معي في قصري

"But please promise never to desert me"

ولكن من فضلك وعدني بأنك لن تتركني أبدًا

They gladly accepted the invitation.

لقد قبلوا الدعوة بكل سرور.

The king's son was smitten with the princess.

كان ابن الملك معجبًا بالأميرة.

He adored the charms of the peerless princess.

لقد كان يعشق سحر الأميرة التي لا مثيل لها.

And he married her after a short time.

وتزوجها بعد فترة قصيرة.

There was no priest at the palace.

لم يكن هناك كاهن في القصر.

So the hymeneal knot was tied by other means.

لقد تم ربط عقدة غشاء البكارة بوسائل أخرى.

A simple exchange of garlands of flowers.

تبادل بسيط لأكاليل الزهور.

The king's son became inexpressibly happy.

وأصبح ابن الملك سعيدًا بشكل لا يوصف.

He delighted in the company of the princess.

كان مسرورًا بصحبة الأميرة.

The prince's friend also had a wife.

وكان لصديق الأمير زوجة أيضًا.

Of course she was living in the upper world.

بالطبع كانت تعيش في العالم العلوي.

But he participated in his friend's happiness.

ولكنه شارك في سعادة صديقه.

The time they spent together passed merrily.

لقد مر الوقت الذي قضوه معًا بمرح.

But they could not live here forever.

ولكنهم لم يتمكنوا من العيش هنا إلى الأبد.

The prince had to return to his kingdom.

وكان على الأمير أن يعود إلى مملكته.

But he knew the return would require some planning.

ولكنه كان يعلم أن العودة سوف تتطلب بعض التخطيط.

The occasion would come with a lot of pomp.

وستأتي هذه المناسبة مع الكثير من الفخامة.

There were going to be many ceremonies.

كان من المقرر أن يكون هناك العديد من الاحتفالات.

Because there was a lot to be celebrated.

لأنه كان هناك الكثير للاحتفال به.

First the prince's friend was going to go.

أولاً كان صديق الأمير سيذهب.

And then he was going to return with the attendants.

وبعد ذلك كان سيعود مع الحاضرين.

Horses, and elephants for the happy pair.

الخيول والفيلة للزوج السعيد.

The prince accompanied his friend.

كان الأمير برفقة صديقه.

Together they went back to the surface.

وعادوا معًا إلى السطح.

And they saw the upper world again.

ورأوا العالم العلوي مرة أخرى.

The two friends bid each other adieu.

ودع الصديقان بعضهما البعض.

The prince returned to his lovely wife.

عاد الأمير إلى زوجته الجميلة.

Before leaving everything had been organized.

قبل المغادرة كان كل شيء منظمًا.

The prince's friend arranged his return.

صديق الأمير رتّب عودته.

He said when he was going to go the embankment.

قال عندما كان ذاهبا إلى الجسر.

He was going to have the horses that they needed.

كان سيحصل على الخيول التي يحتاجونها.

Elephants were going to be there too, and attendants.

وكان من المقرر أن يكون هناك أيضًا الفيلة والمرافقون.

They were going to wait upon the prince and princess.

وكانوا في طريقهم لانتظار الأمير والأميرة.

The snake-jewel gave them the rights to this.

لقد أعطتهم جوهرة الثعبان الحق في هذا.

The prince's friend went back to his country.

عاد صديق الأمير إلى بلاده.

To prepare for the return of his friend.

للتحضير لعودة صديقه.

One day the prince was sleeping.

في أحد الأيام كان الأمير نائما.

He had just had his midday meal.

لقد تناول للتو وجبة الغداء.

The princess had never seen the upper regions.

لم تكن الأميرة قد شاهدت المناطق العليا من قبل.

She felt the desire to see the upper world.

لقد شعرت بالرغبة في رؤية العالم العلوي.

For this she needed the snake-jewel.

ولتحقيق هذه الغاية، كانت بحاجة إلى جوهرة الثعبان.

Only this could help her through the water.

هذا فقط يمكن أن يساعدها في عبور الماء.

The jewel was shining its bright light in the room.

كانت الجوهرة تشرق بضوءها الساطع في الغرفة.

She took the snake-jewel into her hand.

أخذت جوهرة الثعبان في يدها.

And then she left the palace and the garden.

ثم غادرت القصر والحديقة.

She successfully swam to the upper world.

لقد نجحت في السباحة إلى العالم العلوي.

No mortal had caught sight of her.

لم يتمكن أي إنسان من رؤيتها.

At the edge of the water were some steps.

وعلى حافة المياه كانت هناك بعض الخطوات.

The steps were for the convenience of bathers.

كانت الخطوات مخصصة لراحة المستحمين.

And this is also where she sat.

وهنا أيضًا جلست.

She scrubbed her body with the sand.

فركت جسدها بالرمل.

She washed her hair with the fresh water.

غسلت شعرها بالماء العذب.

And she played with the water for fun.

ولعبت بالماء من أجل المتعة.

She walked about on the water's edge.

كانت تمشي على حافة المياه.

And she admired all the scenery around.

وأعجبت بكل المناظر المحيطة بها.

But finally she returned back to her palace.

لكنها عادت في النهاية إلى قصرها.

Her husband was still deep in sleep.

وكان زوجها لا يزال في نوم عميق.

But eventually he had slept enough.

لكن في النهاية كان قد نام بما فيه الكفاية.

She did not tell him about her adventures.

ولم تخبره عن مغامراتها.

The next day her husband fell asleep again.

وفي اليوم التالي نام زوجها مرة أخرى.

And again she paid a visit the upper world.

ومرة أخرى قامت بزيارة العالم العلوي.

And she remained unnoticed by mortal man.

وبقيت دون أن يلاحظها الإنسان الفاني.

Her success was starting to give her courage.

لقد بدأ نجاحها يمنحها الشجاعة.

So she repeated her adventure a third time.

فكررت مغامرتها للمرة الثالثة.

The rajah's son was out hunting that day.

وكان ابن الراجا خارجًا للصيد في ذلك اليوم.

He had his tent not far from the water.

وكان خيمته ليست بعيدة عن الماء.

His attendants were cooking his meal.

وكان مساعدوه يطبخون له طعامه.

So, he wandered about along the water.

فتجول على طول الماء.

Nearby an old woman was gathering sticks.

كانت هناك امرأة عجوز تجمع العصي في مكان قريب.

She was collecting dried branches of trees.

كانت تجمع أغصان الأشجار المجففة.

She needed the sticks for kindling wood.

كانت بحاجة إلى العصي لإشعال الخشب.

This was when the princess came out the water.

في هذه اللحظة خرجت الأميرة من الماء.

She gazed around and she saw a man.

نظرت حولها ورأت رجلاً.

And then she saw there was also a woman.

ثم رأت أن هناك امرأة أيضًا.

The princess knew she didn't want to be seen.

عرفت الأميرة أنها لا تريد أن يراها أحد.

So she went back down to her palace.

فعادت إلى قصرها.

But the rajah's son had caught a glimpse of her.

لكن ابن الراجا لمحها.

And the old woman gathering sticks saw her too.

ورأتها المرأة العجوز التي تجمع الحطب أيضًا.

The rajah's son stood gazing on the waters.

كان ابن الراجا واقفا ينظر إلى المياه.

He had never seen such a beautiful woman.

لم يسبق له أن رأى امرأة جميلة مثلها.

She seemed to him to be a deva-kanyas.

لقد بدت له وكأنها ديفا كانياس.

Heavenly goddesses he had read of in old books.

قرأ عن الآلهة السماوية في الكتب القديمة.

They are said to visit the upper world.

ويقال أنهم يزورون العالم العلوي.

And the upper world is honored to have them.

والعالم العلوي يشرف بوجودهم.

But it is said to happen only rarely.

ولكن يقال أن هذا يحدث نادرا فقط.

The way that angels only visit rarely.

الطريقة التي لا يزورها الملائكة إلا نادرا.

He had seen the princess' unearthly beauty.

لقد رأى جمال الأميرة الخارق للطبيعة.

She had made a deep impression on his heart.

لقد تركت انطباعا عميقا في قلبه.

Although he had seen her only for a moment.

رغم أنه لم يراها إلا للحظة واحدة.

But her beauty distracted his mind.

لكن جمالها شغل تفكيره.

He stood there like a statue, for hours.

لقد وقف هناك مثل التمثال لساعات.

All he could do was gaze into the waters.

كل ما كان بإمكانه فعله هو النظر إلى المياه.

In the hope of seeing the lovely figure again.

على أمل رؤية هذه الشخصية الجميلة مرة أخرى.

But all his time was spent in vain.

لكن كل وقته ضاع سدى.

The princess did not appear again.

ولم تظهر الأميرة مرة أخرى.

The rajah's son became mad with love.

أصبح ابن الراجا مجنونًا بالحب.

He kept muttering, "now here, now gone!"

ظل يتمتم الآن هنا، الآن ذهب

He refused to leave the water's edge.

رفض مغادرة حافة المياه.

His attendants had to forcibly remove him.

اضطر مساعدوه إلى إزالته بالقوة.

They took him to his father's palace.

أخذوه إلى قصر أبيه.

But he was in a state of hopeless insanity.

ولكنه كان في حالة من الجنون اليائس.

He couldn't be made to speak to anyone.

لم يكن من الممكن إجباره على التحدث إلى أي شخص.

And he spent his days sobbing heavily.

وكان يقضي أيامه يبكي بشدة.

No others words came out of his mouth.

ولم تخرج أي كلمات أخرى من فمه.

"Now here, now gone!"

الآن هنا، الآن ذهب

"Now here, now gone!"

الآن هنا، الآن ذهب

You can imagine the rajah's grief.

يمكنك أن تتخيل حزن الراجا.

"What could have deranged my son's mind?"

ما الذي يمكن أن يخل بعقل ابني؟

"'Now here, now gone,' what does it mean?"

الآن هنا، الآن ذهب، ماذا يعني ذلك؟

He could not unravel the words' meaning.

لم يتمكن من فهم معنى الكلمات.

His attendants couldn't decipher the words either.

ولم يتمكن مساعدوه من فهم الكلمات أيضًا.

The land's best physicians were consulted.

تم استشارة أفضل الأطباء في البلاد.

But their consultation had no effect.

ولكن استشاراتهم لم يكن لها أي تأثير.

The sons of æsculapius were not able to help.

ولم يكن أبناء إسكليبيوس قادرين على المساعدة.

No one could ascertain the cause of the madness.

لـم يتمكن أحد من تحديد سبب الجنون.

Without knowing the cause there was no cure.

دون معرفة السبب لم يكن هناك علاج.

The physicians tried to ask the prince.

حاول الأطباء أن يسألوا الأمير.

But all he said was, "now here, now gone!"

ولكن كل ما قاله كان الآن هنا، الآن ذهب

The rajah was distracted with grief.

كان الراجا مشتتًا بالحزن.

Day and night he worried for his son.

كان قلقاً على ابنه ليلاً ونهاراً.

He wished for his son's intellects to return.

كان يتمنى أن يعود عقل ابنه.

A proclamation was made in the capital.

صـدر إعلان في العاصمة.

Town criers were sent into the city.

تـم إرسال المنادين إلى المدينة.

And they beat their drums for attention.

وضربوا طبولهم لجذب الانتباه.

"The rajah's son has lost his mental faculties"

ابن الراجا فقد عقله

"The rajah seeks a cure for his son"

الراجا يبحث عن علاج لابنه

"A reward is offered for the cure"

يتم تقديم مكافأة للعلاج

"The hand of the rajah's daughter"

يد ابنة الراجا

"Her hand comes with half his kingdom"

يدها تأتي بنصف مملكته

The drum was beaten around the city.

تـم قرع الطبل في أنحاء المدينة.

But no one felt they could touch the drum.

ولكن لم يشعر أحد أنهم قادرون على لمس الطبل.

No one knew the cause of his madness.

لـم يعرف أحد سبب جنونه.

At last an old woman came forward.

وأخيرا تقدمت امرأة عجوز.

And she stepped up to touch the drum.

وتقدمت لتلمس الطبلة.

"I will discover the cause of his madness"

سأكتشف سبب جنونه

"And I will cure him from his disease"

وسأشفيه من مرضه

She had seen what happened to the boy.

لقد رأت ما حدث للصبي.

She was at the water's edge that day.

لقد كانت على حافة المياه ذلك اليوم.

It was her who was gathering up sticks.

كانت هي التي تجمع العصي.

This woman had a crack-brained son.

كان لهذه المرأة ابن ذو عقل مجنون.

Her son was named of Phakir-Chand.

وكان اسمها فاكير تشاند.

So she was called Phakir's mother.

فأطلقوا عليها اسم أم فاكير.

The woman was brought before the rajah.

تم إحضار المرأة أمام الراجا.

And the following conversation took place.

و:جرى الحوار التالي

"You are the woman that touched the drum"

أنت المرأة التي لمست الطبل

"You know the cause of my son's madness?"

هل تعرف سبب جنون ابني؟

"Yes, oh incarnation of justice!"

نعم يا تجسيد العدالة

"I know the cause of your son's madness"

أعرف سبب جنون ابنك

"But I will not say the cause of his madness"

ولكن لن أقول سبب جنونه

"First I will cure your son of his madness"

أولاً سأعالج ابنك من جنونه

"How can I believe you are able to?"

كيف يمكنني أن أصدق أنك قادر على ذلك؟

"The best physicians of the land have failed"

لقد فشل أفضل الأطباء في البلاد

"You need not now believe, my king"

لا داعي لأن تؤمن الآن يا ملكي

"Wait till I have performed the cure"

انتظر حتى أنتهي من العلاج

"Many an old woman knows many secrets"

العديد من النساء المسنات يعرفن الكثير من الأسرار

"Secrets wise men are unacquainted with"

أسرار لا يعرفها الحكماء

"Very well, let me see what you can do"

حسنًا، دعني أرى ما يمكنك فعله

"In what time will you perform the cure?"

في أي وقت سوف تقوم بالعلاج؟

"It is impossible to fix the time"

من المستحيل تحديد الوقت

"Ff course I will begin work immediately"

بالطبع سأبدأ العمل على الفور

"But I need your lordship's assistance"

لكنني أحتاج إلى مساعدة سيادتك

"What help do you require from me?"

ما هي المساعدة التي تحتاجها مني؟

"Your lordship will please order a hut"

سيادتكم سوف تطلب كوخًا من فضلك

"Have the hut raised on the embankment of the water"

أنشئوا الكوخ على حافة الماء

"Where your son first caught the disease"

أين أصيب ابنك بالمرض لأول مرة

"I mean to live in that hut for a few days"

أقصد أن أعيش في هذا الكوخ لبضعة أيام

"And please order some of your servants"

وأمر بعض خدمك

"They have to be in attendance at a distance"

يجب عليهم الحضور عن بعد

"Tell them to be about a hundred yards away"

أخبرهم أن يكونوا على بعد مائة ياردة تقريبًا

"That way I can call them over when we need them"

بهذه الطريقة يمكنني الاتصال بهم عندما نحتاجهم

The king had listened attentively.

وكان الملك يستمع باهتمام.

"I will order that to be immediately done"

سآمر أن يتم ذلك على الفور

"Do you want anything else?"

هل تريد شيئًا آخر؟

"Those are all the preparations I need"

هذه كل الاستعدادات التي أحتاجها

"But let me remind you of the agreement"

ولكن دعني أذكرك بالاتفاقية

"You promised the hand of your daughter"

لقد وعدت بيد ابنتك

"And you promised half your kingdom"

ووعدت بنصف مملكتك

"But I can't marry your daughter"

لكن لا يمكنني الزواج من ابنتك

"Because your daughter has to marry a man"

لأن ابنتك يجب أن تتزوج رجلاً

"But I also have a son of marriageable age"

ولكن لدي أيضًا ابن في سن الزواج

"Allow my son to marry your daughter"

اسمح لابني أن يتزوج ابنتك

"Allow him to have half of your kingdom"

اسمح له أن يحصل على نصف مملكتك

The king was agreed with the terms.

وافق الملك على الشروط.

"If you find a cure, he marries my daughter"

إذا وجدت علاجًا، فسوف يتزوج ابنتي

"And half of my kingdom shall be his"

ونصف مملكتي يكون له

A temporary hut was quickly erected.

تم تشييد كوخ مؤقت بسرعة.

The hut was built on the embankment of the water.

تـم بناء الكوخ على حافة الماء.

And Phakir's mother took up her abode.

وأقامت أم فاكير.

An outpost was also erected at some distance.

كـما تم إنشاء نقطة استيطانية على مسافة ما.

Because the woman might require some attendance.

لـأن المرأة قد تحتاج إلى بعض الحضور.

Strict orders were given by Phakir's mother.

وأعطت والدة فاكير أوامر صارمة.

No one was allowed to go near the water.

لـم يُسمح لأحد بالاقتراب من الماء.

Only she was allowed to stay by the water.

كـان مسموحًا لها فقط بالبقاء بجانب الماء.

But let us leave Phakir's mother at the water.

ولكن دعونا نترك أم فاكير عند الماء.

Let us hasten down the subterranean palace.

فـلنسرع إلى أسفل القصر تحت الأرض.

To see what the prince and the princess are doing.

لـرؤية ما يفعله الأمير والأميرة.

The princess did want to go up again.

أرادت الأميرة الصعود مرة أخرى.

But she now knew that it would be dangerous.

لـكنها الآن عرفت أن الأمر سيكون خطيرًا.

And she had given up the idea of a fourth visit.

ولقد تخلت عن فكرة الزيارة الرابعة.

But women generally have greater curiosity.

لـكن النساء عمومًا لديهن فضول أكبر.

And the princess was no exception to the rule.

ولم تكن الأميرة استثناءً من القاعدة.

One day her husband was asleep.

وفي يوم من الأيام كان زوجها نائما.

He always slept after his noonday meal.

كـان ينام دائمًا بعد وجبة الظهيرة.

She took the snake-jewel in her hand.

أخذت جوهرة الثعبان في يدها.

And she rushed out of the palace.

وخرجت مسرعة من القصر.

And she came up to the upper world.

وصعدت إلى العالم العلوي.

There was an upheaval in the waters.

وكان هناك اضطراب في المياه.

And Phakir's mother was on high alert.

وكانت والدة فاكير في حالة تأهب قصوى.

She was hiding in the hut.

كانت مختبئة في الكوخ.

And she was looking through the chinks.

وكانت تنظر من خلال الشقوق.

The princess saw no human being nearby.

لم ترى الأميرة أي إنسان بالقرب منها.

So she came to the bank of the water.

فوصلت إلى ضفة الماء.

Phakir's mother showed herself outside the hut.

وأظهرت والدة فاكير نفسها خارج الكوخ.

And she addressed the princess politely.

وخاطبت الأميرة بكل أدب.

"Come, my child, thou queen of beauty"

تعالي يا طفلتي يا ملكة الجمال

"Come to me, and I will help you to bathe"

تعال إليّ، وسأساعدك على الاستحمام

So saying, she approached the princess.

وقالت ذلك واقتربت من الأميرة.

The princess saw she was just an old woman.

رأت الأميرة أنها مجرد امرأة عجوز.

So she made no resistance to her offer.

لذلك لم تقاوم عرضها.

The old woman was washing the princess' hair.

كانت العجوز تغسل شعر الأميرة.

And she noticed the bright jewel in her hand.

ولاحظت الجوهرة اللامعة في يدها.

"Out the jewel here till you are bathed"

أخرج الجوهرة هنا حتى تستحم

Now the jewel was in the hands of Phakir's mother.

والآن أصبحت الجوهرة في يد والدة فاكير۔

She wrapped the jewel up in a cloth.

لقد لفت الجوهرة بقطعة قماش۔

And she wrapped the cloth around her waist.

ولفت القماش حول خصرها۔

Now the princess was unable to escape.

والآن لم تعد الأميرة قادرة على الهروب۔

And Phakir's mother gave the signal.

وأعطت أم فاكير الإشارة۔

The attendants rushed to the water.

هرع الموظفون إلى الماء۔

And they took the princess captive.

وأخذوا الأميرة أسيرة۔

The news soon reached the city.

وسرعان ما وصل الخبر إلى المدينة۔

"Phakir's mother had captured a water-nymph"

أم فاكير أمسكت بحورية ماء

And the people rejoiced at the news.

وفرح الناس بالخبر۔

All came to see the"daughter of the immortals"

جاء الجميع لرؤية ابنة الخالدين

She was brought to the palace.

تم جلبها إلى القصر۔

And she was brought to the rajah's son.

وأحضِرت إلى ابن الراجا۔

The rajah's son was still of impaired intellect.

كان ابن الراجا لا يزال يعاني من ضعف في الذكاء۔

But that cloud on his brain soon dissipated.

ولكن تلك السحابة على دماغه سرعان ما تبددت۔

"I have found you! I have found you!"

لقد وجدتك لقد وجدتك

His eyes had been vacant and lusterless.

كانت عيناه فارغة وبلا بريق۔

But now his eyes had the fire of intelligence.

لكن الآن كانت عيناه تحملان نار الذكاء۔

He had almost lost the use of his tongue.

لـقد فقد تقريبًا استخدام لسانه.

"Now here, now gone!" was all he had been able to say.

الآن هنا، الآن ذهب كان كل ما كان قادرًا على قوله.

But this sense too was restored.

ولكن هذا الإحساس عاد أيضاً.

The joy of the rajah knew no bounds.

لـم يكن لفرحة الراجا حدود.

There was great festivity in the city.

كان هناك احتفال كبير في المدينة.

The people praised Phakir-Chand's mother.

وأشاد الناس بأم فاكير تشاند.

And everyone soon expected the marriage.

وسرعان ما توقع الجميع الزواج.

The rajah's son was to wed the water-nymph.

كان من المقرر أن يتزوج ابن الراجا من حورية الماء.

The princess, however, had made a promise.

لـكن الأميرة كانت قد قطعت وعداً.

She told Phakir's mother of her promise.

وأخبرت والدة فاكير بوعدها.

"I won't as much as look at another man"

لن أنظر إلى رجل آخر على الإطلاق

"For one year my vows shall last"

ستستمر نذوري لمدة عام واحد

"The marriage cannot happen in that time"

لا يمكن أن يتم الزواج في ذلك الوقت

The rajah's son was somewhat disappointed.

لـقد كان ابن الراجا محبطًا إلى حد ما.

But he readily agreed to the delay.

ولكنه وافق على التأخير بسهولة.

"Delay enhances the sweetness of the pleasure"

التأخير يزيد من حلاوة المتعة

Of course the princess spent her time in sorrow.

وبطبيعة الحال قضت الأميرة وقتها في الحزن.

She spent her days and nights sighing.

لـقد قضت أيامها ولياليها وهي تتنهد.

And she lamented her idle curiosity.

وكانت تشكو من فضولها الفارغ.

The curiosity that led her to the upper world.

الفضول الذي قادها إلى العالم العلوي.

The curiosity that separated her from her husband.

الفضول الذي فرقها عن زوجها.

She thought of her unfortunate husband.

لقد فكرت في زوجها التعيس.

She had left him all alone below the waters.

لقد تركته وحيدًا تحت المياه.

And she wept bitter tears each day.

وكانت تبكي دموعًا مريرة كل يوم.

She wished that she could run away.

تمنت لو أنها تستطيع الهرب.

But that would have been impossible.

ولكن هذا كان ليكون مستحيلا.

Because she was immured within walls.

لأنها كانت محصورة بين الجدران.

And there were walls within the walls.

وكانت هناك جدران داخل الجدران.

And what use was getting out the palace?

وما فائدة الخروج من القصر؟

She couldn't get to her husband anyway.

لم تتمكن من الوصول إلى زوجها على أية حال.

She didn't have the serpent jewel.

لم يكن لديها جوهرة الثعبان.

The ladies of the palace tried to comfort her.

حاولت سيدات القصر مواساتها.

And Phakir's mother tried to divert her mind.

وحاولت أم فاكير أن تصرف انتباهها.

But their efforts were in vain.

ولكن جهودهم ذهبت سدى.

She took pleasure in nothing.

لم تستمتع بأي شيء.

She hardly spoke to anyone.

بالكاد تحدثت مع أي شخص.

She wept throughout the day.

لقد بكت طيلة اليوم.

And she wept through the night.

وبكت طوال الليل.

The year of her vow was drawing to a close.

كان عام نذرها يقترب من نهايته.

But she was still disconsolate.

لكنها كانت لا تزال يائسة.

The marriage, however, had to be celebrated.

لكن كان لا بد من الاحتفال بالزواج.

The rajah consulted the astrologers.

استشار الراجا المنجمين.

The day and the hour had been decided.

لقد تم تحديد اليوم والساعة.

The nuptial knot was to be tied.

كان من المقرر عقد عقدة الزواج.

Great preparations were made.

لقد تم إجراء استعدادات كبيرة.

The confectioners were busy day and night.

كان الحلوانيون مشغولين ليلًا ونهارًا.

They prepared all sorts of sweetmeats.

لقد قاموا بإعداد كل أنواع الحلويات.

Milkmen supplied the palace with tanks of curds.

قام بائعو الحليب بتزويد القصر بخزانات من اللبن الرائب.

Great quantities of gunpowder were manufactured.

تم تصنيع كميات كبيرة من البارود.

There were going to be grand fireworks.

كان من المقرر أن يكون هناك ألعاب نارية ضخمة.

Stages were erected everywhere.

تم نصب المسارح في كل مكان.

And musicians were selected to play music.

وقد تم اختيار الموسيقيين لعزف الموسيقى.

All the city assumed an air of mirth.

ساد جو من البهجة والمرح المدينة بأكملها.

All looked forward to the festivities.

وكان الجميع يتطلعون للاحتفالات.

We must return out attention to the minister's son.

يتعين علينا أن نعيد اهتمامنا إلى ابن الوزير.

He had left his friend in the subterranean palace.

لقد ترك صديقه في القصر تحت الأرض.

And he had gone to his country.

وكان قد ذهب إلى بلاده.

He was bringing horses and elephants.

وكان يحضر معه الخيول والفيلة.

And he had with him many attendants.

وكان معه كثير من المرافقين.

For the return of the king's son.

من أجل عودة ابن الملك.

And for the return of his lovely princess.

ولعودة أميرته الجميلة.

So that the ceremony had due pomp.

حتى يكون الحفل مهيباً ومحترماً.

The preparations took him many months.

استغرقت الاستعدادات عدة أشهر.

But eventually all was prepared.

ولكن في النهاية كان كل شيء جاهزا.

And the minister's son started on his journey.

وبدأ ابن الوزير رحلته.

He was accompanied by a long train of elephants.

وكان برفقته قطار طويل من الفيلة.

And behind the elephants were horses.

وخلف الفيلة كانت الخيول.

And all the horses had their own attendants.

وكان لكل الخيول خدمها الخاصون.

He reached the water ahead of schedule.

وصل إلى الماء قبل الموعد المحدد.

So he had two or three days to spare.

فكان لديه يومين أو ثلاثة أيام إضافية.

Tents were pitched in the mango slopes.

تم نصب الخيام في منحدرات المانجو.

So the men and cattle had accommodation.

فـكان الرجال والماشية يجدون مأوى.

The minister's son kept his eyes on the water.

كان ابن الوزير ينظر إلى الماء.

The sun of the appointed day sank below the horizon.

غابت شمس اليوم المحدد تحت الأفق.

But there was no sign of the prince.

ولكن لم يكن هناك أي أثر للأمير.

Nor did the princess come to the surface.

ولم تأت الأميرة إلى السطح.

He waited two or three days longer.

انتظر يومين أو ثلاثة أيام أخرى.

Still the prince did not make his appearance.

ولكن الأمير لم يظهر بعد.

What could have happened to his friend?

ماذا قد يحدث لصديقه؟

And where was his beautiful wife?

وأين كانت زوجته الجميلة؟

Had another serpent beaten them to death?

هل ضربهم ثعبان آخر حتى الموت؟

Possibly the mate of the one that had died.

ربما كان رفيق الشخص الذي مات.

Had they somehow lost the serpent-jewel?

هل فقدوا جوهرة الثعبان بطريقة ما؟

Or had they perhaps visited the upper world?

أم أنهم ربما زاروا العالم العلوي؟

And had they been captured in the upper world?

وهل تم القبض عليهم في العالم العلوي؟

Such were the reflections of the prince's friend.

وكانت هذه تأملات صديق الأمير.

The prince's friend was overwhelmed with grief.

لقد غمر الحزن صديق الأمير.

The waters were quite close to the city.

وكانت المياه قريبة جداً من المدينة.

And often the sound of music could be heard.

وفي كثير من الأحيان كان من الممكن سماع صوت الموسيقى.

He asked passers-by what that music meant.

سأل المارة ماذا تعني تلك الموسيقى؟

He was told about the rajah's son.

وأخبر عن ابن الراجا.

And he was told of a wonderful young lady.

وأخبروه عن شابة رائعة.

And he was told they were going to marry.

وقيل له أنهم سوف يتزوجون.

And he was told more about the wonderful lady.

وأخبروه المزيد عن تلك السيدة الرائعة.

She had come out of the waters he was waiting by.

لقد خرجت من المياه التي كان ينتظرها.

The marriage ceremony was in two days.

كان حفل الزفاف بعد يومين.

The minister's son made the connection.

ابن الوزير هو من قام بالربط.

The wonderful young lady was the wife of his friend.

وكانت الشابة الرائعة زوجة صديقه.

He resolved, therefore, to go into the city.

فـقرر، بالتالي، أن يذهب إلى المدينة.

And he was going to find out all he could.

وكان سيحاول معرفة كل ما يمكنه معرفته.

If he could, he would rescue the princess.

لو كان بإمكانه، فسوف ينقذ الأميرة.

He told the attendants to go home.

طلب من الحاضرين أن يذهبوا إلى منازلهم.

And he told them to take the elephants.

وأمرهم بأخذ الفيلة.

And he told them to take the horses.

وأمرهم بأخذ الخيول.

And he himself went to the city.

وذهب هو إلى المدينة.

And he took up his abode in the house of a Brahman.

وأقام في بيت البراهمي.

First, he rested from his journey.

أولاً، استراح من رحلته.

Then the prince's friend had his dinner.

ثم تناول صديق الأمير عشاءه.

And then he spoke to the Brahman.

ثم تحدث إلى البراهمان.

"Throughout the city there are musicians and bands"

في جميع أنحاء المدينة هناك موسيقيون وفرق موسيقية

"What is the cause of all the celebrations?

ما هو سبب كل هذه الاحتفالات؟

The Brahman was rather surprised.

لقد كان البراهمان متفاجئًا إلى حد ما.

"From what part of the world have you come?"

من أي جزء من العالم أتيت؟

"What rock have you been living under?"

ما هي الصخرة التي كنت تعيش تحتها؟

"Have you not heard the wonderful news?"

ألم تسمع الأخبار الرائعة؟

"A young lady of heavenly beauty"

شابة ذات جمال سماوي

"She rose out of the waters"

لقد ارتفعت من المياه

"And she is going to the son of our rajah"

وهي ذاهبة إلى ابن راجا

The prince's friend wanted to know more.

أراد صديق الأمير أن يعرف المزيد.

The information could be useful.

قد تكون المعلومات مفيدة.

"I have not heard of this news"

لم أسمع بهذا الخبر

"I have come from a distant country"

لقد جئت من بلد بعيد

"The story has not reached us yet"

القصة لم تصل إلينا بعد

"Will you kindly tell me the particulars?"

هل يمكنك أن تخبرني بالتفاصيل؟

The Brahman was happy to relay the story.

وكان البراهمان سعيدًا بنقل القصة.

"The rajah's son went out hunting"

ابن الراجا خرج للصيد

"It must have been about this time last year"

لا بد أن الأمر كان في مثل هذا الوقت من العام الماضي

"They pitched their tents by the waters in the suburbs"

نصبوا خيامهم على ضفاف المياه في الضواحي

"One day, the rajah's son was walking near the water"

في أحد الأيام، كان ابن الراجا يمشي بالقرب من الماء

"On this day, he saw a young woman"

في هذا اليوم رأى امرأة شابة

"I have to mention she was of uncommon beauty"

يجب أن أذكر أنها كانت ذات جمال غير عادي

"She had risen from the depth of the waters"

لقد ارتفعت من أعماق المياه

"She gazed about for a minute or two"

نظرت حولها لمدة دقيقة أو دقيقتين

"And then the beautiful lady disappeared"

ثم اختفت السيدة الجميلة

"The rajah's son, however, had seen her"

لكن ابن الراجا رآها

"He had been struck by her heavenly beauty"

لقد انبهر بجمالها السماوي

"And so he became desperately enamored by her"

وهكذا أصبح معجبًا بها بشدة

"Indeed, she had affected him greatly"

لقد أثرت فيه كثيرًا

"And his mental faculties gave way to passion"

ولقد استسلمت قدراته العقلية للعاطفة

"He was carried home as a mad man"

تم نقله إلى المنزل كرجل مجنون

"He spoke no words except a few"

لم يتكلم إلا بكلمات قليلة

"'now here, now gone!' was all he said"

كل ما قاله هو: الآن هنا، الآن ذهب

"The rajah sent for all the best physicians"

أرسل الراجا في طلب أفضل الأطباء

"They tried to restore his son to reason"

حاولوا إعادة ابنه إلى رشده

"But the physicians were powerless"

ولكن الأطباء كانوا عاجزين

"At last the rajah made a proclamation"

وأخيرًا أصدر الراجا إعلانًا

"And he had the drum beat around the kingdom"

وكان يدق الطبل في جميع أنحاء المملكة

"There was a reward for anyone who cured his son"

وكان لمن شفى ابنه أجر

"They would become the rajah's son-in-law"

سوف يصبحون صهر الراجا

"And they would get half the kingdom"

وسوف يحصلون على نصف المملكة

"An old woman answered the call of the drum"

أجابت امرأة عجوز على نداء الطبل

"All knew her as Phakir's mother"

الجميع عرفوها بأنها أم فاكير

"She said she could cure the rajah's son"

قالت إنها تستطيع علاج ابن الراجا

"She had a hut built outside the town"

لقد بنت كوخًا خارج المدينة

"In the suburbs, next to the waters"

في الضواحي، بجانب المياه

"An in the hut she took her abode"

و في الكوخ اتخذت مسكنها

"She also had some huts erected close by"

كما قامت ببناء بعض الأكواخ بالقرب منها

"And in those huts attendants waited"

وفي تلك الأكواخ كان الخدم ينتظرون

"In case she might need their help"

في حال احتاجت إلى مساعدتهم

"It seems the goddess rose from the waters"

يبدو أن الإلهة نهضت من المياه

"Phakir's mother and the attendants seized her"

أم فاكير والخدم أمسكوا بها

"And they carried her in a palki to the palace"

وحملوها في عربة إلى القصر

"The rajah's son saw the water-nymph"

رأى ابن الراجا حورية الماء

"And he was soon restored to his senses"

وسرعان ما عاد إلى رشده

"They would have married there and then"

كانوا سيتزوجون هناك وفي تلك اللحظة

"But the water goddess had made a vow"

لكن إلهة الماء كانت قد قطعت نذرًا

"She wouldn't look at a man for one year"

لن تنظر إلى رجل لمدة عام

"The year of the vow is now over"

لقد انتهى عام النذر الآن

"The music is from the rajah's palace"

الموسيقى من قصر الراجا

"This, in brief, is the story"

هذه هي القصة باختصار

The prince's friend could put the story together.

صديق الأمير استطاع أن يجمع القصة معًا.

"a truly wonderful story!"

قصة رائعة حقا

"So where is Phakir's mother?"

فأين أم فاكير؟

"And where is Phakir-Chand himself?"

وأين فاكير تشاند نفسه؟

"Has he received the hand of the rajah's daughter?"

هل تلقى يد ابنة الراجا؟

"And has he received half the kingdom?"

وهل أخذ نصف المملكة؟

The Brahman could also answer these questions.

يمكن للبراهمان أيضًا الإجابة على هذه الأسئلة.

"No, they have not married yet"

لا، لم يتزوجا بعد

"And he doesn't yet have half the kingdom"

ولم يحصل بعد على نصف المملكة

"And, I should say, he is a dimwitted lad"

ويجب أن أقول إنه شاب غبي

"In fact, no one knows where the lad is"

في الواقع، لا أحد يعرف أين الشاب

"He has been away from home for more than a year"

لقد كان بعيدًا عن المنزل لأكثر من عام

"That is his manner," he explained.

هذه هي طريقته أوضح.

"He stays away for a long time"

يبقى بعيدًا لفترة طويلة

"And then suddenly he comes home"

ثم فجأة يعود إلى المنزل

"And then suddenly he leaves again"

ثم فجأة يغادر مرة أخرى

"I believe his mother expects him to come soon"

أعتقد أن والدته تتوقع أن يأتي قريبًا

This was very useful information.

كانت هذه معلومات مفيدة للغاية.

"What is he like?" he asked.

كيف هو؟ سأل.

"And what does he do when he returns home?"

وماذا يفعل عندما يعود إلى المنزل؟

These questions the Brahman could also answer.

هذه الأسئلة كان بإمكان البراهمان أيضًا الإجابة عليها.

"Well, he is about your height"

حسنًا، إنه في نفس طولك تقريبًا

"Though he is somewhat younger than you"

على الرغم من أنه أصغر منك قليلاً

"He wears a small piece of cloth round his waist"

يرتدي قطعة قماش صغيرة حول خصره

"And he rubs his body with ashes"

ويفرك جسده بالرماد

"He carries the branch of a tree in his hand"

يحمل في يده غصن شجرة

"And there is a tune to which he dances"

وهناك لحن يرقص عليه

"He comes to the door of the hut of his mother"

يأتي إلى باب كوخ أمه

"And he sings 'dhoop! dhoop! dhoop!'"

'dhoop dhoop dhoop' وهو يغني

"His articulation is very indistinct"

نطقه غير واضح للغاية

"'Come, stay with your mother,' she says"

تعال، ابق مع والدتك، قالت

"And he always gives the same answer"

ويعطي نفس الإجابة دائمًا

"'No, I won't remain,' he says unintelligibly"

لا، لن أبقى، يقول بشكل غير مفهوم.

"You should hear him when he wants to say yes"

يجب أن تسمعه عندما يريد أن يقول نعم

"To answer in the affirmative he says 'hoom'"

للإجابة بالإيجاب يقول هوم

A flood of light entered the prince's friend.

دخل طوفان من الضوء إلى صديق الأمير.

He now saw very well how matters stood.

لقد رأى الآن جيدًا كيف كانت الأمور.

The princess must have taken the snake-jewel.

يبدو أن الأميرة قد أخذت جوهرة الثعبان.

And she must have left the palace alone.

ولابد أن تكون قد غادرت القصر بمفردها.

And she was captured without the king's son.

وتم القبض عليها دون ابن الملك.

Phakir's mother must have the snake-jewel.

لا بد أن والدة فاكير لديها جوهرة الثعبان.

His friend was still below the water.

وكان صديقه لا يزال تحت الماء.

The prince had no means of escape.

ولم يكن أمام الأمير أي وسيلة للهروب.

He could imagine his friends desolate state.

كان بإمكانه أن يتخيل حالة أصدقائه البائسة.

And he could imagine how hopeless he must be.

ويمكنه أن يتخيل مدى اليأس الذي قد يشعر به.

The prince's friend was filled with grief.

كان صديق الأمير مملوءًا بالحزن.

But that was not cause to give up hope.

ولكن هذا لم يكن سببا للتخلي عن الأمل.

Perhaps he could rescue his friend.

ربما يستطيع انقاذ صديقه.

"I must get the jewel from the old woman"

يجب أن أحصل على الجوهرة من المرأة العجوز

"Can I not do it by personating Phakir-Chand?"

هل يمكنني أن أفعل ذلك من خلال تجسيد شخصية فاكير تشاند؟

"His mother is expecting him soon"

والدته تنتظره قريبًا

"Maybe I can rescue the princess the same way"

ربما أستطيع إنقاذ الأميرة بنفس الطريقة

He resolved to act the role of Phakir-Chand.

قرر أن يلعب دور فاكير تشاند.

In the morning he left the Brahman's house.

وفي الصباح غادر منزل البراهمان.

And he went to the outskirts of the city.

وذهب إلى أطراف المدينة.

He divested himself of his usual clothing.

خلع ملابسه المعتادة.

Around his waist he put a narrow piece of cloth.

وضع حول خصره قطعة ضيقة من القماش.

The cloth scarcely reached his knees.

بالكاد وصل القماش إلى ركبتيه.

And he rubbed his body well with ashes.

وفرك جسده جيداً بالرماد.

And finally he broke some twigs off a tree.

وأخيرا كسر بعض الأغصان من الشجرة.

And thus he was ready to play his role.

وبذلك أصبح جاهزًا للقيام بدوره.

He went to the door of the hut of Phakir's mother.

وذهب إلى باب كوخ أم فاكير.

And he commenced the operation by dancing.

وبدأ العملية بالرقص.

He danced in a most violent manner.

لقد رقص بطريقة عنيفة للغاية.

And he sung to the tune of"dhoop! dhoop! dhoop!"

وdhoop dhoop dhoop غنى على أنغام

The dancing attracted the notice of the old woman.

لقد جذب الرقص انتباه المرأة العجوز.

The critical moment had come.

لقد حانت اللحظة الحاسمة.

The old woman looked to her door.

نظرت المرأة العجوز إلى بابها.

"Phakir-Chand, my son, have you come?"

فاكير تشاند، ابني، هل أتيت؟

"my darling; the gods have become propitious to us"

عزيزتي، لقد أصبحت الآلهة مواتية لنا

Her supposed son uttered the monosyllable, "hoom"

نطق ابنها المفترض المقطع الواحد من الكلمة هوم

And he danced more violent than before.

ورقص بشكل أكثر عنفًا من ذي قبل.

And he waved the twig in his hand.

ولوّح بالغصن الذي في يده.

"this time you must not go away"

هذه المرة لا يجب عليك الذهاب بعيدًا

"you must remain with me"

يجب أن تبقى معي

"no, I won't remain," said the prince's friend.

لا، لن أبقى، قال صديق الأمير.

"remain with me," the mother tried again.

ابقى معي حاولت الأم مرة أخرى.

"i'll get you married to the rajah's daughter"

سأزوجك من ابنة الراجا

"will you marry, Phakir-Chand?"

هل ستتزوج يا فاكير تشاند؟

The minister's son replied—"hoom, hoom"

فـأجاب ابن الوزير: هوم هوم

And he danced even more like a madman.

ورقص أكثر كالمجنون.

"will you come with me to the rajah's house?"

هل ستأتي معي إلى منزل الراجا؟

"I'll show you a princess of uncommon beauty"

سأريك أميرة ذات جمال غير عادي

"She rose from the waters"

لقد نهضت من المياه

"hoom, hoom," was the answer from his lips.

هووم، هووم كانت الإجابة من شفتيه.

And his feet stomped violently to"dhoop! dhoop!"

وداس بقدميه بعنف قائلاً: دووب دووب

"Do you wish to see a jewel, Phakir?"

هل ترغب في رؤية جوهرة، فاكير؟

"The crest jewel of the serpent"

جوهرة قمة الثعبان

"The treasure of seven kings"

كنز الملوك السبعة

"hoom, hoom," was the reply.

هووم، هووم كان الرد.

The old woman went back into the hut.

عادت المرأة العجوز إلى الكوخ.

And she brought out the snake-jewel.

وأخرجت جوهرة الثعبان.

She put the jewel into the hand of her supposed son.

وضعت الجوهرة في يد ابنها المفترض.

The minister's son took the snake-jewel.

أخذ ابن الوزير جوهرة الثعبان.

He wrapped the jewel up in the piece of cloth.

لف الجوهرة في قطعة القماش.

And he wrapped the cloth around his waist.

ولفّ الثوب حول وسطه.

Phakir's mother was delighted beyond measure.

لقد كانت والدة فاكير في غاية السعادة.

Her son had come at just the right time.

لقد جاء ابنها في الوقت المناسب.

She went to the rajah's house.

ذهبت إلى بيت الراجا.

She announced the news of Phakir's appearance.

وأعلنت خبر ظهور فاكير.

And also in order to show Phakir the princess.

وأيضاً من أجل إظهار فاكير الأميرة.

They were given access to the rajah's palace.

لقد تم منحهم حق الوصول إلى قصر الراجا.

And all parts of the palace were open to them.

وكانت جميع أجزاء القصر مفتوحة لهم.

The old woman had saved the rajah's son.

لقد أنقذت المرأة العجوز ابن الراجا.

So she was the most important person in the kingdom.

فكانت هي الشخص الأكثر أهمية في المملكة.

She took her supposed son around the palace.

أخذت ابنها المفترض في جولة حول القصر.

And she took him to the princess' room.

وأخذته إلى غرفة الأميرة.

Phakir's mother introduced her son to the princess.

قدمت والدة فاكير ابنها إلى الأميرة.

You can imagine the princess was not best impressed.

يمكنك أن تتخيل أن الأميرة لم تكن معجبة بهذا الأمر.

She did not appreciate the company of a madman.

لم تكن تحب صحبة المجنون.

A madman, half naked, and covered in ash.

مجنون، نصف عاري، ومغطى بالرماد.

And he kept dancing in a wild manner.

وظل يرقص بطريقة جنونية.

The three had spent the day together.

لقد أمضى الثلاثة اليوم معًا.

It was soon going to be sunset.

لقد كان من المقرر أن تغرب الشمس قريبا.

The woman asked her son to come with her.

طلبت المرأة من ابنها أن يأتي معها.

But the supposed Phakir-Chand refused to comply.

لكن فاكير تشاند المفترض رفض الامتثال.

He said he would stay there that night.

وقال أنه سيبقى هناك تلك الليلة.

His mother tried to persuade him to come with her.

حاولت والدته إقناعه بالذهاب معها.

But he persisted in his determination.

ولكنه أصر على إصراره.

He said he would remain with the princess.

وقال أنه سيبقى مع الأميرة.

Phakir's mother went home without him.

ذهبت والدة فاكير إلى المنزل بدونه.

And she told the guards to look after her son.

وطلبت من الحراس أن يعتنوا بابنها.

Eventually all the palace retired to rest.

وفي النهاية تقاعد القصر بأكمله للراحة.

The supposed Phakir spoke to the princess again.

تحدث فاكير المزعوم إلى الأميرة مرة أخرى.

But this time he spoke in his own voice.

لكن هذه المرة تحدث بصوته الخاص.

"Princess! do you not recognize me?"

الأميرة هل لا تعرفيني؟

"I am the prince's friend"

أنا صديق الأمير

"I am the friend of your princely husband"

أنا صديق زوجك الأميري

The princess was astonished for a moment.

لقد اندهشت الأميرة للحظة.

"Who? the prince's friend?"

من؟ صديق الأمير؟

"Oh, my husband's best friend"

أوه، أفضل صديق لزوجي

"Please rescue me from this terrible captivity"

أرجوك أنقذني من هذا الأسر الرهيب

"This is worse than death"

هذا أسوأ من الموت

"All of this is my own fault"

كل هذا خطئي

"Rescue me, oh please, thou best of friends!"

أنقذني، من فضلك، أيها أفضل الأصدقاء

She then burst into tears.

ثم انفجرت بالبكاء.

The prince's friend spoke again.

وتحدث صديق الأمير مرة أخرى.

"Do not be disconsolate"

لا تكن يائسًا

"I will try my best to rescue you"

سأبذل قصارى جهدي لإنقاذك

"I will try to have you out of here tonight"

سأحاول إخراجك من هنا الليلة

"But you must do whatever I tell you"

ولكن يجب عليك أن تفعل كل ما أقوله لك

The princess trusted the prince's friend.

الأميرة وثقت بصديق الأمير.

"I will do anything you tell me"

سأفعل أي شيء تطلبه مني

After this the supposed Phakir left the room.

بعد ذلك غادر فاكير المفترض الغرفة.

He passed through the courtyard of the palace.

مرّ بفناء القصر.

Some of the guards challenged him.

بعض الحراس تحديوه.

"hoom hoom!" he replied.

هووم هووم أجاب.

"I'm just going out for a minute"

سأخرج لمدة دقيقة فقط

"And then I will come back again"

وبعد ذلك سأعود مرة أخرى

They understood that it was the madcap Phakir.

لقد فهموا أنه كان فاكير المجنون.

True to his word he did come back shortly.

وفيا بكلمته فقد عاد قريبا.

And again he went to the princess.

وذهب مرة أخرى إلى الأميرة.

An hour afterwards he again went out.

وبعد ساعة خرج مرة أخرى۔

And again he was challenged by the guards.

ومرة أخرى تم تحديه من قبل الحراس۔

He made the same reply as at the first time.

فأجاب بنفس الإجابة التي أجاب بها في المرة الأولى۔

The guards began to talk among themselves.

بدأ الحراس بالتحدث فيما بينهم۔

"This Phakir surely has no sense"

هذا فاكير بالتأكيد ليس لديه أي حس

"He will go out and come in all night"

سوف يخرج ويعود طوال الليل

"Let us leave him to do what he likes"

دعونا نتركه يفعل ما يحلو له

"There's no use guarding him all night"

لا فائدة من حراسته طوال الليل

The minister's son had worn down the guards.

لقد أنهك ابن الوزير الحراس۔

And he was looking for a way to escape.

وكان يبحث عن طريقة للهروب۔

He kept going in and out until three at night.

ظل يدخل ويخرج حتى الساعة الثالثة ليلاً۔

This time there were no guards there.

هذه المرة لم يكن هناك حراس هناك۔

Because all the guards had fallen asleep.

لأن جميع الحراس كانوا نائمين۔

He was overjoyed at the auspicious circumstance.

لقد كان في غاية السعادة بسبب الظروف الميمونة۔

Then he went back to the princess.

ثم عاد إلى الأميرة۔

"Now, princess, is the time for escape"

الآن، يا أميرتي، حان وقت الهروب

"The guards are all asleep"

الحراس جميعهم نائمون

"You must mount on my back"

يجب عليك أن تركب على ظهري

"Tie the locks of your hair round my neck"

اربطي خصلات شعرك حول رقبتي

"And keep tight hold of me"

وامسكني جيدا

The princess did what she was asked of.

لقد فعلت الأميرة ما طلب منها.

He passed unchallenged through the courtyard.

لقد مر عبر الفناء دون أي تحدي.

And he had a lovely burden on his back.

وكان يحمل عبئا جميلا على ظهره.

Eventually he got to the gate of the palace.

وفي النهاية وصل إلى بوابة القصر.

And he went through without being challenged.

ومضى دون أن يواجه أي تحديات.

Then they went to the outskirts of the city.

ثم ذهبوا إلى أطراف المدينة.

Eventually he reached the outer suburbs.

وفي نهاية المطاف وصل إلى الضواحي الخارجية.

They reached the water from which the princess had risen.

وصلوا إلى الماء الذي خرجت منه الأميرة.

The princess rejoiced at her escape.

فرحت الأميرة بهروبها.

But she was still trembling with fear.

لكنها كانت لا تزال ترتجف من الخوف.

The prince's friend untied the snake-jewel.

قام صديق الأمير بفك جوهرة الثعبان.

And together they ascended into the water.

وصعدا معًا إلى الماء.

And soon they found back to the subterranean palace.

وسرعان ما عادوا إلى القصر تحت الأرض.

You can imagine how happy the prince was.

يمكنك أن تتخيل مدى سعادة الأمير.

He had nearly died of grief.

لقد كاد أن يموت من الحزن.

And you can imagine the princess' happiness too.

ويمكنك أن تتخيل سعادة الأميرة أيضًا.

All the three of them were mad with joy.

وكان الثلاثة في غاية السعادة.

For three days they remained in the palace.

وبقوا في القصر لمدة ثلاثة أيام.

And they retold the prince the whole story.

وأخبروا الأمير بالقصة كاملة.

They told of how the princess was seized.

وأخبروا كيف تم القبض على الأميرة.

They told him of her captivity in the palace.

فأخبروه بأسرها في القصر.

They described the marriage that was planned.

ووصفوا الزواج الذي كان مخططا له.

They told him of the old woman.

أخبروه عن المرأة العجوز.

And they told him all about her Phakir-Chand.

وأخبروه بكل شيء عن فاكير تشاند.

They told him how he had impersonated him.

أخبروه كيف انتحل شخصيته.

And they told him how he freed the princess.

وأخبروه كيف حرر الأميرة.

I don't need to tell you how grateful they were.

لا أحتاج إلى أن أخبرك بمدى امتنانهم.

The prince's friend truly was a good friend.

وكان صديق الأمير صديقًا جيدًا حقًا.

They thanked him in the warmest terms.

شكروه بأحر العبارات.

And they vowed to always follow his counsel.

وتعهدوا بأن يتبعوا نصيحته دائمًا.

They were all resolved to return home.

وكانوا جميعا عازمين على العودة إلى ديارهم.

They wanted to return to their native country.

أرادوا العودة إلى وطنهم.

The king's son, the minister's son, and the princess.

ابن الملك وابن الوزير والأميرة.

They left the subterranean palace together.

غادروا القصر تحت الأرض معًا.

They lighted the passage with the snake-jewel.

أضاءوا الممر بجوهرة الثعبان.

And they made their way to the upper world.

واتجهوا إلى العالم العلوي.

They had neither elephants nor horses waiting for them.

ولم يكن لديهم أفيال ولا خيول في انتظارهم.

So they had no choice but to travel on foot.

لذلك لم يكن أمامهم خيار سوى السفر سيرًا على الأقدام.

The two friends had been bred in the lap of luxury.

لقد نشأ الصديقان في أحضان الرفاهية.

Both of them found walking troublesome.

كلاهما وجد المشي صعبًا.

But the princess found it infinitely more troublesome.

ولكن الأميرة وجدت الأمر أكثر إزعاجًا إلى حد كبير.

She was used to even finer treatment.

لقد اعتادت على معاملة أرقى من ذلك.

The stones of the road were too rough for her.

كانت حجارة الطريق خشنة للغاية بالنسبة لها.

And the rough stones wounded her tender feet.

والحجارة الخشنة جرحت قدميها الرقيقتين.

Eventually her feet became very sore.

في نهاية المطاف أصبحت قدميها مؤلمة للغاية.

At times the king's son carried her on his shoulders.

وفي بعض الأحيان كان ابن الملك يحملها على كتفيه.

The load he was carrying was of course lovely.

الحمل الذي يحمله كان جميلا بالطبع.

But although lovely, she was heavy to carry.

ولكن على الرغم من أنها كانت جميلة، إلا أنها كانت ثقيلة للحمل.

And she could not be carried a great distance.

ولم يكن من الممكن حملها لمسافة كبيرة.

And therefore she too had to walk often.

ولذلك كان عليها أيضًا أن تمشي كثيرًا.

One evening they arrived beneath a tree.

وفي أحد الأمسيات وصلوا تحت شجرة.

There were no visible signs of human habitations.

ولم تكن هناك أي علامات مرئية على وجود مساكن بشرية.

So they decided to make the tree their sleeping place.

فـقرروا أن يجعلوا من الشجرة مكاناً لنومهم.

The prince's friend offered to keep guard.

عرض صديق الأمير أن يكون حارسًا.

"Both of you can go to sleep"

يمكنكما الذهاب إلى النوم

"I will keep watch over you both tonight"

سأراقبكما الليلة

"In order to prevent any danger"

من أجل منع أي خطر

The royal couple soon dozed off.

وسرعان ما نام الزوجان الملكيان.

And they were locked in the arms of sleep.

وكانوا محبوسين في أحضان النوم.

The faithful friend of the prince did not sleep.

الصديق المخلص للأمير لم ينم.

He stayed awake and watched for danger.

لـقد بقي مستيقظا ويراقب الخطر.

It so happened they camped under a special tree.

لـقد حدث أنهم خيموا تحت شجرة خاصة.

In the tree swung the nest of two birds.

فـي الشجرة تأرجح عش طائرين.

The immortal birds Bihangama and Bihangami.

الطيور الخالدة بيهانجاما وبيهانجامي.

These birds were endowed with human speech.

لـقد تم تزويد هذه الطيور بالكلام البشري.

And they could also see into the future.

وكانوا قادرين أيضًا على رؤية المستقبل.

The minister's son listened the bird's conversation.

لكان ابن الوزير يستمع إلى حديث الطائر.

He was more than a little astonished at what he heard!

لـقد اندهش أكثر من قليل مما سمع

Bihangama: "The prince's friend risked his own life"

بـيهانجاما :صديق الأمير خاطر بحياته

"He did everything for the safety of his friend"

لقد فعل كل شيء من أجل سلامة صديقه

"But more dangers will befall the king's son"

ولكن المزيد من المخاطر ستصيب ابن الملك

"And he will find it difficult to save the prince"

وسوف يجد صعوبة في إنقاذ الأمير

Bihangami: "Why is that?"

بيهانجامي: لماذا هذا؟

Bihangama: "Many dangers await the king's son"

بيهانجاما: مخاطر كثيرة تنتظر ابن الملك

"The prince's father will hear of his son's approach"

سيسمع والد الأمير عن اقتراب ابنه

"He will send for him an elephant and some horses"

سيرسل إليه فيلًا وبعض الخيول

"And he will arrange attendants to meet him"

وسيرتب له حراسًا لاستقباله

"The king's son will ride the elephant"

ابن الملك سيركب الفيل

"But he will fall from the back of the elephant"

لكنه سيسقط من ظهر الفيل

"And he will die from his fall from the elephant"

ويموت من سقوطه عن الفيل

Bihangami: "But suppose someone prevented this?"

بيهانجامي: ولكن ماذا لو منع أحدهم هذا؟

"Suppose the king's son is not going to ride on the elephant"

افترض أن ابن الملك لن يركب الفيل

"What might happen if he rides on a horse instead?"

ماذا قد يحدث لو ركب على حصان بدلاً من ذلك؟

"Will he not in that case be saved?"

فهل ينجو في تلك الحالة؟

Bihangama: "Yes, in that case he would escape that fate"

بيهانجاما: نعم، في هذه الحالة سوف ينجو من هذا المصير

"But then a fresh danger would await him"

ولكن بعد ذلك سينتظره خطر جديد

"When the king's son is in sight of his father's palace"

وعندما يكون ابن الملك أمام قصر أبيه

"When he is in the act of passing through the lion-gate"

عندما يكون في طور المرور عبر بوابة الأسد

"In that moment the lion-gate will fall upon him"

في تلك اللحظة سوف يسقط عليه باب الأسد

"And the stones will crush him to death"

والأحجار ستسحقه حتى الموت

Bihangami: "But suppose someone gets there first"

بيهانجامي: لكن لنفترض أن أحدهم وصل إلى هناك أولاً

"Suppose someone destroys the lion-gate"

لنفترض أن أحدهم دمر بوابة الأسد

"If that happens the king's son couldn't go through the lion-gate"

إذا حدث ذلك، فلن يتمكن ابن الملك من المرور عبر بوابة الأسد

"Will not the king's son in that case be saved?"

أفلا ينجو ابن الملك في تلك الحالة؟

Bihangama: "Yes, in that case he would escape his fate"

بيهانجاما: نعم، في هذه الحالة سوف ينجو من مصيره

"But then a fresh danger would await him"

ولكن بعد ذلك سينتظره خطر جديد

"When the king's son reaches the palace"

عندما يصل ابن الملك إلى القصر

"When he sits at a feast prepared for him"

حين يجلس على وليمة أعدت له

"The head of a fish will be cooked for him"

سيُطهى له رأس سمكة

"He will put into his mouth the head of the fish"

فيضع رأس السمكة في فمه

"But the head of the fish will stick in his throat"

ولكن رأس السمكة سيعلق في حلقه

"And he will choke to death on the head of the fish"

ويختنق على رأس الحوت حتى الموت

Bihangami: "But suppose someone snatches the fish"

بيهانجامي: لكن لنفترض أن أحدهم خطف السمكة

"Suppose someone takes the head of the fish from his plate"

لنفترض أن أحدهم أخذ رأس السمكة من طبقه

"Suppose he can't put the fish's head in his mouth"

افترض أنه لا يستطيع وضع رأس السمكة في فمه

"Will not the king's son in that case be saved?"

أفلا ينجو ابن الملك في تلك الحالة؟

Bihangama: "Yes, in that case he will escape his fate"

بـيهانجاما :نعم، في هذه الحالة سوف ينجو من مصيره

"But a fresh danger would await him"

ولكن خطر جديد ينتظره

"When the prince and princess retire after dinner"

عندما يتقاعد الأمير والأميرة بعد العشاء

"When they go into their sleeping apartment"

عندما يذهبون إلى شقتهم النائمة

"They will lie together in bed"

سوف ينامون معًا في السرير

"A terrible cobra will come into the room"

سوف يدخل كوبرا رهيب إلى الغرفة

"And the cobra will bite the king's son to death"

وسوف يعض الكوبرا ابن الملك حتى الموت

Bihangami: "But suppose someone was in the room"

بـيهانجامي :لكن لنفترض أن شخصًا ما كان في الغرفة

"Suppose this person was waiting for the snake"

افترض أن هذا الشخص كان ينتظر الثعبان

"And suppose that this person cuts the snake into pieces"

و لنفترض أن هذا الشخص يقطع الحية إلى قطع

"Will not the king's son in that case be saved?"

أفلا ينجو ابن الملك في تلك الحالة؟

Bihangama: "Yes, in that case he will escape his fate"

بـيهانجاما :نعم، في هذه الحالة سوف ينجو من مصيره

"In that case the life of the king's son will be saved"

في هذه الحالة سوف تنجو حياة ابن الملك

"But he who saves him can't repeat these words"

ولكن من ينقذه لا يستطيع أن يردد هذه الكلمات

"If he tells his secret he will be turned into marble"

إذا أخبر بسرّه، سيتحوّل إلى رخام

Bihangami: "Can the statue be returned to life?"

بـيهانغامي :هل يمكن إرجاع التمثال إلى الحياة؟

Bihangama: "Yes, the marble statue can be restored to life"

بيهانجاما: نعم، يمكن استعادة التمثال الرخامي إلى الحياة

"The princess will give birth to a child"

الأميرة ستلد طفلاً

"They must wash the statue with the blood of the infant"

يجب أن يغسلوا التمثال بدم الطفل

The prophetical birds had spoken until that point.

حتى تلك اللحظة كانت الطيور النبوية تتحدث.

But then they were interrupted by the craw of crows.

ولكن بعد ذلك قاطعهم صراخ الغربان.

The eastern sky tinted in a reddish hue.

السماء الشرقية ملونة باللون الأحمر.

And the travelers beneath the tree bestirred themselves.

فأثار المسافرون تحت الشجرة نشاطهم.

The prophetic conversation came to an end.

وانتهى الحديث النبوي.

But the prince's friend had heard everything.

لكن صديق الأمير سمع كل شيء.

The next morning they continued their journey.

وفي صباح اليوم التالي واصلوا رحلتهم.

The prince, the princess, and the prince's friend.

الأمير والأميرة وصديق الأمير.

Soon they met the king's procession.

وبعد قليل التقوا بموكب الملك.

There was an elephant, a horse, and a palki.

كان هناك فيل وحصان وحصان.

And there was a large number of attendants.

وكان هناك عدد كبير من الحاضرين.

These animals and men had been sent by the king.

لقد تم إرسال هؤلاء الحيوانات والرجال من قبل الملك.

The king heard his son was with his friend.

سمع الملك أن ابنه كان مع صديقه.

And he had heard that his son had married.

وسمع أن ابنه تزوج.

And he heard they were not far from the capital.

فسمع أنهم ليسوا بعيدين عن العاصمة.

The elephant had been richly caparisoned.

لقد تم تجهيز الفيل بشكل غني.

The elephant was intended for the prince.

وكان الفيل مخصصا للأمير.

The framework of the palki was of silver.

وكان إطار البالكي من الفضة.

The palki was meant for the princess.

كانت البالكي مخصصة للأميرة.

And the horse was for the prince's friend.

و كان الحصان لصديق الأمير.

The prince was about to mount on the elephant.

وكان الأمير على وشك ركوب الفيل.

But then his friend spoke to him.

ولكن بعد ذلك تحدث إليه صديقه.

"Allow me to ride on the elephant, please"

اسمح لي أن أركب الفيل، من فضلك

"And you can ride back on horseback"

ويمكنك العودة على ظهر الخيل

The prince was not a little surprised.

ولم يكن الأمير متفاجئًا على الإطلاق.

The proposal had been made in a very cold manner.

لقد تم تقديم الاقتراح بطريقة باردة جدًا.

Maybe his friend felt a little too entitled.

ربما شعر صديقه بأنه يستحق ذلك أكثر من اللازم.

And the king's son was slightly annoyed.

وكان ابن الملك منزعجا قليلا.

But he remembered what his friend had done for him.

ولكنه تذكر ما فعله صديقه من أجله.

And he remembered how he saved the princess.

وتذكر كيف أنقذ الأميرة.

So he mounted the horse without objecting.

فركب الحصان دون أن يعترض.

But his mind became somewhat alienated from him.

لكن عقله أصبح منفصلاً عنه إلى حد ما.

The procession towards the capital started again.

انطلق الموكب نحو العاصمة مرة أخرى.

After some time they came in sight of the palace.

وبعد مرور بعض الوقت، ظهروا أمام أنظار القصر.

The lion-gate had been gaily adorned.

لقد تم تزيين بوابة الأسد بشكل مبهج.

There was a grand reception for the prince.

وكان هناك استقبال كبير للأمير.

And the princess was equally anticipated.

وكانت الأميرة منتظرة بنفس القدر.

But the prince's friend seemed to have an objection.

ولكن يبدو أن صديق الأمير كان لديه اعتراض.

"I want the lion-gate to be broken down"

أريد أن يُكسر باب الأسد

The prince was astounded at the proposal.

لقد اندهش الأمير من الاقتراح.

The request was very out of the ordinary.

وكان الطلب خارجا عن المألوف تماما.

And he had given no reason for his demand.

ولم يقدم أي سبب لطلبه.

But he remembered all his friend had done for him.

لكنّه تذكّر كلّ ما فعله صديقه من أجله.

And he remembered how he saved the princess.

وتذكر كيف أنقذ الأميرة.

So he complied with the wish of his friend.

فامتثل لرغبة صديقه.

And the beautiful lion-gate was torn down.

وهُدِم باب الأسد الجميل.

But his mind became even more estranged from him.

لكن عقله أصبح أكثر غربة عنه.

The procession now went into the palace.

والآن توجه الموكب إلى القصر.

The king gave a warm reception to his son.

استقبل الملك ابنه استقبالا حارا.

He welcomed his daughter-in-law equally warmly.

ورحب بزوجة ابنه بنفس القدر من الحفاوة.

And he was very pleased to see the prince's friend.

وكان سعيدًا جدًا برؤية صديق الأمير.

The story of their adventures was related.

وقد تم سرد قصة مغامراتهم.

The king expressed great astonishment at the tale.

أبدى الملك دهشته الكبيرة من هذه القصة.

And his courtiers were equally impressed.

ولقد أعجب به رجال حاشيته أيضًا.

All praised the minister's son's devotion.

وأشاد الجميع بإخلاص ابن الوزير.

And the ladies of the palace praised the princess.

وأشادت سيدات القصر بالأميرة.

The connoisseurs of beauty praised the princess.

وأشاد خبراء الجمال بالأميرة.

Her complexion was a mixture of milk and vermilion.

كان لون بشرتها مزيجًا من الحليب واللون القرمزي.

Her neck was like that of a swan.

وكان عنقها مثل عنق البجعة.

Her eyes were like those of a gazelle.

وكانت عيناها مثل عيون الغزال.

Her lips were as red as the berry bimba.

كانت شفتيها حمراء مثل التوت بيمبا.

Her cheeks were as lovely as they could be.

كانت خدودها جميلة بقدر ما يمكن أن تكون.

And her nose was straight and high.

وكان أنفها مستقيما ومرتفعا.

Her hair reached down to her ankles.

وصل شعرها إلى كاحليها.

Her walk was as graceful as that of a young elephant.

كانت مشيتها رشيقة مثل مشية فيل صغير.

The princess whom destiny had brought to them.

الأميرة التي أحضرها القدر لهم.

They sat around her wanting to know everything.

جلسوا حولها يريدون أن يعرفوا كل شيء.

And they put to her a thousand questions.

وطرحوا عليها ألف سؤال.

They asked her about her parents.

سألوها عن والديها.

They asked her about the subterranean palace.

سألوها عن القصر تحت الأرض.

And they asked her all about the serpent.

وسألوها عن كل شيء عن الحية.

The serpent which had killed all her relatives.

الثعبان الذي قتل كل أقاربها.

Soon it was time for the new arrivals to dine.

وبعد قليل حان وقت تناول الطعام للقادمين الجدد.

The dinner was served up in dishes of gold.

تم تقديم العشاء في أطباق من الذهب.

All sorts of delicacies were on the table.

كانت كل أنواع الأطعمة الشهية موجودة على الطاولة.

The most conspicuous dish was the head of a rohita fish.

وكان الطبق الأكثر وضوحا هو رأس سمكة الروهيتا.

The large fish's head was placed in a golden cup.

تم وضع رأس السمكة الكبيرة في كأس ذهبي.

And the cup was placed near the prince's plate.

ووضع الكأس بالقرب من طبق الأمير.

All were eating and retelling the adventure.

كان الجميع يأكلون ويروون المغامرة.

And suddenly the prince's friend snatched the head.

وفجأة قام صديق الأمير بخطف الرأس.

He took the fish's head from the prince's plate.

أخذ رأس السمكة من طبق الأمير.

"Let me, prince, eat this rohita's head"

دعني يا أمير آكل رأس هذا الروهيتا

The king's son was quite indignant.

وكان ابن الملك غاضبًا جدًا.

But he remembered all his friend had done for him.

لكنّه تذكّر كلّ ما فعله صديقه من أجله.

And he remembered how he saved the princess.

وتذكر كيف أنقذ الأميرة.

And so he made no objection to the request.

ولم يعترض على الطلب.

But he could not hide his terrible rage.

ولكنه لم يستطع إخفاء غضبه الشديد.

Of course the prince's friend noticed this.

وبطبيعة الحال لاحظ صديق الأمير هذا.

But there was nothing else he could have done.

ولكن لم يكن هناك شيء آخر يستطيع أن يفعله.

His conduct, however strange, was necessary.

لكن سلوكه، على الرغم من غرابته، كان ضروريا.

It was for the safety of his friend's life.

وكان ذلك من أجل سلامة حياة صديقه.

Nor could he tell his friend the reason.

ولم يستطع أن يخبر صديقه بالسبب.

Else he would be transformed into a marble statue.

وإلا فإنه سيتحول إلى تمثال من الرخام.

Soon the dinner was going to be over.

كان العشاء سينتهي قريبا.

The prince's friend had one more request.

وكان لصديق الأمير طلب آخر.

The two friends had spent every night together.

لقد أمضى الصديقان كل ليلة معًا.

But tonight he wanted to go to his own house.

لكن الليلة أراد أن يذهب إلى بيته.

The prince was also shocked at his strange conduct.

لقد صدم الأمير أيضًا من سلوكه الغريب.

But he remembered all his friend had done for him.

لكنّه تذكّر كلّ ما فعله صديقه من أجله.

And he remembered how he saved the princess.

وتذكر كيف أنقذ الأميرة.

And he also agreed to this request of his friend.

ووافق أيضًا على طلب صديقه هذا.

The prince's friend, however, had other plans.

لكن صديق الأمير كان لديه خطط أخرى.

He had no intentions of going to his own house.

لم يكن لديه أي نية للذهاب إلى منزله.

He was resolved to avert the last peril.

لقد عزم على تجنب الخطر الأخير.

The last thing to threaten the life of his friend.

الشيء الأخير الذي يهدد حياة صديقه.

Accordingly, he took a sword into his hand.

وبناء على ذلك، أخذ سيفًا في يده.

And he stealthily entered the royal room.

ودخل خلسةً إلى الغرفة الملكية.

The room of the prince and the princess.

غرفة الأمير والأميرة.

He ensconced himself under the bedstead.

كان يجلس تحت السرير.

The bed was furnished with mattresses of down.

كان السرير مفروشًا بمراتب من الريش.

The mosquito curtains were of the richest silk.

كانت ستائر البعوض مصنوعة من أجود أنواع الحرير.

And all the bedding was laced with gold.

وكانت جميع أغطية الأسرة مزينة بالذهب.

Soon the prince and princess came into the bedroom.

وبعد قليل دخل الأمير والأميرة إلى غرفة النوم.

They undressed themselves and went to bed.

خلعوا ملابسهم وذهبوا إلى السرير.

And soon the royal couple were asleep.

وبعد قليل كان الزوجان الملكيان نائمين.

At midnight he heard the slithering of a snake.

وفي منتصف الليل سمع صوت ثعبان يزحف.

The sound was coming from a water passage.

كان الصوت قادمًا من ممر مائي.

A snake of gigantic size entered the room.

دخلت ثعبان ذو حجم ضخم الغرفة.

The serpent climbed up the frame of the bed.

صعد الثعبان على إطار السرير.

The minister's son rushed out with the sword.

خرج ابن الوزير حاملاً السيف.

And he killed the serpent with one blow.

فقتل الحية بضربة واحدة.

And then he cut the snake into smaller pieces.

ثم قام بتقطيع الثعبان إلى قطع صغيرة.

He put the pieces in the dish for holding betel-leaves.

وضع القطع في الطبق المخصص لحفظ أوراق التنبول.

But as he did this, he spilled a drop of blood.

ولكن عندما فعل ذلك، أراق قطرة من الدم.

The drop of blood fell on the breast of the princess.

سقطت قطرة الدم على صدر الأميرة.

Because the mosquito curtains had not been let down.

لأن ستائر البعوض لم تُنزل.

He worried for the health of the princess.

كان قلقًا على صحة الأميرة.

The blood might be of some sort of poison.

ربما يكون الدم عبارة عن نوع من السم.

So he resolved to lick up the blood.

فقرر أن يلعق الدم.

But he could not look at the naked princess.

ولكنه لم يستطع النظر إلى الأميرة العارية.

It would have been a great sin.

لقد كان ذلك ليكون خطيئة عظيمة.

So he blindfolded himself with seven-fold cloth.

فغطى عينيه بسبعة قطع من القماش.

And he licked off the drop of blood.

ولعق قطرة الدم.

But just at this time the princess awoke.

ولكن في تلك اللحظة استيقظت الأميرة.

Her scream roused her husband from his sleep.

صراخها أيقظ زوجها من نومه.

And he could not believe what he was seeing.

ولم يستطع أن يصدق ما كان يراه.

The prince fell into a great rage.

لقد وقع الأمير في غضب شديد.

And he was prepared to kill his friend.

وكان مستعدًا لقتل صديقه.

But he gave his friend a chance to speak.

ولكنه أعطى صديقه فرصة للتحدث.

"Please, my friend, restrain your anger"

من فضلك يا صديقي، كبح غضبك

"I have done this only to save your life"

لقد فعلت هذا فقط لإنقاذ حياتك

The prince was more confused than before.

وكان الأمير أكثر ارتباكًا من ذي قبل.

"I do not understand what you mean"

لا أفهم ما تقصده

"From the time we came out of the subterranean palace"

منذ خروجنا من القصر الجوفي

"You have been behaving in a most extraordinary way"

لقد كنت تتصرف بطريقة غير عادية للغاية

"First, you insisted on riding my elephant"

أولاً، أصريت على ركوب فيلي

"The elephant my father had sent for me"

الفيل الذي أرسله والدي لي

"I thought it was vain of you to ask"

اعتقدت أنه من الغرور منك أن تسأل

"But I remembered what you had done for me"

ولكنني تذكرت ما فعلته من أجلي

"And I decided to let the matter pass"

وقررت أن أترك الأمر يمر

"And instead I rode back on horseback"

وبدلا من ذلك عدت على ظهر الخيل

"Secondly, you insisted on destroying the lion-gate"

ثانيًا، أصررتم على تدمير بوابة الأسد

"The lion-gate my father had adorned for me"

بوابة الأسد التي زينها لي والدي

"I thought it was strange of you to ask"

اعتقدت أنه من الغريب منك أن تسأل

"But I remembered what you had done for me"

ولكنني تذكرت ما فعلته من أجلي

"And I decided to let the matter pass"

وقررت أن أترك الأمر يمر

"And I had the lion-gate destroyed"

ولقد دمر بوابة الأسد

"Thirdly, at dinner you behaved most shamefully"

ثالثًا، لقد تصرفت بشكل مخجل للغاية أثناء العشاء.

"You snatched the rohita's head from my plate"

لقد انتزعت رأس الروهيتا من طبقتي

"And you insisted on eating the fish head"

و أصريت على أكل رأس السمكة

"I thought you felt too entitled"

اعتقدت أنك تشعر بأنك مستحق جدًا

"But I remembered what you had done for me"

ولكنني تذكرت ما فعلته من أجلي

"So I decided to let the matter pass"

لذلك قررت أن أترك الأمر يمر -

"You then pretended that you were going home"

ثم تظاهرت بأنك ذاهب إلى المنزل

"And I was very glad you were going home"

وكنت سعيدًا جدًا بعودتك إلى المنزل

"Because you had made yourself very disagreeable"

لأنك جعلت نفسك مزعجًا جدًا

"And now you are actually in my bedroom"

والآن أنت في الواقع في غرفة نومي

"You are bending over the naked bosom of my wife"

أنت تنحني فوق صدر زوجتي العاري

"You must have had some evil plan"

لا بد أن لديك خطة شريرة

"And now you pretend you are saving my life"

والآن تتظاهر بأنك تنقذ حياتي

"But I don't believe you want to save my life"

لكنني لا أعتقد أنك تريد إنقاذ حياتي

"I believe you want to destroy my wife's chastity"

أعتقد أنك تريد تدمير عفة زوجتي

The prince's friend knew how things looked.

صديق الأمير كان يعرف كيف تبدو الأمور-

"Oh, do not harbor such thoughts in your mind"

أوه، لا تضع مثل هذه الأفكار في ذهنك

"Please do not think badly against me"

من فضلك لا تفكر بالسوء ضدي

"The gods know what I have done"

الآلهة تعرف ما فعلته

"They know I did it to save your life"

إنهم يعلمون أنني فعلت ذلك لإنقاذ حياتك

"You would see the reasonableness of my conduct"

سوف ترى معقولية سلوكي

"But I don't have liberty to state my reasons"

ولكن ليس لدي الحرية في ذكر أسبابي

The prince asked him to explain himself.

طلب منه الأمير أن يشرح نفسه.

"And why are you not at liberty?"

ولماذا لست حرًا؟

"Who has put a seal upon your mouth?"

من ختم على فمك؟

And the prince's friend answered.

فأجاب صديق الأمير.

"Destiny has put a seal upon my mouth"

لقد ختم القدر فمي

"If I told you, I would be transformed into marble"

إذا قلت لك، سأتحول إلى رخام

The prince grew angrier with his friend.

لقد أصبح الأمير غاضبًا من صديقه.

"You should be transformed into a marble statue!"

يجب أن تتحول إلى تمثال من الرخام

"You must take me to be a simpleton"

يجب أن تعتبرني شخصًا ساذجًا

"You can't expect me to believe this nonsense"

لا يمكنك أن تتوقع مني أن أصدق هذا الهراء

The minister's son made one last request.

وقدم ابن الوزير طلبًا أخيرًا.

"Do you wish me then, friend, for me to tell you?

هل تريد مني إذن يا صديقي أن أخبرك؟

"You would make your friend turn into stone?"

هل تريد أن تحول صديقك إلى حجر؟

The prince wanted to hear the reason.

أراد الأمير أن يسمع السبب.

He did not care about the consequences.

لم يهتم بالعواقب.

"Tell me, or else you are a dead man"

أخبرني وإلا فأنت رجل ميت

The prince's friend wanted to clear his name.

أراد صديق الأمير تبرئة اسمه.

He wanted no foul accusations brought against him.

لم يكن يريد توجيه أي اتهامات باطلة ضده.

And he deemed it his duty to reveal the secret.

ورأى أنه من واجبه أن يكشف السر.

Even if this would put his life at risk.

حتى لو كان هذا من شأنه أن يعرض حياته للخطر.

He again warned the prince not to ask him.

وحذر الأمير مرة أخرى من أن يطلب منه ذلك.

But the prince remained inexorable.

لكن الأمير ظل ثابتًا على موقفه.

The prince's friend then told him his secret.

ثم أخبر صديق الأمير بسرّه.

"While sleeping under a lofty tree one night"

أثناء النوم تحت شجرة عالية في إحدى الليالي

"I overheard a conversation between two birds.

سمعت محادثة بين طائرين.

"The prophesizing birds Bihangama and Bihangami"

الطيور المتنبئة بيهانجاما وبيهانجامي

"Bihangama predicted all the dangers in your life"

تنبأ بيهانجاما بكل المخاطر في حياتك

"First the bird predicted your father would send an elephant"

أولاً، تنبأ الطائر أن والدك سيرسل فيلًا

"The bird said you would fall from the elephant"

قال الطائر أنك ستسقط من الفيل

"And the bird said you would die from the fall"

وقال الطائر أنك ستموت من السقوط

At this point the minister's son's legs turned to stone.

في هذه اللحظة تحولت ساقا ابن الوزير إلى حجر.

"See? my legs have already turned to stone"

أرأيت؟ ساقاي تحولتا إلى حجر بالفعل

"Go on with your story," said the prince.

استمر في قصتك قال الأمير.

And the prince's friend continued the story.

وأكمل صديق الأمير القصة.

"The bird said the lion-gate would be gaily decorated"

قال الطائر أن بوابة الأسد ستكون مزينة بشكل مبهج

"And the bird said the lion-gate would collapse on you"

وقال الطائر أن بوابة الأسد ستنهار عليك

"If the lion-gate had fallen on you, you would have died"

لو سقط عليك باب الأسد لكنت مت

At this point the minister's son's torso turned to stone.

في هذه اللحظة تحول جسد ابن الوزير إلى حجر.

But the prince insisted the minister's son continues.

لكن الأمير أصر على استمرار نجل الوزير.

"Go on with your story," said the prince.

استمر في قصتك قال الأمير.

"The bird said there would be the head of a fish"

قال الطائر أنه سيكون هناك رأس سمكة

"And the bird predicted you would choke on the fish"

وتنبأ الطائر بأنك ستختنق بالسمكة

Now his head was the only thing not of stone.

والآن أصبح رأسه هو الشيء الوحيد الذي لم يكن مصنوعا من الحجر.

"See? my whole body has turned to stone"

أرأيت؟ لقد تحول جسدي كله إلى حجر

"If I continue, I will become a man of stone"

إذا واصلت فسوف أصبح رجلاً من حجر

"Do you wish me to tell the rest"

هل تريد مني أن أخبرك بالباقي؟

"Go on with your story," said the prince.

استمر في قصتك قال الأمير.

"Very well, I will go on to the end"

حسنًا، سأستمر حتى النهاية

"But you may repent after I tell you"

ولكن يمكنك التوبة بعد أن أخبرك

"And you may wish to restore me to life"

وربما تريد أن تعيدني إلى الحياة

"I will tell you how to reverse the spell"

سأخبرك كيف تعكس التعويذة

"In a few months the princess will bear a child"

بعد بضعة أشهر ستلد الأميرة طفلاً

"Wait for the birth of the child"

انتظر ولادة الطفل

"Besmear my statue with the infant's blood"

ادهنوا تمثالي بدم الرضيع

"Only then will I be restored back to life"

حينها فقط سأعود إلى الحياة

The last word left his lips, and he turned to stone.

الكلمة الأخيرة خرجت من شفتيه، وتحول إلى حجر.

The princess jumped out of bed.

قفزت الأميرة من السرير.

She opened the vessel for betel-leaves and spices.

فتحت الوعاء لتأخذ منه أوراق التنبول والتوابل.

And she saw the pieces of a serpent.

فرأت قطع الحية.

The prince and the princess were now convinced.

لقد اقتنع الأمير والأميرة الآن.

They saw the good faith of their departed friend.

لقد رأوا حسن نية صديقهم الراحل.

They saw the benevolence of his actions.

لقد رأوا حسن أفعاله.

They went to the marble statue.

ذهبوا إلى التمثال الرخامي.

But the statue of their friend was lifeless.

ولكن تمثال صديقهم كان بلا حياة.

They let out a loud cry lamentation.

فأطلقوا صرخة عالية من الندم.

But their cries were to no purpose.

ولكن صراخهم لم يجدي نفعا.

Because the statue was not moved by tears.

لأن التمثال لم يتأثر بالدموع.

The prince and princess knew what they had to do.

لقد عرف الأمير والأميرة ما يجب عليهما فعله.

They concealed the marble figure in a safe place.

قاموا بإخفاء التمثال الرخامي في مكان آمن.

And they waited for the birth of their child.

وكانوا ينتظرون ميلاد طفلهم.

In process of time the hour came.

مع مرور الوقت جاءت الساعة.

The princess's travail had arrived.

لقد وصل مخاض الأميرة.

The princess bore a beautiful boy.

أنجبت الأميرة ولدًا جميلًا.

The child was the perfect image of his mother.

وكان الطفل صورة مثالية لأمه.

The beauty of their child was striking.

لقد كان جمال طفلهم مذهلاً.

And they were in awe of him.

وكانوا في رهبة منه.

They would have spared his life.

لقد كانوا سيبقون على حياته.

But they remembered their best friend.

لكنهم تذكروا صديقهم المفضل.

They remembered all he had done for them.

لقد تذكروا كل ما فعله لهم.

But now he was a lifeless stone.

ولكنه الآن أصبح حجرًا بلا حياة.

And they remembered the vows they had made.

فـتذكروا عهودهم التي قطعوها.

And they cut the child into two.

وقطعوا الطفل إلى نصفين.

They besmeared the statue with the child's blood.

لقد لطخوا التمثال بدماء الطفل.

And their friend became animated back to life.

وعاد صديقهم إلى الحياة.

They were glad to see him alive again.

لقد كانوا سعداء لرؤيته حيًا مرة أخرى.

But the prince's friend was overwhelmed with grief.

لكن صديق الأمير كان غارقًا في الحزن.

Because he saw the new-born in a pool of blood.

لأنه رأى المولود الجديد في بركة من الدماء.

So he picked up the dead infant.

ف‍أخذ الطفل الميت.

He carefully wrapped the child in a towel.

ل‍ف الطفل بعناية في منشفة.

And he resolved to get the child restored to life.

وعزم على إعادة الطفل إلى الحياة.

He consulted all the physicians of the country.

استشار جميع أطباء البلاد.

They all told him the same thing.

ل‍قد قالوا له جميعا نفس الشيء.

A cure can be found for any illness.

ي‍مكن إيجاد علاج لأي مرض.

But life requires the spark of life.

ل‍كن الحياة تحتاج إلى شرارة الحياة.

When the spark is gone, it is beyond their jurisdiction.

ع‍ندما تختفي الشرارة، يصبح الأمر خارج نطاق اختصاصهم.

And so they had to go on with their lives.

ولذلك كان عليهم أن يواصلوا حياتهم.

Eventually the prince's friend returned to his wife.

وفي نهاية المطاف عاد صديق الأمير إلى زوجته.

She was a devoted worshipper of the goddess kali.

ك‍انت تعبد الإلهة كالي بإخلاص.

She was the only one who could return life.

ل‍قد كانت هي الوحيدة التي استطاعت أن تعيد الحياة.

His wife was living in a distant town.

وكانت زوجته تعيش في بلدة بعيدة.

So he set out on a journey to the town.

ف‍خرج في رحلة إلى المدينة.

His wife still lived in her father's house.

ولا تزال زوجته تعيش في بيت أبيها.

Adjoining the house there was a garden.

وكان بجوار المنزل حديقة.

And in the garden there was a tree.

وفي الحديقة كانت هناك شجرة.

The child had been stored in that tree.

ل‍قد تم تخزين الطفل في تلك الشجرة.

His wife was overjoyed to see her husband.

كانت زوجته في غاية السعادة لرؤية زوجها.

She had not seen him for a long time.

لم تراه منذ وقت طويل.

But she was surprised when she saw him.

ولكنها تفاجأت عندما رأته.

Her husband was very melancholy that day.

وكان زوجها حزينًا جدًا في ذلك اليوم.

He spoke very little to his wife.

لقد تحدث قليلا جدا مع زوجته.

And his wife knew that he was not himself.

وعرفت زوجته أنه ليس هو نفسه.

He was brooding over something in his mind.

كان يفكر في شيء ما في ذهنه.

She asked the reason for his melancholy.

سألته عن سبب حزنه.

But he kept quiet, and wouldn't tell her.

ولكنه ظل صامتا ولم يخبرها.

One night they were lying together in bed.

في إحدى الليالي كانا مستلقيين معًا في السرير.

The wife got up and left the marital bed.

قامت الزوجة وخرجت من فراش الزوجية.

She opened the door and went into the garden.

فتحت الباب ودخلت إلى الحديقة.

Her husband had not been able to sleep well.

ولم يكن زوجها قادرا على النوم جيدا.

Therefore he awoke from the movement of his wife.

فاستيقظ من حركة زوجته.

He heard her leave in the dead of the night.

سمعها تغادر في منتصف الليل.

And he was determined to follow her.

وكان مصمما على متابعتها.

But he was also determined not to be noticed.

ولكنه كان مصمما أيضا على عدم لفت الانتباه.

She went to a temple of the goddess kali.

ذهبت إلى معبد الإلهة كالي.

The temple was at no great distance from her house.

ولم يكن المعبد على مسافة كبيرة من منزلها۔

She worshipped the goddess with flowers.

كانت تعبد الإلهة بالزهور۔

And she worshiped the goddess with sandal-wood perfume.

وكانت تعبد الإلهة بعطر الصندل۔

"Oh mother kali! have mercy upon me"

يا أم كالي ارحميني

"Deliver me out of all my troubles"

نجّني من كل ضيقاتي

The goddess replied to the woman.

ردت الإلهة على المرأة۔

"Why, what further grievance have you?

لماذا، ما هي الشكوى الأخرى التي لديك؟

"You long prayed for the return of your husband"

لقد صليت طويلاً من أجل عودة زوجك

"And your prayers have been answered"

ولقد استجيب لدعائك

"Your husband has returned to you"

لقد عاد إليك زوجك

"So then, what ails thee now?"

إذن، ما الذي يزعجك الآن؟

The woman answered the goddess.

أجابت المرأة الإلهة۔

"True, oh mother, my husband has come to me"

صحيح يا أمي، زوجي جاء إليّ

"But he has come to me in a melancholy mood"

لكنه جاء إليّ في مزاج حزين

"He hardly speaks to me when I speak to him"

إنه بالكاد يتحدث معي عندما أتحدث إليه

"He takes no delight in me when he is with me"

لا يفرح بي عندما يكون معي

"All he does is sit melancholy in a corner"

كل ما يفعله هو الجلوس حزينًا في الزاوية

The goddess replied to her devotee.

ردت الإلهة على مُريدها۔

"Ask your husband why he feels melancholy"

اسألي زوجك لماذا يشعر بالحزن

"When he tells you, let me know the reason"

عندما يخبرك، أخبرني السبب

The minister's son overheard the conversation.

سمع ابن الوزير المحادثة۔

But he stayed unnoticed by the goddess.

ولكنه بقي دون أن تلاحظه الإلهة۔

And his wife did not notice him either.

ولم تلاحظه زوجته أيضًا۔

He quietly slunk away before his wife.

لقد تسلل بهدوء بعيدًا عن زوجته۔

And he returned back to bed before her.

وعاد إلى فراشه قبلها۔

The following day the wife asked her husband.

و:في اليوم التالي سألت الزوجة زوجها

"My dear husband, why are you in a melancholy mood?"

زوجي العزيز، لماذا أنت في مزاج حزين؟

Her husband retold the whole story.

لقد روى زوجها القصة كاملة۔

He told her about the jewel serpent.

أخبرها عن جوهرة الثعبان۔

He told her about the subterranean palace.

أخبرها عن القصر تحت الأرض۔

He told her about the princess being captured.

أخبرها عن القبض على الأميرة۔

He told her how he freed the princess.

أخبرها كيف حرر الأميرة۔

And he told her about Bihangama and Bihangami.

وأخبرها عن بيهانجاما وبيهانجامي۔

He told her how he had turned to stone.

أخبرها كيف تحول إلى حجر۔

And he told her how he was returned back to life.

وأخبرها كيف عاد إلى الحياة۔

So he told her also about the killing of the child.

فأخبرها أيضًا عن مقتل الطفل۔

That night his wife left the bed again.

وفي تلك الليلة غادرت زوجته السرير مرة أخرى.

And she returned to the goddess kali's temple.

وعادت إلى معبد الإلهة كالي.

And she told the goddess of her husband's melancholy.

وأخبرت الإلهة بحزن زوجها.

The goddess listened intently to what was said.

استمعت الإلهة باهتمام إلى ما قيل.

"Bring the child here and I will restore it to life"

أحضروا الطفل إلى هنا وسأعيده إلى الحياة

The next night she left the marital bed again.

وفي الليلة التالية غادرت الفراش الزوجي مرة أخرى.

She went to the tree in the garden.

ذهبت إلى الشجرة في الحديقة.

And she took the child from the tree.

وأخذت الطفل من الشجرة.

And she took the child to the goddess kali.

وأخذت الطفل إلى الإلهة كالي.

And the goddess kali returned the child back to life.

وأعادت الإلهة كالي الطفل إلى الحياة.

The prince's friend was entranced with joy.

لقد سُرِرَ صديق الأمير فرحًا.

He picked up the reanimated child.

التقط الطفل الذي أعيد إنعاشه.

And he ran as fast as he could to his friend.

وركض بأسرع ما يمكن إلى صديقه.

And he gave him his child, alive and well.

وأعطاه ولده حياً ومعافى.

They all rejoiced with exceedingly great joy.

فـفرح الجميع فرحاً عظيماً جداً.

And they lived together happily till the day of their death.

وعاشوا معًا بسعادة حتى يوم وفاتهم.

The Indignant Brahman
البراهمان الغاضب

There was once a poor Brahman.

كان هناك ذات مرة براهمان فقير.

This poor Brahman had a wife.

كان لهذا البراهمان الفقير زوجة.

And he also had four children.

وكان لديه أيضًا أربعة أطفال.

He was a very poor man.

لقد كان رجلاً فقيراً جداً.

And he had no resources in the world.

ولم تكن لديه أي موارد في العالم.

He lived from the charity of others.

كان يعيش من صدقة الآخرين.

During marriages he earned well.

خلال الزواج كان يكسب جيدا.

And he earned well during funerals.

وكان يكسب رزقه جيدا أثناء الجنازات.

But his parishioners did not marry daily.

ولكن أبناء رعيته لم يكونوا يتزوجون يومياً.

And they did not die every day either.

ولم يموتوا كل يوم أيضًا.

It was difficult to make the two ends meet.

لقد كان من الصعب التوفيق بين الطرفين.

His wife often rebuked him.

وكانت زوجته توبخه كثيرا.

"Why can you not support me?"

لماذا لا تستطيع أن تدعمني؟

"Our children run around naked"

أطفالنا يركضون عراة

"And they suffer from hunger"

وهم يعانون من الجوع

Though poor, he was a good man.

رغم أنه كان فقيرًا، إلا أنه كان رجلاً صالحًا.

And he was diligent in his devotions.

وكان مجتهداً في عباداته.

Every day he said his prayers.

وكان يقول صلواته كل يوم.

He prayed at the same time each day.

كان يصلي في نفس الوقت كل يوم.

His tutelary deity was the Goddess Durga.

كانت معبودته الوصائية هي الإلهة دورجا.

She is the consort of Shiva.

وهي زوجة شيفا.

She is the creative energy of the universe.

إنها الطاقة الإبداعية للكون.

Every day he wrote the name of Durga.

كل يوم كان يكتب اسم دورجا.

He wrote the name in red ink.

كتب الإسم بالحبر الأحمر.

At least one hundred and eight times.

مائة وثماني مرات على الأقل.

He did not drink or eat till he did this.

لم يشرب ولم يأكل حتى فعل هذا.

throughout the day he uttered prayers.

كان يردد الصلوات طيلة اليوم.

"O Durga! have mercy upon me"

يا دورجا ارحمني

He prayed whenever he felt anxious.

كان يصلي كلما شعر بالقلق.

And he often felt anxious.

وكان يشعر بالقلق في كثير من الأحيان.

Because he lived in poverty.

لأنه عاش في فقر.

He prayed when his worries were too much.

لقد صلى عندما كانت همومه كثيرة.

And there were many things he worried about.

وكان هناك الكثير من الأشياء التي كانت تقلقه.

He worried about his wife and children.

كان قلقًا على زوجته وأولاده.

And he worried about supporting them.

وكان قلقًا بشأن دعمهم.

One day he was very sad.

ذات يوم كان حزينًا جدًا.

On this day he went to a forest.

وفي هذا اليوم ذهب إلى الغابة.

The forest was far outside the village.

وكانت الغابة بعيدة خارج القرية.

He let out all his grief.

لقد أخرج كل حزنه.

And he wept bitter tears.

وبكى دموعًا مريرة.

"O Durga! O Mother Bhagavati!"

يا دورغا يا أم بهاغافاتي

"Please put an end to my misery?"

من فضلك ضع حدا لبؤسي؟

"I wish I were alone in the world"

أتمنى أن أكون وحدي في العالم

"Then my poverty wouldn't worry me"

ثم لن يقلقني فقري

"But thou hast given me a wife"

ولكنك أعطيتني زوجة

"And my wife has given me children"

وزوجتي أنجبت لي أطفالاً

"O Mother, I beg of you"

يا أمي أتوسل إليك

"Give me the means to support them"

أعطوني الوسائل لدعمهم

Shiva and his wife Durga happened to be there.

لقد كان شيفا وزوجته دورجا متواجدين هناك.

They were taking their morning walk.

لقد كانوا في نزهتهم الصباحية.

The Goddess Durga saw the Brahman at a distance.

رأت الإلهة دورجا البراهمان من مسافة بعيدة.

"O Lord of Kailas, do you see that Brahman?"

يا رب كايلاس، هل ترى هذا البراهمان؟

"He is always taking my name on his lips"

إنه يأخذ اسمي دائمًا على شفتيه

"He prays I deliver him from his troubles"

يدعو أن أنقذه من مشاكله

"Can we not do something for the poor Brahman?"

هل لا يمكننا أن نفعل شيئًا من أجل البراهمي الفقير؟

"He is oppressed with many cares"

إنه مثقل بالهموم الكثيرة

"And he deeply cares for his growing family"

وهو يهتم بشدة بعائلته المتنامية

"We should make his life more comfortable"

يجب أن نجعل حياته أكثر راحة

"Because the poor man never has enough to eat"

لأن الرجل الفقير لا يملك ما يكفي من الطعام

"And his family doesn't have enough to eat either"

وعائلته ليس لديها ما يكفي من الطعام أيضًا

"Let us give him a pot"

فلنعطيه قدرًا

"A pot with an infinite supply of murukku"

وعاءٌ فيه إمدادٌ لا ينضب من الموروكو

The divine consort was right.

لقد كان الزوج الإلهي على حق.

The Lord of Kailas agreed to the proposal.

وافق سيد كايلاس على الاقتراح.

On the spot he created a magical pot.

وفي الحال صنع وعاءً سحريًا.

Durga went to the poor Brahman.

ذهبت دورجا إلى البراهمي الفقير.

"O Brahman! My loyal devotee"

يا براهمان مُخلصي المُخلص

"I have often thought of your pitiable case"

لقد فكرت كثيرًا في حالتك المزرية

"Your repeated prayers have moved my compassion"

صلواتك المتكررة حركت شفقتي

"Here is a pot for you"

هذا وعاء لك

"You must turn the pot upside down"

يجب عليك قلب القدر رأسًا على عقب

"And then you must shake the pot"

وبعد ذلك يجب عليك أن تهز القدر

"The finest murukku will pour out"

سوف يتدفق أرقى موروكو

"The murukku will keep pouring out forever"

سوف يستمر تدفق الموروكو إلى الأبد

"Until you put the pot upright again"

حتى تعيد وضع القدر في مكانه مرة أخرى

"You can eat as much murukku as you like"

يمكنك أن تأكل ما تشاء من الموروكو

"Your wife and children will hunger no more"

لن تجوع زوجتك وأولادك بعد الآن

"And you can sell the murukku if you like"

ويمكنك بيع الموروكو إذا أردت

The Brahman was delighted beyond measure.

لقد كان البراهمان مسرورًا للغاية.

He had received a truly valuable treasure.

لقد حصل على كنز ثمين حقا.

He made his deepest obeisance to the goddess.

وقد قدم أعمق عبادته للإلهة.

And he expressed his eternal gratefulness.

وأعرب عن امتنانه الأبدي.

The Brahman had started walking home.

بدأ البراهمان بالسير إلى منزله.

But first he had to test his magical pot.

لكن كان عليه أولاً أن يختبر قدرته السحرية.

He wanted to see if the pot really worked.

أراد أن يرى ما إذا كان الوعاء يعمل حقًا.

He turned the pot upside down.

قلب القدر رأسا على عقب.

And he shook the pot, as instructed.

ثم هز القدر كما أمره.

Lo and behold! The pot really did work.

ها هو القدر يعمل فعلاً.

The finest murukku fell to the ground.

سقط أرقى موروكو على الأرض.

He tied the sweetmeat in his sheet.

ربط الحلوى في ملاءته.

And he walked on, towards his village.

ومشى نحو قريته.

By noon the Brahman had gotten hungry.

بحلول الظهر كان البراهمان قد أصبح جائعًا.

But he could not eat without his ablutions.

ولكنه لا يستطيع أن يأكل إلا على وضوء.

First, he had to say his prayers.

أولاً، كان عليه أن يقول صلواته.

There was an inn on his way.

وكان هناك نزل في طريقه.

Close to the inn there was a water tank.

كان هناك خزان مياه بالقرب من النزل.

So, he intended to halt there.

لذلك، كان ينوي التوقف هناك.

In order to bathe and say his prayers.

من أجل الاستحمام وقول صلواته.

After this he could eat all the murukku.

بعد ذلك أصبح بإمكانه أن يأكل كل الموروكو.

The Brahman sat at the innkeeper's shop.

جلس البراهمان في متجر صاحب النزل.

The shopkeeper was smoking tobacco.

وكان صاحب المتجر يدخن التبغ.

He put the pot near the shopkeeper.

وضع القدر بالقرب من صاحب المتجر.

And he asked him to look after the pot.

وطلب منه أن يعتني بالوعاء.

"Please take special care of this pot"

يرجى الاعتناء بهذا القدر بشكل خاص

"I must bathe and say my prayers"

يجب أن أستحم وأقول صلواتي

"Please look after this pot for me"

من فضلك اعتني بهذا القدر من أجلي

"Make sure nothing happens to this pot"

تأكد من عدم حدوث أي شيء لهذه الوعاء

He thought it was a strange request.

اعتقد أنه طلب غريب.

But he agreed to look after the pot.

ولكنه وافق على الاعتناء بالوعاء.

And the Brahman gave him the pot.

وأعطاه البراهمي القدر.

He besmeared his body with mustard oil.

دهن جسده بزيت الخردل.

And he went to do his ablutions.

وذهب ليتوضأ.

The innkeeper grew curious about the pot.

أصبح صاحب النزل فضوليًا بشأن القدر.

"This pot must have something valuable in it"

لا بد أن هذا القدر يحتوي على شيء ثمين

"Why else would he be so careful?"

ولماذا يكون حذرا إلى هذه الدرجة؟

His curiosity had been excited.

لقد أثار فضوله.

So, he opened the pot.

ففتح القدر.

To his surprise the pot was empty.

لقد فوجئ بأن الوعاء كان فارغا.

"What can be the meaning of this?"

ماذا يمكن أن يكون معنى هذا؟

"Why does he care so much for an empty pot?"

لماذا يهتم كثيرًا بالوعاء الفارغ؟

He began to examine the pot more carefully.

بدأ بفحص الوعاء بعناية أكبر.

During his inspection he turned the pot upside down.

أثناء التفتيش، قلب القدر رأسًا على عقب.

And then the finest murukku fell out from the pot.

وبعد ذلك سقط أرقى الموروكو من الوعاء.

And the murukku didn't stop falling out.

ولم يتوقف الموروكو عن السقوط

The innkeeper called his wife and children.

نادى صاحب الفندق على زوجته وأولاده.

He wanted them to witness what had happened.

أراد منهم أن يشهدوا ما حدث.

An unexpected stroke of good fortune!

ضربة حظ غير متوقعة

The pot gave copious showers of sugared paddy.

أعطت الوعاء كميات وفيرة من الأرز المحلى.

He filled all his pots and jars.

ملأ جميع أوانيه وجراره.

He knew he had to have this pot.

لقد كان يعلم أنه يجب عليه أن يحصل على هذه القدرة.

So, he replaced the pot with another one.

لذلك، قام باستبدال الوعاء بآخر.

He had a pot of the same size and color.

وكان عنده وعاء من نفس الحجم واللون.

The Brahman had finished his ablutions.

لقد انتهى البراهمان من الوضوء.

He had performed all of his devotions.

لقد أدى جميع عباداته.

He came back to the shop in wet clothes.

لقد عاد إلى المتجر بملابس مبللة.

He was still reciting holy texts of the Vedas.

كان لا يزال يتلو النصوص المقدسة من الفيدا.

He put back on his dry clothes.

ارتدى ملابسه الجافة مرة أخرى.

In red ink he wrote the name of Durga.

وكتب اسم دورجا بالحبر الأحمر.

He wrote her name one hundred and eight times.

كتب اسمها مائة وثماني مرات.

After doing this he broke his fast.

وبعد أن فعل ذلك أفطر.

And he ate the murukku he had in his sheet.

وأكل الموروكو الذي كان في سريره.

He was refreshed from the meal.

لـقد انتعش من الوجبة.

Now he could resume his journey home.

الآن يمكنه أن يستأنف رحلته إلى المنزل.

So he called to the innkeeper.

فـنادى على صاحب الفندق.

"Please could I get my pot back"

من فضلك هل يمكنني استعادة قدرتي

The innkeeper gave him back his pot.

أعاد له صاحب الفندق وعاءه.

"There, sir, here is your pot"

هناك يا سيدي، هنا قدرتك

"The pot is exactly where you had put it"

الوعاء موجود بالضبط حيث وضعته

"Your pot is just as you left it"

وعاءك كما تركته تمامًا

"I made sure no one has touched your pot"

لقد تأكدت من عدم لمس أحد لوعائك

The Brahman didn't suspect a thing.

لـم يشك البراهمان في أي شيء.

He picked up the pot.

لـقد التقط القدر.

And he proceeded on his journey home.

ثم واصل رحلته إلى منزله.

On his journey he had to think.

فـي رحلته كان عليه أن يفكر.

He congratulated his good fortune.

هنأ على حظه السعيد.

"My wife will be most pleasantly surprised!"

ستكون زوجتي متفاجئة للغاية

"The children will devour the murukku!"

الأطفال سوف يلتهمون الموروكو

"I shall soon become rich"

سأصبح غنيًا قريبًا

"I will be able to lift my head up high"

سأكون قادرًا على رفع رأسي عالياً

The pains of travelling had been reduced.

لقد تم تخفيف آلام السفر.

Now his problems were much more pleasant.

والآن أصبحت مشاكله أكثر متعة.

Only anticipation made the journey difficult.

كان الترقب فقط هو ما جعل الرحلة صعبة.

He finally reached his home again.

لقد وصل أخيرا إلى منزله مرة أخرى.

He called to his wife and children.

نادى على زوجته وأولاده.

"Look at what I have brought"

انظروا ماذا أحضرت

"This pot is an unfailing source of wealth".

إن هذا القدر هو مصدر لا ينضب للثروة.

"We will never have to struggle again"

لن نضطر إلى النضال مرة أخرى

"I will turn the pot upside down"

سأقلب القدر رأسًا على عقب

"And then you will see something.

وبعد ذلك سوف ترى شيئا.

"Something you've never seen before"

شيء لم تره من قبل

"A stream of the finest murukku will flow"

سيتدفق تيار من أجود أنواع الموروكو

You can imagine what his wife was thinking.

يمكنك أن تتخيل ما كانت تفكر فيه زوجته.

"My husband has gone mad," she thought.

لقد جن زوجي فكرت.

She was soon confirmed in her opinion.

وسرعان ما تأكدت من رأيها.

Nothing fell from the pot, as promised.

لم يسقط شيء من القدر كما وعدنا.

He turned the pot upside down again and again.

لقد قلب القدر رأسًا على عقب مرارًا وتكرارًا.

The Brahman was overwhelmed with grief.

لقد غمر الحزن البراهمان.

He realized that he had been tricked.

أدرك أنه قد تم خداعه.

The innkeeper must have swapped the pot.

لا بد أن صاحب النزل قد قام بتبديل الوعاء.

He must have stolen Durga's pot.

لابد أنه سرق وعاء دورجا.

And he must have replaced the pot with a normal one.

ولابد أن يكون قد استبدل الوعاء بآخر عادي.

He went back to the innkeeper the next day.

ثم عاد إلى صاحب النزل في اليوم التالي.

And he accused him of having changed his pot.

واتهمه بتغيير قدره.

At first the innkeeper acted surprised.

في البداية تصرف صاحب النزل وكأنه مندهش.

Then he pretended to be angry at the accusation.

ثم تظاهر بالغضب من التهمة.

Finally, he chased him out of his shop.

وأخيرًا، طرده من متجره.

He had no way of getting the pot back.

لم تكن لديه أي وسيلة لاستعادة القدر.

The Brahman knew what he had to do.

لقد عرف البراهمان ما يجب عليه فعله.

He went to see the goddess Durga again.

ذهب لرؤية الإلهة دورجا مرة أخرى.

Siva and Durga honored him with their presence.

لقد شرفه شيفا ودورجا بحضورهما.

Durga spoke to the poor Brahman.

تحدثت دورجا إلى البراهمي الفقير.

"So, you have lost the pot I gave you"

لذا، لقد فقدت الوعاء الذي أعطيتك إياه

"I take pity on your situation"

أشفق على حالتك

"Here is another magical pot"

هذا وعاء سحري آخر

"Take this pot, and make good use of it"

خذ هذه القدر، واستفد منها جيدًا

The Brahman was elated with joy.

كان البراهمان مسرورًا للغاية.

He made obeisance to the divine couple.

وسجد للزوجين الإلهيين.

And he took the pot with him.

وأخذ القدر معه.

Again he had to see if the pot worked.

مرة أخرى كان عليه أن يرى ما إذا كان الوعاء يعمل.

He turned the pot upside down.

قلب القدر رأسا على عقب.

And he shook the pot as before.

ورجّ القدر كما فعل من قبل.

And he waited for the murukku to fall out.

وانتظر سقوط الموروكو.

But no, horror of horrors!

ولكن لا، رعب من الرعب

Murukku did not fall from the pot.

لم يسقط موروكو من الوعاء.

Instead of murukku, demons jumped out.

بدلاً من الموروكو، قفز الشياطين.

They began to beat the astonished Brahman.

فبدأوا بضرب البراهمان المذهول.

The Brahman received punches and kicks.

تلقى البراهمان اللكمات والركلات.

But he kept his presence of mind.

ولكنه حافظ على حضور ذهنه.

He turned the pot the right way up.

لقد قلب القدر إلى الاتجاه الصحيح.

And he covered the pot up again.

ثم غطى القدر مرة أخرى.

Fortunately his quick thinking worked.

لحسن الحظ أن تفكيره السريع نجح.

The demons disappeared as soon as he did this.

اختفى الشياطين فور قيامه بهذا.

The Brahman tried to understand what this meant.

حاول البراهمان أن يفهم ما يعنيه هذا۔

It must be to punish the innkeeper!

لا بد من معاقبة صاحب النزل

So he went to the innkeeper again.

فذهب إلى صاحب الفندق مرة أخرى۔

He gave him the new pot.

أعطاه الوعاء الجديد۔

He begged of him to look after the pot.

وتوسل إليه أن يعتني بالوعاء۔

Just like he had done before.

تمامًا كما فعل من قبل۔

He went for his ablutions and prayers.

ذهب إلى الوضوء والصلاة۔

The innkeeper was delighted.

كان صاحب النزل مسرورًا۔

He had been given a second godsend.

لقد أعطيت له هبة ثانية من الله۔

He agreed to take the greatest care of the pot.

وافق على أن يولي القدر أكبر قدر من العناية۔

He waited for the Brahman to go.

كان ينتظر رحيل البراهمان۔

And he called his wife and children.

ودعا زوجته وأولاده۔

"This is another pot from the Brahman"

هذه إناء آخر من البراهمان

"This time I hope it is not murukku"

هذه المرة أتمنى ألا يكون موروكو

"I hope this pot is full of sandesa"

أتمنى أن يكون هذا الوعاء مليئًا بالسانديسا

"Come, be ready with the baskets"

تعالوا، كونوا مستعدين بالسلال

"I will turn the pot upside down"

سأقلب القدر رأسًا على عقب

"And then I will shake the pot"

وبعد ذلك سأهز القدر

And he did what he said he would do.

وفعل ما قال أنه سيفعله.

But the room did not fill with food.

ولكن الغرفة لم تمتلئ بالطعام.

This time the room filled with demons.

هذه المرة كانت الغرفة مليئة بالشياطين.

The demons caught hold of the innkeeper.

استولى الشياطين على صاحب النزل.

And the demons also caught his family.

والشياطين أيضا استولوا على عائلته.

And the demons beat them mercilessly.

وضربهم الشياطين بلا رحمة.

They would have completely destroyed the shop.

لقد قاموا بتدمير المتجر بالكامل.

But the victims ran to the Brahman.

لكن الضحايا ركضوا إلى البراهمان.

The Brahman had returned from his ablutions.

لقد عاد البراهمان من وضوئه.

The Brahman showed mercy to them.

وأظهر البراهمان رحمته لهم.

And he accepted their request.

وقبل طلبهم.

But there was one condition to his help.

ولكن كان هناك شرط واحد لمساعدته.

"I will only help if I get my pot back"

سأساعد فقط إذا استعدت قدرتي

The innkeeper didn't have much choice.

لم يكن أمام صاحب النزل الكثير من الخيارات.

He had to accept the Brahman's conditions.

وكان عليه أن يقبل شروط البراهمان.

The Brahman put the pot upright again.

أعاد البراهمان الوعاء إلى وضعه الطبيعي مرة أخرى.

And he put the lid on the pot.

ووضع الغطاء على القدر.

He took his pot back from the innkeeper.

أخذ وعاءه من صاحب الفندق.

And he returned back to his village.

وعاد إلى قريته.

Now the Brahman had two magical pots.

والآن أصبح لدى البراهمان وعاءان سحريان.

The Brahman shut the door of his house.

أغلق البراهمان باب بيته.

And he called his family again.

واتصل بعائلته مرة أخرى.

He turned the murukku-pot upside down.

لقد قلب وعاء الموروكو رأسًا على عقب.

And he shook the murukku-pot as before.

وهز القدر كما فعل من قبل.

This time the magic pot worked.

هذه المرة نجحت القدرة السحرية.

An endless stream of the finest murukku.

تيار لا نهاية له من أرقى الموروكو.

The family devoured the sweetmeat.

التهمت العائلة الحلوى.

They ate to their hearts' content.

لقد أكلوا حتى شبعوا.

All the pots and pans were filled.

كانت جميع الأواني والمقالي مملوءة.

The next day the Brahman became confectioner.

وفي اليوم التالي أصبح البراهمان صانع حلوى.

He opened a shop in his house.

فتح محلاً في منزله.

And he sold the best murukku.

وباع أفضل الموروكو.

The whole village came to the Brahman's house.

وجاءت القرية بأكملها إلى منزل البراهمان.

They all wanted to buy the wonderful murukku.

أرادوا جميعًا شراء الموروكو الرائع.

They had never seen such murukku in their life.

لم يروا مثل هذا الموروكو في حياتهم قط.

It was the most delicious murukku they ever had.

لـقد كان ألذ موروكو تناولوه على الإطلاق.

No one had ever made anything like this dessert.

لم يصنع أحد من قبل شيئًا مثل هذه الحلوى.

The reputation of the Brahman's murukku spread.

انتشرت شهرة موروكو البراهمي.

Soon people from outside the city came.

وبعد قليل جاء الناس من خارج المدينة.

Cartloads of the sweetmeat were sold every day.

تم بيع كميات كبيرة من الحلويات كل يوم.

The Brahman quickly became very rich.

سرعان ما أصبح البراهمان غنيًا جدًا.

He built a large brick house.

لـقد بنى بيتًا كبيرًا من الطوب.

And he lived like a nobleman of the land.

وعاش مثل أحد نبلاء البلاد.

Once, however, his luck almost changed.

ولكن في إحدى المرات، تغير حظه تقريبًا.

His children had taken the wrong pot.

لـقد أخذ أطفاله القدر الخطأ.

A large number of demons came out.

خرج عدد كبير من الشياطين.

And they caught hold of the Brahman's wife.

فـأمسكوا بزوجة البراهمي.

And they also caught his children.

وألقوا القبض على أولاده أيضًا.

They were striking them mercilessly.

وكانوا يضربونهم بلا رحمة.

Fortunately the Brahman came back into the house.

لـحسن الحظ عاد البراهمان إلى المنزل.

He turned the pot back to its proper position.

أعاد القدر إلى موضعه الصحيح.

He wanted to prevent a similar catastrophe.

أراد أن يمنع وقوع كارثة مماثلة.

So the Brahman had a private room built.

لـذلك قام البراهمان ببناء غرفة خاصة.

And he put the pot in a secret place.

ووضع القدر في مكان سري.

Mortals, however, do not have the luck of Gods.

لكن البشر ليس لديهم حظ الآلهة.

Uninterrupted prosperity is not their fortune.

إن الرخاء المتواصل ليس من نصيبهم.

The demon-pot had been put out of the way.

لقد تم إخراج وعاء الشيطان من الطريق.

But why might accident not befall the murukku pot?

ولكن لماذا لا يقع حادث في وعاء الموروكو؟

One day the Brahman and his wife were absent.

في أحد الأيام كان البراهمان وزوجته غائبين.

The children decided to shake the pot.

قرر الأطفال هز القدر.

Each of them wanted to do the honors.

كل واحد منهم أراد أن يقوم بالواجب.

So there was a fight to get the pot.

فكان هناك صراع للحصول على القدر.

In the struggle the pot fell to the ground.

وفي الصراع سقط الوعاء على الأرض.

Like any other earthen pot, it broke.

مثل أي وعاء فخاري آخر، انكسر.

Eventually the Braham came back home again.

وفي نهاية المطاف عاد براهام إلى منزله مرة أخرى.

You can imagine how the news grieved him.

يمكنك أن تتخيل مدى حزنه عند سماع هذا الخبر.

Of course the children were well cudgeled.

بالطبع كان الأطفال مهذبين بشكل جيد.

But anger could not replace the pot.

ولكن الغضب لم يستطع أن يحل محل القدر.

After some days he went to the forest again.

وبعد بضعة أيام ذهب إلى الغابة مرة أخرى.

He offered many a prayer for Durga's favor.

قدم العديد من الصلوات من أجل نيل رضا دورجا.

At last Siva and Durga appeared to him.

وأخيراً ظهر له شيفا ودورجا.

They listened to how the pot had been broken.

لقد استمعوا إلى كيفية كسر القدر.

Durga decided to give him another pot.

قررت دورجا أن تعطيه وعاءًا آخر.

But this pot was accompanied with a caution.

ولكن هذا القدر كان مصحوبا بحذر.

"Brahman, take care of this pot"

براهمان، اعتني بهذه القدر

"Do not break or lose this pot again"

لا تكسر أو تفقد هذا القدر مرة أخرى

"Next time I will not give you another pot"

في المرة القادمة لن أعطيك وعاءًا آخر

The Brahman made obeisance to the Gods.

كان البراهمان يسجد للآلهة.

And he went straight back to his house.

وعاد مباشرة إلى بيته.

This time he did not halt at the innkeepers'.

هذه المرة لم يتوقف عند أصحاب النزل.

He shut the door of his house.

أغلق باب بيته.

He called his family to him.

ن ادى على عائلته.

And he turned the pot upside down.

وقلب القدر رأسا على عقب.

And then he began to shake the pot.

وبعد ذلك بدأ يهز القدر.

They were only expecting murukku.

لقد كانوا يتوقعون فقط الموروكو.

But this time it was not murukku.

ولكن هذه المرة لم يكن موروكو.

A stream of beautiful sandesa poured out.

تدفقت سيل من مياه السانديسا الجميلة.

It was the finest sandesa you can imagine.

لقد كانت أفضل سانديسا يمكنك تخيلها.

It truly was the food of Gods.

لقد كان حقا طعام الآلهة.

The Brahman set up another shop.

أنشأ البراهمان متجرًا آخر.

Now he was selling sandesa.

الآن كان يبيع الساندیسا.

The fame of his shop soon drew large crowds.

سرعان ما اجتذبت شهرة متجره حشودًا كبيرة.

People came from all over the country.

جاء الناس من جميع أنحاء البلاد.

At all festivals and marriage feasts.

في جميع المهرجانات والأعياد الزفاف.

And at all funeral celebrations in the area.

وفي جميع مراسم الجنازة في المنطقة.

No one bought any other sandesa.

لم يشتري أحد أي سانديسا أخرى.

All day long the pot produced sandesa.

طوال اليوم أنتجت الوعاء سانديسا.

Gigantic jars were filled with sweet.

كانت الجرار الضخمة مليئة بالحلويات.

And the jars were sent all over the country.

وأرسلت الجرار إلى جميع أنحاء البلاد.

The Brahman's wealth made the Zemindar jealous.

ثروة البراهمي جعلت الزميندار يشعر بالغيرة.

In these days all villages had a Zemindar.

في تلك الأيام كان لكل قرية زمندار.

He had heard strange things about the sandesa.

لقد سمع أشياء غريبة عن الساندیسا.

He heard the dessert came from a magic pot.

سمع أن الحلوى جاءت من وعاء سحري.

So he devised a plan to get this pot.

لذلك وضع خطة للحصول على هذه القدرة.

His son was going to get married.

وكان ابنه سوف يتزوج.

To celebrate there was a great feast.

وللاحتفال كان هناك وليمة عظيمة.

Many hundreds of people were invited.

لقد تمت دعوة مئات الأشخاص.

Mountain-loads of sandesa were required.

كانت هناك حاجة إلى كميات هائلة من السانديسا.

The Zemindar made a proposal to the Brahman.

قدم الزميندار اقتراحًا إلى البراهمان.

"Bring the magical pot to my house"

أحضروا الوعاء السحري إلى منزلي

At first the Brahman refused to bring the pot.

في البداية رفض البراهمي إحضار القدر.

But the Zemindar insisted.

لكن الزميندار أصر.

"I will have hundreds of guests"

سوف يكون لدي مئات الضيوف

"I will need mountains of sandesa"

سأحتاج إلى جبال من السانديسا

"More sandesa than you can carry"

سانديسا أكثر مما يمكنك حمله

"Bring the vessel to my house"

أحضروا السفينة إلى منزلي

"It will be easier for you and me"

سيكون الأمر أسهل بالنسبة لي ولك

Eventually the Brahman agreed.

وفي نهاية المطاف وافق البراهمان.

Himalayas of sandesa were shaken out.

تم هز جبال الهيمالايا في سانديسا.

But the Zemindar got hold of the pot.

ولكن الزميندار استولى على القدر.

The Zemindar insulted the Brahman.

لقد أهان الزميندار البراهمان.

And he chased him out of his house.

وطرده من بيته.

The Brahman didn't give vent to anger.

لم يكن البراهمان يسمح بالتنفيس عن غضبه.

Instead, he quietly went back to his house.

وبدلاً من ذلك، عاد بهدوء إلى منزله.

He went to the private room.

ذهب إلى الغرفة الخاصة.

And he took out the demon-pot.

وأخرج إناء الشيطان.

He came back to the Zemindar's house.

لقد عاد إلى بيت الزميندار.

And he went to the door of the Zemindar.

وذهب إلى باب الزماندار.

He turned the pot upside down.

قلب القدر رأسا على عقب.

And then shook the magical pot.

ثم هز الوعاء السحري.

A hundred demons fell out of the pot.

سقط مئة شيطان من القدر.

The chaos was impossible to describe.

كانت الفوضى من المستحيل وصفها.

The unearthly visitors flooded the party.

لقد غمر الزوار غير العاديين الحفلة.

They caught hundreds of the guests.

لقد ألقوا القبض على المئات من الضيوف.

And the demons beat them mercilessly.

وضربهم الشياطين بلا رحمة.

The women were dragged by their hair.

تم سحب النساء من شعرهن.

The Zemindar was chased from room to room.

تم مطاردة الزميندار من غرفة إلى غرفة.

The demons' mischief was getting out of hand.

لقد أصبح أذى الشياطين خارجا عن السيطرة.

Someone had to put an end to their mischief.

كان لابد على شخص ما أن يضع حدًا لتصرفاتهم المشاغبة.

Else all the men would have been killed.

وإلا لكان جميع الرجال قد قتلوا.

And the house would have been torn to the ground.

وكان البيت ليُهدم إلى الأرض.

The Zemindar fell at the feet of the Brahman.

سقط الزميندار عند قدمي البراهمان.

And he begged to be shown mercy.

وطلب الرحمة.

The Brahman showed him great mercy.

وأظهر له البراهمان رحمة عظيمة.

And he put the demons back in the pot.

وأعاد الشياطين إلى القدر.

The Zemindar never disturbed the Brahman again.

لـم يزعج الزميندار البراهمان مرة أخرى.

Nor was he disturbed by anyone else.

ولم يزعجه أحد آخر.

And he lived for many happy years.

وعاش سنوات عديدة سعيدة.

The Story of the Rakshasas
قصة الراكشاسا

There was once a poor dimwitted Brahman.

كان هناك ذات مرة براهمان فقير غبي.

This dimwitted man had a wife, but no children.

كان لهذا الرجل الغبي زوجة، ولكن ليس لديه أطفال.

But him not having children was probably for the best.

لكن عدم إنجابه للأطفال ربما كان هو الأفضل.

Because he was barely able to meet his own needs.

لأنه كان بالكاد قادرا على تلبية احتياجاته الخاصة.

And he could hardly supply enough for his wife.

وكان بالكاد يستطيع توفير ما يكفي لزوجته.

But his dimwittedness was not even his biggest problem.

لكن غباءه لم يكن مشكلته الأكبر.

This dimwitted man was also a rather lazy man!

وكان هذا الرجل الغبي رجلاً كسولًا إلى حد ما أيضًا

He was averse to making any long journeys.

كان يكره القيام بأي رحلات طويلة.

Had he travelled further he might have had enough.

لو سافر أكثر ربما كان قد حصل على ما يكفي.

He could have got presents from rich men.

كان بإمكانه الحصول على هدايا من الرجال الأغنياء.

This would have enabled them to live comfortably.

وهذا كان من شأنه أن يمكّنهم من العيش بشكل مريح.

There was a great king in a neighbouring country.

كان هناك ملك عظيم في بلد مجاور.

The mother of the great king had just died.

لقد توفيت والدة الملك العظيم للتو.

So this king was celebrating the funeral obsequies.

وكان هذا الملك يحتفل بالجنازة.

And the funeral was celebrated with great pomp.

وأقيمت جنازته بكل فخامة واحتفال.

Brahmans and beggars were coming from faraway lands.

وكان البراهمة والمتسولون يأتون من بلاد بعيدة.

They all came expecting to receive rich presents.

لـقد جاءوا جميعًا على أمل الحصول على هدايا ثمينة۔

The Brahman's wife requested him to also go.

طلبت زوجة البراهمان منه أن يذهب أيضًا۔

"Seize this opportunity and get us a little money"

اغتنم هذه الفرصة واحصل لنا على القليل من المال

But his constitutional indolence stood in the way.

لـكن كسله الدستوري وقف في طريقه۔

The woman, however, gave her husband no rest.

ولكن المرأة لم تترك لزوجها أي فرصة للراحة۔

Finally she extorted from him the promise.

وأخيرا انتزعت منه الوعد۔

He promised his wife that he would go.

وعد زوجته أنه سيذهب۔

The good woman, accordingly, cut down a plantain tree.

وبناءً على ذلك، قامت المرأة الطيبة بقطع شجرة الموز۔

And she burnt the plantain tree to ashes.

وأحرقت شجرة الموز حتى تحولت إلى رماد۔

With the ashes she cleaned the clothes of her husband.

بـاستخدام الرماد قامت بتنظيف ملابس زوجها۔

And she made his clothes as white as any cleaner could.

وجعلت ملابسه بيضاء كالثلج مثل أي منظف۔

Her husband was going to the palace of a great king.

وكان زوجها ذاهبا إلى قصر ملك عظيم۔

The king could not be approached by men in rags.

لـم يكن من الممكن أن يقترب من الملك الرجال الذين يرتدون الخرق۔

Besides, Brahman are bound to appear neat and clean.

عـلاوة على ذلك، من المفترض أن يبدو البراهمان أنيقًا ونظيفًا۔

At last, one morning the Brahman left his house.

وأخيرًا، في أحد الصباحات، غادر البراهمان منزله۔

And he made his way to the palace of the great king.

واتجه في طريقه إلى قصر الملك العظيم۔

I have already mentioned he was a dimwitted man.

لـقد ذكرت بالفعل أنه كان رجلاً غبيًا۔

He did not inquire which road he should take.

ولم يسأل أي طريق ينبغي أن يسلك۔

Instead, he walked on and on without directions.

وبدلًا من ذلك، استمر في المشي دون توجيهات.

And he followed wherever his nose pointed him.

وتبعه حيثما أشار إليه أنفه.

I don't need to say he was not on the right road.

لا أحتاج إلى أن أقول أنه لم يكن على الطريق الصحيح.

The regions he wandered became less and less inhabited.

وأصبحت المناطق التي تجول فيها أقل سكانًا.

Soon he met no human being for many miles.

وبعد فترة قصيرة لم يقابل أي إنسان على بعد أميال عديدة.

But there were many other things he saw there.

لكن كان هناك العديد من الأشياء الأخرى التي رآها هناك.

Things he had never seen in all his life.

أشياء لم يشاهدها قط في حياته كلها.

He saw hillocks of cowries on the roadside.

لقد رأى تلالاً من المحار على جانب الطريق.

Cowries were shells used as money in those times.

كان الكوري عبارة عن أصداف كانت تستخدم كعملة في تلك الأوقات.

He kept going and saw hillocks of jewels.

استمر في السير فرأى تلالاً من الجواهر.

Next, he saw hillocks of four-anna pieces.

وبعد ذلك، رأى تلالاً من قطع الآنا الأربعة.

Further along were hillocks of eight-anna pieces.

وعلى مسافة أبعد كانت هناك تلال من قطع الثماني آنا.

And further yet were hillocks of rupees.

وأبعد من ذلك كانت هناك تلال من الروبيات.

But the Brahman's surprise did not end there.

ولكن مفاجأة البراهمان لم تنته عند هذا الحد.

Next there was a hill of burnished gold-mohurs.

وبعد ذلك كان هناك تلة من الصخور الذهبية المصقولة.

The burnished gold-mohurs were shining brightly.

كانت الأحجار الكريمة الذهبية المصقولة تلمع بشكل ساطع.

Because the gold-mohurs had been freshly minted.

لأن العملات الذهبية كانت قد سُكّت حديثًا.

Close to the hill of gold-mohurs was a large house.

كان هناك منزل كبير بالقرب من تل الموهور الذهبي.

The house looked like the palace of a powerful king.

كان المنزل يبدو وكأنه قصر ملك قوي.

At the door stood a lady of exquisite beauty.

عند الباب وقفت سيدة ذات جمال رائع.

The lady, seeing the Brahman, said;

قالت السيدة عندما رأت البراهمان:

"Come to me, my beloved husband"

تعال إليّ يا زوجي الحبيب

"You married me when I was young"

لقد تزوجتني عندما كنت صغيرا

"But you never came back after our marriage"

ولكنك لم تعد أبدًا بعد زواجنا

"Though I have been daily expecting you"

على الرغم من أنني كنت أنتظرك يوميًا

"Blessed be this day," said the lady.

مبارك هذا اليوم قالت السيدة.

"On this day I see the face of my husband"

في هذا اليوم أرى وجه زوجي

"Come, my sweet, come in," she asked of him.

تعال يا حبيبي، تعال إلى الداخل، سألته.

"You must be fatigued from your long journey"

لا بد أنك متعب من رحلتك الطويلة

"Wash your feet and rest, and eat and drink"

اغسلوا أرجلكم واستريحوا وكلوا واشربوا

"And after that we shall make ourselves merry"

وبعد ذلك سوف نجعل أنفسنا سعداء

The Brahman was astonished beyond measure.

لقد اندهش البراهمان إلى حد لا يمكن قياسه.

He had no recollection marrying twice.

لم يكن لديه أي ذكريات عن الزواج مرتين.

He remembered marrying the wife he left at home.

تذكر أنه تزوج من زوجته التي تركها في المنزل.

But he did not remember marrying this lady.

ولكنه لم يتذكر أنه تزوج هذه السيدة.

But he remembered that he was a Kulin Brahman.

ولكنه تذكر أنه كان كولين براهمان.

Perhaps his father got him married as a child.

ربما أن والده زوجه عندما كان طفلاً.

But what he thought did not matter much.

ولكن ما كان يعتقده لم يكن مهمًا كثيرًا.

The woman was certain he was her husband.

وكانت المرأة متأكدة أنه زوجها.

And he had no reason to say he was not her husband.

ولم يكن لديه سبب ليقول أنه ليس زوجها.

Because her beauty was more than he could fathom.

لأن جمالها كان أكثر مما يستطيع أن يتصوره.

As beautiful as the Goddesses of Indra's heaven.

جميلة مثل آلهة سماء إندرا.

And he was sure that she was wealthy too.

وكان متأكداً أنها كانت غنية أيضاً.

These thoughts went through the Brahman's mind.

لقد دارت هذه الأفكار في ذهن البراهمان.

But the lady interrupted his flow of thought.

ولكن السيدة قاطعت تدفق أفكاره.

"Are you doubting whether I am your wife?"

هل تشك في أنني زوجتك؟

"Have you lost all memories of that happy event?

هل فقدت كل ذكريات هذا الحدث السعيد؟

"All the pomp and circumstance of our nuptials"

كل البهاء والاحتفالات في حفل زفافنا

"Come in, beloved; this is your house"

ادخل يا حبيبي، هذا بيتك

"Because whatever is mine is thine also"

لأن كل ما هو لي فهو لك أيضًا

The fair lady easily persuaded the Brahman.

تمكنت السيدة الجميلة من إقناع البراهمان بسهولة.

And he succumbed to her loving entreaties.

واستسلم لتوسلاتها المحبة.

And he went into the house of the lady.

ودخل بيت السيدة.

The house was not an ordinary one.

لم يكن المنزل عاديًا.

The house was in fact a magnificent palace.

وكان المنزل في الواقع قصرًا رائعًا.

All the apartments were large and lofty.

كانت جميع الشقق كبيرة ومرتفعة.

Every room in the palace was richly furnished.

كانت كل غرفة في القصر مفروشة بشكل غني.

But one thing surprised the Brahman very much.

ولكن هناك شيء واحد فاجأ البراهمان كثيرًا.

There was no other person in all the house.

لم يكن هناك شخص آخر في البيت بأكمله.

The only one there was the lady herself.

وكان الشخص الوحيد هناك هي السيدة نفسها.

He could not account for the strange phenomenon.

لم يتمكن من تفسير هذه الظاهرة الغريبة.

They meet anyone on their walks either.

ويقابلون أي شخص أثناء نزهتهم أيضًا.

The fact was that the lady was not a human being.

والحقيقة أن السيدة لم تكن إنسانة.

What the lady really was was a Rakshasi.

في الحقيقة كانت السيدة راكشاسي.

She had eaten up the king and queen.

لقد أكلت الملك والملكة.

And she had eaten all the members of the royal family.

وكانت قد أكلت جميع أفراد العائلة المالكة.

And gradually she had eaten their servants too.

وبدأت تأكل خدمهم تدريجيا أيضا.

This was why there were no humans far and wide.

ولهذا السبب لم يكن هناك بشر في كل مكان.

The Rakshasi and the Brahman now lived together.

والآن يعيش الراكشاسي والبراهمي معًا.

After a week the former said to the latter;

وبعد أسبوع قال الأول للأخير:

"I am very anxious to see my sister"

أنا متشوق جدًا لرؤية أختي

"As you know, my sister is your other wife"

كما تعلم، أختي هي زوجتك الأخرى

"You must go and fetch my sister; your other wife"

يجب عليك أن تذهب وتأخذ أختي؛ زوجتك الأخرى

"Then we shall all live together happily"

ثم سنعيش جميعا معا بسعادة

"You must go to get her early tomorrow"

يجب عليك الذهاب لإحضارها مبكرًا غدًا

"I will give you clothes and jewels for her"

سأعطيك ملابس ومجوهرات لها

Next morning the Brahman set out for his home.

وفي صباح اليوم التالي، انطلق البراهمان إلى منزله.

He was furnished with fine clothes.

لقد تم تزويده بملابس جميلة.

And he wore around his wrists costly ornaments.

وكان يرتدي حول معصميه الحلي الثمينة.

The poor woman was in great distress.

وكانت المرأة المسكينة في حالة من الضيق الشديد.

The funeral ceremony of the king's mother was over.

انتهت مراسم جنازة والدة الملك.

All the Brahmans and Pandits had returned.

لقد عاد جميع البراهمة والبانديت.

And they were loaded with donations.

وكانت محملة بالتبرعات.

But her husband had not returned.

ولكن زوجها لم يعد.

No one could give any news of him.

لم يتمكن أحد من إعطاء أي أخبار عنه.

Because no one had seen him there.

لأنه لم يره أحد هناك.

The woman therefore could only come to one conclusion.

لذلك لم تستطع المرأة إلا التوصل إلى نتيجة واحدة.

He must have been murdered on the road by highwaymen.

لا بد أنه قُتل على الطريق على يد قطاع الطرق.

She was in this terrible suspense.

لقد كانت في هذا الترقب الرهيب.

But then one day she heard some rumors.

ولكن ذات يوم سمعت بعض الشائعات.

People in her village were talking about her husband.

وكان الناس في قريتها يتحدثون عن زوجها.

They said they saw him coming back.

قالوا أنهم رأوه عائدا.

And they said he was dressed in fine clothes.

وقالوا أنه كان يرتدي ملابس جميلة.

And they said he had fine jewels for his wife.

وقالوا إنه كان يملك مجوهرات ثمينة لزوجته.

And sure enough the Brahman soon appeared.

وبالفعل ظهر البراهمان قريبًا.

And he was carrying fine jewels for his wife.

وكان يحمل مجوهرات ثمينة لزوجته.

On seeing his wife the Brahman thus accosted her;

وعندما رأى البراهمان زوجته، خاطبها بهذه الطريقة؛

"Come with me, my dearest wife"

تعالي معي يا زوجتي العزيزة

"I have found my first wife"

لقد وجدت زوجتي الأولى

"She lives in a stately palace"

إنها تعيش في قصر فخم

"Near her palace are hillocks of rupees"

بالقرب من قصرها توجد تلال من الروبيات

"And there is a large hill of gold-mohurs"

وهناك تلة كبيرة من الذهب

"Why should you pine away in wretchedness?"

لماذا يجب عليك أن تذبل في البؤس؟

"Why would you stay in this horrible place?"

لماذا بقيت في هذا المكان الرهيب؟

"Come with me to the house of my first wife"

تعال معي إلى بيت زوجتي الأولى

"There we shall all live together happily"

هناك سوف نعيش جميعا معا بسعادة

At first, she thought her half-witted man had gone mad.

في البداية، اعتقدت أن زوجها الذي كان ضعيف العقل قد أصيب بالجنون.

She could not imagine the hillocks of rupees.

لم تتمكن من تخيل كميات الروبيات.

And she could not imagine a hill of gold-mohurs.

ولم تكن قادرة على تخيل تلة من الذهب.

But then she saw how he was beautifully dressed.

ولكن بعد ذلك رأت كيف كان يرتدي ملابس جميلة.

Beautiful clothes of exquisite silks and satins.

ملابس جميلة من الحرير والساتان الرائع.

Ornaments set with diamonds and precious stones.

زينة مرصعة بالماس والأحجار الكريمة.

Clothes fit for the queen of the land.

ملابس تليق بملكة الأرض.

Clothes only princesses were in the habit of putting on.

كانت الأميرات معتادات على ارتداء الملابس فقط.

She concluded in her mind that something was amiss:

وخلصت في ذهنها إلى أن هناك شيئًا ما خطأ:

Her stupid husband must have been tricked.

لا بد أن زوجها الغبي قد تعرض للخداع.

He must have fallen into the meshes of a Rakshasi.

لا بد أنه وقع في شباك راكشاسي.

The Brahman, however, insisted his wife went with him.

لكن البراهمي أصر على أن تذهب زوجته معه.

"Feel free to stay here and pine away in poverty"

لا تتردد في البقاء هنا والعيش في فقر

"As for me, I will return to the palace of my first wife"

أما أنا فسأعود إلى قصر زوجتي الأولى

The good woman did her best to stop her husband.

لقد بذلت المرأة الصالحة قصارى جهدها لمنع زوجها.

But in the end she resolved to go with him.

ولكن في النهاية قررت الذهاب معه.

Perhaps she could judge the matter better at the palace.

ربما استطاعت أن تحكم على الأمر بشكل أفضل في القصر.

They set out accordingly the next morning.

وانطلقوا وفقا لذلك في صباح اليوم التالي.

They went the same road the Brahman had travelled.

لقد سلكوا نفس الطريق الذي سلكه البراهمان.

The woman was not a little surprised by what she saw.

She saw the hillocks of cowries and of jewels.

ولم تكن المرأة متفاجئة على الإطلاق بما رأته.

And she saw hillocks of eight-anna pieces.

لقد رأت تلالاً من المحار والجواهر.

And she saw the hillocks of rupees too.

ورأت تلالاً من قطع الثماني آنا.

And last of all she saw a lofty hill of gold-mohurs.

ورأت أيضًا تلال الروبيات.

She saw also an exceedingly beautiful lady.

وأخيراً رأت تلة عالية من الصخور الذهبية.

The lady of the palace was hastening towards her.

ورأت أيضًا سيدة جميلة للغاية.

The lady fell on the neck of the Brahman woman.

وكانت سيدة القصر تسرع نحوها.

And she wept tears of joy, and said:

سقطت السيدة على رقبة المرأة البراهمية.

"Welcome, beloved sister!"

ف:بكت دموع الفرح وقالت

"This is the happiest day of my life!"

مرحبا بك أختي الحبيبة

"I see the face of my dearest sister again!"

هذا هو أسعد يوم في حياتي

The husband and his two wives entered the palace.

أرى وجه أختي العزيزة مرة أخرى

Now he was lodged in a stately mansion.

دخل الزوج وزوجتاه القصر.

The most delectable food appeared, as if by enchantment.

وكان يقيم الآن في قصر فخم.

He was caressed and endeared by his two wives.

ظهرت أشهى الأطعمة، وكأنها سحر.

Both wives did their best to make him happy.

لقد كان محبوباً ومدللاً من قبل زوجتيه.

Both wives did their best to make him comfortable.

لقد بذلت كلتا الزوجتين قصارى جهدهما لإسعاده.

His two wives were competing for his love.

بذلت كلتا زوجتيهما قصارى جهدهما لجعله مرتاحًا.

وكانت زوجتيه تتنافسان على حبه.

The Brahman had a jolly time of it.

لقد أمضى البراهمان وقتًا ممتعًا.

He was steeped in an ocean of enjoyment.

لقد كان غارقًا في محيط من المتعة.

The Brahman lived in this state of Elysian pleasure.

لقد عاش البراهمان في هذه الحالة من المتعة الإليزية.

Some fifteen or sixteen years he spent this way.

لقد أمضى بهذه الطريقة حوالي خمسة عشر أو ستة عشر عامًا.

During this time his two wives presented him with two
sons.

خلال هذه الفترة أنجبت له زوجتيه ولدين.

The Rakshasi's son was the elder.

وكان ابن الراكشاسي هو الأكبر.

He looked more like a god than a human being.

لقد كان يبدو مثل الإله أكثر من كونه إنسائًا.

He was named Sahasra-Dal.

لقد تم تسميته ساهسرا دال.

His name meant the thousand-branched.

اسمه يعني الألف فرع.

The son of the Brahman woman was a year younger.

وكان ابن المرأة البراهمية أصغر منها بسنة.

He was named Champa-Dal

تم تسميته تشامبا دال

His name meant the branch of a champaka tree.

اسمه يعني فرع شجرة الشامباكا.

The two brothers loved each other dearly.

لقد أحب الأخوين بعضهما البعض بشدة.

They were both sent to the same school.

لقد تم إرسالهما إلى نفس المدرسة.

The school was several miles distant from the palace.

كانت المدرسة على بعد عدة أميال من القصر.

Every day they rode their two little ponies to school.

كل يوم كانوا يركبون حصانيهما الصغيرين إلى المدرسة.

The Brahman woman had always been suspicious.

لقد كانت المرأة البراهمية دائمًا مشبوهة.

A thousand little circumstances gave her clues.

ألف حالة صغيرة أعطتها أدلة.

She knew her sister-in-law was not a human being.

لقد عرفت أن أخت زوجها ليست إنسانة.

She was sure her sister-in-law was a Rakshasi.

كانت متأكدة أن أخت زوجها كانت من راكشاسي.

But her suspicion had not yet ripened into certainty.

ولكن شكوكها لم تنضج بعد إلى يقين.

Because the Rakshasi exercised great self-restraint.

لأن الراكشاسي مارسوا ضبط النفس بشكل كبير.

She never did anything which human beings did not do.

لم تفعل أبدًا أي شيء لم يفعله البشر.

But she couldn't hide her demonic nature forever.

لكنها لم تتمكن من إخفاء طبيعتها الشيطانية إلى الأبد.

Her demonic nature was eventually going to reveal itself.

طبيعتها الشيطانية كانت ستكتشف عن نفسها في نهاية المطاف.

The Brahman had little to keep him busy.

لم يكن لدى البراهمان الكثير مما يجعله مشغولاً.

In order to pass his time he went hunting.

من أجل قضاء وقته ذهب للصيد.

The first day he returned with an antelope.

في اليوم الأول عاد مع الظباء.

The antelope was laid in the courtyard of the palace.

تم وضع الظبي في فناء القصر.

The Rakshasi saw the antelope with great interest.

لقد رأى الراكشاسي الظبي باهتمام كبير.

At the sight of the raw meat her mouth began to water.

عندما رأت اللحم النيء بدأ فمها يسيل لعاباً.

The antelope was never taken to the kitchen.

لم يتم أخذ الظبي إلى المطبخ أبدًا.

Instead, the Rakshasi took the antelope to another room.

وبدلاً من ذلك، أخذ الراكشاسي الظبي إلى غرفة أخرى.

In this room she began devouring the antelope.

وفي هذه الغرفة بدأت في التهام الظباء.

The Brahman woman saw everything from a secret room.

لقد رأت المرأة البراهمية كل شيء من غرفة سرية.

Her Rakshasi sister tore a leg off the antelope.

مزقت أختها الراكشاسية ساق الظبي.

She saw how she opened her tremendous jaw.

لقد رأت كيف فتحت فكها الهائل.

And in one mouthful she swallowed up the leg.

وفي لقمة واحدة ابتلعت الساق.

The other limbs were devoured in the same manner.

وتم التهام الأطراف الأخرى بنفس الطريقة.

And opening her jaw even further, she swalled the body.

وفتحت فكها أكثر، وابتلعت الجثة.

Only a little bit of the meat was kept for the kitchen.

لم يتم الاحتفاظ إلا بالقليل من اللحوم للمطبخ.

On the second day the Brahman caught another antelope.

وفي اليوم الثاني، اصطاد البراهمان ظبيًا آخر.

On the third day the Brahman caught another antelope.

وفي اليوم الثالث، اصطاد البراهمان ظبيًا آخر.

The Rakshasi was unable to restrain her appetite.

لم تتمكن الراكشاسي من كبح شهيتها.

The raw flesh brought out her demonic nature.

أظهر اللحم النيء طبيعتها الشيطانية.

And she devoured each antelope like the last.

وأكلت كل ظبي مثل الأخير.

On the third day the Brahman woman expressed her surprise.

وفي اليوم الثالث، أعربت المرأة البراهمية عن دهشتها.

"Nearly three whole antelopes have disappeared"

اختفى ما يقرب من ثلاثة ظباء كاملة

"All that is left is a little bit of meat"

كل ما تبقى هو القليل من اللحم

The Rakshasi did not appreciate the accusation.

لم يتقبل الراكشاسي هذا الاتهام.

"Do I eat raw flesh?" she asked fiercely.

هل آكل لحمًا نيئًا؟ سألت بشراسة.

"Perhaps you do eat raw flesh," replied the Brahman woman.

ربما تأكل لحمًا نيئًا، أجابت المرأة البراهمية.

"I have nothing to prove the contrary"

ليس لدي ما يثبت العكس

The Rakshasi knew she had been discovered.

عرف الراكشاسي أنه تم اكتشافها.

Her eyes became even fiercer than before.

أصبحت عيناها أكثر شراسة من ذي قبل.

And she vowed to get her revenge.

وتعهدت بالانتقام.

The Brahman woman concluded her fate was sealed.

لقد خلصت المرأة البراهمية إلى أن مصيرها قد تم تحديده.

She thought her husband would meet the same fate.

اعتقدت أن زوجها سيلقى نفس المصير.

She did not expect her son to be spared either.

ولم تكن تتوقع أن ينجو ابنها أيضًا.

That night she hardly slept at all.

في تلك الليلة لم تنم إطلاقا.

The Rakshasi had prevented her from seeing her husband.

لقد منعها الراكشاسي من رؤية زوجها.

Early next morning Champa-Dal went to school.

في الصباح الباكر التالي ذهب شامبا دال إلى المدرسة.

Before he went to school she gave her son a golden bottle.

قبل أن يذهب إلى المدرسة أعطت ابنها زجاجة ذهبية.

In the golden bottle was her own breast milk.

في الزجاجة الذهبية كان حليب ثديها.

"Carefully watch the colour of the milk"

راقب لون الحليب بعناية

"If the milk turns red, your father has been killed"

إذا تحول الحليب إلى اللون الأحمر، فقد قُتل والدك

"If the milk turns redder, then I have been killed"

إذا تحول الحليب إلى اللون الأحمر، فقد قُتلت

"If the milk turns red you must gallop away"

إذا تحول الحليب إلى اللون الأحمر، يجب عليك الركض بعيدًا

"Gallop as fast as your horse can carry you"

اركض بأسرع ما يمكن لحصانك أن يحملك

"If you do not run away, you will be devoured"

إذا لم تهرب، فسوف تُلتهم

That morning the Rakshasi made a suggestion to her husband.

وفي ذلك الصباح قدمت الراكشاسي اقتراحًا لزوجها.

"Let us bathe in the river this morning"

دعونا نستحم في النهر هذا الصباح

She would not take no for an answer.

لن تقبل بالرفض.

The river was some distance from the palace.

وكان النهر على مسافة ما من القصر.

The Brahman followed her as meekly as a lamb.

لقد تبعها البراهمان بخنوع كالحمل.

The Brahman woman saw that her doom was near.

رأت المرأة البراهمية أن مصيرها أصبح قريبًا.

But it was beyond her power to avert the catastrophe.

ولكن كان الأمر يفوق قدرتها على تجنب الكارثة.

The Brahman and the Rakshasi did indeed reach the river.

لقد وصل البراهمان والراكشاسي بالفعل إلى النهر.

Soon after the Rakshasi changed into her real dimensions.

وبعد فترة وجيزة تحولت راكشاسي إلى أبعادها الحقيقية.

She tore the Brahman limb from limb.

لقد مزقت عضو البراهمان إرباً إرباً.

She devoured him like she had devoured the antelope.

لقد التهمته كما التهمت الظبي.

Then she ran back to her palace.

ثم ركضت عائدة إلى قصرها.

The wive's fate was the same as the Brahman's.

وكان مصير الزوجة هو نفس مصير البراهمان.

Young Champ Dal had done as his mother instructed.

لقد فعل البطل الصغير دال كما أرشدته والدته.

He was diligently observing the golden bottle.

كان يراقب الزجاجة الذهبية بعناية.

He paid special attention to the colour of the milk.

اهتم بشكل خاص بلون الحليب.

He was horror-struck to find the milk redden a little.

لقد أصيب بالرعب عندما وجد الحليب قد تحول إلى اللون الأحمر قليلاً.

"My father has been killed," he cried.

لقد قُتل والدي، صرخ.

Soon after the milk completely reddened.

وبعد فترة وجيزة تحول الحليب إلى اللون الأحمر تماما.

"Now my mother has been killed too," he cried.

والآن قُتلت أمي أيضًا، صرخ.

Quickly he rushed to mount his pony.

أسرع ليركب حصانه.

His half-brother, Sahasra-Dal, was surprised.

لقد تفاجأ أخوه غير الشقيق، ساهسرا دال.

"Where are you going, Champa?"

إلى أين أنت ذاهب يا شامبا؟

"Why are you crying, brother?"

لماذا تبكي يا أخي؟

"Let me accompany you to wherever you are going"

دعني أرافقك أينما كنت ذاهبًا

But Champa-Dal now feared his brother.

لكن شامبا دال أصبح الآن خائفًا من أخيه.

"Oh! do not come to me," he objected.

أوه لا تأتي إليّ، اعترض.

"Your mother has devoured my father and mother"

أمك أكلت أبي وأمي

"Don't you come and devour me"

لا تأتي وتلتهمني

"I will not devour you," he promised his brother.

لن آكلك وعد أخاه.

"I'll save you," he promised his brother.

سأنقذك وعد أخاه.

And he galloped after his brother, Champa-Dal.

وركض خلف أخيه شامبا دال.

Soon his mother, the Rakshasi, appeared at a distance.

وبعد قليل ظهرت أمه، الراكشاسي، من مسافة بعيدة.

She demanded Champa-Dal to come to her.

طلبت من شامبا دال أن يأتي إليها.

But Champa-Dal knew better than to go to the Rakshasi.

لكن شامبا دال كان يعلم أنه من الأفضل عدم الذهاب إلى راكشاسي.

"Champa-Dal will not come to you, but I will"

لن يأتي إليك شامبا دال، لكنني سأأتي

And instead, Sahasra-Dal went to his mother.

وبدلاً من ذلك، ذهب ساهسرا دال إلى والدته.

The young prince always carried a sword with him.

وكان الأمير الشاب يحمل معه دائمًا سيفًا.

With his sword he cut off his mother's head.

لقد قطع رأس أمه بسيفه.

Champa-Dal had not stayed to witness this.

ولم يبقَ شامبا دال ليشهد هذا.

He had galloped off as far as his pony could carry him.

لقد انطلق مسرعًا إلى أقصى حد يمكن أن يحمله حصانه.

Because he was running for his life.

لأنه كان يركض لإنقاذ حياته.

But Sahasra-Dal soon caught up with his brother.

لكن سرعان ما تمكن ساهسرا دال من اللحاق بأخيه.

And he told him that his mother was no more.

وأخبره أن أمه لم تعد موجودة.

This was small consolation to Champa-Dal.

وكان هذا بمثابة عزاء صغير لشامبا دال.

The Rakshasi had already devoured both his parents.

لقد التهم الراكشاسي والديه بالفعل.

But he could still not trust Sahasra-Dal's friendship.

ولكنه لا يزال لا يستطيع أن يثق بصداقة ساهسرا ـدال.

They both rode as fast as their horses could carry them.

لقد ركبا كلاهما بأسرع ما يمكن أن تحمله خيولهما.

And their horses could carry them very far.

ويمكن لخيولهم أن تحملهم لمسافات بعيدة جدًا.

Because their horses were Pakshirajes horses.

لأن خيولهم كانت خيول باكشيراج.

Pakshirajes horses are the kings of birds.

خيول الباكشيراج هي ملوك الطيور.

On their horses they travelled over hundreds of miles.

سافروا على خيولهم مئات الأميال.

An hour or two before sundown they reached a village.

قبل ساعة أو ساعتين من غروب الشمس وصلوا إلى قرية.

Here they became the guests of a respectable family.

وهنا أصبحوا ضيوفًا لعائلة محترمة.

But the two brothers saw the family was in gloom.

لكن الأخوين رأيا أن العائلة كانت في حالة من الكآبة.

Something was agitating the family very much.

كان هناك شيء يزعج العائلة كثيرًا.

Some of the family held private consultations.

أجرى بعض أفراد العائلة استشارات خاصة.

And others in the family were weeping.

وكان آخرون في العائلة يبكون.

The mother was the eldest lady in the house.

وكانت الأم هي السيدة الأكبر سنا في المنزل.

"I will go, as I am the eldest," she said.

سأذهب، فأنا الأكبر، قالت.

"I have lived long enough"

لقد عشت طويلاً بما فيه الكفاية

"At most my life would be cut short by a year or two"

على الأكثر ستكون حياتي قصيرة بعام أو عامين

The youngest member of the house was a little girl.

وكان أصغر عضو في المنزل فتاة صغيرة.

"I will go, as I am young," she said.

سأذهب، فأنا شابة، قالت.

"I am useless to the family"

أنا عديم الفائدة للعائلة

"If I die, I shall not be missed"

إذا متُّ، فلن أفتقدني

The head of the house was the son of the old lady.

وكان رب البيت ابن السيدة العجوز.

"I am the representative of the family," he said.

أنا ممثل العائلة، قال.

"It is but reasonable that I should give up my life"

من المعقول أن أتخلى عن حياتي

He also had a younger brother.

وكان له أخ أصغر أيضًا.

"You are the pillar of the family," he said.

أنت عمود العائلة، قال۔

"If you go the whole family is ruined"

إذا ذهبت، فسوف تدمر العائلة بأكملها

"It is not reasonable that you should go"

ليس من المعقول أن تذهب

"I will go, as I shall not be much missed"

سأذهب، لأنني لن أفتقد كثيرًا

The two strangers listened to all this conversation.

كان الغريبان يستمعان إلى كل هذا الحديث۔

You can imagine their curiosity was not little.

يمكنك أن تتخيل أن فضولهم لم يكن قليلا۔

They wondered what the discussion could be about.

وتساءلوا عما يمكن أن يكون موضوع المناقشة۔

Sahasra-Dal took the risk of being thought meddlesome.

لقد خاض ساهسرا دال مخاطرة اعتباره متطفلاً۔

"What is the subject of your consultations?"

ما هو موضوع استشاراتك؟

"What is the reason for your deep miserable?"

ما هو سبب تعاستك العميقة؟

"Why are your words full of countenances?"

لماذا كلماتك مليئة بالوجوه؟

The head of the house gave the following answer.

ف:أجاب رب البيت بالجواب التالي

"There is something you must know, me worthy guests"

هناك شيء يجب أن تعرفوه، أيها الضيوف الكرام

"These lands are infested by a terrible Rakshasi"

هذه الأراضي موبوءة بركشاسي رهيب

"This Rakshasi has depopulated all the regions here"

لقد أدى هذا الراكشاسي إلى إخلاء جميع المناطق هنا

"This town, too, would have been depopulated"

هذه المدينة أيضًا كانت ستصبح خالية من السكان

"But that our king became suppliant to the Rakshasi"

ولكن ملكنا أصبح متوسلاً إلى الراكشاسي

"He begged her to show mercy to us his people"

توسل إليها أن تظهر الرحمة لنا شعبه

The Rakshasi replied to the king.

رد الراكشاسي على الملك.

"I will consent to show mercy to your subjects"

سأوافق على إظهار الرحمة لرعيتك

"But there is one condition for my mercy"

ولكن هناك شرط واحد لرحمتي

"Every night I demand one human being"

كل ليلة أطالب بإنسان واحد

"I don't mind if it is a male or a female"

لا يهمني إن كان ذكرًا أم أنثى

"Put the human being in a temple for me to feast"

ضع الإنسان في معبد لأتناوله

"If I get a human being every night I will rest satisfied"

إذا حصلت على إنسان كل ليلة سأرتاح راضيًا

"Promise me this and I will commit no further depredations"

وعدني بهذا ولن أرتكب المزيد من التعديات

"Your subjects will be spared from my ravenous hunger"

سوف يتم إنقاذ رعيتك من جوعي الشديد

"Our king had no other alternative than to agree"

لم يكن أمام ملكنا خيار آخر سوى الموافقة

"What human can ever hope to contend against a Rakshasi?"

ما هو الإنسان الذي يمكن أن يأمل في المنافسة ضد راكشاسي؟

"From that day the king made a new law"

ومن ذلك اليوم أصدر الملك قانونًا جديدًا

"Every family has to send one member to the temple"

يجب على كل عائلة أن ترسل أحد أفرادها إلى المعبد

"To appease the wrath of the terrible Rakshasi"

لتهدئة غضب الراكشاسي الرهيب

"To satisfy the endless hunger of the Rakshasi"

لإشباع الجوع اللامتناهي للراكشاسي

"All the families in this neighbourhood have had their turn"

لقد حصلت جميع العائلات في هذا الحي على دورها

"This night it is the turn of our family"

هذه الليلة جاء دور عائلتنا

"One of us is to devote ourself to destruction"

أحدنا أن يكرّس نفسه للتدمير

"We are therefore discussing who should go to the Rakshasi"

لذلك نحن نناقش من يجب أن يذهب إلى راكشاسي

"You can now perceive the cause of our distress"

يمكنك الآن إدراك سبب محنتنا

The two friends consulted together for a few minutes.

تشاور الصديقان معًا لبضع دقائق.

After this time they concluded their consultation.

وبعد هذا الوقت انتهوا من استشاراتهم.

Sahasra-Dal was the spokesman for the brothers.

وكان ساهسرا دال المتحدث باسم الإخوة.

"Most worthy host, do not any longer be sad"

أيها المضيف الكريم، لا تحزن بعد الآن

"You have been very kind to us"

لقد كنت لطيفًا جدًا معنا

"We have resolved to requite your hospitality"

لقد قررنا أن نرد لكم حسن ضيافتكم

"We will go to the temple instead of you"

سنذهب إلى المعبد بدلاً منك

"We shall go as your representatives"

سنذهب كممثلين لكم

"We will become the food of the Rakshasi"

سنصبح طعامًا للراكشاسي

The whole family protested against the proposal.

احتجّت العائلة بأكملها على الاقتراح.

They declared that guests were like gods.

وأعلنوا أن الضيوف كانوا مثل الآلهة.

"The host must ensure the comfort of the guests"

يجب على المضيف ضمان راحة الضيوف

"The guests must not suffer for the host"

لا ينبغي للضيوف أن يتألموا من أجل المضيف

But the two strangers could not be persuaded.

ولكن لم يتمكن أحد من إقناع الغريبين.

"We will stand as proxies for your family"

سنكون وكلاء لعائلتك

There was a great deal of objection to the proposal.

وكان هناك قدر كبير من الاعتراض على الاقتراح.

But eventually the guests persuaded their hosts.

ولكن في نهاية المطاف نجح الضيوف في إقناع مضيفهم.

Finally the hosts consented to the arrangement.

وأخيرًا وافق المضيفون على الترتيب.

Sahasra-Dal and Champa-Dal rode off on their horses.

انطلق ساهسرا دال وتشامبا دال على خيولهما.

Immediately after candle light they reached the temple.

وبعد ضوء الشموع مباشرة وصلوا إلى المعبد.

They went into the temple, and shut the door.

فدخلوا الهيكل وأغلقوا الباب.

Sahasra told his brother to go to sleep.

قال السحاسرا لأخيه أن يذهب للنوم.

"I will guard over your sleep"

سأحرس نومك

"I will watch out for the terrible Rakshasi"

سأكون حذرًا من راكشاسي الرهيب

Champa was soon in a fine sleep.

وسرعان ما نام شامبا نومًا عميقًا.

Sahasra lay awake, waiting for the Rakshasi.

كمستيقظًا في انتظار الركشاسي Sahasra ان.

Nothing happened during the early hours of the night.

ولم يحدث شيء خلال الساعات الأولى من الليل.

But then the gong of the king's bell sounded.

ولكن بعد ذلك رن جرس الملك.

It was midnight, the dead hour of the night.

لقد كانت الساعة منتصف الليل، الساعة الميتة من الليل.

Sahasra heard the sound as of a rushing tempest.

سمع ساهسرا صوتًا يشبه صوت العاصفة العاصفة.

He used the knowledge he had of Rakshasas.

لقد استخدم المعرفة التي كان يمتلكها عن الراكشاساس.

He concluded the Rakshasi was nigh.

وخلص إلى أن راكشاسي كان قريبًا.

A thundering knock was heard at the door.

سمع صوت طرق قوي على البابُ.

The following words accompanied the knock at the door:

الكلمات التالية رافقت الطرق على الباب:

"How, mow, khow! A human being I smell"

كيف، يا إلهي أشتم رائحة إنسان

"Who keeps guard inside this temple?"

من يحرس داخل هذا المعبد؟

To this question Sahasra-Dal made the following reply:

وأجاب ساهسرا دال على هذا السؤال بما يلي:

"Sahasra-Dal keeps guard inside this temple"

السهاسرا دال يحرس داخل هذا المعبد

"Champa-Dal keeps guard inside this temple"

تشامبا دال يحرس داخل هذا المعبد

"Two winged horses keep guard inside this temple"

حصانان مجنحان يحرسان داخل هذا المعبد

Rakshasa blood flowed through Sahasra-Dal's veins.

تدفق دم الراكشاسا في عروق ساهسرا دال.

The Rakshasi knew Sahasra-Dal was not human.

عرف الراكشاسي أن ساهاسرا دال ليس إنسانًا.

And so the Rakshasi turned away with a groan.

وهكذا استدار الراكشاسي بعيدًا مع تأوه.

After an hour the Rakshasi returned to the temple.

بعد ساعة عاد الراكشاسي إلى المعبد.

The Rakshasi thundered at the door again.

هدر الراكشاسي عند الباب مرة أخرى.

"How, mow, khow! A human being I smell"

كيف، يا إلهي أشتم رائحة إنسان

"Who keeps guard inside this temple?"

من يحرس داخل هذا المعبد؟

To this question Sahasra-Dal again replied:

وأجاب ساهسرا دال على هذا السؤال مرة أخرى:

"Sahasra-Dal keeps guard inside this temple"

السهاسرا دال يحرس داخل هذا المعبد

"Champa-Dal keeps guard inside this temple"

تشامبا دال يحرس داخل هذا المعبد

"Two winged horses keep guard inside this temple"

حصانان مجنحان يحرسان داخل هذا المعبد

The Rakshasi again groaned and went away.

أطلق الراكشاسي أنينًا مرة أخرى وذهب بعيدًا.

At two o'clock the Rakshasi appeared once more.

وفي الساعة الثانية ظهر الراكشاسي مرة أخرى.

And at three o'clock the Rakshasi came again.

وفي الساعة الثالثة جاء الراكشاسي مرة أخرى.

Each time the Rakshasi made the same inquiry.

في كل مرة كان الراكشاسي يقوم بنفس الاستفسار.

And each time the Rakshasi left with a groan.

وفي كل مرة كان الراكشاسي يغادر مع تأوه.

After three o'clock, however, Sahasra-Dal felt very sleepy.

ومع ذلك، بعد الساعة الثالثة، شعر ساهسرا دال بالنعاس الشديد.

He could not any longer keep awake.

لم يعد بإمكانه البقاء مستيقظا.

He therefore roused Champa.

ولذلك أيقظ شامبا.

And he told him to keep guard over the temple.

وأمره بحراسة الهيكل.

"The Rakshasi will come again in an hour"

سوف يأتي الراكشاسي مرة أخرى في غضون ساعة

"The Rakshasi will ask who keeps guard here"

سوف يسأل الراكشاسي من يحرس هنا

"You must mention Sahasra's name first"

يجب عليك ذكر اسم ساهسرا أولاً

Having given these instructions he went to sleep.

وبعد أن أعطى هذه التعليمات ذهب إلى النوم.

At four o'clock the Rakshasi again made her appearance.

في الساعة الرابعة ظهر الراكشاسي مرة أخرى.

The Rakshasi thundered at the door, and said:

هدر الراكشاسي عند الباب وقال:

"How, mow, khow! A human being I smell"

كيف، يا إلهي أشتم رائحة إنسان

"Who keeps guard inside this temple?"

من يحرس داخل هذا المعبد؟

Champa-Dal was in a terrible fright.

كان شامبا دال في حالة خوف شديد.

He had forgotten the instructions of his brother.

لقد نسي تعليمات أخيه.

"Champa-Dal keeps guard inside this temple"

تشامبا دال يحرس داخل هذا المعبد

"Sahasra-Dal keeps guard inside this temple"

السهاسرا دال يحرس داخل هذا المعبد

"Two winged horses keep guard inside this temple"

حصانان مجنحان يحرسان داخل هذا المعبد

The Rakshasi uttered a shout of exultation.

أطلق الراكشاسي صرخة فرح.

And the Rakshasi laughed how only demons can laugh.

وضحك الراكشاسي كما يضحك الشياطين فقط

With a dreadful noise the door broke open.

مع ضجيج مروع انفتح الباب.

The noise roused Sahasra from his sleep.

أيقظ الضجيج سهاسرا من نومه.

Within a moment he sprung to his feet.

وفي غضون لحظة قفز على قدميه.

He had his sword with him not only by day.

وكان يحمل سيفه معه ليس فقط في النهار.

He had his sword with him by night too.

وكان معه سيفه في الليل أيضًا.

His sword was as supple as a palm-leaf.

وكان سيفه مرنًا مثل سعف النخيل.

And he cut off the head of the Rakshasi.

وقطع رأس الراكشاسي.

The huge mountain of a body fell to the ground.

سقط الجبل الضخم من الجسد على الأرض.

The body made a great noise when it fell.

لقد أحدث الجسد ضجيجًا كبيرًا عندما سقط

And the body covered many surrounding acres.

وغطى الجسد مساحات واسعة من الأراضي المحيطة.

Sahasra-Dal kept the severed head of the Rakshasi.

ابرأس الركثاسي المقطوع Sahasra-Dal حتفظ

And he slept again with the head near him.

ثم نام مرة أخرى والرأس بجانبه.

Early in the morning some wood-cutters came.

في الصباح الباكر جاء بعض الحطابين.

The wood-cutters were passing near the temple.

وكان الحطابون يمرون بالقرب من المعبد.

The wood-cutters saw the huge body on the ground.

رأى الحطابون الجسد الضخم على الأرض.

So they walked towards the temple.

فذهبوا نحو المعبد.

Soon they saw that it was a carcass.

وسرعان ما رأوا أنها كانت جثة.

The carcass of the terrible Rakshasi.

جثة راكشاسي الرهيبة.

The Rakshasi that had nearly depopulated the land.

الراكشاسي الذين كانوا على وشك إخلاء الأرض من السكان.

There had been a bounty for this Rakshasi.

لقد كانت هناك مكافأة لهذا الراكشاسي.

The king offered the hand of his daughter.

عرض الملك يد ابنته.

And the king had offered half the kingdom.

وعرض الملك نصف المملكة.

He would trade it all for the head of the Rakshasi.

كان مستعدًا لتداول كل شيء مقابل رأس الراكشاسي.

The wood-cutters saw no claimant at hand.

ولم يجد الحطابون أي مطالبة في متناول اليد.

So they went to get the reward.

فذهبوا ليحصلوا على المكافأة.

Each wood-cutter cut off a limb from the Rakshasi.

كل قاطع حطب يقطع فرعًا من الراكشاسي.

And each wood-cutter went to the king.

وذهب كل حطاب إلى الملك.

And each wood-cutter tried to claim the reward.

وحاول كل حطاب أن يحصل على المكافأة.

"I am the destroyer of the great man eater"

أنا مدمر آكل البشر العظيم

"I have come to claim my reward"

لقد جئت للمطالبة بمكافأتي

The king knew there could only be one hero.

كان الملك يعلم أنه لا يمكن أن يكون هناك إلا بطل واحد.

So he made an inquiry with his minister.

فسأل وزيره.

"What family's turn was it last night?"

ما هو دور العائلة الليلة الماضية؟

"And who is the head of that family?"

ومن هو رب تلك العائلة؟

The king's minister set out to find the family.

انطلق وزير الملك للبحث عن العائلة.

He brought the head of the family to the king.

فأحضر رئيس العائلة إلى الملك.

And the head of the family told of his guests.

وأخبر رب الأسرة عن ضيوفه.

"Last night two youthful travelers came to me"

في الليلة الماضية، جاء إليّ مسافران شابان

"We offered to be their hosts for the night"

لقد عرضنا أن نكون مضيفين لهم طوال الليل

"Soon they discovered the problem we had"

سرعان ما اكتشفوا المشكلة التي كانت لدينا

"And they volunteered to take our place"

وتطوعوا ليحلوا محلنا

"They went to the temple, instead of one of us"

ذهبوا إلى المعبد، بدلاً من واحد منا

The king took his men to the temple.

أخذ الملك رجاله إلى المعبد.

The door of the temple was broken open.

لقد انكسر باب المعبد.

They found the two brothers sleeping.

ووجدوا الأخوين نائمين.

And the horses were safe in the temple too.

وكانت الخيول آمنة في المعبد أيضًا.

And the head of the Rakshasi was there too.

وكان رئيس الراكشاسي هناك أيضًا.

There was no doubt about who had killed the monster.

لم يكن هناك شك حول من قتل الوحش.

The real hero had been discovered.

لقد تم اكتشاف البطل الحقيقي.

And the king kept true to his word.

وأوفى الملك بكلمته.

He gave the hand of his daughter to Sahasra-Dal.

أعطى يد ابنته لسهاسرا دال.

And he gave him half his kingdom too.

وأعطاه نصف مملكته أيضًا.

Champa-Dal remained with his friend.

بقي شامبا دال مع صديقه.

And he rejoiced in Sahasra-Dal's prosperity.

وفرح بازدهار ساهسرا دال.

And they lived together happily for some time.

وعاشوا معاً بسعادة لبعض الوقت.

But one day a misunderstanding arose between them.

ولكن في يوم من الأيام حدث سوء تفاهم بينهما.

The queen-mother had a certain maid-servant.

وكان للملكة الأم خادمة معينة.

This maid-servant was the most useful domestic.

كانت هذه الخادمة هي الخادمة الأكثر فائدة في المنزل.

She could turn her hand to any task.

كان بإمكانها أن تلجأ إلى أي مهمة.

And she had uncommon strength for a woman.

وكانت تمتلك قوة غير عادية بالنسبة لامرأة.

Her intelligence was not lacking either.

ولم يكن ذكاءها ناقصا أيضا.

And she had a remarkable amount of energy.

وكانت تمتلك كمية كبيرة من الطاقة.

She would have been quickly missed in the palace.

لقد كان من الممكن أن يتم افتقادها بسرعة في القصر.

The zenana was completely dependent on her.

وكانت الزنانة تعتمد عليها كليا.

Hence her services were highly valued.

ومن ثم كانت خدماتها موضع تقدير كبير.

The queen-mother appreciated her very much.

لقد كانت الملكة الأم تقدرها كثيرًا.

And the ladies of the palace valued her too.

وكانت سيدات القصر يقدرونها أيضًا.

But this valuable woman was not a woman.

ولكن هذه المرأة القيمة لم تكن امرأة.

What this woman was was a Rakshasi.

كانت هذه المرأة راكشاسي.

She had put on the appearance of a woman.

لقد كانت تبدو كامرأة.

She had her own nefarious reasons for doing this.

لقد كانت لديها أسبابها الشريرة الخاصة للقيام بهذا.

And then she took service in the royal household.

وبعد ذلك أخذت الخدمة في البيت الملكي.

At night she used to assume her own real form.

وفي الليل كانت تتخذ شكلها الحقيقي.

When everyone in the palace was asleep.

عندما كان الجميع في القصر نائمين.

And then she went about in search of food.

وبعد ذلك ذهبت للبحث عن الطعام.

Because her hunger was not satisfied at the palace.

لأن جوعها لم يشبع في القصر.

A Rakshasi needs much more food than a man or woman.

يحتاج الراكشاسي إلى قدر أكبر من الطعام مقارنة بالرجل أو المرأة.

At this time Champa-Dal had no wife.

في هذا الوقت لم يكن لدى شامبا دال زوجة.

So he often slept outside the zenana.

فكان ينام خارج الحرام في كثير من الأحيان.

He was not far from the outer gate of the palace.

ولم يكن بعيدًا عن البوابة الخارجية للقصر.

And from there he could observe her.

ومن هناك استطاع أن يراقبها.

He saw her devouring sundry goats and sheep.

لقد رآها تلتهم الكثير من الماعز والأغنام.

And he saw her devouring horses and elephants.

ورآها تأكل الخيول والفيلة.

This of course was not good for the maid-servant.

وهذا بالطبع لم يكن جيدا بالنسبة للخادمة.

Champa-Dal was in the way of her supper.

كان شامبا دال عائقًا في طريق عشائها.

So she was determined to get rid of him.

لذلك قررت التخلص منه.

One day she went to the queen-mother.

ذهبت ذات يوم إلى الملكة الأم.

"Queen-mother," she said to her.

الملكة الأم، قالت لها.

"I can no longer work in the palace"

لم يعد بإمكاني العمل في القصر

"Why?" asked the queen-mother.

لماذا؟ سألت الملكة الأم.

"What is the matter, Dasi" she wanted to know.

ما الأمر يا داسي أرادت أن تعرف.

"How can I go on without you?"

كيف يمكنني الاستمرار بدونك؟

"Tell me your reasons for leaving"

أخبرني عن أسباب رحيلك

The maid-servant explained her situation.

شرحت الخادمة وضعها.

"I am but a poor woman in this palace"

أنا مجرد امرأة فقيرة في هذا القصر

"A woman like me can't preserve her honour here"

امرأة مثلي لا تستطيع الحفاظ على شرفها هنا

"Your son-in-law has a friend, Champa-Dal"

صهرك لديه صديق، شامبا دال

"He always cracks indecent jokes with me"

إنه دائمًا يطلق النكات البذيئة معي

"I would rather beg for my rice than to lose my honour"

أفضل أن أتوسل للحصول على أرزّي من أن أفقد شرفي

"If Champa-Dal remains in the palace I must go away"

إذا بقي شامبا دال في القصر، يجب أن أرحل

The maid-servant was irreplicable in the palace.

كانت الخادمة لا يمكن تكرارها في القصر.

The queen-mother knew what sacrifice to make.

عرفت الملكة الأم حجم التضحية التي يجب عليها تقديمها.

Champa-Dal was going to have to leave the palace.

كان يتعين على شامبا دال أن يغادر القصر.

And she told Sahasra-Dal all her reasons.

وأخبرت ساهسرا دال بكل أسبابها.

"Champa-Dal is a bad man"

شامبا دال رجل سيء

"His character and morals are loose"

شخصيته وأخلاقه متزعزعة

"He must leave this palace at once"

يجب عليه مغادرة هذا القصر على الفور

Sahasra-Dal did his best to persuade her otherwise.

بذل ساهسرا دال قصارى جهده لإقناعها بخلاف ذلك.

He earnestly pleaded on behalf of his friend.

لقد دافع بشدة عن صديقه.

But his efforts were in vain.

ولكن جهوده كانت بلا جدوى.

The queen-mother had made up her mind.

لقد اتخذت الملكة الأم قرارها.

He had to be driven out of the palace.

كان لا بد من طرده من القصر.

Sahasra-Dal had not the courage to tell his friend.

ولم يكن لدى ساهسرا دال الشجاعة ليخبر صديقه.

He therefore wrote a letter to him.

فكتب له رسالة.

In the letter he was vague about the reason.

وفي الرسالة كان غامضا بشأن السبب.

But either way, he was going to have to leave.

ولكن على أية حال، كان عليه أن يرحل.

Champa-Dal went to have a bath.

ذهب شامبا دال للاستحمام.

And the letter was put in his room.

ووضعت الرسالة في غرفته.

Champa-Dal was grieved upon reading the letter.

حزن شامبا دال عندما قرأ الرسالة.

He mounted his fleet of horses.

ركب أسطوله من الخيول.

And on his horses he left the palace.

وعلى خيوله خرج من القصر.

Champa's horses were uncommonly fleet.

كانت خيول شامبا سريعة بشكل غير عادي.

Soon he had traversed thousands of miles.

وبعد فترة وجيزة، كان قد عبر آلاف الأميال.

And eventually he reached a new city.

وفي نهاية المطاف وصل إلى مدينة جديدة.

He stood at the gateway of a magnificent palace.

كان واقفا عند بوابة القصر العظيم.

He dismounted from his horse.

نزل عن حصانه.

And he entered the palace.

ودخل القصر.

But in the palace he met not a single creature.

ولكن في القصر لم يقابل أي مخلوق.

He went from apartment to apartment.

انتقل من شقة إلى شقة.

All the rooms were richly furnished.

تم تأثيث جميع الغرف بشكل غني.

But none of the rooms were lived in.

ولكن لم يكن هناك أي شخص مسكون في أي من الغرف.

But in the end he came to a different room.

ولكن في النهاية وصل إلى غرفة أخرى.

In this room there was a young lady.

كانت هناك سيدة شابة في هذه الغرفة.

The young lady was of heavenly beauty.

وكانت الشابة ذات جمال سماوي.

And she was lying down on a splendid bedstead.

وكانت مستلقية على سرير فاخر.

The beautiful young lady was asleep.

وكانت الشابة الجميلة نائمة.

Champa-Dal looked upon the sleeping beauty.

نظر شامبا دال إلى الجميلة النائمة.

He was captivated by what he was seeing.

لقد كان مفتونًا بما كان يرى.

He had not seen any woman so beautiful.

لم يرى امرأة جميلة مثلها.

Upon the bed there were two sticks.

وعلى السرير كان هناك عصوان.

The two sticks were near the woman's head.

وكانت العصيان بالقرب من رأس المرأة.

One of the sticks was made of silver.

كانت إحدى العصي مصنوعة من الفضة.

And the other stick was made of gold.

والعصا الأخرى كانت مصنوعة من الذهب.

Champa took the silver stick into his hand.

أخذ شامبا العصا الفضية في يده.

And with the stick he touched the body of the lady.

وبالعصا لمس جسد السيدة.

But no change was perceptible to her sleep.

ولكن لم يكن هناك أي تغيير ملحوظ في نومها.

He then took up the gold stick.

ثم أخذ العصا الذهبية.

And with the stick he touched the body of the lady.

وبالعصا لمس جسد السيدة.

This time the young lady did awake.

هذه المرة استيقظت الشابة.

Eyeing the stranger, she inquired who he was.

نظرت إلى الغريب وسألت من هو.

"I am Champa-Dal," he told her.

أنا شامبا دال، قال لها.

"There was once a poor dimwitted Brahman"

كان هناك ذات مرة براهمان فقير غبي

"This dimwitted man had a wife, but no children"

كان لهذا الرجل الأحمق زوجة، ولكن ليس لديه أطفال

"But him not having children was probably for the best"

لكن عدم إنجابه أطفالًا ربما كان هو الأفضل

"Because he was barely able to meet his own needs"

لأنه بالكاد كان قادرًا على تلبية احتياجاته الخاصة

"And he could hardly supply enough for his wife"

وكان بالكاد يستطيع توفير ما يكفي لزوجته

"But his dimwittedness was not even his biggest problem"

ولكن غباءه لم يكن حتى أكبر مشاكله

And he continued the story as we have followed it.

وأكمل القصة كما تابعناها.

"My mother concluded her fate was sealed"

خلصت والدتي إلى أن مصيرها قد تم تحديده

"And she thought my father would meet the same fate"

وكانت تعتقد أن والدي سيلقى نفس المصير

"And she did not expect me to be spared either"

ولم تكن تتوقع أن أنجو أنا أيضًا

"That night she hardly slept at all"

في تلك الليلة لم تنم على الإطلاق

"The Rakshasi had prevented her from seeing my father"

لقد منعها الراكشاسي من رؤية والدي

"Early next morning I went to school"

في الصباح الباكر التالي ذهبت إلى المدرسة

"Before I went to school she gave me a golden bottle"

قبل أن أذهب إلى المدرسة أعطتني زجاجة ذهبية

"In the golden bottle was her own breast milk"

في الزجاجة الذهبية كان حليب ثديها

"I was told to carefully watch the colour of the milk"

لقد قيل لي أن أراقب لون الحليب بعناية

And he continued the story as we have followed it.

وأكمل القصة كما تابعناها.

"We will stand as proxies for your family"

سنكون وكلاء لعائلتك

"There was a great deal of objection to our proposal"

كان هناك قدر كبير من الاعتراض على اقتراحنا

"But eventually we persuaded our hosts"

ولكن في النهاية نجحنا في إقناع مضيفينا

"Finally the hosts consented to the arrangement"

وأخيرًا وافق المضيفون على الترتيب

And he continued the story as we have followed it.

وأكمل القصة كما تابعناها.

"So I often slept outside the zenana"

لذلك كنت أنام خارج الحرام كثيرًا

"I was not far from the outer gate of the palace"

لم أكن بعيدًا عن البوابة الخارجية للقصر

"And from there I could observe her"

ومن هناك تمكنت من مراقبتها

"I saw her devouring sundry goats and sheep"

رأيتها تأكل الكثير من الماعز والأغنام

"And I saw her devouring horses and elephants"

ورأيتها تأكل الخيول والفيلة

And he continued the story as we have followed it.

وأكمل القصة كما تابعناها.

"One day a letter was put in my room"

في أحد الأيام، وُضعت رسالة في غرفتي

"I was grieved upon reading the letter"

لقد حزنت عندما قرأت الرسالة

"I mounted my fleet of horses"

ركبت أسطولي من الخيول

"And on my horses he left the palace"

وعلى خيلي غادر القصر

"My horse are uncommonly fleet"

حصاني سريع بشكل غير عادي

"Soon I had traversed thousands of miles"

سرعان ما قطعت آلاف الأميال

"And eventually I reached a new city"

وفي النهاية وصلت إلى مدينة جديدة

And he continued the story as we have followed it.

وأكمل القصة كما تابعناها.

"I took the silver stick into his hand"

أخذت العصا الفضية في يده

"And with the stick I touched your body"

وبالعصا لمست جسدك

"But no change was perceptible to your sleep"

ولكن لم يكن هناك أي تغيير ملحوظ في نومك

"I then took up the gold stick"

ثم أخذت العصا الذهبية

And with the stick he touched your body.

وبالعصا لمس جسدك.

"This time you did awake from your sleep"

هذه المرة استيقظت من نومك

The young lady had listened to Champa-Dal's story.

لقد استمعت الشابة إلى قصة شامبا دال.

The young lady was in fact a princess.

وكانت الشابة في الواقع أميرة.

"Unhappy man! why have you come here?"

أيها الرجل التعيس لماذا أتيت إلى هنا؟

"This is the country of Rakshasas"

هذه هي بلاد الراكشاساس

"No less than seven hundred Rakshasas live here"

لا يقل عدد سكان راكشاسا الذين يعيشون هنا عن سبعمائة

"Every morning the Rakshasas leave"

كل صباح يغادر الراكشاسا

"They go to the other side of the ocean"

إنهم يذهبون إلى الجانب الآخر من المحيط

"And they search for provisions there"

ويبحثون عن الطعام هناك

"And before dusk they return again"

وقبل الغسق يعودون مرة أخرى

"My father was king in these regions"

كان والدي ملكًا في هذه المناطق

"His kingdom had millions of subjects"

كانت مملكته تضم ملايين الرعايا

"They lived in flourishing towns and cities"

لقد عاشوا في المدن والبلدات المزدهرة

"But some years ago the Rakshasas invaded"

ولكن منذ بضع سنوات غزت قبيلة راكشاسا

"And they devoured all the subjects of the kingdom"

وأكلوا كل رعايا المملكة

"The Rakshasas devoured my father and my mother"

الراكشاسا التهموا والدي وأمي

"The Rakshasas devoured my brothers and sisters"

الراكشاسا التهموا إخوتي وأخواتي

"And they devoured all the cattle of the country"

وأكلوا كل ماشية الأرض

"There is no living human being in these regions"

لا يوجد إنسان حي في هذه المناطق

"I am the last human living left"

أنا آخر إنسان على قيد الحياة

"I too would have been devoured long ago"

أنا أيضًا كنت سأُفترس منذ زمن طويل

"But an old Rakshasi took a liking to me"

لكن أحد رجال راكشاسي العجوز أعجب بي

"She prevents the other Rakshasas from eating me"

إنها تمنع الراكشاسا الآخرين من أكلي

"Do you see those sticks of silver and gold?"

هل ترى تلك العصي الفضية والذهبية؟

"Every morning she kills me with the silver stick"

كل صباح تقتلني بالعصا الفضية

"Every evening she re-animates me with the gold stick"

في كل مساء تُعيد إحيائي بالعصا الذهبية

"I do not know how to advise you"

لا أعرف كيف أنصحك

"If the Rakshasas see you, you are a dead man"

إذا رآك الراكشاسا، فأنت رجل ميت

Then they talked in a very affectionate manner.

ثم تحدثوا بطريقة حنونة للغاية.

And they laid their heads together.

ووضعوا رؤوسهم معًا.

And they thought to devise a means of escape.

فـفكروا في إيجاد وسيلة للنجاة.

Some way to get out of the hands of the Rakshasas.

بـعض الطرق للخروج من أيدي الراكشاسا.

The hour of the return of the Rakshasas was coming.

لـقد حانت ساعة عودة الراكشاسا.

The seven hundred flesh-eaters were soon returning.

وسرعان ما عاد السبعمائة من آكلي اللحوم.

Keshavati called out to Champa-Dal.

كيشافاتي تنادي على شامبا دال.

(Because that was the name of the princess)

((لأن هذا كان اسم الأميرة

"Hide yourself in the heaps of the sacred trefoil"

اختبئ في أكوام البرسيم المقدس

But first Champ Dal picked up the silver stick.

لكن أولاً التقط تشامب دال العصا الفضية.

He touched Keshavati with the silver stick.

لقد لمس كشافاتي بالعصا الفضية.

And as soon as he touched her, she died.

وبمجرد أن لمسها ماتت.

Then he went to the center of the temple of Siva.

ثم ذهب إلى وسط معبد شيفا.

And he hid beneath the heaps of sacred trefoil.

واختبأ تحت أكوام البرسيم المقدس.

From his hiding place he heard the sound of wind rushing.

ومن مخبئه سمع صوت الريح العاصفة.

Then he heard terrible noises in the palace.

ثم سمع أصواتًا رهيبة في القصر.

The Rakshasas had come home from their hunt.

لقد عاد الراكشاسا إلى منزلهم من رحلة الصيد.

They had filled their stomachs with meat.

لقد ملئوا بطونهم باللحم.

Sundry goats, sheep, cows, horses, buffaloes.

الماعز والأغنام والأبقار والخيول والجاموس المتنوعة.

And they had devoured elephants too.

وكانوا قد التهموا الفيلة أيضًا.

The old Rakshasi returned to the palace too.

عاد الراكشاسي القديم إلى القصر أيضًا.

She went to the room of the sleeping princess.

ذهبت إلى غرفة الأميرة النائمة.

And she woke her with the stick made of gold.

وأيقظتها بالعصا المصنوعة من ذهب.

"Hye, mye, khye! A human being I smell"

هي، ماي، خاي أشمّ إنسانًا

"I am the only human being here," said the princess.

أنا الإنسان الوحيد هنا، قالت الأميرة.

"Eat me if you like," added Keshavati.

كلني إذا أردت، أضافت كيشافاتي.

To this the Rakshasi replied:

ف:أجابه الراكشاسي

"Let me eat up your enemies"

دعني آكل أعدائك

"Why should I eat you?" she asked the princess.

لماذا يجب أن آكلك؟ سألت الأميرة.

She laid herself down on the ground.

ألقت نفسها على الأرض.

She was as long and high as the Vindhya Hills.

كانت طويلة ومرتفعة مثل تلال فينديا.

And in this position she fell asleep.

وفي هذا الوضع نامت.

The other Rakshasas and Rakshasis soon fell asleep too.

وسرعان ما نام الراكشاسا والراكشاسيس الآخرون أيضًا.

Because they were tired from their gigantic labour.

لأنهم كانوا متعبين من عملهم الضخم.

Keshavati also composed herself to sleep.

كما هدأت كشافاتي نفسها للنوم.

But Champa did not dare to come out from under the leaves.

ولكن شامبا لم يجرؤ على الخروج من تحت الأوراق.

And he tried his best to pray to the god of repose.

وحاول جاهدا أن يصلي إلى إله الراحة.

At daybreak all seven hundred Rakshasas got up again.

عند الفجر، نهض جميع الراكشاسا السبعمائة مرة أخرى.

They went on their usual predatory excursion.

لقد ذهبوا في رحلتهم المفترسة المعتادة.

And along with them went the old Rakshasi.

ومعهم ذهب الراكشاسي العجوز.

But first the old Rakshasi picked up the silver stick.

ولكن أولاً التقط الراكشاسي العجوز العصا الفضية.

And she touched Keshavati with the silver stick.

ولمست كشافاتي بالعصا الفضية.

Soon the coast was clear for Champa-Dal.

وبعد قليل أصبح الساحل خاليا بالنسبة لشامبا دال.

And he dared to come out from under the pile of leaves.

وأراد أن يخرج من تحت كومة الأوراق.

He walked back into the room of the princess.

عاد إلى غرفة الأميرة.

And he touched her with the golden stick.

ولمسها بالعصا الذهبية.

And the princess revived from her death again.

وعادت الأميرة إلى الحياة من موتها.

They sauntered about in the gardens.

لقد كانوا يتجولون في الحدائق.

They enjoyed the cool breeze of the morning.

لقد استمتعوا بنسيم الصباح البارد.

They bathed in a lucid pool of water.

لقد استحموا في بركة من الماء الصافي.

And they ate and drank food in the palace.

وأكلوا وشربوا الطعام في القصر.

And they spent the day in sweet converse.

وقضيا اليوم في محادثة حلوة.

And they concocted a plan for their deliverance.

ووضعوا خطة لإنقاذهم.

Keshavaity was going to speak to the old Rakshasi.

كان كيشافايتي على وشك التحدث إلى راكشاسي العجوز.

She was going to ask on what a Rakshasa's life depended.

لقد كانت ستسأل عن ما تعتمد عليه حياة الراكشاسا.

And with that secret they were going to act accordingly.

وبهذا السر كانوا سيتصرفون وفقًا لذلك.

The hour of the return of the Rakshasas was coming again.

لقد حانت ساعة عودة الراكشاسا مرة أخرى.

And events unfolded as they had the evening before.

وتوالى الأحداث كما كانت في الليلة السابقة.

The seven hundred flesh-eaters were returning to the palace.

وكان السبعمائة من آكلي لحوم البشر عائدين إلى القصر.

Champ Dal touched Keshavati with the silver stick.

لمس تشامب دال كيشافاتي بالعصا الفضية۔

She died like the had died the night before.

لقد ماتت مثلما ماتت في الليلة السابقة۔

Champa-Dal went to the centre of the temple of Siva.

ذهب تشامبا دال إلى مركز معبد شيفا۔

He hid beneath the heaps of sacred trefoil again.

اختبأ مرة أخرى تحت أكوام البرسيم المقدس۔

He heard the sound of wind rushing.

سمع صوت الريح العاصفة۔

And he heard terrible noises in the palace.

وسمع أصواتاً رهيبة في القصر۔

The Rakshasas had come home from their hunt.

لقد عاد الراكشاسا إلى منزلهم من رحلة الصيد۔

They had filled their stomachs with meat.

لقد ملئوا بطونهم باللحم۔

Sundry goats, sheep, cows, horses, buffaloes.

الماعز والأغنام والأبقار والخيول والجاموس المتنوعة۔

And they had devoured elephants too.

وكانوا قد التهموا الفيلة أيضًا۔

The old Rakshasi returned to the palace too.

عاد الراكشاسي القديم إلى القصر أيضًا۔

She went to the room of the sleeping princess.

ذهبت إلى غرفة الأميرة النائمة۔

And she woke her with the stick made of gold.

وأيقظتها بالعصا المصنوعة من ذهب۔

"Hye, mye, khye! A human being I smell"

هي، ماي، خاي أشمّ إنسانًا

"I am the only human being here," said the princess.

أنا الإنسان الوحيد هنا، قالت الأميرة۔

"Eat me if you like," added Keshavati.

كلني إذا أردت، أضافت كيشافاتي۔

To this the Rakshasi replied:

ف:أجابه الراكشاسي

"Let me eat up your enemies"

دعني آكل أعدائك

"Why should I eat you?" she asked the princess.

لماذا يجب أن آكلك؟ سألت الأميرة۔

She laid herself down on the ground.

ألقت نفسها على الأرض۔

And she looked like a part of the Himalaya mountains.

وبدت وكأنها جزء من جبال الهيمالايا۔

Keshavati had a phial of heated mustard oil.

كان لدى كيشافاتي قارورة من زيت الخردل الساخن۔

And she approached the foot of the Rakshasi.

واقتربت من سفح الراكشاسي۔

"Mother, your feet are sore from walking"

أمي، قدميك تؤلمك من المشي

"Let me rub your sore feet with oil"

دعني أفرك قدميك المؤلمتين بالزيت

And she began to rub with oil the Rakshasi's feet.

وبدأت تدهن قدمي الراكشاسي بالزيت۔

Then a few tear-drops fell from the eyes of the princess.

ثم سقطت بعض الدموع من عيني الأميرة۔

And the tear-drops landed on the monster's legs.

وسقطت الدموع على ساقي الوحش۔

The Rakshasi tasted the tear-drops with her lips.

تذوقت الراكشاسي الدموع بشفتيها۔

And she found the tear-drops tasted briny.

ووجدت أن الدموع كانت ذات طعم مالح۔

"Why are you weeping, darling?" asked the Rakshasi.

لماذا تبكي يا عزيزتي؟ سأل الراكشاسي۔

"What aileth thee?" she wanted to know.

ما الذي يزعجك؟ أرادت أن تعرف۔

The princess tried to stop herself from crying.

حاولت الأميرة منع نفسها من البكاء۔

"Mother, I am weeping because you are old"

أمي، أنا أبكي لأنك عجوز

"When you die one of the Rakshasas will devour me"

عندما تموت، سوف يلتهمني أحد الراكشاسا

"When I die?! Don't be foolish, girl"

عندما أموت؟ لا تكوني حمقاء يا فتاة

"Don't you know that Rakshasas never die?"

ألا تعلم أن الراكشاساس لا يموتون أبدًا؟

"We are not naturally immortal"

نحن لسنا خالدين بطبيعتنا

"There is a secret to our strength"

هناك سر لقوتنا

"But no human can unravel this secret"

ولكن لا يمكن لأي إنسان أن يكشف هذا السر

"But let me tell you the secret"

ولكن دعني أخبرك بالسر

"So that you are comforted a little"

لكي تتعزوا قليلاً

"Do you see the pool of water in the palace?"

هل ترى بركة الماء في القصر؟

"In that pool of water is a Sphatikasthamba"

في تلك البركة من الماء يوجد Sphatikasthamba

"The Sphatikasthambha is deep in the water"

عميق في الماء Sphatikasthambha

"And on the Sphatikasthambha are two bees"

نحلتان Sphatikasthambha وعلى

"A human being would have to dive into the water"

يجب على الإنسان أن يغوص في الماء

"The human being would have to bring the bees onto dry land"

كان على الإنسان أن يجلب النحل إلى اليابسة

"Then the human being would have to kill the two bees"

ثم يجب على الإنسان أن يقتل النحلتين

"But not a drop of their blood must touch the ground"

ولكن لا ينبغي أن تلمس قطرة من دمائهم الأرض

"Only then can a human kill a Rakshasa"

عندها فقط يمكن للإنسان أن يقتل راكشاسا

"But if the blood touches the ground, a thousand Rakshasas will rise"

ولكن إذا لامس الدم الأرض، فسوف ينهض ألف راكشاسا

"But what human will find out this secret?"

ولكن أي إنسان سوف يكتشف هذا السر؟

"And what human can achieve this feat?"

و أي إنسان يستطيع تحقيق هذا الإنجاز؟

"No human knows the secret to the life of a Rakshasa"

لا أحد يعرف سر حياة الراكشاسا

"And no human can achieve such a feat"

ولا يمكن لأي إنسان أن يحقق مثل هذا الإنجاز

"So there is no reason to be sad, my darling"

لذا لا داعي للحزن يا عزيزتي

"I am practically immortal," she confirmed.

أنا خالدة عمليا، أكدت.

Keshavati treasured the secret in her memory.

احتفظت كشافاتي بالسر في ذاكرتها.

And then she went back to sleep.

ثم عادت إلى النوم.

Next morning the Rakshasas, as usual, went away.

في صباح اليوم التالي، غادر أفراد عائلة راكشاسا، كما جرت العادة.

Champa came out of his hiding-place.

خرج شامبا من مخبئه.

And he roused Keshavati from her sleep.

وأيقظ كشافاتي من نومها.

The princess told him the secret she had learnt.

أخبرته الأميرة بالسر الذي تعلمته.

Champa-Dal immediately started to prepare himself.

بدأ شامبا دال على الفور في تحضير نفسه.

He brought to the pool a knife.

أحضر سكينًا إلى البركة.

And he brought a quantity of ashes.

وأحضر كمية من الرماد.

He took off his heavy clothes.

خلع ملابسه الثقيلة.

He put a drop or two of mustard oil into each ear.

وضع قطرة أو قطرتين من زيت الخردل في كل أذن.

To prevent water from entering into his ears.

لمنع دخول الماء إلى أذنيه.

He swam out into the middle of the water.

لقد سبح إلى منتصف الماء.

And from there he dove down into the pool.

ومن هناك غاص إلى البركة.

Soon he reached the top of the crystal pillar.

وسرعان ما وصل إلى قمة العمود البلوري.

And on Sphatikasthambha were the two bees.

وعلى سباتيكاستامبا كان هناك النحلتان.

He caught hold of the two bees he found there.

أمسك بالنحلتين اللتين وجدهما هناك.

And he swam up again in a singular breath.

وسبح مرة أخرى بنفس واحد.

He took the knife he had left at the edge of the water.

أخذ السكين الذي تركه على حافة الماء.

And over the ashes he cut up the bees.

وفوق الرماد قطع النحل.

A drop or two of the blood fell from the bees.

سقطت قطرة أو قطرتان من الدم من النحل.

But their blood did not touch the ground.

ولكن دمائهم لم تصل إلى الأرض.

Instead, their blood landed on the ashes.

وبدلاً من ذلك، هبطت دمائهم على الرماد.

A terrible scream was heard at a distance.

سمع صراخ رهيب من مسافة بعيدة.

The scream was the wailing of the Rakshasas.

وكان الصراخ هو عويل الراكشاسا.

They were all running home as fast as they could.

لقد كانوا جميعًا يركضون إلى منازلهم بأسرع ما يمكن.

They wanted to prevent the bees from being killed.

أرادوا منع قتل النحل.

But they could not reach the palace in time.

ولكنهم لم يتمكنوا من الوصول إلى القصر في الوقت المناسب.

Because the bees had already perished.

لأن النحل قد هلك بالفعل.

The moment the bees were killed, all the Rakshasas died.

في اللحظة التي قتلت فيها النحل، مات كل الراكشاسا.

Their carcases fell on the very spot they were standing.

سقطت جثثهم في نفس المكان الذي كانوا واقفين فيه.

Their carcases now blocked the gateway of the palace.

وأصبحت جثثهم الآن تسد بوابة القصر.

In this manner the seven hundred Rakshasas were destroyed.

وبهذه الطريقة تم تدمير السبعمائة راكشاسا.

Afterwards Champa-Dal and Keshavati got married.

وبعد ذلك تزوج شامبا دال وكيشافاتي.

They made the traditional exchange of garlands of flowers.

قاموا بتبادل تقليدي لأكاليل الزهور.

The princess had never been out of the house.

الأميرة لم تكن خارج المنزل أبدًا.

So she naturally expressed a desire to see the outer world.

فأبدت بشكل طبيعي رغبتها في رؤية العالم الخارجي.

Every morning and evening they went on long walks.

كل صباح ومساء كانوا يذهبون في جولات طويلة.

There was a large river Keshavati wished to bathe in.

كان هناك نهر كبير أرادت كيشافاتي الاستحمام فيه.

As she bathed one of Keshavati's hairs came off.

وبينما كانت تستحم، سقطت إحدى شعرات كيشافاتي.

There was a special custom in those times.

وكان هناك عادة خاصة في تلك الأوقات.

A woman never threw away a hair away by itself.

لم تتخلص المرأة من شعرة واحدة بمفردها.

A sea-shell was floating in the water.

كانت هناك صدفة بحرية تطفو في الماء.

So Keshavati tied the strand of hair to the sea-shell.

لذلك قامت كيشافاتي بربط خصلة الشعر إلى صدفة البحر.

And then the couple returned to the palace.

وبعد ذلك عاد الزوجان إلى القصر.

Meanwhile the sea-shell floated down the stream.

وفي هذه الأثناء كانت الصدفة البحرية تطفو في مجرى النهر.

And in due time the sea-shell reached another bathing spot.

وفي الوقت المناسب وصلت المحارة إلى مكان آخر للاستحمام.

This was the bathing spot Sahasra-Dal went to.

كان هذا هو مكان الاستحمام الذي ذهب إليه ساهسرا دال.

Here Champa-Dal's brother performed his ablutions.

هنا قام شقيق شامبا دال بالوضوء.

On this day Sahasra-Dal was in the water.

في هذا اليوم كان ساهسرا دال في الماء.

He was bathing and swimming with his friends.

كان يستحم ويسبح مع أصدقائه.

And so the sea-shell floated past the men.

وهكذا طفت القوقعة البحرية أمام الرجال.

The men were in a playful mood that day.

وكان الرجال في مزاج مرح ذلك اليوم.

"Whoever gets to the sea-shell first wins"

من يصل إلى صدفة البحر أولاً يفوز

And so they all swam towards the sea-shell.

وهكذا سبحوا جميعا نحو صدفة البحر.

Sahasra-Dal was the strongest swimmer among his friends.

كان ساهسرا دال السباح الأقوى بين أصدقائه.

And so he was the first the reach the sea-shell.

فكان أول من وصل إلى صدفة البحر.

Examining the seashell, he found a hair tied to it.

وعند فحصه للصدفة، وجد شعرة مربوطة بها.

But it was a hair of extraordinary length.

ولكنه كان شعرًا بطول غير عادي.

He had never seen such a long hair.

لم يسبق له أن رأى شعرًا طويلًا كهذا.

The strand of hair was exactly seven cubits long.

وكان طول الشعرة سبعة أذرع بالضبط

"This strand of hair must belong to a woman"

لا بد أن خصلة الشعر هذه تنتمي إلى امرأة

"And this woman must be very remarkable"

ولا بد أن تكون هذه المرأة رائعة للغاية

"I must see who this remarkable woman is"

يجب أن أرى من هي هذه المرأة الرائعة

Sahasra-Dal was determined to find the remarkable woman.

كان ساهسرا دال مصمماً على العثور على المرأة الرائعة.

He went home from the river in a pensive mood.

عاد إلى منزله من النهر في حالة تفكير عميق.

And he did not proceed to the zenana for breakfast.

ولم يتوجه إلى الحرام للفطور.

Instead he remained in the outer part of the palace.

وبدلًا من ذلك بقي في الجزء الخارجي من القصر.

The queen-mother heard about Sahasra-Dal's meloncholy.

سمعت الملكة الأم عن حزن ساهسرا دال.

And she heard he had not come to breakfast.

وسمعت أنه لم يأت لتناول الإفطار.

So she went to him and asked the reason.

فذهبت إليه وسألته عن السبب.

He showed her the strand of hair he had found.

أراها خصلة الشعر التي وجدها.

"I must see the woman who's head this strand of hair adorned"

يجب أن أرى المرأة التي تزين رأسها خصلة الشعر هذه

The queen-mother was happy to help her son-in-law.

وكانت الملكة الأم سعيدة بمساعدة صهرها.

"Very well," she said to him.

حسنًا، قالت له.

"You shall soon have that lady in the palace"

سوف تحصل على تلك السيدة في القصر قريبًا

"I promise you to bring her here"

أعدك بإحضارها إلى هنا

The queen mother already had a plan.

وكانت الملكة الأم لديها خطة بالفعل.

Her favourite maid-servant would be good at the job.

ستكون خادمتها المفضلة جيدة في القيام بهذه المهمة.

Because this maid-servant was very resourceful.

لأن هذه الخادمة كانت ذات حيلة كبيرة.

Of course the queen-mother did not really know her maid.

وبطبيعة الحال فإن الملكة الأم لم تكن تعرف خادمتها حقًا.

She did not know her favourite maid was a Rakshasi.

لم تكن تعلم أن خادمتها المفضلة هي راكشاسي.

"Please find the owner of this strand of hair," she asked.

من فضلك ابحث عن صاحب هذا الشعر سألت.

And her maid-servant more than politely agreed.

ووافقت خادمتها بكل أدب.
"It would my pleasure to find this woman"
سيكون من دواعي سروري العثور على هذه المرأة
"I will soon bring her to the palace"
سأحضرها إلى القصر قريبًا
"I will need a boat build from Hajol wood"
سأحتاج إلى بناء قارب من خشب الهاجول
"The oars of the boat must be made from Mon-Paban wood"
يجب أن تكون مجاديف القارب مصنوعة من خشب مون بابان
The boat makers soon made the boat.
سرعان ما قام صانعو القوارب بصنع القارب.
And the boat was launched on the stream.
وأطلق القارب على النهر.
The maid-servant went on board of the boat.
صعدت الخادمة على متن السفينة.
With her she took some baskets of wicker.
وأخذت معها بعض السلال الخوصية.
The baskets of wicker were of curious workmanship.
كانت سلال الخوص مصنوعة بطريقة غريبة.
She also took with her some sweetmeats.
وأخذت معها أيضًا بعض الحلويات.
Into the sweetmeats some poison had been mixed.
لقد تم خلط بعض السم في الحلويات.
She snapped her fingers thrice.
لقد نقرت بأصابعها ثلاث مرات.
And then she uttered the following charm:
ث:م نطقت بالسحر التالي
"Boat of Hajol! Oars of Mon Paban!"
قارب هاجول مجاذيف مون بابان
"Take me to the Ghat,"
خذني إلى الغات
"The Ghat in which Keshavati bathes"
الغاط الذي تستحم فيه كيشافاتي
The boat heeded to her command.
استجاب القارب لأمرها.
And the boat flew like lightning over the waters.

وطار القارب كالبرق فوق المياه ـ

And the boat left many towns and cities behind.

وتركت السفينة وراءها مدنًا وقرى كثيرة.

At last the boat stopped at a bathing-place.

وأخيرا توقف القارب في مكان الاستحمام.

The Rakshasi maid-servant had reached her goal.

لقد وصلت خادمة راكشاسي إلى هدفها.

She concluded it was the bathing ghat of Keshavati.

وخلصت إلى أنها كانت غاط الاستحمام لكيشافاتي.

She landed with the sweetmeats in her hand.

هبطت مع الحلويات في يدها.

She went to the gate of the palace, and cried aloud:

ف:ذهبت إلى بوابة القصر وصرخت بصوت عال

"Oh Keshavati! Keshavati! I am your aunt"

يا كشافاتي أنا عمتك

"Oh Keshavati, I am your mother's sister"

يا كشافاتي، أنا أخت أمك

"I have come to see you, my darling"

لقد جئت لرؤيتك يا عزيزتي

"I have come after so many years"

لقد أتيت بعد سنوات عديدة

"Are you home, Keshavati?" she asked.

هل أنت في المنزل، كيشافاتي؟ سألت.

The princess heard the words of the false-aunt.

سمعت الأميرة كلام العمة الكاذبة.

She came out of her room and to the entrance of the palace.

خرجت من غرفتها إلى مدخل القصر.

She had no doubt that it was really her aunt.

لم يكن لديها شك في أنها كانت عمتها حقًا.

And she embraced and kissed her aunt.

واحتضنت عمتها وقبلتها.

They both wept rivers of joy.

لقد بكى كلاهما نهرًا من الفرح.

Although you should know the Rakshasi wept first.

على الرغم من أنك يجب أن تعرف أن الراكشاسي بكى أولاً.

Keshavati wept with her out of empathy.

بكت كشافاتي معها تعاطفًا.

Champa-Dal also believed the Rakshasi to be her aunt.

كما اعتقدت تشامبا دال أيضًا أن الراكشاسي هي عمتها.

They all ate and drank and enjoyed the happy occasion.

لقد أكلوا وشربوا واستمتعوا بالمناسبة السعيدة.

And then they took rest in the middle of the day.

ثم استراحوا في منتصف النهار.

And they celebrated again in the evening.

وأحتفلوا مرة أخرى في المساء.

The next day the celebrations continued at breakfast.

وفي اليوم التالي استمرت الاحتفالات عند الإفطار.

Champa-Dal had a habit of sleeping after breakfast.

كان لدى شامبا دال عادة النوم بعد الإفطار.

Towards afternoon, the supposed aunt said to Keshavati:

وفي فترة ما بعد الظهر، قالت العمة المفترضة لكيشافاتي:

"Let us both go to the river and wash ourselves:

فلنذهب معًا إلى النهر ونغتسل:

Keshavati replied, "How can we go now?"

فأجابت كشافاتي: كيف يمكننا أن نذهب الآن؟

"My husband is sleeping," she explained.

زوجي نائم أوضحت.

"Do not worry about your husband's sleep," said the aunt.

لا تقلقي بشأن نوم زوجك، قالت العمة.

"Let him sleep as much as he likes"

دعه ينام بقدر ما يريد

"Let me put these sweetmeats near his bedside"

دعني أضع هذه الحلويات بجانب سريره

"That way, when he awakes, he has something to eat"

بهذه الطريقة، عندما يستيقظ، يكون لديه ما يأكله

Then they then went to the river-side.

ثم ذهبوا بعد ذلك إلى ضفة النهر.

They went close to the spot where the boat was.

ذهبوا بالقرب من المكان الذي كان القارب.

From a distance Keshavati saw the baskets of wicker-work.

ومن مسافة بعيدة رأى كيشافاتي سلال الخوص.

"Aunt, what beautiful things are those!"

عمتي، ما أجمل هذه الأشياء

"I wish I could get some of those wicker baskets"

أتمنى أن أحصل على بعض من تلك السلال الخوصية

Her aunt happily obliged her.

استجابت عمتها لطلبها بكل سرور۔

"Come, my child, and look at the wicker baskets"

تعال يا ابني وانظر إلى سلال الخوص

"You can have as many baskets as you like"

يمكنك الحصول على عدد السلال الذي تريده

Keshavati at first refused to go into the boat.

في البداية رفضت كيشافاتي الدخول إلى القارب۔

But her aunt was very persuasive.

ولكن عمتها كانت مقنعة للغاية۔

And finally she went onto the boat.

وأخيرا صعدت إلى القارب۔

But once on the boat her aunt did a strange thing.

ولكن بمجرد وصولها إلى القارب، فعلت عمتها شيئًا غريبًا۔

The aunt snapped her fingers thrice and said:

ن:قرت العمة بأصابعها ثلاث مرات وقالت

"Boat of Hajol! Oars of Mon-Paban!"

قارب هاجول مجاذيف مون بابان

"Take me to the Ghat,"

خذني إلى الغات

"The Ghat in which Sahasra-Dal bathes"

الغاط الذي يستحم فيه ساهسرا دال

And the boat heeded to her command.

واستجابت السفينة لأمرها۔

And the boat flew like an arrow over the waters.

وطار القارب كالسهم على المياه۔

Keshavati was frightened and began to cry.

كانت كشافاتي خائفة وبدأت بالبكاء۔

But the boat went on despite her crying.

لكن القارب استمر في رحلته رغم بكائها۔

And the boat left behind many towns and cities.

وتركت السفينة وراءها مدنًا وقرى كثيرة۔

In a trice the boat reached its destination.

وفي لحظة وصل القارب إلى وجهته.

The ghat where Sahasra-Dal was in the habit of bathing.

الغات حيث كان ساهسرا دال معتادًا على الاستحمام.

Keshavati was taken to the palace.

تم اصطحاب كشيافاتي إلى القصر.

Sahasra-Dal admired her beauty and the length of her hair.

أعجب ساهسرا دال بجمالها وطول شعرها.

And the ladies of the palace tried their best to comfort her.

وحاولت سيدات القصر قدر استطاعتها مواساتها.

But she set up a loud cry of protest.

لكنها أطلقت صرخة احتجاجية عالية.

And she wanted to be taken back to her husband.

وأرادت العودة إلى زوجها.

Finally she saw that she had been taken captive.

وأخيراً أدركت أنها قد تم أسرها.

So she spoke to the ladies of the palace.

فتحدثت إلى سيدات القصر.

"Upon marriage I made a vow to my husband"

عند الزواج قطعت عهداً لزوجي

"I promised not to look upon the face of any other man"

لقد وعدت ألا أنظر إلى وجه أي رجل آخر

"I promised to uphold this vow for six months"

لقد وعدت بالوفاء بهذا العهد لمدة ستة أشهر

She was then lodged away from the others in the palace.

وتم عزلها بعد ذلك عن الآخرين في القصر.

And she was given a small house to live in.

وأعطيت بيتًا صغيرًا لتعيش فيه.

The window of the house overlooked the road.

كانت نافذة البيت تطل على الطريق.

There she spent the livelong day.

أمضت هناك يومها كله.

And there she spent the livelong night.

وقضت هناك ليلتها بأكملها.

Because she had very little sleep.

لأنها لم تنام إلا قليلا.

Because her time was spent in sighing and weeping.

لأن وقتها كان يقضى بالتنهد والبكاء.

In the meantime Champa-Dal awoke from his sleep.

وفي هذه الأثناء استيقظ شامبا دال من نومه.

He was distracted with the grief of not finding his wife.

لقد انشغل بالحزن لعدم عثوره على زوجته.

His suspicions turned to the aunt of Keshavati.

توجهت شكوكه نحو عمة كشافاتي.

He knew she was a cheat and an impostor.

لقد عرف أنها كانت غشاشه ومحتالة.

It must have been her who carried away Keshavati.

لا بد أنها هي التي حملت كشافاتي.

He did not eat the sweetmeats left for him.

ولم يأكل من الحلويات التي تركت له.

Because he suspected the sweets to have been poisoned.

لأنه يشتبه في أن الحلويات مسمومة.

He threw one of the sweets to a crow.

ألقى إحدى الحلويات إلى الغراب.

The moment the crow ate the sweet, it dropped down dead.

عندما أكل الغراب الحلوى سقط ميتا.

This confirmed his suspicion of the pretend aunt.

وقد أكد هذا شكوكه بشأن العمة المزيفة.

Maddened with grief, he rushed out of the house.

لقد أصيب بالجنون من الحزن، فخرج مسرعا من المنزل.

He was determined to go wherever his feet took him.

لقد كان مصمماً على الذهاب إلى أي مكان تأخذه قدماه.

Like a madman he blubbered, "Oh Keshavati! Oh Keshavati!"

كالمجنون، بكى قائلاً: يا كشافاتي يا كشافاتي

He travelled on foot day after day.

كان يسافر سيرًا على الأقدام يومًا بعد يوم.

And he followed whatever way his feet took him.

وكان يتبع حيثما توجهته قدماه.

Six months he spent travelling in this wearisome manner.

أمضى ستة أشهر مسافرًا بهذه الطريقة المرهقة.

After six month he reached the capital of Sahasra-Dal.

وبعد ستة أشهر وصل إلى العاصمة ساهسرا دال۔

He passed by the gate of the palace.

مرّ ببوابة القصر۔

And from the road he could see a small house.

ومن الطريق استطاع أن يرى بيتًا صغيرًا۔

And from in the house he could hear sighs.

ومن داخل البيت كان يسمع التنهدات۔

Champa-Dal instantly recognized his wife.

تعرف شامبا دال على زوجته على الفور۔

And Keshavita instantly recognized her husband.

وتعرفت كيشافيتا على زوجها على الفور۔

Keshavita told her husband everything that had happened.

أخبرت كيشافيتا زوجها بكل ما حدث۔

"The woman asked to go bathing after breakfast"

طلبت المرأة الاستحمام بعد الإفطار

"At the river there was a boat"

كان هناك قارب عند النهر

"The woman persuaded me onto the boat"

أقنعتني المرأة بالصعود على متن القارب

"And then the boat took us to this place"

ثم أخذنا القارب إلى هذا المكان

"I realized that I had been made captive"

أدركت أنني أصبحت أسيرًا

"So I told them of my vows to you"

فأخبرتهم بعهودي لك

"But tomorrow will be the end of six month"

ولكن غدا سيكون نهاية الستة أشهر

There was a custom in those days.

وكان هناك عادة في تلك الأيام۔

The fulfilments of vows were publicly recited.

وقد تم تلاوة الوفاء بالنذور علناً۔

This was normally fulfilled by a learned Brahman.

كان يتم تحقيق ذلك عادة من قبل براهمان المتعلم۔

They planned for Champa-Dal to take on this role.

لقد خططوا لشامبا دال لتولي هذا الدور۔

And so that evening the palace drum was beat.

وفي ذلك المساء قُرع طبول القصر.

The king wanted a learned Brahman to make a recitation.

أراد الملك أن يقوم أحد علماء البراهمة بإلقاء تلاوة.

The story of Keshavati on the fulfilment of her vow.

قصة كشافاتي حول الوفاء بنذرها.

Champa-Dal touched the drum and volunteered.

لمس شامبا دال الطبلة وتطوع.

"I will make the recitation of Keshavita's vows"

سأقوم بتلاوة عهود كيشافيتا

The next morning all assembled in the courtyard.

وفي صباح اليوم التالي، اجتمع الجميع في الفناء.

The old king and the queen mother.

الملك العجوز والملكة الأم.

Sahasra-Dal and his wife were there.

وكان ساهسرا دال وزوجته هناك.

All the courtiers and the learned Brahmans of the country.

جميع رجال الحاشية والبراهمة المتعلمين في البلاد.

All royalty was under a huge canopy of silk.

كان جميع أفراد العائلة المالكة تحت مظلة ضخمة من الحرير.

Kashavati was also there, but behind a veil.

وكانت كاشافاتي هناك أيضًا، ولكن خلف حجاب.

So that she wouldn't be exposed to the rude gaze of people.

لكي لا تتعرض لنظرات الناس الوقحة.

Champa-Dal, the reciter, sat on a dais.

كان شامبا دال، القارئ، يجلس على المنصة.

And he began to tell the story of Keshavati.

وبدأ يروي قصة كشافاتي.

"There was once a poor dimwitted Brahman"

كان هناك ذات مرة براهمان فقير غبي

"This dimwitted man had a wife, but no children"

كان لهذا الرجل الأحمق زوجة، ولكن ليس لديه أطفال

"But him not having children was probably for the best"

لكن عدم إنجابه أطفالًا ربما كان هو الأفضل

"Because he was barely able to meet his own needs"

لأنه بالكاد كان قادرًا على تلبية احتياجاته الخاصة

"And he could hardly supply enough for his wife"

وكان بالكاد يستطيع توفير ما يكفي لزوجته

"But his dimwittedness was not even his biggest problem"

ولكن غباءه لم يكن حتى أكبر مشاكله

And he continued the story as we have followed it.

وأكمل القصة كما تابعناها.

And sometimes he turned around to Keshavati.

وأحيانا كان يتجه إلى كشافاتي.

And he asked her if he was telling the story correctly.

وسألها إذا كان يروي القصة بشكل صحيح.

And she told him he was telling the story correctly.

وأخبرته أنه يروي القصة بشكل صحيح.

"The Brahman woman concluded her fate was sealed"

خلصت المرأة البراهمية إلى أن مصيرها قد تم تحديده

"And she thought her husband would meet the same fate"

وكانت تعتقد أن زوجها سيلقى نفس المصير

"And she did not expect her son to be spared either"

ولم تكن تتوقع أن ينجو ابنها أيضًا

"That night she hardly slept at all"

في تلك الليلة لم تنم على الإطلاق

"The Rakshasi had prevented her from seeing her husband"

لقد منعها الراكشاسي من رؤية زوجها

"Early next morning Champa-Dal went to school"

في الصباح الباكر التالي ذهب شامبا دال إلى المدرسة

"Before he went to school, she gave her son a golden bottle"

قبل أن يذهب إلى المدرسة، أعطت ابنها زجاجة ذهبية

"In the golden bottle was her own breast milk"

في الزجاجة الذهبية كان حليب ثديها

"Carefully watch the colour of the milk"

راقب لون الحليب بعناية

During the recitation the Rakshasi maid-servant grew pale.

أثناء التلاوة، شحب وجه خادمة راكشاسي.

She perceived that her real character was going to be discovered.

لقد أدركت أن شخصيتها الحقيقية سوف يتم اكتشافها.

And Sahasra-Dal was astonished at the knowledge of the reciter.

ولقد دهش ساهسرا دال من علم القارئ.

The reciter clearly told the history of the prince's life.

وقد روى القارئ قصة حياة الأمير بشكل واضح.

"A drop or two of the blood fell from the bees"

سقطت قطرة أو قطرتان من الدم من النحل

"But their blood did not touch the ground"

ولكن دمائهم لم تمس الأرض

"Instead, their blood landed on the ashes"

بدلا من ذلك، هبطت دمائهم على الرماد

"A terrible scream was heard at a distance"

سمعت صرخة رهيبة من بعيد

"The scream was the wailing of the Rakshasas"

كانت الصرخة بمثابة عويل الراكشاسا

"They were all running home as fast as they could"

كانوا جميعًا يركضون إلى منازلهم بأسرع ما يمكن

"They wanted to prevent the bees from being killed"

أرادوا منع قتل النحل

"But they could not reach the palace in time"

ولكنهم لم يتمكنوا من الوصول إلى القصر في الوقت المناسب

"Because the bees had already been killed"

لأن النحل كان قد قُتل بالفعل

"The moment the bees were killed, all the Rakshasas died"

في اللحظة التي قُتلت فيها النحل، مات جميع الراكشاسا

"Their carcasses fell on the very spot they were standing"

سقطت جثثهم في نفس المكان الذي كانوا واقفين فيه

"Their carcasses now blocked the gateway of the palace"

جثثهم الآن سدت بوابة القصر

"In this manner the seven hundred Rakshasas were destroyed"

وبهذه الطريقة تم تدمير السبعمائة راكشاسا

All where enthralled by the story of the Rakshasas.

كان الجميع مفتونين بقصة الراكشاسا.

Because the story was being told by a true storyteller.

لأن القصة كانت يرويها راوي حقيقي.

All enjoyed the story except for the maid-servant.

استمتع الجميع بالقصة باستثناء الخادمة.

Because her real character was bound to be discovered.

لأن شخصيتها الحقيقية كان من المفترض أن يتم اكتشافها.

"Champa-Dal touched the drum and volunteered.

لمس شامبا دال الطبلة وتطوع.

"I will make the recitation of Keshavita's vows"

سأقوم بتلاوة عهود كيشافيتا

"The next morning all assembled in the courtyard"

في صباح اليوم التالي اجتمع الجميع في الفناء

"The old king and the queen mother"

الملك العجوز والملكة الأم

"Sahasra-Dal and his wife were there"

كان ساهسرا دال وزوجته هناك

"All the courtiers and the learned Brahmans of the country"

جميع رجال الحاشية والبراهمة المتعلمين في البلاد

"All royalty was under a huge canopy of silk"

كان جميع أفراد العائلة المالكة تحت مظلة ضخمة من الحرير

"Kashavati was also there, but behind a veil"

كانت كاشافاتي هناك أيضًا، ولكن خلف حجاب

"So that she wouldn't be exposed to the rude gaze of people"

حتى لا تتعرض لنظرات الناس الوقحة

"Champa-Dal, the reciter, sat on a dais"

جلس شامبا دال، القارئ، على المنصة

"And he began to tell the story of Keshavati"

وبدأ يروي قصة كشافاتي

Sahasra-Dal jumped up from his seat.

قفز ساهسرا دال من مقعده.

And he embraced the reciter of the story.

واحتضن صاحب القصة.

"You can be none other than my brother Champa-Dal"

لا يمكنك أن تكون سوى أخي شامبا دال

Then the prince was inflamed with rage.

ثم غضب الأمير بشدة.

He ordered the maid-servant to come into his presence.

وأمر الخادمة أن تأتي إلى حضرته.

A hole the height of a man was dug in the ground.

حفرت حفرة في الأرض بارتفاع رجلٍ.

And the maid-servant was put into the hole, standing.

وألقيت الأمة في الجحر واقفة.

Prickly thorns were heaped around her.

كانت الأشواك الشائكة متراكمة حولها.

Up to the crown of her head she was covered in thorns.

كانت مغطاة بالأشواك حتى قمة رأسها.

In this way the maid-servant was buried alive.

بهذه الطريقة تم دفن الخادمة حية.

After this all lived happily together for many years.

وبعد ذلك عاش الجميع معًا بسعادة لسنوات عديدة.

Sahasra-Dal and his princess, and Champa-Dal and
Keshavati.

ساهاسرا دال وأميرته، وتشامبا دال وكيشافاتي.

The Story of Swet and Bachanta
قصة سويت وباشانتا

There was once upon a time a rich merchant.

كان هناك ذات مرة تاجر غني.

This rich merchant had only one son.

كان لهذا التاجر الغني ابن واحد فقط.

And he loved his only son very much.

وكان يحب ابنه الوحيد كثيرًا.

He gave to his son whatever he wanted.

لقد أعطى لابنه كل ما أراد.

Of course his son wanted a beautiful house.

بالطبع أراد ابنه منزلًا جميلًا.

And he also wanted to have a large garden.

وأراد أيضًا أن تكون له حديقة كبيرة.

So a beautiful house was built for him.

فتم بناء له بيت جميل.

And a fine garden was made for him too.

وأُنشئت له حديقة جميلة أيضًا.

The merchant's son was pleased with the garden.

كان ابن التاجر مسرورًا بالحديقة.

And he enjoyed walking in the garden.

وكان يستمتع بالمشي في الحديقة.

One day a bird's nest caught his attention.

ذات يوم لفت انتباهه عش طائر.

This bird happens to be called Toontooni.

يToontooni طلق على هذا الطائر اسمُ.

He put his hand into the small bird's nest.

وضع يده في عش الطائر الصغير.

And in the nest he found an egg.

وفي العش وجد بيضة.

He took the egg out of its nest.

أخرج البيضة من عشها.

There was an almirah in the wall of his house.

وكان في حائط بيته خزانة.

So he put the egg in the almirah.

ثم وضع البيضة في الخزانة.

He closed the door of the almirah.

أغلق باب الخزانة.

And then he thought no more of the egg.

وبعد ذلك لم يعد يفكر في البيضة.

The merchant's son had a house of his own.

وكان ابن التاجر يملك بيتًا خاصًا به.

But he had a house without a household.

ولكن كان له بيت بلا أهل.

So in his house there was no cook.

فلم يكن في بيته طباخ.

But he had no need for his own cook.

ولكنه لم يكن في حاجة إلى طباخ خاص به.

Because his mother regularly sent him food.

لأن والدته كانت ترسل له الطعام بانتظام.

In the morning she sent him breakfast.

وفي الصباح أرسلت له الفطور.

And every day she had dinner sent to him.

وكانت ترسل له العشاء كل يوم.

One day the egg in the almirah burst.

في أحد الأيام انفجرت البيضة الموجودة في الخزانة.

But it was not a bird that came out of the egg.

ولكن لم يكن الطائر الذي خرج من البيضة.

Out of the egg came a beautiful infant.

خرج من البيضة طفل جميل.

The infant was not a bird, but a human girl.

الطفل لم يكن طائرًا، بل فتاة بشرية.

But the merchant's son knew nothing of the event.

ولكن ابن التاجر لم يكن يعلم شيئًا عن الحادثة.

He had forgotten everything about the egg.

لقد نسي كل شيء عن البيضة.

The door of the wall-almirah had been kept closed.

لقد ظل باب الحائط مغلقا.

However, the merchant's son did not lock the door.

ولكن ابن التاجر لم يغلق الباب.

The child grew up within the wall-almirah.

نشأ الطفل داخل جدار الخزانة۔

She had no knowledge of the merchant's son.

ولم تكن لديها أي علم بابن التاجر۔

Nor did she know of anyone else.

ولم تكن تعرف أحدا آخر۔

When the child could walk it grew curious.

عندما أصبح الطفل قادرًا على المشي أصبح فضوليًا۔

And out of curiosity she opened the door.

ومن باب الفضول فتحت الباب۔

That day, too, the mother had sent breakfast.

وفي ذلك اليوم أيضًا أرسلت الأم وجبة الإفطار۔

And the breakfast had been put on the floor.

ووضعت وجبة الإفطار على الأرض۔

The child saw the food that was on the floor.

رأى الطفل الطعام الذي كان على الأرض۔

Of course the child ate from the food.

وبطبيعة الحال أكل الطفل من الطعام۔

And then the child returned into the wall.

ثم عاد الطفل إلى الحائط

The merchant's mother always made a lot of food.

كانت والدة التاجر تصنع دائمًا الكثير من الطعام۔

It was more food than he could possibly eat.

لقد كان الطعام أكثر مما يمكنه أن يأكله۔

So he didn't notice that any food was missing.

لذلك لم يلاحظ أن هناك أي طعام مفقود۔

The girl of the wall-almirah came out every day.

وكانت فتاة الحائط-الخزانة تخرج كل يوم۔

And every day she ate a part of the food.

وكانت تأكل كل يوم جزءا من الطعام۔

After eating the food she returned to the almirah.

وبعد أن أكلت الطعام عادت إلى الخزانة۔

But with time the girl got older and older.

لكن مع مرور الوقت أصبحت الفتاة أكبر سناً وأكبر سناً۔

And with age she got bigger and bigger.

ومع التقدم في السن أصبحت أكبر وأكبر۔

And the bigger she got the hungrier she got.

وكلما كبرت، كلما ازداد جوعها.

And she began to eat more of the food each day.

وبدأت تأكل كمية أكبر من الطعام كل يوم.

Eventually the merchant's son noticed the missing food.

وفي نهاية المطاف لاحظ ابن التاجر اختفاء الطعام.

But he had no way of knowing where the food went.

ولكن لم تكن لديه أي وسيلة لمعرفة أين ذهب الطعام.

The last thing he suspected was a girl from inside the almirah.

الشيء الأخير الذي اشتبه به هو فتاة من داخل الخزانة.

And so he came to a very different conclusion.

وهكذا توصل إلى نتيجة مختلفة تماما.

"Why is mother sending such a small quantity of food?".

لماذا ترسل الأم هذه الكمية الصغيرة من الطعام؟

And he had a message sent to his mother.

وأرسل رسالة إلى والدته.

"Why am I being sent insufficient food?".

لماذا لا يصلني طعام كاف؟.

"And why is the dish served so slovenly?".

ولماذا يتم تقديم الطبق بهذه الطريقة غير المتقنة؟.

Of course we know why the food was insufficient.

بالطبع نحن نعلم لماذا كان الطعام غير كاف.

And we know why the food was presented slovenly.

ونحن نعلم لماذا تم تقديم الطعام بطريقة غير جيدة.

The girl from in the wall ate from his food.

أكلت الفتاة من داخل الحائط من طعامه.

And as she ate she fingered the rice and curry.

وبينما كانت تأكل، كانت تتحسس الأرز والكاري.

And she always hurried back into her cell in the wall.

وكانت تعود دائمًا مسرعة إلى زنزانتها في الحائط

So that she would not be seen by anyone.

لكي لا يراها أحد.

She had no time to put the rice in proper order.

لم يكن لديها الوقت لوضع الأرز بالترتيب الصحيح.

The mother was astonished at her son's complaint.

دهشت الأم من شكوى ابنها.

She gave him more than he could eat.

لقد أعطته أكثر مما يستطيع أن يأكل.

The food was served up on a silver plate.

تم تقديم الطعام على طبق فضي.

And she neatly arranged the food herself.

ورتبت الطعام بنفسها بعناية.

But her son repeated the same complaint again.

لكن ابنها كرر نفس الشكوى مرة أخرى.

Day after day he complained of the small portions.

يوما بعد يوم كان يشكو من صغر حجم الأجزاء.

Day after day he complained of the messy food.

يوما بعد يوم كان يشكو من الطعام الفوضوي.

And so his mother began to suspect foul play.

وهكذا بدأت والدته تشك في أن الأمر متعمد.

She told her son to watch over the food.

طلبت من ابنها مراقبة الطعام.

"See if anyone is eating your food".

انظر هل يأكل أحد طعامك

The next day a servant brought the food.

وفي اليوم التالي أحضر الخادم الطعام.

The servant laid the food in a clean place.

وضع الخادم الطعام في مكان نظيف.

Normally the merchant's son took a bath.

عادة ما يستحم ابن التاجر.

But this day he did not go for a bath.

ولكن في هذا اليوم لم يذهب للاستحمام.

Instead, on this day he hid himself nearby.

وبدلاً من ذلك، في هذا اليوم، اختبأ في مكان قريب.

From his hiding place he could see the food.

ومن مكان اختبائه كان بإمكانه رؤية الطعام.

The merchant's son did not have to wait for long.

ولم يكن على ابن التاجر أن ينتظر طويلاً.

Soon he saw the wall-almirah open.

وسرعان ما رأى جدار الخزانة مفتوحا.

And he saw a beautiful damsel step out.

ورأى فتاة جميلة تخرج.

She could not have been more than sixteen.

لم يكن عمرها أكثر من ستة عشر عامًا.

She sat on the carpet by the breakfast.

جلست على السجادة بجانب وجبة الإفطار.

And she began to eat from the food left on the floor.

وبدأت تأكل من الطعام المتروك على الأرض.

The merchant's son came out of his hiding-place.

خرج ابن التاجر من مخبئه.

And the damsel could not escape from him.

ولم تستطع الفتاة الفرار منه.

"Who are you, beautiful creature?".

من أنت أيها المخلوق الجميل؟

"You do not seem to be earth-born".

لا يبدو أنك مولود على الأرض

"Are you one of the daughters of the gods?".

هل أنت إحدى بنات الآلهة؟

The girl replied, "I do not know who I am".

فأجابت الفتاة: لا أعرف من أنا.

"But there is one thing I do know," the girl continued.

ولكن هناك شيء واحد أعرفه، تابعت الفتاة.

"One day I found myself in the almirah in the wall".

في أحد الأيام وجدت نفسي في الخزانة الموجودة في الحائط

"And since then I have been living in the wall".

ومنذ ذلك الحين وأنا أعيش في الجدار.

The merchant's son thought her story was strange.

اعتقد ابن التاجر أن قصتها غريبة.

But then he thought a bit more about the story.

لكن بعد ذلك فكر قليلاً في القصة.

And he remembered what happened sixteen years ago.

وتذكر ما حدث قبل ستة عشر عامًا.

He remembered the nest of the toontoori bird.

تذكر عش طائر التونتوري.

And he remembered finding an egg in the nest.

وتذكر أنه وجد بيضة في العش.

And he remembered putting the egg in the almirah.

وتذكر أنه وضع البيضة في الخزانة.

The wall-almirah girl was of uncommon beauty.

كانت فتاة الحائط-الخزانة ذات جمال غير عادي.

And the merchant's son was struck by her beauty.

فأعجب ابن التاجر بجمالها.

Her beauty made a deep impression on his mind.

لقد تركت جمالها انطباعا عميقا في ذهنه.

And he resolved in his mind to marry her.

وعزم في نفسه على الزواج منها.

From then on the girl didn't stay in the almirah.

منذ ذلك الحين لم تعد الفتاة تبقى في الغرفة.

She was given a room in the merchant's son's house.

وأعطيت غرفة في بيت ابن التاجر.

The next day the merchant's son wrote a message.

وفي اليوم التالي كتب ابن التاجر رسالة.

And he had the message sent to his mother.

وأرسل الرسالة إلى والدته.

You can guess the general theme of the message.

يمكنك تخمين الموضوع العام للرسالة.

The merchant's son said he would like to get married.

قال ابن التاجر أنه يريد الزواج.

The mother of the merchant's son reproached herself.

وبخت أم ابن التاجر نفسها.

She had not tried to find a wife for his son.

ولم تحاول أن تجد زوجة لابنها.

She felt she should have thought of his marriage.

شعرت أنها كان ينبغي أن تفكر في زواجه.

And so she promptly replied to her son's message.

فأجابت على الفور على رسالة ابنها.

She and her father were going to send out ghataks.

كانت هي ووالدها على وشك إرسال الغاتاكس.

The ghataks were going to go to different countries.

كان الغاتاكس في طريقهم إلى بلدان مختلفة.

There they were going to look for suitable brides.

هناك كانوا يبحثون عن العرائس المناسبة.

But the merchant's son said there would be no need.

لكن ابن التاجر قال أنه لن تكون هناك حاجة لذلك.

He had secured himself a lovely young lady.

لقد حصل على فتاة شابة جميلة.

If they had no objection, he would introduce her to them.

إذا لم يكن لديهم اعتراض، فسوف يقدمها لهم.

And so the young lady was taken to the merchant's house.

وبعد ذلك تم أخذ الفتاة إلى بيت التاجر.

The merchant and his wife welcomed the stranger.

رحب التاجر وزوجته بالغريب.

And they were also struck by her unmatched beauty.

ولقد أذهلهم أيضًا جمالها الذي لا مثيل له.

The girl was of perfect loveliness and grace.

كانت الفتاة في غاية الجمال والنعمة.

The parents made no questions to her birth.

ولم يتساءل والداها عن ولادتها.

And the nuptials were celebrated there and then.

وأقيم حفل الزفاف هناك وفي تلك اللحظة.

In the course of time the merchant's son had two sons.

مع مرور الوقت أصبح لابن التاجر ولدان.

The elder of the sons he named Swet.

وكان أكبر أبنائه هو الذي سماه سويت.

And the younger son he named Basanta.

وأما ابنه الأصغر فقد سماه باسنتا.

After the passing of more time the old merchant died.

وبعد مرور المزيد من الوقت توفي التاجر العجوز.

So the merchant's son now became the merchant.

فأصبح ابن التاجر الآن التاجر.

And after some time his mother died too.

وبعد فترة من الوقت توفيت أمه أيضًا.

Swet and Basanta grew up to be fine lads.

لقد نشأ سويت وباسانتا ليصبحا شابين رائعين.

And the elder son was in due time married.

وتزوج الابن الأكبر في الوقت المناسب.

Sometime after Swet's marriage his mother also died.

وبعد فترة من زواج سويت توفيت والدته أيضًا.

The girl from in the wall was no more.

لم تعد الفتاة الموجودة في الحائط موجودة.

The widower lost no time in marrying again.

ولم يضيع الأرمل أي وقت في الزواج مرة أخرى.

And he had a new young and beautiful wife.

وكان له زوجة جديدة شابة وجميلة.

Swet's wife was older than his stepmother.

كانت زوجة سويت أكبر سناً من زوجة أبيه.

So his wife became the mistress of the house.

فأصبحت زوجته سيدة البيت.

The stepmother was like all stepmothers are.

كانت زوجة الأب مثل كل زوجات الأب.

She hated Swet and Basanta with a perfect hatred.

لقد كرهت سويت وباسانتا كراهية شديدة.

And the two ladies also couldn't stand each other.

والسيدتان أيضا لم تستطيعا أن تطيق بعضهما البعض.

It so happened one day that a fisherman came.

وفي أحد الأيام، جاء صياد.

The fisherman brought to the merchant a fish.

أحضر الصياد سمكة إلى التاجر.

This fish was of singular and remarkable beauty.

كانت هذه السمكة ذات جمال فريد ومذهل.

It was unlike any other fish that had been seen.

لقد كان مختلفًا عن أي سمكة أخرى تم رؤيتها.

And the fish had other qualities too.

وكانت الأسماك لها صفات أخرى أيضًا.

The fisherman explained the wonders of the fish.

شرح الصياد عجائب السمك.

"Two things will happen if you eat this fish".

سيحدث شيئان إذا أكلت هذه السمكة

"When you laugh maniks will drop from your mouth".

عندما تضحك، سوف تتساقط الكلمات من فمك.

"And when you weep pearls will drop from your eyes".

وعندما تبكي، سوف تتساقط اللؤلؤ من عينيك.

The merchant was astounded by what he had heard.

لقد اندهش التاجر مما سمع.

And he wanted the wonderful properties of the fish.

وأراد الخصائص الرائعة للسمكة.

And so he bought the fish at one thousand rupees.

فـاشترى السمك بألف روبية.

And he put the fish into the hands of Swet's wife.

ووضع السمكة في يد زوجة سويت.

Because Swet's wife was the mistress of the house.

لأن زوجة سويت كانت سيدة المنزل.

He strictly instructed her to cook the fish well.

لقد أوصى بشدة بطهي السمك جيدًا.

And he told her to give the fish to him alone to eat.

وأمرها أن تعطيه السمك وحده ليأكله.

The house-mother however knew the fish's secret.

لكن ربة المنزل عرفت سر السمكة.

She had overheard what the fisherman had said.

لقد سمعت ما قاله الصياد.

Secretly she made a different plan in her mind.

لقد خططت سراً لخطة مختلفة في ذهنها.

She was going to cook the fish for her husband.

كانت ستقوم بطبخ السمك لزوجها.

And she was going to share the fish with his brother.

وكانت ستتقاسم السمك مع أخيه.

For her father-in-law she was going to prepare a frog.

كانت ستقوم بإعداد ضفدع لحميها.

Soon she had finished cooking the marvelous fish.

وبعد قليل انتهت من طهي السمك الرائع.

And she had finished cooking a frog too.

وكانت قد انتهت من طهي الضفدع أيضًا.

But from the kitchen she could hear a squable.

ولكن من المطبخ كان بإمكانها سماع صراخ.

She could hear who it was that was arguing.

استطاعت أن تسمع من كان يتجادل.

Her stepmother-in-law and her husband's brother.

زوجة أبيها وشقيق زوجها.

And she understood the cause of the argument.

وأدركت سبب الخلاف.

Basanta was still but a young lad.

لكان باسانتا لا يزال شابًا صغيرًا.

But he was passionately fond of his pigeons.

ولكنه كان مولعًا بحمامه بشدة.

And he tamed his pigeons very well.

وقد روّض حمامه جيداً.

Nonetheless, one of his pigeons had escaped.

ومع ذلك، فقد تمكن أحد الحمام من الفرار.

And the pigeon flew into his stepmother's room.

وطار الحمام إلى غرفة زوجة أبيه .

His stepmother hid the pigeon in her clothes.

أخفت زوجة أبيها الحمامة في ملابسها.

Basanta rushed after the pigeon into the room.

هرع باسانتا خلف الحمامة إلى الغرفة.

And he loudly demanded to have the pigeon back.

وطالب بصوت عالٍ باستعادة الحمامة.

His stepmother denied having the pigeon.

زوجة أبيه أنكرت وجود الحمامة.

Swet, however, did know she had the pigeon.

لكن سويت كانت تعلم أنها تمتلك الحمامة.

And the older brother forcibly took the bird.

والأخ الأكبر أخذ الطائر بالقوة.

And he freed the pigeon from her clothes.

وأخرج الحمامة من ثيابها.

And he gave the pigeon back to his brother.

وأعاد الحمامة إلى أخيه.

The stepmother cursed and swore, and added;

فـ:شتمت زوجة الأب وأقسمت وأضافت

"Wait until the head of the house comes home".

انتظر حتى يعود رب البيت إلى البيت".

"He will get no water till he sheds your blood".

لن يحصل على الماء حتى يسفك دمك.

Swet's wife called her husband and said to him;

ا:تصلت زوجة سويت بزوجها وقالت له

"My dearest lord, that woman is a most wicked woman".

سيدي العزيز، هذه المرأة هي امرأة شريرة للغاية.

"And she has boundless influence over my father-in-law".

وإنها تتمتع بنفوذ لا حدود له على حمي.

"She will make him do what she has threatened".

ستجعله يفعل ما هددته به.

"All our lives are in imminent danger".

حياتنا كلها في خطر وشيك.

"But let us first eat a little," she added.

ولكن دعونا نأكل قليلاً أولاً، أضافت.

"And then let us all three run away from this place".

ثم دعونا جميعًا الثلاثة نهرب من هذا المكان.

Swet forthwith called Basanta to him.

اتصل سويت على الفور بباسانتا.

And he told him what he had heard from his wife.

وأخبره بما سمع من امرأته.

They resolved to run away before nightfall.

قرروا الهروب قبل حلول الليل.

The woman placed before her husband the fish.

وضعت المرأة السمكة أمام زوجها.

And her brother-in-law ate of the fish too.

وأكل صهرها من السمك أيضًا.

And they ate of the fish heartily.

وأكلوا من السمك بشهية.

The woman packed up all her jewels in a box.

قامت المرأة بتعبئة جميع مجوهراتها في صندوق.

There was only one horse in the stables.

لم يكن هناك سوى حصان واحد في الإسطبلات.

But the horse was of uncommon fleetness.

ولكن الحصان كان ذو سرعة غير عادية.

They could all sit on the horse together.

وكان بإمكانهم جميعًا الجلوس على الحصان معًا.

Swet held the reins of the horse.

كان سويت يمسك بزمام الحصان.

The woman sat in the middle of the horse.

جلست المرأة في وسط الحصان.

And she had the jewel-box in her lap.

وكانت صندوق المجوهرات في حجرها.

And Basanta sat on the rear of the horse.

وجلس باسنتا على مؤخرة الحصان.

The horse galloped with the utmost swiftness.

لكان الحصان يركض بأقصى سرعة.

They passed through many a plain and noted town.

لـقد مروا عبر العديد من المدن السهلية والشهيرة.

After midnight they found themselves in a forest.

وبعد منتصف الليل وجدوا أنفسهم في الغابة.

And they were not far from the banks of a river.

ولم يكونوا بعيدين عن ضفاف النهر.

Here the most untoward event took place.

وهنا وقع الحدث الأكثر سوءًا.

Swet's wife began to feel the pains of child-birth.

بدأت زوجة سويت تشعر بآلام الولادة.

They dismounted from the horse without delay.

ترجلوا عن الحصان دون تأخير.

And within an hour Swet's wife gave birth to a son.

وفي غضون ساعة أنجبت زوجة سويت ابنا.

What were the two brothers to do in this forest?

ماذا كان على الأخوين أن يفعلوا في هذه الغابة؟

They knew that a fire had to be kindled.

لـقد علموا أنه لا بد من إشعال النار.

The mother and the new-born baby needed warmth.

لكانت الأم والطفل حديث الولادة بحاجة إلى الدفء.

But from where was there fire to be gotten?

ولكن من أين يمكن الحصول على النار؟

There were no human habitations visible.

ولم تكن هناك أية مساكن بشرية مرئية.

Nonetheless, a fire had to be procured.

ومع ذلك، كان لا بد من إشعال النار.

And it was the winter month of December.

وكان شهر ديسمبر في الشتاء.

The mother and the baby would certainly perish.

من المؤكد أن الأم والطفل سوف يموتون.

Swet told Basanta to sit beside his wife.

طلب سويت من باسانتا أن يجلس بجانب زوجته.

And he set out in the darkness of the night.

وانطلق في ظلمة الليل۔

And he went in search of wood to make a fire.

وذهب يبحث عن حطب لإشعال النار۔

Swet walked many a mile through the darkness.

سار سويت عدة أميال عبر الظلام۔

But despite the distance he saw no human habitations.

ولكن على الرغم من المسافة لم يرى أي مسكن بشري۔

But eventually his eyes were given some help.

ولكن في نهاية المطاف حصلت عيناه على بعض المساعدة۔

The genial light of Sukra somewhat illumined his path.

أضاء ضوء سوكرا اللطيف طريقه إلى حد ما۔

And he saw at a distance what seemed a large city.

ورأى من بعيد ما بدا وكأنه مدينة كبيرة۔

He was congratulating himself on his journey's end.

كان يهنئ نفسه على نهاية رحلته۔

And he congratulated himself for finding fire.

وهنأ نفسه على العثور على النار۔

The fire that was going to benefit his poor wife.

النار التي كانت ستعود بالنفع على زوجته المسكينة۔

His wife that was lying cold in the forest.

زوجته التي كانت ترقد في البرد في الغابة۔

The fire that was going to save his new-born child.

النار التي كانت ستنقذ طفله حديث الولادة۔

The new-born baby born into the coldness.

الطفل حديث الولادة ولد في البرد۔

Suddenly an elephant shot across his path.

وفجأة، انطلق فيل عبر طريقه۔

The elephant was gorgeously caparisoned.

لقد كان الفيل مرتديًا ملابس رائعة۔

And the elephant gently picked him with his trunk.

وأمسكه الفيل بخرطومه بلطف۔

He placed him on the rich howdah on its back.

ووضعه على الهودج الكبير على ظهره۔

The elephant then walked rapidly towards the city.

ثم سار الفيل بسرعة نحو المدينة۔

Swet was quite taken aback by the events.

لقد فوجئت سويت بالأحداث.

He did not understand the elephant's actions.

لم يفهم تصرفات الفيل.

And he wondered what was in store for him.

وتساءل عما ينتظره.

A crown is that which was in store for him.

التاج هو ما كان في انتظاره.

He was being taken to the chief city of a kingdom.

لقد تم نقله إلى المدينة الرئيسية للمملكة.

In this kingdom every morning a king was elected.

فـي هذه المملكة كان يتم انتخاب ملك كل صباح.

Because the kings of this city lasted but a day.

لأن ملوك هذه المدينة لم يدوموا إلا يوما واحدا.

Every night the new king joined the queen in her room.

وفي كل ليلة كان الملك الجديد ينضم إلى الملكة في غرفتها.

And every morning the previous king was found dead.

وفي كل صباح كان يتم العثور على الملك السابق ميتا.

No one knew what caused the deaths of the kings.

لـم يكن أحد يعرف سبب وفاة الملوك.

Not even the queen knew what caused their death.

ولم تكن الملكة تعلم سبب وفاتهم.

So this kingdom had its own king-maker.

فـكان لهذه المملكة صـانع ملكها الخاص.

The elephant who suddenly took hold of Swet.

الفيل الذي استولى فجأة على سويت.

Early in the morning the elephant roamed about.

فـي الصباح الباكر كان الفيل يتجول.

Sometimes the elephant went to distant places.

فـي بعض الأحيان كان الفيل يذهب إلى أماكن بعيدة.

And every evening the elephant returned with a man.

وفي كل مساء كان الفيل يعود ومعه رجل.

The man on the elephant's became their king.

وأصبح الرجل على الفيل ملكهم.

The elephant majestically marched through the streets.

سـار الفيل بمهابة عبر الشوارع.

A crowd of people welcomed their new king.

استقبل حشد من الناس ملكهم الجديد۔

But Swet did not yet understand their cheers.

ولكن سويت لم يفهم هتافاتهم بعد۔

The elephant entered the kingdom's palace.

دخل الفيل إلى قصر المملكة۔

And the elephant placed Swet on the throne.

ووضع الفيل سويت على العرش۔

Amid much rejoicing he was proclaimed king.

وفي وسط الكثير من الفرح أُعلن ملكًا۔

But there were lamentations in the crowd too.

ولكن كانت هناك رثاءات في الحشد أيضًا۔

In the course of the day he heard of the curse.

وفي أثناء النهار سمع عن اللعنة۔

The nightly death of every newly elected king.

الموت الليلي لكل ملك جديد منتخب۔

But Swet was possessed of great discretion.

لكن سويت كان يتمتع بقدر كبير من الحكمة۔

And he had the courage not to try an escape.

وكان لديه الشجاعة لعدم محاولة الهروب۔

He took every precaution that he could take.

لقد اتخذ كل الاحتياطات التي كان بوسعه اتخاذها۔

But he did not know how to avert the catastrophe.

ولكنه لم يعرف كيف يتجنب الكارثة۔

And he knew not what expedients to adopt.

ولم يكن ما هي الحلول التي يجب أن يتخذها۔

Because he didn't know the nature of the danger.

لأنه لم يكن يعلم طبيعة الخطر۔

He resolved, however, upon two things;

ولكنه قرر أمرين؛

He was going to go armed into the bedchamber.

كان ينوي أن يدخل إلى غرفة النوم مسلحًا۔

And he was going to stay awake the whole night.

وكان سيبقى مستيقظًا طوال الليل۔

The queen was young and of exquisite beauty.

وكانت الملكة شابة وجميلة للغاية۔

Guileless and benevolent was the expression of her face.

كان تعبير وجهها بريئًا وخيّرًا.

It was impossible to attribute her any malice.

كان من المستحيل أن ننسب إليها أي حقد.

No one believed she caused all the kings' deaths.

لم يصدق أحد أنها كانت السبب في وفاة جميع الملوك.

In the queen's chamber Swet spent an agreeable evening.

أمضى سويت أمسية ممتعة في غرفة الملكة.

As the night advanced the queen fell asleep.

ومع تقدم الليل، نامت الملكة.

But Swet kept awake, and was on the alert.

لكن سويت ظل مستيقظا، وكان في حالة تأهب.

He looked at every creek and corner of the room.

لقد نظر إلى كل جدول وزاوية من الغرفة.

And he expected every minute to be murdered.

وكان يتوقع أن يتم قتله في كل دقيقة.

But the queen did not rise to murder him.

ولكن الملكة لم تنهض لتقتله.

And no one entered the room to murder him either.

ولم يدخل أحد الغرفة ليقتله أيضًا.

Nor did he feel anything other than sleepiness.

ولم يشعر بشيء سوى النعاس.

But in the dead of night he perceived something.

ولكن في منتصف الليل أدرك شيئًا.

A thread was coming out the queen's nostril.

كان هناك خيط يخرج من فتحة أنف الملكة.

The thread was so thin that it was almost invisible.

كان الخيط رقيقًا جدًا حتى أنه كان غير مرئي تقريبًا.

Slowly the thread reached several yards in length.

وببطء وصل الخيط إلى عدة ياردات في الطول.

And eventually all the thread came out.

وفي نهاية المطاف خرج كل الخيوط

Only then did the thread begin to grow thicker.

حينها فقط بدأ الخيط يصبح أكثر سمكا.

Soon the thread took on its real shape.

وسرعان ما اتخذ الخيط شكله الحقيقي.

The thread was in fact a huge serpent.

وكان الخيط في الواقع ثعبانًا ضخمًا.

Immediately Swet cut off the head of the serpent.

فـقام سويت بقطع رأس الثعبان على الفور.

The body of the serpent wriggled violently.

تحرك جسد الثعبان بعنف.

He sat quiet in the room, expecting other adventures.

جلس بهدوء في الغرفة، متوقعًا مغامرات أخرى.

But nothing else happened the rest of the night.

ولكن لم يحدث شيء آخر بقية الليل.

The queen slept longer than usual.

لقد نامت الملكة لفترة أطول من المعتاد.

Because she had been relieved of the huge snake.

لأنها كانت قد تخلصت من الثعبان الضخم.

Early next morning the ministers came.

وفي الصباح الباكر التالي جاء الوزراء.

They were expecting to hear of the king's death.

وكانوا ينتظرون سماع خبر وفاة الملك.

The ladies of the bedchamber knocked at the door.

طرقت سيدات غرفة النوم على الباب.

But to their astonishment Swet come out.

ولكن لدهشتهم خرج سويت.

The folk learned the mystery of all the kings' deaths.

عرف الناس سر وفاة جميع الملوك.

And now the country rejoiced their permanent king.

والآن فرحت البلاد بملكها الدائم.

There is a strange thing you probably noticed.

هناك شيء غريب ربما لاحظته.

Swet did not remember his wife he left behind.

لم يتذكر سويت زوجته التي تركها خلفه.

It is a strange thing, nevertheless it is true.

إنه أمر غريب، لكنه صحيح.

Nor did he remember the defenceless new-born babe.

ولم يتذكر الطفل حديث الولادة الأعزل.

And he did not remember his brother either.

ولم يتذكر أخاه أيضًا.

He had no time to remember when the elephant came.

لم يكن لديه وقت ليتذكر متى جاء الفيل.

On the first night he had to worry for his own life.

في الليلة الأولى كان عليه أن يقلق على حياته.

And now the crown brought on his forgetfulness.

والآن جلب التاج على نسيانه.

But he had entrusted his wife and child to Basanta.

ولكنه كان قد عهد بزوجته وطفله إلى باسانتا.

And his brother sat waiting for many weary hours.

وجلس أخوه ينتظر لساعات طويلة متعبة.

Every moment he expected to see Swet return with fire.

في كل لحظة كان يتوقع أن يرى سويت يعود بالنار.

But the whole night passed away without his return.

لكن الليل كله انقضى دون عودته.

At sunrise he went to the bank of the river.

وعند شروق الشمس ذهب إلى ضفة النهر.

There he anxiously looked about for his brother.

هناك كان يبحث بقلق عن أخيه.

But his waiting and searching were all in vain.

لكن انتظاره وبحثه كان بلا جدوى.

Distressed beyond measure, he wept at the riverside.

كان في حالة من الحزن الشديد، فبكي على ضفة النهر.

As he was weeping a boat was passing by.

وبينما هو يبكي مر قارب.

In the boat a merchant was returning from business.

كان في القارب تاجر عائدا من العمل.

The boat was not far from the shore.

لم يكن القارب بعيدًا عن الشاطئ.

So the merchant could see Basanta weeping.

وبذلك تمكن التاجر من رؤية باسانتا يبكي.

Something struck the attention of the merchant.

لقد لفت شيء انتباه التاجر.

By the weeping man appeared to be a pile of pearls.

وظهر من الرجل الباكي كومة من اللؤلؤ.

The merchant requested the boatman to halt.

طلب التاجر من القارب أن يتوقف.

And the merchant went to the weeping man.

وذهب التاجر إلى الرجل الباكي.

By the weeping man was in fact a pile of pearls.

وكان الرجل الباكي في الواقع عبارة عن كومة من اللؤلؤ.

And the pearls were of the highest quality.

وكانت اللآلئ من أعلى مستويات الجودة.

And another thing astonished the merchant.

وأمر آخر أذهل التاجر.

The pile of pearls grew larger every second.

كانت كومة اللؤلؤ تنمو أكبر كل ثانية.

Because the man was crying, but not tears.

لأن الرجل كان يبكي، ولكن ليس دموعًا.

Because his tears turned to pearls on the ground.

لأن دموعه تحولت إلى لؤلؤ على الأرض.

The merchant stowed away the pearls into his boat.

قام التاجر بتخزين اللآلئ في قاربه.

Then the merchant got his servants to help him.

ثم طلب التاجر من خدمه أن يساعدوه.

And together they captured the crying man.

وتمكنوا معًا من القبض على الرجل الباكي.

They put him on board of the vessel.

وضعوه على متن السفينة.

And he tied him to one of the ship's masts.

وربطه إلى أحد صواري السفينة.

Basanta, of course, tried his best to resist.

وبطبيعة الحال، حاول باسانتا بكل ما في وسعه أن يقاوم.

But what could he do against so many sailors?

ولكن ماذا كان بإمكانه أن يفعل ضد هذا العدد الكبير من البحارة؟

He thought of his brother who never returned.

كان يفكر في أخيه الذي لم يعد أبدًا.

He thought of his sister-in-law in the forest.

كان يفكر في أخت زوجته في الغابة.

And he thought of his newly born niece.

وفكر في ابنة أخته المولودة حديثًا.

And he cried even more bitterly than before.

وبكى بكاءً أشد من ذي قبل.

His weeping mightily pleased the merchant.

لـقد أسعد البكاء التاجر كثيرًا۔

Because even more pearls were falling to the ground.

لـأن المزيد من اللآلئ كانت تتساقط على الأرض۔

And the merchant became richer and richer.

وأصبح التاجر غنيا أكثر فأكثر۔

Eventually the merchant reached his native town.

وفي نهاية المطاف وصل التاجر إلى بلدته الأصلية۔

When they got there he confined Basanta in a room.

وعندما وصلوا هناك، حبس باسانتا في غرفة۔

At stated hours every day he had him whipped.

وفي ساعات محددة من كل يوم كان يتم جلده۔

In order to make him shed yet more tears.

من أجل جعله يذرف المزيد من الدموع۔

And every tear converted into a bright pearl.

وتحولت كل دمعة إلى لؤلؤة لامعة۔

The merchant one day said to his servants;

قـ:ال التاجر ذات يوم لعبيده

"The fellow is making me rich by his weeping".

هذا الرجل يجعلني غنيًا ببكائه

"Let us see what he gives me by laughing".

دعونا نرى ماذا يعطيني بالضحك۔

Accordingly, he began to tickle his captive.

وبناءً على ذلك، بدأ بدغدغة أسيره۔

Upon being tickled Basanta began to laugh.

عندما تم دغدغته بدأ باسانتا بالضحك۔

Of course he was not laughing out of happiness.

وبطبيعة الحال لم يكن يضحك من السعادة۔

But none the less maniks dropped from his mouth.

ولكن مع ذلك كانت الكلمات تتساقط من فمه۔

After this Basanta was not just whipped anymore.

بـعد هذا لم يعد باسانتا مجرد جلد۔

Now he was alternately whipped and tickled.

الآن تم جلده ودغدغته بالتناوب۔

All day and far into the night he was exploited.

ظل يتعرض للاستغلال طوال اليوم وحتى وقت متأخر من الليل۔

The merchant's wealth increased day and night.

زادت ثروة التاجر ليلًا ونهارًا.

Soon he became the wealthiest man in the land.

وسرعان ما أصبح أغنى رجل في البلاد.

But let us return to Basanta's subjugation later.

ولكن دعونا نعود إلى استعباد باسانتا لاحقًا.

Now let us turn our attention to Swet's wife.

والآن دعونا نوجه انتباهنا إلى زوجة سويت.

Swet's abandoned wife was still in the forest.

كانت زوجة سويت المهجورة لا تزال في الغابة.

She had just given birth to her child.

لقد ولدت طفلها للتو.

But now she was alone in the forest.

لكنها الآن أصبحت وحيدة في الغابة.

First her husband had abandoned her.

أولاً تخلى عنها زوجها.

And now her brother-in-law abandoned her too.

والآن تخلى عنها شقيق زوجها أيضًا.

Imagine how overwhelmed with grief she felt.

تخيل مدى الحزن الذي شعرت به.

Alone, and in a forest, far from civilization.

وحيدًا، وفي غابة، بعيدًا عن الحضارة.

Her case was indeed deserving of sympathy.

وكانت قضيتها تستحق التعاطف بالفعل.

She wept rivers of sad and lonely tears.

لقد بكت أنهارًا من الدموع الحزينة والوحيدة.

Excessive grief, however, brought her relief.

لكن الحزن المفرط جلب لها الراحة.

She fell asleep with the new-born in her arms.

لقد نامت مع طفلها حديث الولادة بين ذراعيها.

While she was deep in sleep another tragedy took place.

بينما كانت في نوم عميق حدثت مأساة أخرى.

It so happened that the Kotwal was passing by.

لقد حدث أن كوتوال كان يمر.

He had recently suffered his own misfortune.

لقد عانى مؤخرًا من سوء حظه.

But his misfortune was of a different nature.

ولكن مصيبته كانت من طبيعة مختلفة.

The children his wife bore died shortly after birth.

مات الأطفال الذين أنجبتهم زوجته بعد وقت قصير من ولادتهم.

And he was now going to bury the last infant.

وكان الآن على وشك دفن الطفل الأخير.

He was heading to the banks of the river.

وكان متجها إلى ضفاف النهر.

The place where the other infants were buried.

المكان الذي دفن فيه الأطفال الآخرون.

But then he saw the woman sleeping in the forest.

ولكن بعد ذلك رأى المرأة نائمة في الغابة.

And in her arms he saw her holding a baby.

وفي ذراعيها رآها تحمل طفلاً.

The infant was a lively and beautiful boy.

وكان الطفل صبيًا نشيطًا وجميلًا.

His liveliness did not disturb his mother's sleep.

لم يزعج نشاطه نوم والدته.

The Kotwal wanted the lovely infant very much.

لقد أراد كوتوال الطفل الجميل بشدة.

He quietly took the child from his mother.

أخذ الطفل من أمه بهدوء.

And in her arms he placed his own dead child.

ووضع بين ذراعيها طفله الميت.

Of course this is not what he could tell his wife.

بالطبع هذا ليس ما يستطيع أن يقوله لزوجته.

"We both thought that our son had died".

كنا نعتقد أن ابننا قد مات.

"And I carried his body to the river bank".

وحملت جثته إلى ضفة النهر

"And that was when a miracle occurred".

وعندها حدثت المعجزة.

"Once more our son opened his young eyes".

مرة أخرى فتح ابننا عينيه الصغيرتين.

"And now we have a beautiful and lively boy".

والآن لدينا ولد جميل وحيوي.

But Swet's wife did not know the true events.

لكن زوجة سويت لم تكن تعلم الأحداث الحقيقية.

When she woke she held the dead child in her arms.

عندما استيقظت كانت تحمل الطفل الميت بين ذراعيها.

And she thought it was her child that had died.

وكانت تعتقد أن طفلها هو الذي مات.

The distress of her mind may easily be imagined.

من السهل تصور مدى الضيق الذي تشعر به.

The whole world became dark to her.

لقد أصبح العالم كله مظلما بالنسبة لها.

She was distracted by the loss of her child.

لقد كانت مشغولة بفقدان طفلها.

And in her distraction she formed a resolution.

وفي انشغالها توصلت إلى قرار.

She had resolved to take her own life.

لقد قررت أن تنتحر.

The river was not far from where she had slept.

ولم يكن النهر بعيدًا عن المكان الذي نامت فيه.

And she determined to drown herself in the river.

وقررت أن تغرق نفسها في النهر.

She took in her hand the bundle of jewels.

أخذت في يدها حزمة من المجوهرات.

And then she proceeded to the river-side.

وبعد ذلك توجهت إلى ضفة النهر.

An old Brahman was at no great distance.

لم يكن هناك براهمان قديم على مسافة كبيرة.

The Brahman was performing his morning ablutions.

كان البراهمان يؤدي وضوئه الصباحي.

He noticed the woman going into the water.

لقد لاحظ المرأة تدخل الماء.

Naturally he thought that she was going to bathe.

وبطبيعة الحال كان يعتقد أنها سوف تستحم.

But then he saw her going into the deep waters.

ولكن بعد ذلك رآها تذهب إلى المياه العميقة.

Something akin to suspicion arose in his mind.

لقد نشأ شيء يشبه الشك في ذهنه.

The Brahman discontinued his devotions.

توقف البراهمان عن عباداته.

He too waded out towards the river's depth.

لقد خاض هو أيضًا نحو عمق النهر.

And he ordered the woman to come to him.

وأمر المرأة أن تأتي إليه.

Swet's wife heard the old man calling her.

سمعت زوجة سويت الرجل العجوز يناديها.

So she retraced her steps to the old man.

فعادت أدراجها إلى الرجل العجوز.

"What were your intentions?" asked the Braham.

ما هي نواياك؟ سأل براهام.

And the woman confirmed his suspicions.

وأكدت المرأة شكوكه.

"I was going to put an end to my life".

كنت سأنهي حياتي

And she thanked the Brahman for saving her.

وشكرت البراهمان على إنقاذها.

"Accept these jewels as a sign of appreciation".

تقبل هذه الجواهر كعلامة تقدير

The Brahman accepted the sign of appreciation.

لقد قبل البراهمان علامة التقدير.

But he was more interested in her story.

لكن كان مهتما بقصتها أكثر.

And at his request she related her story.

وبناء على طلبه روت له قصتها.

She had escaped from her stepmother in law.

لقد هربت من زوجة أبيها.

In the forest she gave birth to a child.

وفي الغابة أنجبت طفلاً.

First her husband went looking for fire.

أولاً ذهب زوجها للبحث عن النار.

But her husband never came back to her.

ولكن زوجها لم يعد إليها أبدًا.

Then her brother-in-law looked for her husband.

ثم بحث صهرها عن زوجها.

But her brother-in-law did not return either.

ولكن صهرها لم يعد أيضًا.

Eventually she fell asleep with her child.

وفي نهاية المطاف نامت مع طفلها.

But when she woke her child was dead.

ولكن عندما استيقظت كان طفلها ميتا.

And that's when she decided to drown herself.

وهنا قررت أن تغرق نفسها.

She felt the relieve of telling her fate.

لقد شعرت بالارتياح عندما أخبرت مصيرها.

The Brahman invited the woman to his house.

دعا البراهمان المرأة إلى منزله.

And the woman was accepted into his family.

وقُبلت المرأة في عائلته.

The Brahman's wife treated her like a daughter.

تعاملت زوجة البراهمان معها وكأنها ابنتها.

And she spent years with her new family.

وأمضت سنوات مع عائلتها الجديدة.

Swet spend those years in his kingdom.

لقد قضى سويت تلك السنوات في مملكته.

Basanta spent those years being tortured.

أمضى باسانتا تلك السنوات يتعرض للتعذيب.

And the adopted son of the Kotwal grew up.

ونشأ الابن المتبنى للكوتوال.

The Brahman's house was not far from the Kotwal's.

لم يكن منزل البراهمان بعيدًا عن منزل كوتوال.

So the Kotwal's son met the Brahman's adopted daughter.

وهكذا التقى ابن كوتوال بابنة البراهمان بالتبني.

And the lad thought he fell in love with her.

وظن الشاب أنه وقع في حبها.

He spoke to his father about the woman.

وتحدث مع والده عن المرأة.

And the father spoke to the Brahman about the woman.

وتحدث الأب إلى البراهمان عن المرأة.

The Brahman's rage knew no bounds.

لم يكن لغضب البراهمان حدود.

"What is this insolence!" the Brahman protested.

ما هذه الوقاحة احتج البراهمان.

"Your son is the son of an infidel".

ابنك ابن كافر

"How can he aspire to the hand of a Brahman's daughter!?".

كيف يمكنه أن يطمح إلى الحصول على يد ابنة براهمان؟

"A dwarf may as well aspire to catch hold of the moon!".

قد يطمح القزم أيضًا إلى الاستيلاء على القمر.

But the Kotwal's son determined to have her by force.

لكن ابن كوتوال قرر أن يأخذها بالقوة.

One day he scaled the wall of the Brahman's house.

ذات يوم تسلق جدار منزل البراهمي.

He got upon the thatched roof of the cow-house.

صعد إلى سقف القش لبيت الأبقار.

And from that lofty position he reconnoitered.

ومن ذلك المكان المرتفع كان يستكشف المكان.

And he saw two young calves below him.

فـرأى تحته عجلين صغيرين.

And he overheard the conversation of two young calves.

وسمع حديث عجلين صغيرين.

"Men accuse us of brutish ignorance and immorality".

يتهمنا الرجال بالجهل الوحشي والفساد الأخلاقي.

"But in my opinion men are fifty times worse".

ولكن في رأيي أن الرجال أسوأ بخمسين مرة.

"What makes you say so, brother?" the calf asked.

ما الذي يجعلك تقول ذلك يا أخي؟ سأل العجل.

"Have you witnessed instances of human depravity?".

هل شهدت حالات من الانحطاط البشري؟

"Who is a greater monster than the Kotwal's son?".

من هو الوحش الأعظم من ابن كوتوال؟.

"The same lad standing on the thatched roof".

نفس الشاب الواقف على السطح القشّي.

"The roof of this hut above our heads".

سقف هذا الكوخ فوق رؤوسنا.

"I thought he was just the son of our Kotwal".

اعتقدت أنه كان مجرد ابن كوتوال الخاص بنا.

"I never heard that he was exceptionally vicious".

لم أسمع أبدًا أنه كان شريرًا إلى هذه الدرجة.

"You may have never heard of his wickedness".

ربما لم تسمع أبدًا عن شره.

"But now you will hear of his wickedness from me".

ولكن الآن سوف تسمعون مني بشره

"This wicked lad is now making immoral plans".

هذا الشاب الشرير يقوم الآن بتنفيذ خطط غير أخلاقية.

"He is trying get married to his own mother!".

إنه يحاول الزواج من والدته.

The First Calf then related the whole story.

ثم روى العجل الأول القصة كاملة.

And the inquisitive Second Calf listened.

واستمع العجل الثاني الفضولي.

And the calf told Swet's and Basanta's story.

وحكى العجل قصة سويت وباسانتا.

"A merchant built a house for his son"

بنى التاجر بيتًا لابنه

"In the garden of the house was a Toontooni bird"

في حديقة المنزل كان هناك طائر تونتوني

"In the nest of the Toontooni bird was an egg"

في عش طائر تونتوني كانت هناك بيضة

"The merchant's son put the egg in a almirah"

وضع ابن التاجر البيضة في الخزانة

"Out of the egg came a beautiful girl"

خرجت من البيضة فتاة جميلة

"Eventually the merchant's son married this beautiful girl"

وفي النهاية تزوج ابن التاجر من هذه الفتاة الجميلة

"Together they had two children; Swet and Basanta"

كان لديهم طفلان معًا؛ سويت وباسانتا

"Some time later the grandfather of the children died"

بعد فترة من الوقت توفي جد الأطفال

"Some time later again their grandmother died too"

وبعد فترة من الوقت ماتت جدتهم أيضًا

"At the right time, the oldest son, Swet, got married"

في الوقت المناسب، تزوج الابن الأكبر، سويت

"His mother, the Toontooni woman, died sometime later"

توفيت والدته، امرأة تونتوني، بعد فترة من الوقت

"Soon after their father married a younger woman"

بعد فترة وجيزة تزوج والدهم من امرأة أصغر سناً

"But their new stepmother hated her stepsons"

لكن زوجة أبيهم الجديدة كانت تكره أبناء زوجها

"And she also hated her new stepdaughter-in-law"

وكانت تكره زوجة ابنها الجديدة أيضًا

"One day a fisherman happened to visit the merchant"

في أحد الأيام، صادف أن زار صياد التاجر

"The Fisherman had sold the merchant a magical fish"

باع الصياد للتاجر سمكة سحرية

"Whoever ate the fish would laugh maniks"

من أكل السمك ضحك ضحكة حمقاء

"And whoever ate the fish would weep pearls"

ومن أكل السمك بكى اللؤلؤ

"The same day there was an argument over some pigeons"

في نفس اليوم كان هناك جدال حول بعض الحمام

"The stepmother was terribly vengeful to her stepsons"

كانت زوجة الأب تنتقم بشدة من أبنائها

"And she swore revenge on her stepsons"

و أقسمت على الانتقام من أبنائها

"That day Swet, his wife, and Basanta escaped"

في ذلك اليوم هرب سويت وزوجته وباسانتا

"But before leaving they ate the magical fish"

ولكن قبل أن يغادروا أكلوا السمكة السحرية

"On their journey Swet's wife gave birth to a baby boy"

في رحلتهم، أنجبت زوجة سويت طفلاً ذكرًا

"Swet went to look for wood to make a fire"

ذهب سويت للبحث عن الخشب لإشعال النار

"But he was carried away by an elephant"

ولكنه حمله فيل

"He was taken to a Queen haunted by a snake"

تم نقله إلى ملكة مسكونة بثعبان

"But he succeeded in killing the serpent"

لكنه نجح في قتل الثعبان

"And so he became king of the land"

وهكذا أصبح ملكًا للأرض

"Basanta went looking for his brother"

ذهب باسانتا يبحث عن أخيه

"But he was captured by a merchant"

ولكن تم القبض عليه من قبل تاجر

"And now he's flogged and tickled daily"

والآن يتم جلده ودغدغته يوميًا

"And he cries pearls and laughs maniks"

ويبكي اللؤلؤ ويضحك المانيك

"The Kotwal's son had died that night"

لقد مات ابن كوتوال في تلك الليلة

"So the Kotwal exchanged the two babies"

لذلك قام الكوتوال بتبادل الطفلين

"The mother couldn't bear the loss of her child"

لم تستطع الأم تحمل فقدان طفلها

"So she made the decision to drown herself"

لذلك اتخذت قرارًا بإغراق نفسها

"But there was a Brahman that saved her life"

ولكن كان هناك براهمان أنقذ حياتها

"And this Brahman took her into his home"

وأخذها هذا البراهمان إلى منزله

"The Kotwal's son grew up a hardy boy"

نشأ ابن كوتوال صبيًا قويًا

"And he fell in love with the woman"

ووقع في حب المرأة

"And now he stands on the roof"

والآن هو يقف على السطح

"And he's intent on having the woman"

وهو عازم على الحصول على المرأة

All this the Kotwal's son heard.

كل هذا سمعه ابن كوتوال.

And he was struck with horror.

فأصيب بالرعب.

He forthwith got down from the thatch.

نزل على الفور من القش.

And he went home to his father.

وذهب إلى بيت أبيه.

And he said he must speak with the king.

وقال أنه يجب أن يتحدث مع الملك.

The father protested against the request.

احتج الأب على الطلب.

But he got an interview with the king.

ولكنه حصل على مقابلة مع الملك.

He told the king about the two calves.

وأخبر الملك عن العجلين.

And he repeated the whole story.

وكرر القصة كاملة.

The king now remembered his poor wife.

وتذكر الملك الآن زوجته المسكينة.

So a servant was sent to the Brahman.

فأرسل خادمًا إلى البراهمان.

And the Brahman was richly rewarded.

وقد تم مكافأة البراهمان بسخاء.

And his wife was brought back to the palace.

وأعيدت زوجته إلى القصر.

His wife was put in her proper position.

ووضعت زوجته في مكانها المناسب.

And she became queen of the kingdom.

وأصبحت ملكة المملكة.

The reputed son of the Kotwal was readopted.

تم إعادة تبني الابن المزعوم لكوتوال.

And he was proclaimed heir to the throne.

وأعلن وريثًا للعرش.

Basanta was brought out of the dungeon.

تم إخراج باسانتا من الزنزانة.

And the wicked merchant was buried alive.

ودفن التاجر الشرير حياً.

And thorns were put in his burying-place.

ووضعوا له شوكاً في قبره.

And all lived together happily for many years.

وعاش الجميع معًا بسعادة لسنوات عديدة.

Swet, his wife and son, and Basantas.

سويت وزوجته وابنه وباسانتاس.

The Evil Eye of Sani
العين الشريرة للساني

Once upon a time Sani and Lakshmi fell out with each other.

ذات مرة، كان ساني ولاكشمي مختلفين مع بعضهما البعض.

Sani, also known as Saturn, is the God of bad luck.

ساني، المعروف أيضًا باسم زحل، هو إله الحظ السيئ.

And Lakshmi is the Goddess of good luck.

ولاكشمي هي إلهة الحظ السعيد.

And these two Gods fell out with each other in heaven.

وهذان الإلهان وقعا في خلاف مع بعضهما البعض في السماء.

Sani said he was higher in rank than Lakshmi.

قال ساني أنه كان أعلى رتبة من لاكشمي.

And Lakshmi said she was higher in rank than Sani.

وقالت لاكشمي أنها كانت أعلى رتبة من ساني.

But there were just as many Gods as there were Goddesses.

ولكن كان هناك عدد من الآلهة مثلما كان هناك عدد من الآلهة.

Therefore the dispute could not be settled in heaven.

ولذلك لم يكن من الممكن تسوية النزاع في السماء.

The contending deities agreed to refer the matter to humans.

واتفق الآلهة المتنازعة على إحالة الأمر إلى البشر.

The humans had a name for wisdom and justice.

وكان للإنسان اسم للحكمة والعدالة.

There lived at that time upon earth a man named Sribatsa.

كان يعيش في ذلك الوقت على الأرض رجل اسمه سريباتسا.

(Sri is another name of Lakshmi).

((سري هو اسم آخر لـ لاكشمي.

(And"batsa" is another word for child).

((وباتسا كلمة أخرى تعني طفل.

(so Sribatsa literally means"the child of fortune").

((لذا فإن سريباتسا تعني حرفيًا طفل الحظ.

Sribatsa had as much wisdom as he had wealth.

كان سريباتسا يتمتع بالحكمة بقدر ما كان يتمتع بالثروة.

And he was as fair as he was rich, too.

وكان عادلاً مثلما كان غنياً أيضاً.

He was therefore a good judge for the dispute.

لقد كان بذلك قاضيًا جيدًا للنزاع.

And the God and Goddess agreed he could judge their case.

واتفق الإله والإلهة على أنه يستطيع الحكم في قضيتهما.

One day, accordingly, Sribatsa was contacted.

وفي أحد الأيام، تم الاتصال بسريباتسا.

He was told that Sani and Lakshmi would come to him.

وقيل له أن ساني ولاكشمي سيأتيان إليه.

And he was told they wished for him to settle their dispute.

وقيل له أنهم يريدون منه أن يحسم نزاعهم.

This put Sribatsa in a delicate situation.

وهذا وضع سريباتسا في موقف حساس.

He could say Sani was higher in rank than Lakshmi.

يمكنه أن يقول أن ساني كان أعلى رتبة من لاكشمي.

But then she would be angry with him and forsake him.

ولكنها بعد ذلك سوف تغضب منه وتتخلى عنه.

He could say Lakshmi was higher in rank than Sani.

يمكنه أن يقول أن لاكشمي كانت أعلى رتبة من ساني.

But then Sani would cast his evil eye upon him.

ولكن بعد ذلك سوف يلقي ساني عينه الشريرة عليه.

He made up his mind not to say anything directly.

لقد قرر عدم قول أي شيء بشكل مباشر.

The god and the goddess had to observe his actions.

وكان على الإله والإلهة أن يراقبا أفعاله.

And from his actions they could gather their opinions.

ومن أفعاله استطاعوا أن يستنتجوا آراءهم.

Sribatsa ordered two chairs to be made.

أمر سريباتسا بصنع كرسيين.

One of the chairs was made from gold.

كان أحد الكراسي مصنوعًا من الذهب.

And the other chair was made from silver.

والكرسي الآخر كان مصنوعا من الفضة.

And he placed the two chairs beside himself.

ووضع الكرسيين بجانبه.

The day came when Sani and Lakshmi visited Sribatsa.

وجاء اليوم الذي زار فيه ساني ولاكشمي سريباتسا.

He told Sani to sit upon the silver chair.

طلب من ساني أن يجلس على الكرسي الفضي.

And he told Lakshmi to sit upon the gold chair.

وطلب من لاكشمي أن تجلس على الكرسي الذهبي.

Sani became mad with rage, and spoke angrily;

لقد جن جنون ساني وتحدث بغضب؛

"You consider me lower in rank than Lakshmi"

أنت تعتبرني أقل مرتبة من لاكشمي

"I will cast my eye on you for three years"

سألقي عليك نظرة لمدة ثلاث سنوات

"We shall see how you fare at the end of that period"

سنرى كيف ستكون أحوالك في نهاية تلك الفترة

The god then went away in great anger.

ثم ذهب الإله في غضب شديد.

Lakshmi, before she went away, said to Sribatsa;

قالت لاكشمي لسريباتسا قبل أن تذهب

"My child, do not fear. I'll befriend you"

يا بني، لا تخف سأصادقك .

The god and the goddess then went away.

ثم ذهب الإله والإلهة.

Sribatsa spoke to his wife, Chantamani;

تحدث سريباتسا إلى زوجته شانتاماني؛

"Dearest, the evil eye of Sani will be upon me"

عزيزتي، عين الشر من ساني ستكون عليّ

"I had better go away from the house"

من الأفضل أن أبتعد عن المنزل

"If I stay evil will befall you and me"

إذا بقيت فسوف يصيبك الشر وأنا

"But if I go, evil will overtake me only"

ولكن إن ذهبت فلن يصيبني إلا الشر

Chintamani said, "it cannot be that way"

قال تشينتاماني لا يمكن أن يكون الأمر كذلك

"Wherever you go, I will go with you"

أينما ذهبت، سأذهب معك

"Your good luck shall be my good luck"

حظك السعيد سيكون حظي السعيد

"And your bad luck shall be my bad luck"

وسوف يكون حظك السيئ هو حظي السيئ

The husband tried hard to persuade his wife to stay.

حاول الزوج جاهدا إقناع زوجته بالبقاء.

But all his efforts were of no use.

ولكن كل جهوده كانت بلا فائدة.

She refused to abandon her husband.

رفضت التخلي عن زوجها.

Sribatsa told his wife to make an opening in their mattress.

طلب سريباتسا من زوجته أن تصنع فتحة في فراشهما.

And he told her to stow away all their money and jewels.

وطلب منها أن تخبئ كل أموالهم ومجوهراتهم.

On the eve of leaving their house, Sribatsa invoked
Lakshmi.

في عشية مغادرة منزلهم، استحضر سريباتسا لاكشمي.

Upon being invoked, Lakshmi forthwith appeared.

وعند استدعائها، ظهرت لاكشمي على الفور.

"Mother Lakshmi, the evil eye of Sani is upon us"

الأم لاكشمي، عين الشر من ساني علينا

"We are going away into exile"

نحن ذاهبون إلى المنفى

"Please befriend us, and take care of our property"

يرجى أن تصبح صديقًا لنا، وأن تعتني بممتلكاتنا

The goddess of good luck answered.

أجابت إلهة الحظ السعيد.

"Do not fear; I'll befriend you"

لا تخف، سأصبح صديقًا لك

"In the end all will be right"

في النهاية كل شيء سيكون على ما يرام

They then set out on their journey.

ثم انطلقوا في رحلتهم.

Sribatsa rolled up the mattress and put it on his head.

لف سريباتسا المرتبة ووضعها على رأسه.

They had not gone many miles when they saw a river.

لم يكن قد مضى على مسيرهم سوى أميال قليلة عندما رأوا النهر.

There was a canoe with a man sitting in it.

كان هناك زورق وكان رجل يجلس فيه.

The travelers requested the ferryman to take them across.

طلب المسافرون من صاحب العبارة أن يأخذهم إلى الجانب الآخر.

The ferryman said he could only take one at a time.

قال صاحب العبارة أنه لا يستطيع أن يأخذ إلا شخصًا واحدًا في كل مرة.

"Tere are three of you," he objected.

أنتم ثلاثة، اعترض.

"There is you, your wife, and your mattress"

هناك أنت وزوجتك وفراشك

Sribatsa proposed in what order they should ferry over the river.

اقترح سريباتسا الترتيب الذي ينبغي أن يعبروا به النهر.

"First my wife should be taken across the river"

أولاً يجب أن نأخذ زوجتي عبر النهر

"After my wife, take the mattress across the river"

بعد زوجتي، خذ المرتبة عبر النهر

"And then you can take me across the river"

وبعد ذلك يمكنك أن تأخذني عبر النهر

But the ferryman would not hear of it.

ولكن صاحب العبارة لم يستمع إلى ذلك.

"Only one at a time," he repeated.

واحدة فقط في كل مرة كرر.

"First let me take across the mattress"

أولاً دعني أحمل المرتبة عبر

Sribatsa saw no reason to object to the proposal.

ولم ير سريباتسا أي سبب للاعتراض على الاقتراح.

The ferryman started taking the mattress across the river.

بدأ صاحب العبارة بنقل المرتبة عبر النهر.

He had reached halfway across the river.

لقد وصل إلى منتصف الطريق عبر النهر.

But then, from nowhere, a fierce gale arose.

ولكن بعد ذلك، من العدم، نشأت عاصفة عنيفة.

The ferryman lost control of his canoe.

فـقد صاحب العبارة السيطرة على زورقه.

The mattress was blown into the river.

تـم نفخ الفراش في النهر.

The river carried everything away with it.

لـقد حمل النهر كل شيء معه.

And the ferrymen, canoe, and mattress were never seen again.

ولم يتم رؤية رجال العبارة والقارب والفراش مرة أخرى.

But that was not even the strangest events.

ولكن لم تكن تلك حتى الأحداث الأكثر غرابة.

Because the river also disappeared into thin air.

لـأن النهر اختفى أيضًا في الهواء.

Where there was water there was now dry ground.

حيث كان هناك ماء، كانت هناك الآن أرض جافة.

Sribatsa knew the evil eye of Sani had been watching.

عرف سريباتسا أن عين ساني الشريرة كانت تراقب.

Sribatsa and his wife had not a pice in their pockets.

ولم يكن لدى سريباتسا وزوجته أي نقود في جيوبهما.

Together, impoverished, they went to a nearby village.

ذهبوا معًا فقراءً إلى قرية قريبة.

The village was dwelt in mostly by wood-cutters.

كانت القرية مأهولة في الغالب بعمال قطع الأخشاب.

At sunrise the woodcutters went to cut wood.

عند شروق الشمس ذهب الحطابون لقطع الخشب.

And the wood they cut they sold in a faraway town.

والخشب الذي قطعوه كانوا يبيعونه في مدينة بعيدة.

Sribatsa asked to work with the wood-cutters.

طلب سريباتسا العمل مع الحطابين.

And the wood-cutters agreed to let him cut wood.

ووافق الحطابون على السماح له بقطع الخشب.

He could fell trees as well as the best of them.

كان قادرًا على قطع الأشجار بأفضل ما يمكن.

But Sribatsa was different from the wood-cutters.

لكن سريباتسا كان مختلفًا عن الحطابين.

The wood-cutters cut any and every sort of wood.

يقوم قاطعو الأخشاب بقطع كل أنواع الخشب.

But Sribatsa cut only the precious types of wood.

لكن سريباتسا لم يقطع إلا الأنواع الثمينة من الخشب.

His efforts were focused on cutting down sandal-wood.

تركزت جهوده على قطع خشب الصندل.

The wood-cutters brought to market large loads of common wood.

قام قاطعو الأخشاب بإحضار كميات كبيرة من الخشب الشائع إلى السوق.

Sribatsa brought only a few pieces of sandal-wood to the market.

لم يحضر سريباتسا إلى السوق سوى قطع قليلة من خشب الصندل.

He was paid a great deal more money than the others.

لقد تم دفع له مبلغًا كبيرًا من المال أكثر من الآخرين.

Things went on this way for some days.

واستمرت الأمور على هذا النحو لعدة أيام.

And the wood-cutters became jealous of Sribatsa.

وأصبح الحطابون يغارون من سريباتسا.

In their jealousy they plotted against Sribatsa.

في غيرتهم تآمروا ضد سريباتسا.

And finally they drove Sribatsa and his wife from the village.

وأخيرًا، طردوا سريباتسا وزوجته من القرية.

Sribatsa and his wife made their way to another village.

توجه سريباتسا وزوجته إلى قرية أخرى.

In this village there were many women that weaved.

في هذه القرية كان هناك العديد من النساء اللواتي ينسجن.

Here Chintamani made herself useful by spinning cotton.

هنا جعلت تشينتاماني نفسها مفيدة من خلال غزل القطن.

Chintamani was an intelligent and skillful woman.

كانت تشينتاماني امرأة ذكية وماهرة.

So she spun finer thread than the other women.

فكانت تغزل خيوطًا أدق من خيوط النساء الأخريات.

And she got paid more money than the other women.

وحصلت على أموال أكثر من النساء الأخريات۔

This roused the envy of the native women of the village.

وقد أثار هذا حسد النساء الأصليات في القرية۔

But the envy of the other women was not all.

ولكن حسد النساء الأخريات لم يكن كل شيء۔

Sribatsa wanted to gain the good grace of the weavers.

أراد سريياتسا أن يحظى بقبول النساجين۔

So he invited the women that spun cotton to a feast.

فـقام بدعوة النساء اللواتي ينسجن القطن إلى وليمة۔

The dishes of the feat were all cooked by his wife.

تـم طهي جميع أطباق هذا العمل من قبل زوجته۔

Chintamani was a good weaver, and an excellent in cook.

كان تشينتاماني نساجًا جيدًا، وطاهٍ ممتازًا۔

She placed the delicacies before the women.

وضعت الأطعمة الشهية أمام النساء۔

And the barbarous weavers were quite charmed.

ولقد سحر النساجون البرابرة تمامًا۔

The men went to their homes with their bellies full.

وذهب الرجال إلى منازلهم وبطونهم ممتلئة۔

But when they got home, they reproached their wives.

ولكن عندما وصلوا إلى منازلهم، وبخوا زوجاتهم۔

"Why do you not cook like the wife of Sribatsa"

لماذا لا تطبخين مثل زوجة سريياتسا

And the men called their wives good-for-nothing women.

وكان الرجال يسمون زوجاتهم نساءً فاسقات۔

This made the women hate Chintamani the more.

وهذا جعل النساء يكرهن تشينتاماني أكثر۔

One day Chintamani went to the river-side.

ذات يوم ذهب تشينتاماني إلى ضفة النهر۔

She wanted to bathe along with the other women of the village.

أرادت أن تستحم مع بقية نساء القرية۔

A boat had been lying on the bank, stranded on the sand.

كانت هناك قارب ملقى على الضفة، عالقا على الرمال۔

The boat had been stranded there for many days.

لقد كانت السفينة عالقة هناك لعدة أيام.

They had tried to move the boat, but in vain.

لقد حاولوا تحريك القارب، ولكن دون جدوى.

It so happened that Chintamani touched the boat.

لقد حدث أن تشينتاماني لمس القارب.

It was an accident, for she did not mean to touch the boat.

لقد كان حادثًا، لأنها لم تكن تقصد أن تلمس القارب.

But whether she meant to or not, the boat moved.

ولكن سواء كانت تقصد ذلك أم لا، فقد تحرك القارب.

And soon the boat was heading off to the river.

وبعد قليل كان القارب متجها إلى النهر.

The boatmen were astonished by what they had seen.

لقد اندهش أصحاب القارب مما رأوه.

They thought that the woman had uncommon power.

ظنوا أن المرأة تمتلك قوة غير عادية.

And so they thought she might be useful in future.

ولذلك اعتقدوا أنها قد تكون مفيدة في المستقبل.

They therefore caught hold of her, against her will.

فأمسكوا بها رغماً عنها.

And they put her in the boat, and rowed off.

فأدخلوها في السفينة وانطلقوا.

The women of the village were present for this kidnapping.

وكانت نساء القرية حاضرات أثناء عملية الاختطاف.

But they did not offer Chintamani any assistance.

لكنهم لم يقدموا أي مساعدة لتشينتاماني.

Because Chintamani had put them in a bad light.

لأن تشينتاماني وضعهم في صورة سيئة.

Sribatsa heard how his wife had been carried away by boatmen.

سمع سريباتسا كيف أن البحارة حملوا زوجته بعيدًا.

I will let you imagine how he became mad with grief.

سأترك لك أن تتخيل كيف أصيب بالجنون من الحزن.

He left the village and went to the river-side.

غادر القرية وذهب إلى ضفة النهر.

And he resolved to follow the course of the stream.

وقد عزم على اتباع مجرى النهر.

Along the stream he was sure to meet the kidnappers' boat.

كان متأكداً من مقابلة قارب الخاطفين على طول النهر.

He travelled on and on, along the side of the river.

لقد سافر واستمر في السفر، على طول جانب النهر.

And he travelled till it eventually became dark.

وسافر حتى أصبح الظلام أخيراً.

Where he was there were no huts to be seen.

حيث كان لم تكن هناك أكواخ يمكن رؤيتها.

So he climbed into a tree to sleep for the night.

فصعد إلى شجرة لينام ليلته.

In the next morning he got down from the tree.

وفي الصباح التالي نزل من الشجرة.

At the foot of the tree he saw a Kapila-cow.

عند سفح الشجرة رأى بقرة كابيلا.

A Kapila-cow never has any calves of her own.

البقرة كابيلا لا تنجب أي عجول خاصة بها أبدًا.

But she can be milked at all hours of the day.

ولكن يمكن حلبها في جميع ساعات اليوم.

Sribatsa milked the cow without her objecting.

حلبت سريباتسا البقرة دون اعتراض.

And he drank the milk to his heart's content.

وشرب الحليب حتى شبع.

And then he noticed something else about the cow.

ثم لاحظ شيئًا آخر في البقرة.

The dung of the cow was of a bright yellow color.

وكان روث البقرة ذو لون أصفر فاتح.

In fact, the dung of the cow was made of pure gold.

في الواقع، كان روث البقرة مصنوعًا من الذهب الخالص.

The golden cow dung was still in a soft state.

كان روث البقر الذهبي لا يزال في حالة طرية.

So he was able to write his name in the golden dung.

فأصبح قادرا على كتابة اسمه في الروث الذهبي.

During the course of the day the dung hardened.

خلال النهار تصلبت الروث.

And finally the dung looked like a brick of gold.

وأخيراً أصبح الروث يبدو مثل لبنة من الذهب.

The tree he had slept in grew on the river-side.

كانت الشجرة التي نام عليها تنمو على ضفة النهر.

And the Kapila-cow supplied him with milk all day.

وكانت بقرة كابيلا تزوده بالحليب طوال اليوم.

So Sribatsa decided to wait there for the boat.

لذلك قرر سريباتسا الانتظار هناك من أجل القارب.

In the morning the cow deposited the precious article.

وفي الصباح وضعت البقرة القطعة الثمينة.

And at night the cow deposited the precious article.

وفي الليل وضعت البقرة القطعة الثمينة.

So the gold bricks increased every day.

فكانت الطوب الذهبية تزداد كل يوم.

And on each golden brick he had engraved his name.

وعلى كل لبنة ذهبية نقش اسمه.

He stacked the bricks on top of each other.

قام برص الطوب فوق بعضه البعض.

From a distance it looked like a hillock of gold.

من مسافة بعيدة بدا الأمر وكأنه تلة من الذهب.

But now we must leave Sribatsa to stack his gold.

لكن الآن يجب علينا أن نترك سريباتسا ليجمع ذهبه.

And we must turn our attention to Chintamani.

ويجب علينا أن نوجه اهتمامنا إلى تشينتاماني.

Chintamani was a graceful woman of great beauty.

كانت تشينتاماني امرأة رشيقة ذات جمال عظيم.

She had worried her beauty might be her ruin.

لقد كانت قلقة من أن جمالها قد يكون سبب دمارها.

So she offered a prayer as she was being kidnapped.

لذلك قدمت صلاة عندما تم اختطافها.

"Lakshmi, O Mother Lakshmi! have pity upon me"

لاكشمي، يا أم لاكشمي ارحميني

"Thou hast made me beautiful, you have"

لقد جعلتني جميلة، لقد فعلت ذلك.

"But now my beauty will undoubtedly be my ruin"

لكن الآن جمالي سيكون بلا شك سبب دماري

"I am bound to loss my honor and my chastity"

أنا مضطر لخسارة شرفي وعفتي

"I therefore beseech thee, gracious Mother;"

لذلك أتوسل إليك، أيتها الأم الكريمة؛

"Take my beauty from me, and make me ugly"

خذ جمالي مني واجعلني قبيحًا

"Cover my body with some loathsome disease"

غطي جسدي ببعض الأمراض البغيضة

"That way the boatmen might not touch me"

بهذه الطريقة لن يلمسني البحارة

Chintamani was in the arms of the boatmen.

كان تشينتاماني بين أحضان القارب.

But the Goddess of good fortune heard her prayer.

ولكن إلهة الحظ السعيد سمعت صلاتها.

In the twinkling of an eye her form changed.

في غمضة عين تغير شكلها.

Her naturally beautiful form faded away.

لقد تلاشى شكلها الطبيعي الجميل.

And she was turned into a vile carcass.

فتحولت إلى جثة بائسة.

The boatmen were putting her down in the boat.

كان أصحاب القارب يضعونها في القارب.

They found her body was covered with loathsome sores.

ووجدوا أن جسدها كان مغطى بقروح مقززة.

And the sores were giving out a disgusting stench.

وكانت القروح تصدر رائحة كريهة.

They therefore threw her into the hold of the boat.

فألقوها في عنبر السفينة.

And they left her amongst the cargo of the ship.

وتركوها في وسط السفينة.

Morning and evening they sent her some food.

في الصباح والمساء أرسلوا لها بعض الطعام.

A little boiled rice, and some water to drink.

قليل من الأرز المسلوق، وبعض الماء للشرب.

Chintamani was miserable in the hull of the ship.

كان تشينتاماني بائسًا في بدن السفينة.

But she greatly preferred misery to the alternative.

لكنها فضلت البؤس على البديل.

She would rather be miserable than loss her chastity.

إنها تفضل أن تكون بائسة على أن تفقد عفتها.

The boatmen had gone to some port to sell cargo.

وكان أصحاب القوارب قد ذهبوا إلى أحد الموانئ لبيع البضائع.

While sailing back they caught sight something.

بينما كانوا يعودون أبحروا لفت انتباههم شيء ما.

By the river-side there seemed to be a hillock of gold.

على ضفة النهر يبدو أن هناك تلة من الذهب.

Sribatsa had been keeping watch by the river.

وكان سريباتسا يراقب النهر.

So he was delighted to see a boat approach him.

فكان مسروراً عندما رأى قارباً يقترب منه.

Because he fondly imagined his wife might be on board.

لأنه كان يتخيل بشغف أن زوجته قد تكون على متن الطائرة.

The boatmen went greedily to the hillock of gold.

ذهب أصحاب القارب بشراهة إلى تل الذهب.

Of course Sribatsa told them the gold was his.

بالطبع أخبرهم سريباتسا أن الذهب كان ملكه.

But that didn't help Sribatsa very much.

ولكن هذا لم يساعد سريباتسا كثيرا.

The sailors took him prisoner on the boat.

أسره البحارة على متن القارب.

And they loaded the gold onto their vessel.

وحملوا الذهب على سفينتهم.

They happened to imprison him close to the ugly woman.

لقد سجنوه بالقرب من المرأة القبيحة.

Of course the husband and wife recognized each other.

وبطبيعة الحال تعرف الزوج والزوجة على بعضهما البعض.

In spite of the change Chintamani had undergone.

على الرغم من التغيير الذي حدث لشينتاماني.

And despite their excitement they kept their composure.

ورغم حماسهم إلا أنهم حافظوا على هدوئهم.

And they thought it prudent not to speak to each other.

ورأوا أنه من الحكمة عدم التحدث مع بعضهم البعض.
Instead they communicated their ideas through gestures.
وبدلاً من ذلك، قاموا بتوصيل أفكارهم من خلال الإيماءات.
There is something you should know about the boatmen.
هناك شيء يجب أن تعرفه عن أصحاب القوارب.
These boatmen were very fond of playing at dice.
كان هؤلاء البحارة مولعين جدًا باللعب بالنرد.
Sribatsa appeared to them to be a respectable man.
لقد ظهر لهم سريباتسا كرجل محترم.
So they always asked him to join in the game.
لذلك طلبوا منه دائمًا الانضمام إلى اللعبة.
Sribatsa happened to be an expert dice player.
لقد كان سريباتسا خبيرًا في لعب النرد.
Despite their efforts he won almost every game.
وعلى الرغم من جهودهم فقد فاز في كل مباراة تقريبًا.
You can imagine how the sailors felt about losing.
يمكنك أن تتخيل كيف شعر البحارة بالخسارة.
And in jealousy the boatmen threw him overboard.
وفي حسدٍ من أهل السفينة ألقوه في البحر.
Chintamani saw the men throw her husband overboard.
رأت تشينتاماني الرجال يلقون بزوجها في البحر.
Fortunately for Sribatsa, his wife had great presence of
mind.
لحسن الحظ بالنسبة لسريباتسا، كانت زوجته تتمتع بحضور ذهني كبير.
The boatmen had allowed her a pillow to rest her head.
لقد سمح لها أصحاب القارب باستخدام الوسادة لتريح رأسها.
And she simultaneously threw this pillow into the water.
وألقت هذه الوسادة في الماء في نفس الوقت.
Sribatsa was able to grab hold of the pillow.
كان سريباتسا قادرًا على الإمساك بالوسادة.
And the pillow helped him float down the stream.
وساعدته الوسادة على الطفو أسفل النهر.
Up until nightfall the river carried him downstream.
حتى حلول الليل، كان النهر يحمله في اتجاه مجرى النهر.
At nightfall he arrived at what seemed to be a garden.
وعند حلول الليل وصل إلى ما بدا وكأنه حديقة.

Because it was dark there was nothing he could do.

لأنه كان الظلام حالكًا، لم يكن هناك ما يستطيع فعله.

So all night he stayed in the garden, cold and wet.

لذلك بقي طوال الليل في الحديقة، باردًا ومبللًا.

I should tell you who this garden belonged to.

أريد أن أخبرك لمن تعود ملكية هذه الحديقة.

This was the garden of an old widowed woman.

كانت هذه حديقة امرأة أرملة عجوز.

This woman used to supply flowers for the king.

كانت هذه المرأة تقوم بتزويد الملك بالزهور.

But one day some blight had come over her garden.

ولكن في يوم من الأيام حلت بعض الأمراض على حديقتها.

Almost all the trees and plants ceased flowering.

توقفت جميع الأشجار والنباتات تقريبًا عن التزهير.

She had therefore given up the business she had.

ولهذا السبب تخلت عن العمل الذي كانت تملكه.

And she was no longer the royal flower supplier.

ولم تعد هي الموردة الملكية للزهور.

However, Sribatsa's arrival had rejuvenated her garden.

ومع ذلك، فإن وصول سريباتسا قد أدى إلى تجديد حديقتها.

She could scarcely believe her eyes in the morning.

لم تستطع أن تصدق عينيها في الصباح.

The whole garden was ablaze with flowers again.

كانت الحديقة بأكملها مليئة بالزهور مرة أخرى.

There was no plant that was not in bloom.

لم يكن هناك نبات لا يزهر.

And every tree she had was begemmed with flowers.

وكانت كل شجرة لديها مزينة بالزهور.

She had no way of knowing the cause of the miracle.

ولم تكن لديها وسيلة لمعرفة سبب المعجزة.

And so she took a walk through the garden.

وبعد ذلك قامت بالمشي في الحديقة.

But she soon found the cause of all the flowers.

لكنها سرعان ما وجدت سبب كل الزهور.

At the edge of her garden was a cold, wet man.

وعلى حافة حديقتها كان هناك رجل بارد ومبلل.

He was shivering and almost dead from hypothermia.

كان يرتجف ويكاد يموت من انخفاض حرارة الجسم.

She immediately brought the man into to her cottage.

أدخلت الرجل إلى كوخها على الفور.

And she lighted a fire to give him some warmth.

وأشعلت النار لتمنحه بعض الدفء.

She nursed him and showed him every attention.

لقد احتضنته وأظهرت له كل الاهتمام.

And she ascribed the miracle to his presence.

وأرجعت المعجزة إلى وجوده.

She made him as comfortable as she could.

لقد جعلته يشعر بالراحة قدر استطاعتها.

And then she ran to the king's palace.

ثم ركضت إلى قصر الملك.

She asked to speak to the king's chief servant.

طلبت التحدث مع كبير خدم الملك.

And she told him the good fortune she had had.

وأخبرته بالحظ السعيد الذي حظيت به.

"I can again supply the palace with flowers"

أستطيع أن أزود القصر بالزهور مرة أخرى

Her flowers had been very much missed at the palace.

لقد افتقدنا أزهارها كثيرًا في القصر.

So she was immediately restored to her former position.

فأعيدت على الفور إلى منصبها السابق.

She was again the flower-woman of the royal household.

لقد أصبحت مرة أخرى سيدة الزهور في العائلة المالكة.

Sribatsa spent a few more days recovering his health.

أمضى سريباتسا بضعة أيام أخرى يستعيد فيها صحته.

And eventually he had all his vitality back.

وفي النهاية استعاد كل حيويته.

He asked the woman if he could speak with a minister.

سأل المرأة إذا كان بإمكانه التحدث مع وزير.

So the woman took him to the palace with her.

فأخذته المرأة معها إلى القصر.

One of the king's ministers gave him an appointment.

أعطاه أحد وزراء الملك موعدًا.

And he was at once found to be a man of intelligence.

ولقد تبين على الفور أنه رجل ذو ذكاء.

So was offered a position in the king's service.

فعرض عليه منصب في خدمة الملك.

In fact, he was allowed to choose what job he wanted.

في الواقع، سُمح له باختيار الوظيفة التي يريدها.

He asked to be collector of tolls on the river.

طلب أن يكون جامعاً للرسوم على النهر.

The minister was happy to give Sribatsa the job.

وكان الوزير سعيدًا بإعطاء سريباتسا الوظيفة.

The kingdom needed someone to collect river-tolls.

كانت المملكة بحاجة إلى شخص لجمع رسوم النهر.

And Sribatsa immediately started his new job.

وبدأ سريباتسا عمله الجديد على الفور.

It wasn't long before his plan came to fruition.

ولم يمض وقت طويل قبل أن تتحول خطته إلى واقع.

The boat his wife was on was coming down the river.

وكان القارب الذي كانت زوجته على متنه قادما إلى النهر.

Under the king's authority he detained the boat.

وبأمر الملك احتجز القارب.

And he charged the boatmen with the theft of gold-bricks.

واتهم أصحاب المراكب بسرقة قطع من الذهب.

The king liked the sound of a boat full of gold.

كان الملك يحب صوت القارب الممتلئ بالذهب.

So the king himself came to the river-side.

فجاء الملك بنفسه إلى ضفة النهر.

Even he was amazed by the quantity of gold they had.

حتى أنه اندهش من كمية الذهب التي كانت لديهم.

And every gold brick had Sribatsa's inscription.

وكانت كل قطعة من الذهب تحمل نقش سريباتسا.

At the same time he rescued his wife from the boatmen.

وفي الوقت نفسه أنقذ زوجته من البحارة.

Back on dry land she returned to her previous beauty.

وعندما عادت إلى الأرض الجافة عادت إلى جمالها السابق.

He told the king the story of their misfortune.

وأخبر الملك بقصة مصيبتهم۔

And the king had them as a guest in his palace.

وكان الملك يستضيفهم في قصره۔

The king gave them presents of horses and elephants.

وأعطاهم الملك هدايا من الخيول والفيلة۔

And on the horses and elephants they rode to their country.

وعلى الخيول والفيلة ركبوا إلى بلادهم۔

The evil eye of Sani was now turned away from Sribatsa.

لقد تحولت الآن عين ساني الشريرة بعيدًا عن سريباتسا۔

And he again became what he formerly was.

فعاد كما كان من قبل۔

He was again Sribatsa; the Child of Fortune.

لقد أصبح مرة أخرى سريباتسا؛ طفل الحظ

The Boy whom Seven Mothers Suckled
الطفل الذي أرضعته سبع أمهات

Once on a time there reigned a king who had seven queens.

كان في قديم الزمان ملكًا وكان له سبع ملكات.

He was very sad, for the seven queens were all barren.

لقد كان حزينًا جدًا، لأن الملكات السبع كن جميعهن عاقرًا.

One day, however, he met a holy mendicant.

ولكن ذات يوم، التقى متسولاً مقدساً.

The holy mendicant told the king about a certain forest.

أخبر المتسول المقدس الملك عن غابة معينة.

In this forest there grew a special kind of tree.

في هذه الغابة نمت شجرة من نوع خاص.

On a branch of this tree hung seven mangoes.

على فرع من هذه الشجرة كانت هناك سبع مانجو معلقة.

These mangos could restore the fertilities of his queens.

قد تتمكن هذه المانجو من استعادة الخصوبة لملكاته.

But the king had to pluck the mangoes himself.

ولكن كان على الملك أن يقطف المانجو بنفسه.

The king followed the advice of the mendicant.

اتبع الملك نصيحة المتسول.

And he set off to go to the forest with the mango tree.

وانطلق نحو الغابة حيث شجرة المانجو.

Soon he had found the tree the mendicant spoke of.

وسرعان ما وجد الشجرة التي تحدث عنها المتسول.

And he plucked the seven mangoes that grew upon one branch.

ثم قطف السبع حبات المانجو التي نمت على غصن واحد.

He gave a mango to each of the queens to eat.

أعطى المانجو لكل واحدة من الملكات لتأكلها.

In a short time the king's heart was filled with joy.

وفي وقت قصير امتلأ قلب الملك بالفرح.

He was told that the seven queens were all with child.

فأخبروه أن الملكات السبع جميعهن حوامل.

One day the king was out hunting.

ذات يوم كان الملك خارجًا للصيد.

On his path he saw a young lady of peerless beauty.

وفي طريقه رأى فتاة شابة ذات جمال لا مثيل له.

He instantly fell in love with the beautiful woman.

لقد وقع في حب المرأة الجميلة على الفور.

And he brought her to his palace, and married her.

فـأتى بها إلى قصره وتزوجها.

This lady was, however, not a human being.

لكن هذه السيدة لم تكن إنسانًا.

But what this woman was was a Rakshasi.

لكن ما كانت عليه هذه المرأة هو أنها كانت راكشاسي.

But the king of course did not know this.

ولكن الملك بطبيعة الحال لم يكن يعلم هذا.

The king became dotingly fond of her.

وأصبح الملك يحبها بشدة.

And he did whatever she told him to do.

وفعل كل ما قالت له أن يفعله.

One day she made a very particular request of the king.

فـي أحد الأيام تقدمت بطلب خاص جدًا للملك.

"You say that you love me more than anyone else"

أنت تقول أنك تحبني أكثر من أي شخص آخر

"Let me see whether you really love me as much as you say"

دعني أرى هل تحبني حقًا بقدر ما تقول؟

"If you love me, make your seven other queens blind"

إذا كنت تحبني، فاجعل ملكاتك السبع الأخريات أعمى

"And once they are blind, let them be killed"

وإذا أصبحوا عميانًا، فليُقتَلوا

The king became very sad at the terrible request.

حزن الملك كثيرًا بسبب هذا الطلب الرهيب.

He was especially sad because the queens were all pregnant.

لـقد كان حزينًا بشكل خاص لأن الملكات كن جميعهن حوامل.

But he had no choice but to comply with her request.

ولكن لم يكن أمامه خيار سوى الامتثال لطلبها.

The eyes of the queens were plucked out of their sockets.

لـقد تم اقتلاع عيون الملكات من محاجرها.

And the queens were delivered up to the chief minister.

وسُلِّمَت الملكات إلى رئيس الوزراء۔

It was up to the chief minister to destroy the queens.

كان الأمر متروكًا لرئيس الوزراء لتدمير الملكات۔

But the chief minister was a merciful man.

لكن رئيس الوزراء كان رجلاً رحيماً۔

In the side of the hill there was secret a cave.

وفي جانب التل كان هناك كهف سري۔

Instead of killing the queens, the minister hid them.

وبدلا من قتل الملكات، قام الوزير بإخفائهم۔

In course of time the eldest of the seven queens gave birth.

وبمرور الوقت، أنجبت الملكة الأكبر من بين الملكات السبع۔

"What shall I do with the child," said she.

ماذا أفعل بالطفل؟ قالت۔

"we are blind and are dying for want of food?"

نحن عميان ونموت من نقص الطعام؟

"Let me kill the child," she proposed.

دعني أقتل الطفل اقترحت۔

"let us all eat of the child's flesh" she added.

فلنأكل جميعاً من لحم الطفل أضافت۔

Just as she said she would, she killed the infant.

وكما قالت أنها ستفعل، قتلت الطفل۔

She gave to each of her sister-queens a part of the child.

أعطت لكل واحدة من أخواتها الملكات جزءًا من الطفل۔

And the sister queens ate their part of the child.

وأكلت الملكات الأخوات نصيبهن من الطفل۔

But the youngest queen did not eat her share.

ولكن الملكة الأصغر لم تأكل نصيبها۔

Instead, she laid her part of the child beside her.

وبدلًا من ذلك، وضعت جزءًا من الطفل بجانبها۔

In a few days the second queen also was delivered of a child.

وفي غضون أيام قليلة ولدت الملكة الثانية أيضًا طفلًا۔

She did with her child as her eldest sister had done with
hers.

لقد فعلت مع طفلها كما فعلت أختها الكبرى مع طفلها۔

So did the third, the fourth, the fifth, and the sixth queen.

وهكذا فعلت الملكة الثالثة والرابعة والخامسة والسادسة.

Eventually the seventh queen gave birth to a son.

وفي نهاية المطاف أنجبت الملكة السابعة ابنا.

But she did not follow the example of her sister-queens.

لكنها لم تحذو حذو شقيقاتها الملكات.

Instead, she resolved to raise the child.

وبدلاً من ذلك، قررت تربية الطفل.

The other queens demanded their portions of the newly-born.

وطالبت الملكات الأخريات بحصصهن من المولود الجديد.

But she still had the portions she had not eaten.

لكنها لا تزال تحتفظ بالأجزاء التي لم تأكلها.

And she gave her sister-queens back their children's parts.

وأعادت إلى أخواتها الملكات أجزاء أبنائهن.

The other queens at once perceived that their portions were dry.

وأدركت الملكات الأخريات على الفور أن حصصهن كانت جافة.

Therefore the parts could not be of the newly born child.

لذلك لا يمكن أن تكون الأجزاء من الطفل حديث الولادة.

"I have decided not to kill me child," she explained.

لقد قررت أن لا أقتل طفلي، أوضحت.

"I will not eat him, but try to raise him instead"

لن آكله، بل سأحاول تربيته بدلاً من ذلك

The others were glad to hear this news.

وكان الآخرون سعداء لسماع هذا الخبر.

They all said that they would help her in nursing the child.

وقالوا جميعا أنهم سوف يساعدونها في إرضاع الطفل.

And so the child was suckled by seven mothers.

فأرضع الطفل من سبع أمهات.

And the child became the hardiest and strongest boy that ever lived.

وأصبح الطفل أقوى وأقوى طفل عاش على الإطلاق.

In the meantime the Rakshasi-queen was doing infinite mischief.

وفي هذه الأثناء كانت ملكة راكشاسي تقوم بأعمال شريرة لا نهاية لها.

And she got the royal household into all sorts of trouble.

وأدخلت العائلة المالكة في كل أنواع المشاكل.

What she ate at the royal table did not fill her capacious stomach.

ما أكلته على المائدة الملكية لم يملأ معدتها الواسعة.

She therefore, in the darkness of night, went hunting.

فذهبت للصيد في ظلمة الليل.

Gradually she ate up all the members of the royal family.

تدريجيا، أكلت جميع أفراد العائلة المالكة.

She ate all the king's servants, and his attendants.

فأكلت جميع عبيد الملك وحاشيته.

She ate all his horses, elephants, and cattle.

أكلت كل خيوله وأفياله وماشيته.

And eventually only her royal consort and the king were left.

وفي النهاية لم يبق سوى زوجها الملكي والملك.

After that she used to go out in the evenings into the city.

وبعد ذلك كانت تخرج في المساء إلى المدينة.

And she ate up stray human beings wherever she found any.

وكانت تأكل الضالين من البشر أينما وجدتهم.

The king was left without any servants.

وأصبح الملك بلا خدم.

There was no person left to cook for him.

ولم يبق أحد ليطبخ له.

Because no one would accept this job.

لأن لا أحد يقبل هذه الوظيفة.

But at last someone volunteered their services.

ولكن في النهاية تطوع شخص ما بخدماته.

The boy who had been suckled by seven mothers.

الطفل الذي أرضعته سبع أمهات.

He had now grown up to be a stalwart youth.

لقد أصبح الآن شابًا قويًا.

He attended on the king and prepared his food.

كان يخدم الملك ويجهز له الطعام.

But he took every care while with the queen.

ولكنه اهتم بكل شيء أثناء وجوده مع الملكة.

And he made sure that she did not swallow him up.

وتأكد من أنها لم تبتلعه.

The Rakshasi-queen seized her victims only at night.

كانت ملكة راكشاسي تقبض على ضحاياها في الليل فقط

So the boy he went home long before nightfall.

فعاد الصبي إلى منزله قبل حلول الليل بوقت طويل.

So she had to find another way to get rid of the boy.

لذلك كان عليها أن تجد طريقة أخرى للتخلص من الصبي.

The boy always boasted that he could do any work.

كان الصبي يتفاخر دائمًا بأنه قادر على القيام بأي عمل.

So the queen invented a disease for herself.

لذلك اخترعت الملكة مرضًا لنفسها.

She said that there was a cure for her disease.

قالت أن هناك علاج لمرضها.

But she said the cure was not easy to get.

لكنها قالت إن العلاج ليس من السهل الحصول عليه.

This made the boy even more interested in the task.

وهذا جعل الصبي أكثر اهتماما بالمهمة.

She said there was a melon which cured her disease.

قالت أن هناك بطيخًا يعالج مرضها.

The melon was twelve cubits in length.

وكان البطيخ اثني عشر ذراعا طولا.

But the stone of the lemon was thirteen cubits long.

وأما نواة الليمون فكان طولها ثلاثة عشر ذراعاً.

The fruit could only be gotten from her mother.

لم يكن من الممكن الحصول على الفاكهة إلا من والدتها.

And her mother lived on the other side of the ocean.

وأمها كانت تعيش على الجانب الآخر من المحيط

She gave him a letter of introduction to her mother.

أعطته رسالة تعريفية لأمها.

But actually the note told her to eat the boy.

لكن في الواقع كانت المذكرة تطلب منها أن تأكل الصبي.

The boy had suspected there was some foul play.

لقد اشتبه الصبي في أن هناك جريمة ما.

So he tore up the letter and proceeded on his journey.

فمزق الرسالة وواصل رحلته.

The dauntless youth passed through many lands.

لقد مر الشاب الشجاع عبر العديد من الأراضي.

After much travel he stood on the shore of the ocean.

وبعد سفر طويل وصل إلى شاطئ المحيط

On the other side of the ocean was the country of the Rakshasis.

وعلى الجانب الآخر من المحيط كانت بلاد الراكشاسيس.

He then bawled as loud as he could, and said;

ثم صرخ بأعلى صوته وقال

"Granny! granny! come and save your daughter"

جدتي جدتي تعالي وأنقذي ابنتك

"Your daughter, my mother, is dangerously ill"

ابنتك، أمي، مريضة بشكل خطير

On the other side of the ocean an old Rakshasi heard him.

وعلى الجانب الآخر من المحيط سمعه راكشاسي عجوز.

The old Rakshasi crossed the ocean to the boy.

عبر الراكشاسي العجوز المحيط إلى الصبي.

The boy told her the message of the queen.

أخبرها الصبي برسالة الملكة.

And the Rakshasi took the boy on her back.

فأخذت الراكشاسي الصبي على ظهرها.

She re-crossed the ocean to the land of the Rakshasi.

لقد عبرت المحيط مرة أخرى إلى أرض راكشاسي.

And the boy was at once given the medicinal melon.

وأعطي الصبي على الفور البطيخ الطبي.

The Rakshasi told him to hurry back to her daughter.

طلبت منه الراكشاسي أن يعود مسرعاً إلى ابنتها.

But the boy said he was too tired to keep travelling.

لكن الصبي قال إنه كان متعبًا للغاية ولا يستطيع مواصلة السفر.

And he begged to be allowed to rest one day.

وتوسل للسماح له بالراحة يوما ما.

The old Rakshasi consented to her grandson's wishes.

وافقت الراكشاسي العجوز على رغبات حفيدها.

The boy noticed interesting things in the Rakshasi's room.

لاحظ الصبي أشياء مثيرة للاهتمام في غرفة راكشاسي.

There was a stout club and a rope hanging in the room.

لكان هناك هراوة قوية وحبل معلق في الغرفة.

The boy inquired what the stout club and rope were for.

سأل الصبي عن سبب استخدام الهراوة القوية والحبل.

"Child, with that club and rope I cross the ocean"

يا طفل، مع تلك العصا والحبل أعبر المحيط

"One just has to take the club and the rope in his hands"

كل ما عليك فعله هو أن تأخذ العصا والحبل بين يديك

"And then you have to say the following magical words:"

وبعد ذلك عليك أن تقول الكلمات السحرية التالية:

"O stout club! O strong rope!"

يا هراوة قوية يا حبل قوي

"Take me at once to the other side"

خذني إلى الجانب الآخر على الفور

"Then they will take him to the other side of the ocean"

ثم سيأخذونه إلى الجانب الآخر من المحيط

The boy noticed another interesting thing in the room.

لاحظ الصبي شيئًا آخر مثيرًا للاهتمام في الغرفة.

There was a bird in a cage in the corner of the room.

وكان هناك طائر في قفص في زاوية الغرفة.

The boy also wanted to know what this bird was for.

وأراد الصبي أيضًا أن يعرف ما هو هذا الطائر.

"The bird contains a secret, my child"

الطائر يحمل سرًا يا بني

"But that secret must not be disclosed to mortals"

ولكن لا ينبغي الكشف عن هذا السر للبشر

"But how can I hide this secret from my own grandchild?"

ولكن كيف يمكنني إخفاء هذا السر عن حفيدي؟

"That bird, child, contains the life of your mother.

هذا الطائر، يا طفلي، يحتوي على حياة أمك.

"If the bird is killed, your mother will at once die"

إذا قُتل الطائر، ستموت أمك على الفور

Armed with these secrets, the boy went to bed that night.

مسلحًا بهذه الأسرار، ذهب الصبي إلى السرير في تلك الليلة.

Next morning the old Rakshasi went to distant countries.

في صباح اليوم التالي، ذهب الراكشاسي العجوز إلى بلدان بعيدة.

Together with all the other Rakshasis, she went to forage.

ذهبت للبحث عن الطعام برفقة جميع أفراد عائلة راكشاسيس الآخرين.

The boy took down the bird-cage from the ceiling.

قام الصبي بإزالة قفص الطيور من السقف.

And the boy took the club and the rope.

وأخذ الصبي العصا والحبل.

And then he spoke the magic words to the club and rope.

ثم قال الكلمات السحرية للنادي والحبل.

"O stout club! O strong rope!"

يا هراوة قوية يا حبل قوي

"Take me at once to the other side"

خذني إلى الجانب الآخر على الفور

In the twinkling of an eye the boy was put on this side of the ocean.

وفي غمضة عين، تم وضع الصبي على هذا الجانب من المحيط.

He then retraced his steps, back to the queen.

ثم عاد أدراجه، عائداً إلى الملكة.

To her astonishment he really had the medicinal lemon.

لقد فوجئت بأنه كان لديه بالفعل الليمون الطبي.

But the bird in the cage he kept carefully concealed.

لكن الطائر الموجود في القفص أبقاه مخفيًا بعناية.

In the course of time the people of the city came to the king.

وبعد مرور الوقت جاء أهل المدينة إلى الملك.

And they told the king of their troubles.

وأخبروا الملك بمشاكلهم.

"A monstrous bird comes from the palace every evening"

طائر وحشي يأتي من القصر كل مساء

"The bird seizes the people in the streets"

الطائر يستحوذ على الناس في الشوارع

"And the bird swallows the people up whole"

والطائر يبتلع الناس أجمعين

"This has been going on for a long time"

لقد استمر هذا لفترة طويلة

"And now the city has become almost desolate"

والآن أصبحت المدينة خرابًا تقريبًا

The king did not know what this monstrous bird was.

ولم يكن الملك يعرف ما هو هذا الطائر الوحشي.

But the king's servant, the boy, said he knew.

لكن خادم الملك، الصبي، قال إنه يعلم.

"I will kill the monstrous bird," he offered.

سأقتل الطائر الوحشي عرض.

"But the queen has to stand beside us," he added.

ولكن يجب على الملكة أن تقف بجانبنا، أضاف.

The king saw no reason to object to the proposal.

ولم ير الملك سببا للاعتراض على الاقتراح.

And so the queen was made to stand beside the king.

وهكذا تم وضع الملكة بجانب الملك.

The boy then took the bird out from its cage.

ثم أخرج الصبي الطائر من قفصه.

On seeing the bird she fell into a fainting fit.

وعندما رأت الطائر أصيبت بنوبة إغماء.

Then the boy turned to the king, and spoke.

ثم توجه الصبي إلى الملك وتكلم.

"King, you will soon perceive who the monstrous bird is"

أيها الملك، سوف تدرك قريبًا من هو الطائر الوحشي

"You will see what devours your people every evening"

سترى ما يلتهم شعبك كل مساء

"I tear off each limb of this bird"

أقطع كل طرف من أطراف هذا الطائر

"The corresponding limb of the man-eater will fall off"

سوف يسقط الطرف المقابل لآكل البشر

The boy then tore off one leg of the bird in his hand.

ثم قام الصبي بتمزيق ساق واحدة من الطائر الذي كان في يده.

All assembled were astonished at what happened next.

لقد اندهش الجميع مما حدث بعد ذلك.

One of the legs of the queen fell off.

سقطت إحدى أرجل الملكة.

Then the boy squeezed the throat of the bird.

ثم ضغط الصبي على حلق الطائر.

And as he squeezed the bird, the queen gave up the ghost.

وبينما كان يضغط على الطائر، سلمت الملكة روحها.

The boy then retold his history to the king.

ثم أعاد الصبي رواية قصته للملك.

"You used to have seven barren wives"

وكان لك سبع زوجات عاقرات

"To treat their barrenness, you gave them each a mango"

لعلاج عقمهم، أعطيتهم كل واحد منهم مانجو

"And each of your wives fell pregnant with a child"

وكل واحدة من نسائكم حملت بطفل

"However, you then married an eighth wife"

ولكنك تزوجت بعد ذلك زوجة ثامنة

"This wife ordered you to blind your other wives"

هذه الزوجة أمرتك بعمى زوجاتك الأخريات

"And she ordered you to have your other wives killed"

وأمرتكم بقتل نسائكم

"Your minister blinded your seven wives"

وزيرك أعمى زوجاتك السبع

"But he was too good hearted to kill your wives"

لكنه كان طيب القلب لدرجة أنه لم يقتل زوجاتكم

"Your seven wives were taken to a hiding place"

لقد أخذت زوجاتك السبع إلى مكان مخفي

"And in this hiding place they each gave birth"

وفي هذا المخبئ ولدوا كل واحد منهم

"But they were forced to eat their newly born children"

ولكنهم أجبروا على أكل أطفالهم حديثي الولادة

"Only my mother did not let me be eaten"

فقط أمي لم تسمح لي أن آكل

"Instead, I was suckled by seven mothers"

وبدلاً من ذلك، تم إرضاعي من قبل سبع أمهات

"And I grew up strong and capable"

ونشأت قوية وقادرة

"Eventually I came to work in your palace"

في النهاية جئت للعمل في قصرك

"Your wife, my stepmother, sent me on a mission"

زوجتك، زوجة أبي، أرسلتني في مهمة

"She sent me to her mother for a medicine"

أرسلتني إلى والدتها للحصول على الدواء

"However, her mother was a Rakshasi"

ومع ذلك، كانت والدتها من عائلة راكشا

"From her I found the secret of your wife's life"

ومنها وجدت سر حياة زوجتك

"And so I brought the bird that held your wife's life"

وهكذا أحضرت الطائر الذي حمل حياة زوجتك

The king had listened to the story his son told him.

لقد استمع الملك إلى القصة التي أخبره بها ابنه.

The seven queens were brought back to the palace.

تم إرجاع الملكات السبع إلى القصر.

And their eyes were miraculously restored.

وعادت أعينهم إلى حالتها الطبيعية.

The boy that was suckled by seven mothers was crowned.

الطفل الذي أرضعته سبع أمهات توج.

And he was recognized by the king as his rightful heir.

واعترف به الملك كوريث شرعي له.

And they lived together happily.

وعاشوا معاً بسعادة.

The Story of Prince Sobur
قصة الأمير سوبور

Once upon a time there lived a merchant.

ذات مرة كان هناك تاجر يعيش.

This merchant had seven daughters.

كان لهذا التاجر سبع بنات.

One day the merchant asked them a question.

ذات يوم سألهم التاجر سؤالاً.

"From whose fortune do you live?"

من ثروة من تعيش؟

The eldest daughter answered first.

أجابت الابنة الكبرى أولاً.

"Papa, I live from your fortune"

بابا، أنا أعيش من ثروتك

The second daughter gave the same answer.

وأجابت الابنة الثانية نفس الجواب.

The same answer was given by the third daughter.

وأجابت الابنة الثالثة نفس الإجابة.

His fourth daughter also lived from his fortune.

كما عاشت ابنته الرابعة من ثروته.

His fifth daughter was no different.

ولم تكن ابنته الخامسة مختلفة.

And his sixth daughter was like the rest.

وكانت ابنته السادسة مثل الباقيات.

But his youngest daughter surprised him.

لكن ابنته الأصغر فاجأته.

She had a very different answer.

وكان لديها إجابة مختلفة تماما.

"I live from my own fortune"

أنا أعيش من ثروتي الخاصة

He did not like this answer.

لم يعجبه هذا الجواب.

Her answer made the merchant very angry.

لقد أثار جوابها غضب التاجر بشدة.

"You are very ungrateful," he told her.

أنتِ جاحدة جدًا، قال لها.

"See how well you do on your own"

انظر إلى مدى نجاحك بمفردك

"I am kicking you out of my house"

سأطردك من منزلي

"You will not have a rupee in your pocket"

لن يكون لديك روبية واحدة في جيبك

He called his palanquins to come.

لقد نادى على محفاته ليأتوا.

And he ordered them to take the girl away.

وأمرهم أن يأخذوا الفتاة.

"Leave her in the midst of a forest"

اتركها في وسط الغابة

The girl begged to be allowed one thing.

توسلت الفتاة أن يسمح لها بشيء واحد.

"Please let me take my work-box"

من فضلك اسمح لي أن آخذ صندوق عملي

"In the box are my needles and threads"

في الصندوق إبرتي وخيوطي

Her father allowed her to take her box.

سمح لها والدها بأخذ صندوقها.

She got into the seat of the palanquins.

دخلت إلى مقعد المحفة.

And the bearers lifted her up.

فحملها الحاملون.

And they put her onto their shoulders.

ووضعوها على أكتافهم.

As the bearers ran they chanted.

وبينما كان الحاملون يركضون كانوا يهتفون.

"hoon! hoon! hoon! hoon! hoon!"

هون هون هون, هون هون

But they didn't get very far.

ولكنهم لم يصلوا إلى حد بعيد.

An old woman stood in their way.

كانت هناك امرأة عجوز تقف في طريقهم.

She came up to the carriage.

لقد جاءت إلى العربة.

"Where are you taking my daughter?"

إلى أين تأخذ ابنتي؟

She was the maid of the child.

لقد كانت خادمة للطفل.

"We have been given orders by the merchant"

لقد تلقينا أوامر من التاجر

"He told us to take her away"

لقد طلب منا أن نأخذها بعيدًا

"We will leave her in a forest"

سنتركها في الغابة

"We are going to do his bidding"

سوف ننفذ أوامره

"I must go with her," said the old woman.

يجب أن أذهب معها قالت المرأة العجوز.

But the bearers were not sure.

ولكن الحاملين لم يكونوا متأكدين.

Bearers run when they carry a sedan chair.

يركض الحاملون عندما يحملون كرسيًا متحركًا.

"How will you be able to keep pace with us?"

كيف ستتمكن من مواكبتنا؟

The old woman was not deterred.

لم تتراجع المرأة العجوز.

"It does not matter how I do it"

لا يهم كيف أفعل ذلك

"I must go where my daughter goes"

يجب أن أذهب إلى حيث تذهب ابنتي

The youngest daughter begged the bearers.

توسلت الابنة الصغرى لحامليها.

"Please carry my mother with me"

من فضلك احمل أمي معي

And the bearers gracefully agreed.

ووافق الحاملون بكل سرور.

They carried mother and child to the forest.

حملوا الأم وطفلها إلى الغابة.

"hoon! hoon! hoon! hoon! hoon!"

هون هون هون هون هون

In the afternoon they reached a dense forest.

وفي فترة ما بعد الظهر وصلوا إلى غابة كثيفة.

They went deeper and deeper into the forest.

لقد ذهبوا أعمق وأعمق في الغابة.

Towards sunset they reached their goal.

وعند غروب الشمس وصلوا إلى هدفهم.

They stopped at the foot of an old tree.

توقفوا عند سفح شجرة قديمة.

They lowered the girl and the old woman.

أنزلوا الفتاة والمرأة العجوز.

And they left them in the forest.

وتركوهم في الغابة.

Then they retraced their steps home.

ثم عادوا أدراجهم إلى منازلهم.

The merchant's youngest daughter looked around.

نظرت ابنة التاجر الصغرى حولها.

You would not have wanted to be in her shoes.

لم تكن ترغب في أن تكون في مكانها.

Her situation was truly pitiable.

لقد كان وضعها مثيرا للشفقة حقا.

She was hardly fourteen years old.

لم تكن قد تجاوزت الرابعة عشرة من عمرها.

She had grown up in luxury.

لقد نشأت في رفاهية.

But now there was no luxury for her.

ولكن الآن لم يعد هناك أي ترف بالنسبة لها.

She was in the heart of a dark forest.

كانت في قلب غابة مظلمة.

She had not a rupee in her pocket.

ولم يكن في جيبها روبية واحدة.

And she had nothing for protection.

ولم يكن لديها أي شيء للحماية.

Nothing except an old, decrepit, woman.

لا شيء سوى امرأة عجوز، هشة.

Even the trees of the forest pitied her.

حتى أشجار الغابة أشفقت عليها۔

The young girl and old woman sat together.

جلست الفتاة الصغيرة والمرأة العجوز معًا۔

They were at the foot of an old tree.

كانوا عند سفح شجرة قديمة۔

And together they cried over their situation.

وبكوا معًا على حالهم۔

I should say this all happened long ago.

يجب أن أقول أن كل هذا حدث منذ زمن طويل۔

In these times the trees could talk.

في هذه الأوقات أصبحت الأشجار قادرة على التحدث۔

And the old tree spoke to the girl.

وتحدثت الشجرة العجوز إلى الفتاة۔

"Unhappy women, I much pity you"

أيتها النساء التعيسات، أنا أشفق عليكن كثيرًا

"There are wild beasts in this forest"

هناك وحوش برية في هذه الغابة

"Soon they will come out of their lairs"

سوف يخرجون من جحورهم قريبا

"They will roam about for prey"

سوف يتجولون بحثًا عن الفريسة

"And they are sure to devour you two"

ومن المؤكد أنهم سوف يلتهمونكما

"But I can help you, if you want"

لكن يمكنني مساعدتك إذا أردت

"I will make an opening for you"

سأفتح لك

"When you see the opening, go into it"

عندما ترى الفتحة، ادخل إليها

"And then I will close the opening up"

ثم سأغلق الفتحة

"As long as you are in me you'll be safe"

طالما أنك في داخلي ستكون بأمان

"This way the wild beasts can't touch you"

بهذه الطريقة لن تتمكن الوحوش البرية من لمسك

And then the tree split itself in two.

ثم انقسمت الشجرة إلى نصفين.

The two women went inside the tree.

دخلت المرأتان داخل الشجرة.

And the old tree resumed its natural shape.

وعادت الشجرة القديمة إلى شكلها الطبيعي.

The shade of night darkened the forest.

ظل الليل أظلم الغابة.

Everything the tree had said was true.

كل ما قالته الشجرة كان صحيحا.

The wild beasts came out of their lairs.

وخرجت الوحوش من جحورها.

The fierce tiger came out at night.

خرج النمر الشرس في الليل.

The wild bear left his lair.

غادر الدب البري عرينه.

The rhinoceros roamed the forest.

كان وحيد القرن يتجول في الغابة.

The bushy bear was there that night.

وكان الدب الكثيف هناك تلك الليلة.

The great elephant could be heard.

كان من الممكن سماع صوت الفيل العظيم.

And there was the horned buffalo.

وكان هناك الجاموس ذو القرون.

They all growled as they circled the tree.

لقد زأروا جميعًا وهم يدورون حول الشجرة.

They had gotten the scent of human blood.

لقد حصلوا على رائحة الدم البشري.

They could hear the growls of the beasts.

كان بإمكانهم سماع هدير الوحوش.

The beasts came dashing against the tree.

انطلقت الوحوش مسرعة نحو الشجرة.

They broke the old tree's branches.

كسروا أغصان الشجرة القديمة.

Their horns pierced the tree's trunk.

اخترقت قرونهم جذع الشجرة.

They scratched its bark with their claws.

خدشوا لحائه بمخالبهم.

But all their efforts were in vain.

ولكن كل جهودهم كانت بلا جدوى.

The girl and woman were safe in the tree.

وكانت الفتاة والمرأة آمنتين في الشجرة.

Towards dawn the wild beasts went away.

ومع حلول الفجر ذهبت الوحوش البرية.

After sunrise the good tree spoke again.

بعد شروق الشمس تحدثت الشجرة الطيبة مرة أخرى.

"The wild beasts have gone back"

لقد عادت الوحوش البرية

"They are in their lairs again"

لقد عادوا إلى جحورهم مرة أخرى

"But they did their best to torment me"

لكنهم بذلوا قصارى جهدهم لتعذيبي

"The sun has risen up again"

لقد أشرقت الشمس مرة أخرى

"So you can come out now"

لذا يمكنك الخروج الآن

The tree split itself into two again.

انقسمت الشجرة إلى نصفين مرة أخرى.

The girl and the old woman came out.

خرجت الفتاة والمرأة العجوز.

They saw the extent of the damage.

لقد رأوا حجم الضرر.

The tree's branches had been broken off.

لقد تم كسر فروع الشجرة.

The tree's trunk had been pierced.

لقد تم ثقب جذع الشجرة.

The bark had been stripped off.

لقد تم تجريد اللحاء.

"Good mother, we thank you"

الأم الطيبة، نشكرك

"You have been very kind to us"

لقد كنت لطيفًا جدًا معنا

"You gave us shelter from the beasts"

لقد منحتنا المأوى من الوحوش

"But it was at a great cost to yourself"

ولكن كان ذلك بتكلفة كبيرة بالنسبة لك

"You have many wounds from the wilds beasts"

لديك العديد من الجروح من الوحوش البرية

"You must be in great pain?"

يجب أن تكون في ألم كبير؟

Close by there was a flowing river.

وكان هناك نهر متدفق بالقرب منه.

The young girl went to the river bank.

ذهبت الفتاة إلى ضفة النهر.

At the bank of the river she found mud.

وعلى ضفة النهر وجدت الطين.

She covered the tree with the mud.

غطت الشجرة بالطين.

She especially covered the damaged parts.

لقد غطت بشكل خاص الأجزاء التالفة.

The tree thanked her for the treatment.

شكرتها الشجرة على العلاج.

"My good girl, I thank you"

فتاتي الطيبة، أشكرك

"I am greatly relieved of my pain"

لقد تخلصت من آلامي بشكل كبير

"I am, however, more concerned for you"

لكنني أكثر قلقا عليك

"You must be hungry"

لا بد أنك جائع

"You have not eaten since yesterday"

لم تأكل منذ الأمس

"But what can I give you?"

ولكن ماذا يمكنني أن أعطيك؟

"I have no fruit of my own"

ليس لدي ثمار خاصة بي

"But I do have some advice"

ولكن لدي بعض النصائح

"Give the old woman whatever money you have"

أعط المرأة العجوز أي مبلغ من المال لديك

"Let her go into the city"

دعها تذهب إلى المدينة

"In the city she can buy some food"

في المدينة يمكنها شراء بعض الطعام

They explained their situation to the tree.

شرحوا وضعهم للشجرة.

"We have been sent out with no money"

لقد تم إرسالنا بدون أي أموال

But she searched through her work-box anyway.

لكنها بحثت في صندوق عملها على أية حال.

And in the box she found five cowries.

وفي الصندوق وجدت خمسة من المحار.

The tree continued to give its advice.

استمرت الشجرة في تقديم نصيحتها.

"Go with your cowries to the city"

اذهب مع صدفيتك إلى المدينة

"Use the cowries to buy some fried rice"

استخدم المحار لشراء بعض الأرز المقلي

So the old woman went to the city.

فـذهبت المرأة العجوز إلى المدينة.

Fortunately the city was not far away.

ولحسن الحظ أن المدينة لم تكن بعيدة.

She went to the first shopkeeper she found.

ذهبت إلى أول بائع وجدته.

"Please give me five cowries worth of rice"

من فضلك أعطني خمسة أرز بقيمة خمسة أرز

The shopkeeper laughed at her.

ضحك عليها صاحب المتجر.

"Where can rice be had for five cowries?"

أين يمكن الحصول على الأرز مقابل خمسة صدفات؟

"Be off, you old hag," he told her.

اذهبي بعيدا أيها العجوز قال لها.

So she tried to barter at another shop.

فحاولت المقايضة في متجر آخر.

This shopkeeper could see her distress.

كان بإمكان صاحب المتجر أن يرى مدى ضيقها.

And the shopkeeper took pity on her.

فأشفق عليها صاحب المتجر.

She gave her a large quantity of rice.

أعطتها كمية كبيرة من الأرز.

The old woman returned with the rice.

عادت العجوز مع الأرز.

And the tree gave further instructions.

وأعطت الشجرة تعليمات أخرى.

"Eat less than half of the rice"

تناول أقل من نصف كمية الأرز

"Go to the embankments of the river bank"

اذهب إلى ضفاف النهر

"Cast the remaining rice on the river bank"

ألقي الأرز المتبقي على ضفة النهر

They did not understand the sense of it.

ولم يفهموا معناها.

"Why sow the riverbank with rice?"

لماذا نزرع ضفة النهر بالأرز؟

But they did as they were advised.

لكنهم فعلوا كما نصحوهم.

And they threw their rice onto the ground.

وألقوا أرزهم على الأرض.

They spent the day lamenting their fate.

لقد أمضوا يومهم في الحزن على مصيرهم.

Just as before the beasts came out at night.

كما كان الحال من قبل عندما خرجت الوحوش في الليل.

The tree housed them inside of its trunk again.

وأعادتهم الشجرة إلى جذعها مرة أخرى.

Again they mutilated and tortured the tree.

ثم قاموا بتشويه وتعذيب الشجرة مرة أخرى.

But that night something else happened.

ولكن في تلك الليلة حدث شيء آخر.

The women only saw it the next day.

ولم ترى النساء ذلك إلا في اليوم التالي.

The rice had attracted hundreds of peacocks.

لقد جذب الأرز مئات الطاووس.

The peacocks competed for the rice.

تنافس الطاووس على الأرز.

And their feathers fell on the floor.

وريشهم سقط على الأرض.

The tree had known what would happen.

وكانت الشجرة تعرف ما سيحدث.

And the tree advised them what to do next.

ونصحتهم الشجرة بما يجب عليهم فعله بعد ذلك.

"Go back to the bank of the river"

ارجع إلى ضفة النهر

"Go to where you cast the rice"

اذهب إلى المكان الذي ترمي فيه الأرز

"There you will see many feathers"

ستجد هناك العديد من الريش

"Collect all the feathers you can find"

اجمع كل الريش الذي يمكنك العثور عليه

"Use the feathers to make a beautiful fan"

استخدم الريش لصنع مروحة جميلة

"And take the feather-fan to the city"

وخذ مروحة الريش إلى المدينة

The two women did as they were advised.

فعلت المرأتان ما نصحتا به.

It was good the girl had taken her work-box.

لقد كان من الجيد أن الفتاة أخذت صندوق عملها.

In her work-box was some string.

في صندوق عملها كان هناك بعض الخيوط

The tied the feathers together.

ربطوا الريش معًا.

And she had made a fan from the feathers.

وصنعت مروحة من الريش.

She took the feather fan to the city.

أخذت مروحة الريش إلى المدينة.

The son of the king happened to be there.

وكان ابن الملك موجودًا هناك۔

He admired the feathers greatly.

لقد أعجب بالريش كثيرًا۔

He paid a large sum of money for the feathers.

دفع مبلغًا كبيرًا من المال مقابل الريش۔

Each morning a quantity of feathers was collected.

تم جمع كمية من الريش كل صباح۔

And each day a feather fan was made and sold.

وفي كل يوم كان يتم صنع مروحة من الريش وبيعها۔

Within a short time the two women got rich.

في غضون فترة قصيرة من الزمن أصبحت المرأتان ثريتين۔

The tree then advised them to build a house.

ثم نصحتهم الشجرة ببناء منزل۔

"Employ men to burn bricks for you"

استخدم الرجال لحرق الطوب لك

"Get them to cut beams and rafters"

اطلب منهم قطع العوارض والروافد

"Make them plaster the walls with lime"

أجعلهم يطلون الجدران بالجير

In a few months a stately house was built.

في غضون بضعة أشهر تم بناء منزل فخم۔

The tree was pleased for the women.

لقد فرحت الشجرة من أجل النساء۔

"You should add a garden to your house"

يجب عليك إضافة حديقة إلى منزلك

"And you want to be able to store water"

وأنت تريد أن تكون قادرًا على تخزين المياه

"Dig a water tank in your garden"

احفر خزان مياه في حديقتك

The girl had not had much time.

ولم يكن لدى الفتاة الكثير من الوقت۔

So she didn't think of her family.

لذلك لم تفكر في عائلتها۔

The merchant's luck had taken a turn.

لقد تحول حظ التاجر.

The goddess of wealth frowned upon him.

عبست عليه إلهة الثروة.

He was struck by a sudden misfortune.

لقد أصيب بمصيبة مفاجئة.

All at once he lost all of his money.

لقد خسر كل أمواله فجأة.

He was forced to sell his house.

أرغم على بيع منزلهُ.

But he made a great loss on the property.

ولكنه تكبد خسارة كبيرة في الممتلكات.

He and his family were left penniless.

لقد أصبح هو وعائلته بلا مال.

So they were forced to live elsewhere.

فأجبروا على العيش في مكان آخر.

They happened to move to a nearby village.

لقد انتقلوا إلى قرية قريبة.

The palace was not far from their new house.

ولم يكن القصر بعيدًا عن منزلهم الجديد.

But the merchant was not rich anymore.

ولكن التاجر لم يعد غنيا بعد الآن.

And he still had to support his family.

وما زال عليه أن يدعم أسرته.

He had been reduced to doing manual labour.

لقد تم تقليصه إلى القيام بالأعمال اليدوية.

He applied for the job at the palace.

تقدم بطلب للحصول على وظيفة في القصر.

He was going to dig the hole for the water.

كان ينوي حفر حفرة للماء.

His wife also offered to work with him.

وعرضت عليه زوجته أيضًا العمل معه.

But they got there too late to work.

لكنهم وصلوا إلى هناك متأخرين جدًا للعمل.

The water tank had already been finished.

لقد تم الانتهاء من خزان المياه بالفعل.

And they did not know whose house it was.

ولم يعرفوا لمن البيت.

The merchant's daughter was looking out the window.

وكانت ابنة التاجر تنظر من النافذة.

She happened to see her parents in the garden.

لقد صادف أن رأت والديها في الحديقة.

She could see the rags they were wearing.

تمكنت من رؤية الخرق التي كانوا يرتدونها.

Her eyes filled with tears at the sight.

إمتلأت عيناها بالدموع عند هذا المنظر.

She could not believe what she saw.

لم تستطع أن تصدق ما رأته.

Her parents had come to her for work.

لقد جاء والداها إليها من أجل العمل.

She immediately called her servants.

اتصلت على الفور بخدمها.

"Outside in the garden are my parents"

في الخارج في الحديقة والديّ

"Please offer them these fine clothes"

أرجو أن تقدم لهم هذه الملابس الجميلة

"And ask them to come into the palace"

واطلب منهم أن يدخلوا القصر

Her servants did as they were told.

ففعلت عبيدها كما قيل لهم.

But her parents were frightened beyond measure.

لكن والديها كانا خائفين للغاية.

They had seen that the tank was finished.

لقد رأوا أن الخزان قد انتهى.

There used to be a strange tradition.

لقد كان هناك تقليد غريب.

In those days human sacrifices were offered.

وفي تلك الأيام كانت تُقدَّم التضحيات البشرية.

One of those occasions was after digging a pool.

إحدى تلك المناسبات كانت بعد حفر بركة.

You can imagine her parents' fear.

يمكنك أن تتخيل خوف والديها.

They had come to dig the water tank.

لقد جاؤوا لحفر خزان المياه.

But now servants were calling them.

ولكن الآن كان الخدم ينادونهم.

They thought they going to be sacrificed.

ظنوا أنهم سوف يتم التضحية بهم.

"Throw away your rags" they said.

تخلص من خرقك قالوا.

"Here, wear these fine clothes"

تفضل، ارتدي هذه الملابس الجميلة

And their fears increased even more.

وزادت مخاوفهم أكثر.

But they did not have to fear for long.

ولكن لم يكن عليهم أن يخافوا لفترة طويلة.

Their rich daughter came out to meet them.

فخرجت ابنتهم الغنية لاستقبالهم.

She hugged and kissed her parents.

عانقت والديها وقبلتهما.

And she told them everything that had happened.

وأخبرتهم بكل ما حدث.

The father felt that she had been right.

شعر الأب أنها كانت على حق.

"You do live from your own fortune"

أنت تعيش من ثروتك الخاصة

The daughter did not blame her father.

لم تلوم الابنة والدها.

And she gave him a large fortune.

وأعطته ثروة كبيرة.

With the money he moved back to the city.

وبالمال عاد إلى المدينة.

Soon he became a merchant again.

وسرعان ما أصبح تاجرًا مرة أخرى.

And he went to distant countries for trade.

وذهب إلى بلاد بعيدة للتجارة.

One day he got ready for another business venture.

وفي يوم من الأيام كان يستعد لمشروع تجاري آخر.

But that day something strange happened.

ولكن في ذلك اليوم حدث شيء غريب.

The ship was ready to leave the port.

وكانت السفينة جاهزة لمغادرة الميناء.

But for some reason the ship did not move.

ولكن لسبب ما لم تتحرك السفينة.

No one could explain what was happening.

لم يتمكن أحد من تفسير ما كان يحدث.

But the merchant had an idea.

ولكن التاجر كان لديه فكرة.

"Perhaps my daughters would like presents"

ربما ترغب بناتي في الحصول على هدايا

"I need to ask them what they would like"

أحتاج أن أسألهم عما يريدون

He went to see his daughters.

ذهب لرؤية بناته.

He asked them what they would like.

سألهم ماذا يريدون.

And he promised to bring them presents.

ووعدهم بإحضار الهدايا.

But the ship would still not move.

ولكن السفينة لن تتحرك.

He had not asked all his daughters.

ولم يسأل جميع بناته.

His youngest daughter was not there.

ولم تكن ابنته الصغرى هناك.

She was living in a different city.

لقد كانت تعيش في مدينة أخرى.

So he ordered his servants go to her palace.

فأمر عبيده بالذهاب إلى قصرها.

The messenger came at the wrong time.

لقد جاء الرسول في الوقت الخطأ.

The young girl was engaged in devotions.

كانت الفتاة منخرطة في العبادة.

But the messenger asked her anyway.

لكن الرسول سألها على أية حال.

She just told him"sobur"

لقد قالت له فقط سوبور

The meaning of this was"wait"

وكان معنى هذا انتظر

But the messenger didn't know this.

ولكن الرسول لم يعلم هذا.

He thought she wanted something called"sobur"

اعتقد أنها تريد شيئًا يسمى سوبور

So he went back to the city of the merchant.

فعاد إلى مدينة التاجر.

And he delivered the message he received.

وأوصل الرسالة التي وصلته.

"Your daughter wants something called 'sobur'"

ابنتك تريد شيئًا يسمى سوبور

This time the ship could move again.

هذه المرة تمكنت السفينة من التحرك مرة أخرى.

So the merchant started on his travels.

فبدأ التاجر رحلته.

He visited many ports on his journey.

زار العديد من الموانئ في رحلته.

And he made good profits from his trades.

وحقق أرباحًا جيدة من تجارته.

Finding the presents was not difficult.

لم يكن العثور على الهدايا صعبًا.

He found everything his oldest daughters wanted.

لقد وجد كل ما أرادته بناته الأكبر سنا.

But his youngest daughter's wish was difficult.

لكن رغبة ابنته الصغرى كانت صعبة.

He could not find the thing called"sobur"

لم يتمكن من العثور على الشيء المسمى سوبور

He asked at every port he came to.

كان يسأل في كل ميناء يصل إليه.

"Do you have something called 'sobur'?"

هل لديكم شيء يسمى سوبور؟

But the merchants all shook their heads.

لكن التجار جميعا هزوا رؤوسهم.

"We've never heard of 'sobur'"

لم نسمع أبدًا عن sobur

His voyage had almost come to its end.

وكانت رحلته قد وصلت تقريبا إلى نهايتها.

He was soon going to head back home.

وكان على وشك العودة إلى المنزل قريبًا.

But he wanted"sobur" for his daughter.

ولكنه أراد الصبر لابنته.

So he went calling through the streets.

فذهب ينادي في الشوارع.

"Sobur, does anyone have sobur?!"

سوبير، هل يوجد أحد لديه سوبرير؟

The son of the King was in his castle.

وكان ابن الملك في قلعته.

He happened to be looking out the window.

لقد كان ينظر من النافذة.

And the calls attracted his attention.

ولفتت المكالمات انتباهه.

Because his name happened to be Sobur.

لأن اسمه كان سوبور.

He came to the merchant to speak with him.

جاء إلى التاجر ليتحدث معه.

"I have the Sobur that you want"

لدي السوبور الذي تريده

"Take this box, but be careful with it"

خذ هذا الصندوق، ولكن كن حذرًا معه

"In the box is a magical feather fan and mirror"

في الصندوق مروحة ريش سحرية ومرآة

"This is the Sobur your daughter wishes for"

هذا هو السوبور الذي تتمنى ابنتك الحصول عليه

The merchant thanked the prince for the box.

شكر التاجر الأمير على الصندوق.

And he returned back to his country.

وعاد إلى بلاده.

He gave the box to his daughter.

أعطى الصندوق لابنته.

But the daughter didn't think about it.

ولكن ابنتها لم تفكر في هذا الأمر.

She thought it was just a common box.

ظنت أنها مجرد صندوق عادي.

She had forgotten about the messenger.

لقد نسيت الرسول.

But one day she decided to open the box.

ولكن في يوم من الأيام قررت أن تفتح الصندوق.

Inside the box she found a beautiful fan.

وجدت داخل الصندوق مروحة جميلة.

In the feather fan there was a beautiful mirror.

في مروحة الريش كانت هناك مرآة جميلة.

She waved the feather fan to cool herself.

لوحت بمروحة الريش لتبرد نفسها.

And Prince Sobur appeared before her.

وظهر أمامها الأمير سوبور.

"You called me, so here I am," he said.

لقد اتصلت بي، لذا أنا هنا، قال.

"What is it you wish for?" he asked.

ما الذي تتمنى؟ سأل.

She was astonished at what she saw.

لقد دهشت مما رأت.

A handsome prince had suddenly appeared!

لقد ظهر أمير وسيم فجأة.

"Who are you?" she asked the prince.

من أنت؟ سألت الأمير.

"And how did you suddenly appear?"

وكيف ظهرت فجأة؟

The Prince explained what had happened.

وأوضح الأمير ما حدث.

"Your father was looking for 'sobur'"

كان والدك يبحث عن سوبور

"I am prince Sobur," he explained.

أنا الأمير سوبور، أوضح.

"I gave your father a box"

لقد أعطيت والدك صندوقًا

"In this box there is a feather fan and mirror"

في هذا الصندوق مروحة ريش ومرآة

"When you shake the feather fan I will appear"

عندما تهز مروحة الريش سأظهر

She asked the prince to stay as a guest.

طلبت من الأمير البقاء كضيف.

And for two days the prince stayed with her.

وأقام الأمير عندها يومين.

And she entertained him in her palace.

واستقبلته في قصرها.

During that time the two fell in love.

خلال تلك الفترة وقع الاثنان في الحب.

They made their vows to each.

لقد قطعوا عهودهم لبعضهم البعض.

And they became husband and wife.

وأصبحا زوجًا وزوجة.

After this the prince returned to his father.

وبعد ذلك عاد الأمير إلى أبيه.

He told him that he had selected a wife.

وأخبره أنه اختار زوجة.

The day for the wedding was decided.

لقد تم تحديد يوم الزفاف.

All the family was invited.

تمت دعوة جميع أفراد العائلة.

And they had a beautiful wedding.

وكان حفل زفافهم جميلا.

But there was a death in the marriage bed.

ولكن كان هناك موت في فراش الزواج.

The six daughters of the merchant were envious.

كانت بنات التاجر الست يشعرن بالحسد.

They were jealous of their sister's success.

وكانوا يغارون من نجاح أختهم.

So they decided to destroy her happiness.

لذلك قرروا تدمير سعادتها.

They broke several glass bottles.

لقد كسروا عدة زجاجات زجاجية.

And they ground the glass into fine powder.

ثم قاموا بطحن الزجاج حتى أصبح مسحوقا ناعما.

Then they scattered the powder on the bed.

ثم قاموا بنثر المسحوق على السرير.

The prince suspected no danger.

لم يشك الأمير في وجود أي خطر.

He laid himself down in the bed.

وضع نفسه على السرير.

Soon he felt an acute pain.

وسرعان ما شعر بألم حاد.

All of his whole body ached.

كان جسده كله يؤلمه.

The powder had gone through his skin.

لقد تسرب المسحوق من خلال جلده.

The prince became restless through pain.

وأصبح الأمير مضطربًا بسبب الألم.

And he started to kick and scream.

وبدأ بالركل والصراخ.

He was taken away to his own country.

لقد تم نقله إلى بلده.

The king and queen were very worried.

وكان الملك والملكة قلقين للغاية.

They consulted all the kingdom's physicians.

فاستشاروا جميع أطباء المملكة.

But their efforts were in vain.

ولكن جهودهم ذهبت سدى.

Day and night the young prince was screaming.

كان الأمير الشاب يصرخ ليلًا ونهارًا.

No one could ascertain the disease.

لم يتمكن أحد من التأكد من المرض.

So they had no way of knowing the remedy.

لذلك لم يكن لديهم أي وسيلة لمعرفة العلاج.

You can imagine the grief of his wife.

يمكنك أن تتخيل حزن زوجته.

The marriage knot had only just been tied.

لـقد تم عقد عقدة الزواج للتو۔

She thought a terrible disease had attacked him.

ظنت أن مرضًا فظيعًا قد أصابه۔

Then he was carried hundreds of miles away.

ثم تم نقله إلى مسافة مئات الأميال۔

She had never been to his country.

لـم تكن قد ذهبت إلى بلده أبدًا۔

But she was determined to go there.

لـكنها كانت مصممة على الذهاب إلى هناك۔

And she was determined to nurse him better.

وكانت مصممة على رعايته بشكل أفضل۔

She put on the garb of a Sannyasi.

لـقد ارتدت زي السانياسي۔

And she carried a dagger in her hand.

وكانت تحمل خنجرًا في يدها۔

And then she set out on her journey.

وبعدها انطلقت في رحلتها۔

The princess was still relatively young.

وكانت الأميرة لا تزال صغيرة نسبيا۔

She was unaccustomed to long journeys.

لـم تكن معتادة على الرحلات الطويلة۔

And she wasn't used to walking so far.

ولم تكن معتادة على المشي لمسافة بعيدة۔

She soon got weary of walking.

سرعان ما سئمت من المشي۔

So she sat under a tree to rest.

فـجلست تحت شجرة لتستريح۔

On the top of the tree there was a nest.

وكان هناك عش في أعلى الشجرة۔

It was the nest of two divine birds.

لـقد كان عشًا لطائرين إلهيين۔

Bihangami and Bihangama lived here.

عاش بيهانجامي وبيهانجاما هنا۔

They were not in their nest at the time.

ولم يكونوا في عشهم في ذلك الوقت.

But two of their chicks were in the nest.

لكن اثنين من صغارهم كانا في العش.

Suddenly the chicks gave a scream.

وفجأة صرخت الكتاكيت.

This roused the half-drowsy princess.

أيقظ هذا الأميرة نصف النعاس.

The little birds had seen huge serpent.

لقد رأى الطيور الصغيرة ثعبانًا ضخمًا.

The snake was about to climb the tree.

وكان الثعبان على وشك تسلق الشجرة.

This would have been the end of the birds.

لقد كان هذا ليكون نهاية الطيور.

But the Sannyasi took out her dagger.

ولكن السانياسي أخرجت خنجرها.

And she cut the serpent in two.

وقطعت الحية إلى نصفين.

Of course even this frightened the young birds.

وبطبيعة الحال، حتى هذا أخاف الطيور الصغيرة.

And they flew from the nest screaming.

وطاروا من العش وهم يصرخون.

Bihangama and Bihangami were on their way back.

وكان بيهانجاما و بيهانجامي في طريق العودة.

They came sailing through the air.

لقد جاؤوا أبحروا في الهواء.

They thought they already knew what had happened.

ظنوا أنهم يعرفون بالفعل ما حدث.

"I don't expect to see our children"

لا أتوقع أن أرى أطفالنا

"The nest will be empty again"

العش سيكون فارغا مرة أخرى

"All our previous children were eaten"

تم أكل جميع أطفالنا السابقين

"They were eaten by our great enemy the serpent"

لقد أكلهم عدونا العظيم الثعبان

"They will have met the same fate"

سيكونون قد لقوا نفس المصير

"I do not hear the cries of my young ones"

لا أسمع صراخ أطفالي

The two birds got to their nest.

وصل الطائران إلى عشهما۔

And as predicted, the nest was empty.

وكما توقعنا، كان العش فارغًا۔

This seemed to confirm their suspicions.

ويبدو أن هذا يؤكد شكوكهم۔

But soon the young birds returned.

ولكن سرعان ما عادت الطيور الصغيرة۔

The divine birds were pleasantly surprised.

لقد تفاجأت الطيور الإلهية بشكل سار۔

The young birds told them what had happened.

وأخبرهم الطيور الصغيرة بما حدث۔

"There was a young Sannyasi under the tree"

كان هناك سانياسي شاب تحت الشجرة

"He destroyed the serpent"

لقد دمر الحية

"He cut the snake in two with his dagger"

قطع الثعبان إلى نصفين بخنجره

The parents went to foot of the tree.

ذهب الوالدان إلى أسفل الشجرة۔

Two halves of the snake were still there.

وكان نصفي الثعبان لا يزالان هناك۔

"The young Sannyasi has saved our offspring"

لقد أنقذ الشاب سانياسي ذريتنا

"I wish we could do him some service in return"

أتمنى أن نتمكن من تقديم بعض الخدمات له في المقابل

The divine bird Bihangama replied.

أجاب الطائر الإلهي بيهانجاما۔

"We shall do our service to HER"

سوف نقوم بخدمتها

"The Sannyasi under the tree is not a man"

السانياسي تحت الشجرة ليس رجلاً

"The Sannyasi under the tree is a woman"

السانياسي تحت الشجرة هي امرأة

"Last night she got married to Prince Sobur"

لقد تزوجت من الأمير سوبور الليلة الماضية

"Shortly after their marriage he was poisoned"

بعد زواجهما بفترة وجيزة تم تسميمه

"His skin was pierced with small shards of glass"

كان جلده منقوبًا بشظايا صغيرة من الزجاج

"His sisters-in-law envied his wife"

أخوات زوجته يحسدن زوجته

"Her sisters spread the powder over the bed"

أخواتها ينثرن المسحوق على السرير

"He is still suffering from his pain"

لا يزال يعاني من آلامه

"But he is in his native land"

لكنه في وطنه

"And now he is at the point of death"

والآن هو على وشك الموت

"Beneath the tree is his heroic bride"

تحت الشجرة توجد عروسه البطلة

"She is wearing the garb of a Sannyasi"

إنها ترتدي زي السانياسي

"And she is going to nurse him"

وهي سوف ترضعه

The Bihangami asked the Bihangama.

سأل البيهانجامي البيهانجاما.

"Is there no cure for the prince?"

هل لا يوجد علاج للأمير؟

"Yes, there is a cure" replied the Bihangama.

نعم، هناك علاج أجاب البيهانجاما.

"There is hardened dung lying on the ground"

هناك روث متصلب ملقى على الأرض

"She must take this hardened dung"

يجب عليها أن تأخذ هذا الروث المتصلب

"Then she must reduce the dung to powder"

ثم يجب عليها أن تحول الروث إلى مسحوق

"And then she must bathe the prince"

وبعد ذلك يجب عليها أن تستحم الأمير

"She must bathe him in seven jars of water"

يجب عليها أن تغسله في سبع جرار من الماء

"Then she must bathe him in seven jars of milk"

ثم يجب عليها أن تحممه في سبع جرار من الحليب

"Then she must apply the powder to his body"

ثم يجب عليها أن تضع المسحوق على جسده

"After this Prince Sobur will get well"

بعد هذا سوف يتعافى الأمير سوبور

"I have no doubts about this remedy"

ليس لدي أي شك في هذا العلاج

The Bihangami saw a problem though.

لكن البيهانغامي رأى مشكلة.

"The princess is but a young girl"

الأميرة ليست سوى فتاة صغيرة

"She cannot walk such a distance"

لا يمكنها المشي مسافة كهذه

"The journey would take her many days"

ستستغرق الرحلة منها أيامًا عديدة

"By that time the poor prince will have died"

بحلول ذلك الوقت سيكون الأمير المسكين قد مات

"I can," replied the Bihangama.

أستطيع ذلك، أجاب البيهانجاما.

"I will take the young lady on my back"

سأحمل الفتاة على ظهري

"I will fly her to Prince Sobur's city"

سأطير بها إلى مدينة الأمير سوبور

"If she takes no presents, I will fly her back"

إذا لم تأخذ أي هدايا، سأعيدها بالطائرة

The merchant's daughter heard this conversation.

سمعت ابنة التاجر هذا الحديث.

She begged the Bihangama to take her on his back.

توسلت إلى البيهانجاما أن يأخذها على ظهره.

And of course the bird willingly consented.

وبطبيعة الحال وافق الطائر طوعا.

First she gathered some of the birds dung.

أولاً جمعت بعضًا من روث الطيور.
And then she reduced the dung to fine powder.
ثم قامت بتحويل الروث إلى مسحوق ناعم.
She was armed with this potent drug.
لقد كانت مسلحة بهذا المخدر القوي.
And she got on the back of the kind bird.
وركبت على ظهر الطائر اللطيف.

The Bihangama flew as fast as lightning.
كانت البيهانجاما تطير بسرعة البرق.
They soon reached Prince Sobur's city.
وسرعان ما وصلوا إلى مدينة الأمير سوبور.
The young Sannyasi went up to the palace.
صعد الشاب السانياسي إلى القصر.
And she spoke to the guards at the gate.
وتحدثت إلى الحراس على البوابة.
"Send word to the king that I have a drug"
أرسل كلمة إلى الملك أن لدي دواء
"This drug will save the prince's life"
هذا الدواء سوف ينقذ حياة الأمير
"Within hours I will have cured the prince"
خلال ساعات سأتمكن من شفاء الأمير
The king had tried all the best doctors.
لقد حاول الملك جميع الأطباء الأفضل.
But no doctor had been able to cure his son.
ولكن لم يتمكن أي طبيب من علاج ابنه.
So he didn't believe the Sannyasi's words.
لذلك فهو لم يصدق كلام السانياسي.
But his councilors advised him otherwise.
ولكن مستشاريه نصحوه بخلاف ذلك.
The Sannyasi ordered for seven jars of water.
طلب السانياسي سبعة جرار من الماء.
And seven jars of milk were ordered.
وطلبوا سبعة جرار من الحليب.
He poured a jar of water on the prince.
سكب جرة من الماء على الأمير.

And he poured a jar of milk on the prince.

وصب على الأمير جرة من الحليب.

He had a feather from the divine bird.

وكان له ريشة من الطائر الإلهي.

And he used the feather to apply the powder.

واستخدم الريشة لتطبيق المسحوق.

All of the prince's body was covered.

وكان جسد الأمير بأكمله مغطى.

This was repeated another six times.

وقد تكرر هذا ست مرات أخرى.

The last treatment did the magic.

العلاج الأخير فعل السحر.

The prince started to feel well again.

بدأ الأمير يشعر بتحسن مرة أخرى.

The king was happier than words can describe.

وكان الملك أكثر سعادة من أن تصفها الكلمات.

"Give the Sannyasi the finest treasures"

أعطوا السانياسي أروع الكنوز

But the Sannyasi refused to take presents.

لكن السانياسي رفضوا قبول الهدايا.

"Let me have the ring on the prince's finger"

دعني أضع الخاتم في إصبع الأمير

The king and the prince were happy.

وكان الملك والأمير سعداء.

And they gave him what he wanted.

وأعطوه ما أراد.

The merchant's daughter hastened back.

عادت ابنة التاجر مسرعة.

The Bihangama was waiting at the sea-shore.

كان البيهانجاما ينتظر على شاطئ البحر.

They reached the tree of the divine birds.

وصلوا إلى شجرة الطيور الإلهية.

The young bride walked back to her palace.

عادت العروس الشابة إلى قصرها.

The following day she shook the magical feather fan.

وفي اليوم التالي هزت مروحة الريش السحرية.

Just as before, her husband appeared.

كما في السابق، ظهر زوجها.

Of course he was happy to see his wife.

وبطبيعة الحال كان سعيدا برؤية زوجته.

But he was infinitely surprised.

ولكنه فوجئ إلى حد كبير.

She had his ring on her finger.

كان خاتمه في إصبعها.

His own wife was his doctor.

وكانت زوجته طبيبته.

It was his wife that had cured him!

لقد كانت زوجته هي التي شفاه

The prince took his bride to his palace.

أخذ الأمير عروسه إلى قصره.

He forgave his sisters-in-law.

لقد سامح أخوات زوجته.

They lived happily for many years.

لقد عاشوا بسعادة لسنوات عديدة.

And they were blessed with children.

ورزقوا بالأولاد.

The Origins of Opium
أصول الأفيون

Once upon on a time there lived a Rishi.

ذات مرة كان هناك ريشي.

He lived on the banks of the holy Ganges.

كان يعيش على ضفاف نهر الجانج المقدس.

This Rishi was a very religious man.

كان هذا الريشي رجلاً متدينًا للغاية.

He spent his days performing religious rites.

كان يقضي أيامه في أداء الشعائر الدينية.

From sunrise to sunset he sat on the river bank.

من شروق الشمس إلى غروبها كان يجلس على ضفة النهر.

For the whole time he sat engaged in devotion.

لقد جلس طيلة الوقت منخرطًا في العبادة.

At night he took shelter in his hut.

وفي الليل لجأ إلى كوخه.

His hut was made from palm-leaves.

وكان كوخه مصنوعًا من سعف النخيل.

The palms he had grown from saplings.

أشجار النخيل التي زرعها من الشتلات.

There was no one around for miles.

لم يكن هناك أحد حولنا لعدة أميال.

However, in the hut there was a mouse.

ولكن كان هناك فأر في الكوخ.

She lived from what the Rishi left for her.

لقد عاشت على ما تركه لها الريشي.

The Rishi was a kind-hearted man.

وكان الريشي رجلاً طيب القلب.

He would not hurt any living thing.

لن يؤذي أي كائن حي.

So our mouse never ran away from him.

لذلك فإن فأرنا لم يهرب منه أبدًا.

In fact, our mouse went to him.

في الواقع، ذهب فأرنا إليه.

She touched his feet when he was sitting.

لمست قدميه عندما كان جالسا.

And she enjoyed playing with him.

وكانت تستمتع باللعب معه.

The Rishi also liked the little mouse.

كما أحب الريشي الفأر الصغير.

So he wanted to be kind to her.

فأراد أن يكون لطيفًا معها.

And he wanted someone to talk to.

وأراد شخصًا ليتحدث معه.

So he gave her the power of speech.

فأعطاها القدرة على الكلام.

One night the mouse stood up.

في إحدى الليالي وقف الفأر.

She got onto her hind legs.

لقد وقفت على رجليها الخلفيتين.

And she stood in front of the Rishi.

ووقفت أمام الريشي.

And she put her front paws together.

ووضعت كفوفها الأمامية معًا.

"Holy Sage, you have been kind to me"

الحكيم المقدس، لقد كنت لطيفًا معي

"And you have given me human language"

ولقد أعطيتني لغة بشرية

"I hope it doesn't displease your reverence"

أتمنى أن لا يزعج ذلك احترامك

"But I have one more boon to ask"

ولكن لدي نعمة أخرى أطلبها

The Rishi listened to his mouse.

استمع الريشي إلى فأره.

"What is it?" asked the Rishi.

ما هو؟ سأل الريشي.

"Say what you want, little mouse"

قل ما تريد أيها الفأر الصغير

The mouse answered the Rishi.

أجاب الفأر الريشي.

"By day your reverence goes to the river"

في النهار، يذهب احترامك إلى النهر

"And there you practice your devotions"

وهناك تمارس عباداتك

"During this time a cat comes to the hut"

في هذا الوقت تأتي قطة إلى الكوخ

"This cat has been trying to catch me"

هذه القطة تحاول الإمساك بي

"She still has some fear of your reverence"

لا تزال لديها بعض الخوف من احترامك

"Otherwise she would have eaten me long ago"

وإلا لكانت أكلتني منذ زمن طويل

"But I fear the cat will eat me someday"

لكنني أخشى أن تأكلني القطة يومًا ما

"So I have one prayer to ask of you"

لذا لدي صلاة واحدة أريد أن أطلبها منك

"Please may I be changed into a cat!"

من فضلك هل يمكن أن أتحول إلى قطة

"Then I would be a match for my foe"

ثم سأكون ندًا لعدوي

The Rishi understood the mouse's plight.

لقد فهم الريشي محنة الفأر۔

He threw some holy water on the mouse.

ألقى بعض الماء المقدس على الفأر۔

And the mouse instantly turned into a cat.

وتحول الفأر على الفور إلى قطة۔

She had lived as a cat for some days.

لقد عاشت كقطة لعدة أيام۔

One night she went to the Rishi again.

وفي إحدى الليالي ذهبت إلى الريشي مرة أخرى۔

And the Rishi spoke to his pet.

وتحدث الريشي إلى حيوانه الأليف۔

"Well, little kitty, how are you!"

حسنًا، يا قطتي الصغيرة، كيف حالك

"How do you like your present life!"

كيف تحب حياتك الحالية؟

The cat thought about what to say.

فـكرت القطة فيما ستقوله۔

But she didn't have to say anything.

لكنها لم تحتاج إلى قول أي شيء۔

The Rishi could tell by her expression.

يمكن للريشي أن يخبر من خلال تعبير وجهها۔

"Why don't you like it?" asked the sage.

لماذا لا يعجبك ذلك؟ سأل الحكيم۔

"Are you not as strong as the other cats!"

أنت لست قويًا مثل القطط الأخرى

"Yes, I am strong enough," answered the cat.

نعم، أنا قوية بما فيه الكفاية، أجاب القط

"Your reverence has made me a strong cat"

احترامك جعلني قطة قوية

"As strong as any cat in the world"

قوية مثل أي قطة في العالم

"Now I do not fear cats anymore"

الآن لم أعد أخاف القطط

"But now I have got a new foe"

ولكن الآن لدي عدو جديد

"By day your reverence goes to the river"

في النهار، يذهب احترامك إلى النهر

"During this time dogs come to the hut"

في هذا الوقت تأتي الكلاب إلى الكوخ

"These dogs have been barking at me"

هذه الكلاب تنبح علي

"And I have been frightened for my life"

وكنت خائفة على حياتي

"So I have one more prayer to ask of you"

لذا لدي صلاة أخرى لأطلبها منك

"Please may I be changed into a dog!"

من فضلك هل يمكن أن أتحول إلى كلب

The Rishi understood the cat's plight.

لقد فهم الريشي محنة القطة۔

He threw some holy water on the cat.

لقد رمى بعض الماء المقدس على القطة.

And the cat instantly became a dog.

واصبح القط كلبًا على الفور.

She lived as a dog for some days.

لقد عاشت ككلب لبعض الأيام.

But one night she spoke to the Rishi.

ولكن في إحدى الليالي تحدثت إلى الريشي.

"I cannot thank your reverence enough"

لا أستطيع أن أشكر احترامك بما فيه الكفاية

"You have been most kind to me"

لقد كنت لطيفًا جدًا معي

"I was but a poor mouse"

لم أكن سوى فأر فقير

"You not only gave me speech"

لم تمنحني القدرة على الكلام فحسب

"But you also turned me into a cat"

لكنك حولتني أيضًا إلى قطة

"And your kindness didn't end there"

ولم يتوقف لطفك عند هذا الحد

"Then you changed me into a dog"

ثم حولتني إلى كلب

"As a dog, however, I suffer greatly"

لكنني، ككلب، أعاني كثيرًا

"I do not get enough to eat"

لا أحصل على ما يكفي من الطعام

"My only food is what you leave me"

طعامي الوحيد هو ما تتركه لي

"That was fine when I was a mouse"

كان ذلك جيدًا عندما كنت فأرًا

"But you have made me much larger"

لكنك جعلتني أكبر بكثير

"And it is not enough to fill my mouth"

ولا يكفي ملء فمي

"OH your reverence, how I envy those monkeys"

يا إلهي، كم أحسد هؤلاء القرود

"They jump about from tree to tree"

إنهم يقفزون من شجرة إلى شجرة

"They eat all sorts of delicious fruits!"

إنهم يأكلون كل أنواع الفواكه اللذيذة

"Please may reverence not get angry"

من فضلك لا تغضب

"I pray to be changed into an monkey"

أدعو أن أتحول إلى قرد

The sage was a very understanding man.

وكان الحكيم رجلاً متفهماً للغاية.

His heart was filled with patience.

وكان قلبه مليئا بالصبر.

He was happy to grant his pet's wish.

كان سعيدًا بتحقيق رغبة حيوانه الأليف.

He threw some holy water on the dog.

لقد رمى بعض الماء المقدس على الكلب.

And the dog instantly became an monkey.

وأصبح الكلب قردًا على الفور.

Our monkey was at first wild with joy.

كان قردنا في البداية في غاية السعادة.

She leaped from one tree to another.

قفزت من شجرة إلى أخرى.

She sucked every luscious fruit.

لقد امتصت كل الفاكهة اللذيذة.

But her joy was short-lived again.

ولكن فرحتها لم تدم طويلا مرة أخرى.

Summer had brought with it its drought.

لقد جلب الصيف معه الجفاف.

Monkeys find it hard to climb down.

القرود تجد صعوبة في النزول.

So she couldn't drink from the river.

لذلك لم تتمكن من شرب من النهر.

She saw how the wild boars lived.

لقد رأت كيف يعيش الخنازير البرية.

All day they splashed in the water.

لقد قضوا اليوم كله يسبحون في الماء.

She envied their life now.

لقد حسدتهم على حياتهم الآن.

"Oh how happy those wild boars are!"

يا له من سعادة تلك الخنازير البرية

"All day their bodies are cooled"

أجسادهم باردة طوال اليوم

"All day they are refreshed by water"

يتم انتشالهم من الماء طوال اليوم

"How I wish I were a wild boar"

كم أتمنى أن أكون خنزيرًا بريًا

That night she went to the Rishi.

ذهبت إلى الريشي في تلك الليلة.

She recounted her troubles to him.

لقد أخبرته بمشاكلها.

She told him all about the wild boars.

لقد أخبرته بكل شيء عن الخنازير البرية.

"Oh how pleasant their lives must be"

يا لها من حياة ممتعة يجب أن تكون

And she begged to be changed again.

وتوسلت أن تتغير مرة أخرى.

"I pray to be changed into a wild boar"

أدعو أن أتحول إلى خنزير بري

The sage's kindness knew no bounds.

لم يكن لطف الحكيم حدودًا.

and he complied with his pet's request.

وامتثل لطلب حيوانه الأليف.

He threw some holy water on the monkey.

ألقى بعض الماء المقدس على القرد.

And the monkey instantly became a wild boar.

وتحول القرد على الفور إلى خنزير بري.

Our boar was now very content.

لقد أصبح خنزيرنا الآن سعيدًا جدًا.

She kept her body soaking wet.

لقد أبقت جسدها مبللاً.

Every day she went to the river.

كانت تذهب إلى النهر كل يوم.

She splashed about in her favorite element.

لقد كانت تتجول في عنصرها المفضل.

But life is not safe for wild boars.

لكن الحياة ليست آمنة بالنسبة للخنازير البرية.

One day the king was out hunting.

ذات يوم كان الملك خارجًا للصيد.

He was riding on an adorned elephant.

وكان يركب على فيل مزين.

Only by luck did our wild boar escape.

بفضل الحظ فقط تمكن خنزيرنا البري من الهروب.

She thought a lot about her experience.

لقد فكرت كثيرًا في تجربتها.

She dwelt on the dangers of her life.

تحدثت عن مخاطر حياتها.

And she envied the stately elephant.

وكانت تحسد الفيل المهيب.

The elephant was more fortunate than her.

وكان الفيل أكثر حظا منها.

He got to carry the king on his back.

لقد حصل على حمل الملك على ظهره.

Now she longed to be an elephant.

والآن أصبحت تتوق إلى أن تصبح فيلًا.

And at night she besought the Rishi.

وفي الليل توسلت إلى الريشي.

Our elephant was roaming the wilderness.

كان فيلنا يتجول في البرية.

On her adventures she saw the king.

وفي مغامراتها رأت الملك.

Our elephant went towards the king's suite.

ذهب فيلنا نحو جناح الملك.

She had every intention of being caught.

لقد كانت تنوي أن يتم القبض عليها.

The king saw the elephant from a distance.

رأى الملك الفيل من بعيد.

He couldn't help but admire her beauty.

لم يستطع إلا أن يعجب بجمالها.

He gave his orders to his servants.

وأعطى أوامره لخدمه.

"Catch and tame this elephant"

امسك هذا الفيل وقم بترويضه

Our elephant was easily caught.

لقد تم القبض على فيلنا بسهولة.

She was taken into the royal stables.

تم اصطحابها إلى الاسطبلات الملكية.

And she was tamed without any trouble.

وتم ترويضها دون أي مشكلة.

One day the queen had a wish.

ذات يوم كان للملكة أمنية.

She wished to go to the holy Ganges.

كانت ترغب في الذهاب إلى نهر الجانج المقدس.

She wished to bathe in the holy waters.

كانت ترغب في الاستحمام في المياه المقدسة.

The king wanted to accompany his wife.

أراد الملك مرافقة زوجته.

So he made his orders to his servants.

فأصدر أوامره إلى عبيده.

"Bring us the newly caught elephant"

أحضروا لنا الفيل الذي تم اصطياده حديثًا

The king and queen mounted on her back.

ركب الملك والملكة على ظهرها.

Our elephant had gotten her wish.

لقد حصل فيلنا على أمنيته.

Well... she seemed to have gotten her wish.

حسنًا...يبدو أنها حصلت على أمنيتها.

The king had mounted on her back.

وكان الملك راكبا على ظهرها.

But no, the elephant didn't get her wish.

ولكن لا، الفيل لم يحصل على أمنيته.

She looked upon herself as a lordly beast.

لقد نظرت إلى نفسها كوحش سيد.

She could not a woman riding on her back.

لم يكن بوسعها أن تركب امرأة على ظهرها.

It wasn't enough that she was a queen.

لم يكن كافيا أنها كانت ملكة.

She could not bear the idea of it.

لم تستطع أن تتحمل الفكرة.

She felt she had been degraded.

شعرت أنها تعرضت للإهانة.

She jumped up as violently as elephants can.

لقد قفزت بعنف كما يفعل الفيلة.

Both the king and queen fell to the ground.

سقط الملك والملكة على الأرض.

The king carefully picked up the queen.

إلتقط الملك الملكة بعناية.

He took the queen in his arms.

أخذ الملكة بين ذراعيه.

He asked her whether she had been hurt.

سألها إذا كانت قد أصيبت بأذى.

He wiped off the dust from her clothes.

مسح الغبار عن ملابسها.

And he tenderly kissed her a hundred times.

وقبلها بحنان مائة مرة.

Our elephant witnessed the king's caresses.

لقد شهد فيلنا مداعبات الملك.

And she scampered off to the woods.

وهربت إلى الغابة.

She ran as fast as her legs could carry her.

ركضت بأسرع ما يمكن أن تحمله ساقاها.

As she ran, she thought within herself;

وبينما كانت تركض، فكرت في نفسها؛

"I have experienced many different lives"

لقد عشت حياة مختلفة كثيرة

"And I have experienced different happiness"

ولقد عشت سعادة مختلفة

"But those lives cannot be compared"

ولكن لا يمكن مقارنة هذه الأرواح

"A queen is the happiest creature of all"

الملكة هي أسعد مخلوق على الإطلاق

"Of what infinite regard is she the object of!"

ما هو الاهتمام اللانهائي الذي تحظى به؟

"The king lifted her off the ground"

رفعها الملك عن الأرض

"And he carefully took her in his arms"

وأخذها بين ذراعيه بعناية

"He made many tender inquiries to her"

لقد وجه لها العديد من الاستفسارات الحساسة

"And he wiped off the dust from her clothes"

ومسح الغبار عن ثيابها

"And he kissed her a hundred times!"

وقبلها مائة مرة

"Oh, the happiness of being a queen!"

يا لها من سعادة أن أكون ملكة

"I must ask the Rishi to make me a queen!"

يجب أن أطلب من الريشي أن يجعلني ملكة

The sun was just about to set.

وكانت الشمس على وشك الغروب.

Our elephant made it back to the hut.

لقد عاد فيلنا إلى الكوخ.

The Rishi had just finished his devotions.

لقد انتهى الريشي للتو من عباداته.

She fell on the ground at his feet.

سقطت على الأرض عند قدميه.

She was still the little mouse.

لقد كانت لا تزال الفأر الصغير.

And he was still the holy sage.

وكان لا يزال الحكيم المقدس.

"What's the news?" inquired the Rishi.

ما هي الأخبار؟ سأل الريشي.

"Why have you left the king's palace!"

لماذا غادرت قصر الملك؟

Our elephant thought about her words.

فكر فيلنا في كلماته.

"What shall I say to your reverence!"

ماذا أقول لجلالتك؟

"You have been very kind to me"

لقد كنت لطيفًا جدًا معي

"You have granted every wish of mine"

لقد حققت لي كل أمنياتي

"I was a mouse and you gave me speech"

كنت فأرًا وأعطيتني الكلام

"But as a mouse my life was in danger"

ولكن كفأر، كانت حياتي في خطر

"You saved me by turning me into a cat"

لقد أنقذتني بتحويلي إلى قطة

"But as a cat my life was no safer"

لكن كقطة لم تكن حياتي أكثر أمانًا

"And you helped me become a dog"

ولقد ساعدتني في أن أصبح كلبًا

"But as a dog I had not enough to eat"

ولكن ككلب لم يكن لدي ما يكفي من الطعام

"You provided for me again"

لقد وفرت لي احتياجاتي مرة أخرى

"And you turned my into a monkey"

وحولتني إلى قرد

"I had all I could wish to eat"

لقد تناولت كل ما كنت أتمنى أن آكله

"But I had no way of cooling my body"

ولكن لم يكن لدي أي وسيلة لتبريد جسدي

"You helped me with this too"

لقد ساعدتني في هذا أيضًا

"And you turned me into a wild boar"

وحولتني إلى خنزير بري

"Wild boars have a comfortable life"

الخنازير البرية تعيش حياة مريحة

"But they don't live without danger"

ولكنهم لا يعيشون دون خطر

"And again you protected me"

ومرة أخرى حميتني

"And you turned me into an elephant"

وحولتني إلى فيل

"Being an elephant has increased my bulk"

كوني فيلًا زاد من حجمي

"But being an elephant has not increased my happiness"

لكن كوني فيلًا لم يزيد من سعادتي

"I have one more boon to ask of you"

لدي نعمة أخرى أطلبها منك

"It will be the last boon I ask for"

ستكون هذه آخر نعمة أطلبها

"I see now who the happiest creature is"

أرى الآن من هو أسعد مخلوق

"A queen is the happiest in the world"

الملكة هي أسعد امرأة في العالم

"Holy father, please make me a queen"

يا أبانا القديس، من فضلك اجعلني ملكة

"Silly child," answered the Rishi.

طفل أحمق، أجاب الريشي-

"How can I make you a queen!"

كيف يمكنني أن أجعلك ملكة

"Where can I get a kingdom for you!"

أين يمكنني الحصول على مملكة لك

"Where would I find a royal husband!"

أين أجد زوجًا ملكيًا

But the Rishi was still patient.

ولكن الريشي كان لا يزال صبورًا-

"There is one thing I can do for you"

هناك شيء واحد يمكنني أن أفعله من أجلك

"I can change you into a beautiful girl"

أستطيع أن أحولك إلى فتاة جميلة

"You will be as beautiful as a queen"

ستكونين جميلة كالملكة

"You will possess all the charms you need"

ستمتلك كل السحر الذي تحتاجه

"Your charms can captivate a prince's heart"

سحرك قادر على أسر قلب الأمير

"But you must wait for what the gods decide"

ولكن عليك أن تنتظر ما يقرره الآلهة

"They will grant you an interview"

سيمنحونك مقابلة

"Tou will have your chance with a prince!"

ستحصل على فرصتك مع الأمير

Our elephant agreed to the change.

وافق فيلنا على التغيير.

The beast was transformed by the Rishi.

لقد تم تحويل الوحش على يد الريشي.

And now she was a beautiful young lady.

والآن أصبحت شابة جميلة.

The holy sage named her Postomani.

أطلق عليها الحكيم المقدس اسم بوستوماني.

Her name meant 'the poppy-seed lady'.

اسمها يعني سيدة بذور الخشخاش.

Postomani lived in the Rishi's hut.

عاش بوستوماني في كوخ الريشي.

She spent her time tending the flowers.

لقد أمضت وقتها في رعاية الزهور.

And she watered the plants in the garden.

وسقت النباتات في الحديقة.

One day she was sitting at the hut.

وفي يوم من الأيام كانت جالسة في الكوخ.

The Rishi was at the holy Ganges.

وكان الريشي في نهر الجانج المقدس.

A richly dressed man came towards the cottage.

جاء رجل يرتدي ملابس غنية نحو الكوخ.

She stood up to welcome the man.

وقفت للترحيب بالرجل.

And she asked the stranger who he was.

وسألت الغريب من هو؟

"What have you come for?" she asked.

لماذا أتيت؟ سألت.

"I have been on a hunt"

لقد كنت في رحلة صيد

"But we chased the deer in vain"

لكننا طاردنا الغزلان دون جدوى

"Now I am thirsty from the heat"

الآن أنا عطشان من الحر

"I thought that a Rishi lives here"

اعتقدت أن ريشي يعيش هنا

"I had come to ask him for water"

لقد جئت لأطلب منه الماء

"But now I see you live here"

لكنني أرى الآن أنك تعيش هنا

Postomani answered the stranger.

أجاب بوستماني الغريب.

"Look upon this hut as your own"

انظر إلى هذا الكوخ على أنه ملكك

"I am sorry, but we are poor"

أنا آسف، لكننا فقراء

"We cannot offer you any entertainment"

لا يمكننا أن نقدم لك أي ترفيه

"But let me make your visit comfortable"

ولكن دعني أجعل زيارتك مريحة

"Because, I believe you are a king"

لأنني أعتقد أنك ملك

"If I am not mistaken," she added.

إذا لم أكن مخطئا، أضافت.

The stranger smiled in recognition.

ابتسم الغريب عند التعرف عليه.

Postomani then brought a pot of water.

ثم أحضر بوستماني وعاءً من الماء.

She went to wash her royal guest's feet.

ذهبت لتغسل أقدام ضيفها الملكي.

But the visitor did not let her do this.

ولكن الزائر لم يسمح لها بذلك.

"Holy maid, do not touch my feet"

يا فتاة مقدسة، لا تلمسي قدمي

"I am only a Kshatriya," he confessed.

أنا مجرد كشاتريا، اعترف.

"And you are the daughter of a holy sage"

وأنت ابنة حكيم مقدس

"Noble sir;" Postomani begun to confess.

سيدي النبيل، بدأ بوستوماني بالاعتراف.

"I am not the daughter of the Rishi"

أنا لست ابنة الريشي

"And am I not a Brahmani girl either"

وأنا لست فتاة براهمية أيضًا

"There is no harm in me touching your feet"

لا يوجد ضرر في أن ألمس قدميك

"Besides, you are my guest"

بالإضافة إلى ذلك، أنت ضيفي

"And I am bound to wash your feet"

وأنا ملزم بغسل أقدامكم

"Forgive my impertinence," the king wished.

اغفر لي وقاحتي تمنى الملك.

"What caste do you belong to?" he asked.

إلى أي طائفة تنتمي؟ سأل.

"I only know what the sage told me"

أنا أعرف فقط ما قاله لي الحكيم

"I heard my parents were Kshatriyas"

سمعت أن والدي كانا من الكشاتريا

The stranger wanted to know more.

أراد الغريب أن يعرف المزيد.

"May I ask whether your father was a king!"

هل يجوز لي أن أسأل هل كان والدك ملكًا؟

"You have an uncommon beauty," he said.

لديك جمال غير عادي، قال.

"And you possess a stately demeanor"

وأنت تمتلك سلوكًا مهيبًا

"These qualities cannot be worked for"

لا يمكن العمل على هذه الصفات

"It shows that you were born a princess"

هذا يدل على أنك ولدت أميرة

Postomani avoided answering the question.

تجنب بوستوماني الإجابة على السؤال.

Instead she went inside the hut.

وبدلا من ذلك ذهبت إلى داخل الكوخ.

She brought out a tray of delicious fruits.

أخرجت صينية مليئة بالفواكه اللذيذة.

And she set the fruits before the king.

ووضعت الثمار أمام الملك.

The king, however, did not touch the fruits.

ولكن الملك لم يلمس الثمار.

He waited until his question was answered.

انتظر حتى تمت الإجابة على سؤاله.

"I only know what the holy sage says"

أنا أعرف فقط ما يقوله الحكيم المقدس

"He says that my father was a king"

يقول أن والدي كان ملكًا

"But he was overcome in a battle"

ولكنه هُزم في المعركة

"So he, with my mother, fled into the woods"

فهرب هو وأمي إلى الغابة

"My poor father was eaten by a tiger"

لقد أكل النمر والدي المسكين

"My mother closed her eyes as I opened mine"

أغلقت أمي عينيها عندما فتحت عيني

"There was a bee-hive on the tree"

كانت هناك خلية نحل على الشجرة

"I lay at the foot of that tree"

أنا مستلقي عند سفح تلك الشجرة

"Drops of honey fell into my mouth"

سقطت قطرات من العسل في فمي

"The honey maintained the spark inside me"

العسل حافظ على الشرارة بداخلي

"And then the kind Rishi found me"

ثم وجدني ريشي اللطيف

"The holy sage brought me into his hut"

أدخلني الحكيم المقدس إلى كوخه

"This is the simple story of this wretched girl"

هذه هي القصة البسيطة لهذه الفتاة البائسة

"The girl who now stands before the king"

الفتاة التي تقف الآن أمام الملك

"Call not yourself wretched," replied the king.

لا تعتبر نفسك بائسًا، أجاب الملك.

"You are the most beautiful of women"

أنت أجمل النساء

"And you are the loveliest of women"

وأنت أجمل النساء

"You would adorn the grandest palaces"

سوف تزين أعظم القصور

Postomani had gotten her interview.

حصلت بوستوماني على مقابلتها.

She fell in love with the king.

لـقد وقعت في حب الملك.

And the king fell in love with her.

ووقع الملك في حبها.

The Rishi joined them in marriage.

انضم إليهم الريشي في الزواج.

Postomani became the king's favourite queen.

أصبحت بوستوماني الملكة المفضلة للملك.

And the former queen was in disgrace.

وكانت الملكة السابقة في حالة من العار.

But Postomani's happiness was short-lived.

ولكن سعادة بوستوماني لم تدم طويلا.

One day as she was standing by a well.

وفي يوم من الأيام كانت واقفة بجانب بئر.

She was overcome by a moment of giddiness.

لـقد تغلبت عليها لحظة من الدوار.

Fortune had her fall into the water.

لـقد كان الحظ سبباً في سقوطها في الماء.

And she died in the water of the well.

وماتت في ماء البئر.

The Rishi then came to the king.

ثم جاء الريشي إلى الملك.

"O king, grieve not over the past"

يا ملك لا تحزن على الماضي

"What is fixed by fate must come to pass"

ما قدر عليه القدر لابد أن يحدث

"The queen drowned in your well"

غرقت الملكة في بئرك

"But she was not of royal blood"

ولكنها لم تكن من الدم الملكي

"She was born to a family of mice"

ولدت لعائلة من الفئران

"Each evening she came to my hut"

كانت تأتي إلى كوخي كل مساء

"And I gave her the power of speech"

و أعطيتها القدرة على الكلام

"With speech she could express her wishes"

باستخدام الكلام، كانت تستطيع التعبير عن رغباتها

"I changed her according to her wishes"

لقد غيرتها حسب رغبتها

"As a mouse she feared the cat"

كانت تخاف من القطة كالفأر

"And so I changed her into a cat"

وهكذا حولتها إلى قطة

"As a cat she feared the dogs"

كانت تخاف الكلاب كقطة

"And so I changed her into a dog"

وهكذا حولتها إلى كلبة

"As a dog she had not enough to eat"

ككلبة لم يكن لديها ما يكفي من الطعام

"And so I changed her into a monkey"

وهكذا حولتها إلى قرد

"As a monkey she couldn't bear the heat"

كقرد لم تستطع تحمل الحرارة

"And so I changed her into a wild boar"

وهكذا حولتها إلى خنزير بري

"As a boar her life was not safe"

كخنزير بري لم تكن حياتها آمنة

"And so I changed her into an elephant"

وهكذا حولتها إلى فيل

"That was the elephant you caught"

هذا هو الفيل الذي اصطدته

"But as an elephant she was not loved"

ولكن كفيل لم تكن محبوبة

"And so I changed her one last time"

وهكذا قمت بتغييرها للمرة الأخيرة

"I changed her into a beautiful girl"

لقد حولتها إلى فتاة جميلة

"That is the girl that you married"

هذه هي الفتاة التي تزوجتها

"And that is the girl that drowned"

وهذه هي الفتاة التي غرقت

"Take into favor your former queen"

خذ بعين الاعتبار ملكتك السابقة

"And don't worry for my daughter"

ولا تقلق على ابنتي

"I will make her name immortal"

سأجعل اسمها خالدًا

"Let her body remain in the well"

ليبقى جسدها في البئر

"Fill the well up with earth"

املأ البئر بالتراب

"In her flesh there is a seed"

في جسدها بذرة

"From her bones a tree will grow"

من عظامها تنمو شجرة

"We will name this tree after her"

سنسمي هذه الشجرة باسمها

"The tree shall be called 'Posto'"

ستُسمّى الشجرة بوستو

"This means 'the Poppy tree'"

هذا يعني شجرة الخشخاش

"From this tree there will come a drug"

من هذه الشجرة سيأتي دواء

"This drug will be called opium"

هذا الدواء سوف يسمى الأفيون

"Opium will be a powerful medicine"

الأفيون سيكون دواءً قويًا

"People will consume opium in every epoch"

سوف يستهلك الناس الأفيون في كل عصر

"Opium will either be swallowed or smoked"

سيتم إما ابتلاع الأفيون أو تدخينه

"And opium will be a wonderful narcotic"

وسوف يكون الأفيون مخدرًا رائعًا

"Opium will be used till the end of time"

سيتم استخدام الأفيون حتى نهاية الزمان

"You will recognize the opium smoker"

سوف تتعرف على مدخن الأفيون

"He will have many different qualities"

سيكون لديه العديد من الصفات المختلفة

"One quality for each of the animals"

جودة واحدة لكل من الحيوانات

"The animals which Postomani had lived as"

الحيوانات التي عاش بها بوستوماني

"He will be mischievous, like a mouse"

سيكون مؤذًا، مثل الفأر

"He will be fond of milk, like a cat"

سيكون مولعًا بالحليب، مثل القطة

"He will be quarrelsome, like a dog"

سيكون مشاكسًا كالكلب

"He will be filthy, like a monkey"

سيكون قذرًا، مثل القرد

"He will be savage, like a boar"

سيكون متوحشًا، مثل الخنزير

"He will be confident, like an elephant"

سيكون واثقًا، مثل الفيل

"And he will be high-tempered, like a queen"

وسوف يكون سريع الغضب، مثل الملكة

Strike, but Listen First
اضرب ولكن استمع أولاً

There was once a king who had three sons.

كان هناك ملك وكان له ثلاثة أبناء۔

His royal subjects came to him one day and said;

ف:ي أحد الأيام جاء إليه رعيته من الملوك وقالوا له

"Oh incarnation of justice! hear our plea"

يا تجسيدًا للعدالة اسمع ندائنا

"The kingdom is infested with thieves and robbers"

المملكة مليئة باللصوص والقطاع

"Our property is not safe from their thievery"

ممتلكاتنا ليست في مأمن من سرقتهم

"We pray your majesty to catch hold of these thieves"

نطلب من جلالتكم أن تقبضوا على هؤلاء اللصوص

"We beg you punish them to the full extent of the law"

نرجوكم أن تعاقبوهم إلى أقصى حد يسمح به القانون

The king said to his sons, "Oh, my sons, I am old"

قال الملك لأبنائه :يا أبنائي أنا عجوز۔

"But you are all in the prime of manhood"

ولكنكم جميعا في أوج الرجولة

"How is it that my kingdom is full of thieves?"

كيف تكون مملكتي مليئة باللصوص؟

"I look to you to catch hold of these thieves"

أنظر إليك للقبض على هؤلاء اللصوص

The three princes then made up their minds.

ثم اتخذ الأمراء الثلاثة قرارهم۔

They were going to patrol the city every night.

كانوا سيقومون بدورية في المدينة كل ليلة۔

They set up a watch out in the outskirts of the city.

وأقاموا حراسة على أطراف المدينة.

The early part of the night had arrived.

لقد وصل الجزء المبكر من الليل.

So the eldest prince took on his duties.

فتولى الأمير الأكبر مهامه.

He rode upon his horse through the whole city.

ركب على حصانه في جميع أنحاء المدينة.

But did not see a single thief anywhere he looked.

ولكن لم يرى لصًا واحدًا في أي مكان نظر إليه.

He came back to the policing station.

لقد عاد إلى مركز الشرطة.

The middle part of the night had arrived.

لقد وصل الجزء الأوسط من الليل.

So the second prince took on his duties.

فتولى الأمير الثاني مهامه.

And he too rode through every part of the city.

وركب هو أيضًا في كل جزء من المدينة.

But he did not see or hear of a single thief.

ولكنه لم يرى أو يسمع عن لص واحد.

He came also back to the policing station.

وعاد أيضًا إلى مركز الشرطة.

The latter part of the night had arrived.

لقد وصل الجزء الأخير من الليل.

So the youngest prince took on his duties.

فتولى الأمير الأصغر مهامه.

He went near the gate of his father's palace.

وذهب بالقرب من باب قصر أبيه.

There he saw a beautiful woman leaving the palace.

وهناك رأى امرأة جميلة تغادر القصر.

The prince asked the woman, "who are you?"

سأل الأمير المرأة: من أنت؟

"Where are you going at this hour of the night?"

إلى أين أنت ذاهب في هذا الوقت من الليل؟

The woman answered the young prince.

فأجابت المرأة الأمير الشاب.

"I am Rajlakshmi, the guardian deity of this palace"

أنا راجلاكشمي، الإله الحارس لهذا القصر

"The king will be killed this night"

سيتم قتل الملك هذه الليلة

"I am therefore not needed here"

لذلك لا حاجة لي هنا

"And that is why I am going away"

ولهذا السبب سأرحل

The prince did not know what to make of this message.

ولم يعرف الأمير ماذا يفعل بهذه الرسالة.

After a moment's reflection he said to the goddess;

وبعد لحظة من التفكير قال للإلهة:

"But, suppose the king is not killed tonight"

ولكن لنفترض أن الملك لم يُقتَل الليلة

"Have you any objection to return to the palace?"

هل لديك اعتراض على العودة إلى القصر؟

"I have no objection," replied the goddess.

ليس لدي اعتراض أجابت الإلهة.

The prince then begged the goddess to go back.

ثم توسل الأمير إلى الإلهة أن تعود.

And he promised to do his best to protect the king.

ووعد ببذل قصارى جهده لحماية الملك.

Then the goddess entered the palace again.

ثم دخلت الإلهة القصر مرة أخرى.

Within a moment she disappeared into the palace.

وفي غضون لحظة اختفت داخل القصر.

The prince went straight into the palace too.

وذهب الأمير مباشرة إلى القصر أيضًا.

And he went into the bedroom of his royal father.

ودخل إلى غرفة أبيه الملكي.

There his father lay immersed in deep sleep.

وكان والده هناك غارقًا في نوم عميق.

The king had a second, younger wife.

وكان للملك زوجة ثانية أصغر منه سنًا.

This woman was the stepmother of our prince.

كانت هذه المرأة زوجة أب أميرنا.

She was sleeping in another bed in the room.

كانت نائمة في سرير آخر في الغرفة.

There was a light that was burning dimly.

كان هناك ضوء يحترق بشكل خافت.

But then the prince saw something that surprised him!

ولكن بعد ذلك رأى الأمير شيئًا أدهشه

A huge cobra going round and round the golden bedstead.

كوبرا ضخمة تدور حول السرير الذهبي.

The bedstead on which his father was sleeping.

السرير الذي كان ينام عليه والده.

The prince with his sword cut the serpent in two.

قام الأمير بقطع الثعبان إلى نصفين بسيفه.

But he was not satisfied with killing the cobra.

ولكنه لم يكتف بقتل الكوبرا.

So he cut the cobra up into a hundred pieces.

ثم قام بتقطيع الكوبرا إلى مائة قطعة.

And he put the pieces of the cobra inside a pan.

ووضع قطع الكوبرا داخل المقلاة.

But while cutting the cobra a misfortune happened.

ولكن أثناء تقطيع الكوبرا حدث سوء حظ

A drop of blood fell on the breast of his stepmother.

سقطت قطرة دم على صدر زوجة أبيه.

The prince was in great distress by what had happened.

لقد كان الأمير في حالة من الضيق الشديد بسبب ما حدث.

"I have saved my father, but killed my stepmother"

لقد أنقذت والدي، ولكنني قتلت زوجة أبي

How could he remove the drop of blood from her breast?

كيف يستطيع إزالة قطرة الدم من صدرها؟

He wrapped round his tongue a piece of cloth sevenfold.

ولف على لسانه قطعة من القماش سبع مرات.

And with the cloth he licked up the drop of blood.

وبالقطعة القماشية لعق قطرة الدم.

But his stepmother's sleep was not so deep.

ولكن نوم زوجة أبيها لم يكن عميقاً إلى هذا الحد.

And in his attempt to save her he awoke her.

وفي محاولته لإنقاذها أيقظها.

When opening her eyes she saw it was her stepson.

عندما فتحت عينيها رأت أنه ابن زوجها.

The young prince rushed out of the room.

خرج الأمير الشاب مسرعا من الغرفة.

The queen, hated her stepson, the youngest prince.

كانت الملكة تكره ابن زوجها الأمير الأصغر.

And she had every intention to ruin his reputation.

وكانت لديها كل النية لتدمير سمعته.

She called out to her husband, "My lord, my lord"

فنادت زوجها قائلة: سيدي سيدي.

"Are you awake? are you awake? Rouse yourself up"

هل أنت مستيقظ؟ هل أنت مستيقظ؟ استيقظ

"Here is a nice piece of news for you"

هذه قطعة جميلة من الأخبار لك

The king on awaking inquired what the matter was.

وعندما استيقظ الملك سأل عما حدث.

"What the matter is, my lord, let me tell you"

ما الأمر يا سيدي، دعني أخبرك

"Your worthy son was just here in this room"

كان ابنك الكريم هنا في هذه الغرفة

"The youngest prince, of whom you speak so highly"

الأمير الأصغر، الذي تتحدث عنه بإعجاب شديد

"I caught him in the act of touching my breast"

لقد ضبطته وهو يلمس صدري

"I don't doubt he came with wicked intents"

لا أشك في أنه جاء بنوايا شريرة

The king was horror-struck by what he heard.

لقد أصيب الملك بالرعب مما سمع.

The prince went back to where his brothers kept watch.

عاد الأمير إلى حيث كان إخوته يراقبونه.

But he told them nothing of what had happened.

ولكنه لم يخبرهم بشيء عما حدث.

Early in the morning the king called his eldest son.

وفي الصباح الباكر، نادى الملك ابنه الأكبر.

"I entrust my life and my honor to men"

أسلم حياتي وشرفي للرجال

"But what if one of these men prove faithless?

ولكن ماذا لو ثبت أن أحد هؤلاء الرجال غير مؤمن؟

"How should such a man be punished?"

كيف يُعاقب رجلٌ كهذا؟

The eldest prince replied to his father, the king.

فأجاب الأمير الأكبر والده الملك.

"Doubtless such a man's head should be cut off"

لا شك أن رأس مثل هذا الرجل يجب أن يُقطع

"But first you should establish the facts"

ولكن عليك أولاً التأكد من الحقائق

"You must see whether the man is really faithless"

يجب أن ترى ما إذا كان الرجل غير مؤمن حقًا

"What do you mean?" inquired the king.

ماذا تقصد؟ سأل الملك.

"Let your majesty be pleased to listen"

فليكن جلالتكم مسرورًا بالاستماع

Once upon on a time there lived a goldsmith.

ذات مرة كان هناك صائغ ذهب.

This goldsmith had a son who had a wife.

كان لهذا الصائغ ابن متزوج.

His wife had the rare faculty of understanding beasts.

كانت زوجته تمتلك قدرة نادرة على فهم الوحوش.

But she never told anyone about her uncommon gift.

لكنها لم تخبر أحدا أبدا عن هديتها غير العادية.

Not even her husband knew she could understand animals.

حتى زوجها لم يكن يعلم أنها تستطيع فهم الحيوانات.

One night she was lying in bed beside her husband.

وفي إحدى الليالي كانت مستلقية على السرير بجانب زوجها.

From the river by their house she heard a jackal howl.

ومن النهر بجوار منزلهم سمعت عواء ابن آوى.

"There goes a carcass floating on the river"

هناك جثة تطفو على النهر

"There's a diamond ring on the dead man's finger"

هناك خاتم ألماس في إصبع الرجل الميت

"Will anyone take the ring and give me the corpse?"

هل يأخذ أحد الخاتم ويعطيني الجثة؟

The woman understood the jackal's language.

لقد فهمت المرأة لغة ابن آوى.

She got up from bed and went to the river-side.

نهضت من سريرها وذهبت إلى ضفة النهر.

The husband had not been in deep sleep.

ولم يكن الزوج في نوم عميق.

So with his wife's movements he woke up too.

فبحركة زوجته استيقظ هو أيضاً.

And he followed his wife to see where she went.

وتبع زوجته ليرى إلى أين ذهبت.

But he kept his distance, so that he could observe her.

ولكنه أبقى مسافة بينه وبينها حتى يتمكن من مراقبتها.

The woman went into the water next to their house.

ذهبت المرأة إلى المياه بجوار منزلهم.

She tugged the floating corpse towards the shore.

سحبت الجثة العائمة نحو الشاطئ.

And she saw the diamond ring on the finger.

ورأت خاتم الماس في إصبعها.

She was unable to loosen the ring with her hand.

لم تتمكن من فك الخاتم بيدها.

Because the fingers of the dead body had swelled.

لأن أصابع الجثة كانت متورمة.

So she bit off the finger with her teeth.

فقضمت إصبعها بأسنانها.

And she put the dead body upon land, for the jackal.

ووضعت الجثة على الأرض للآوى.

Then she returned to bed, where her husband already was.

ثم عادت إلى السرير، حيث كان زوجها بالفعل.

The young goldsmith lay almost petrified with fear.

كان الصائغ الشاب مستلقيا على الأرض متحجرا تقريبا من شدة الخوف.

He was convinced he was lying next to a Rakshasi.

لقد كان مقتنعا أنه كان مستلقيا بجانب راكشاسي.

He spent the rest of the night tossing in his bed.

أمضى بقية الليل يتقلب في سريره.

And early in the morning spoke to his father.

وفي الصباح الباكر تحدث إلى والده.

"The woman thou hast given me is not a real woman"

المرأة التي أعطيتني ليست امرأة حقيقية

"The woman thou hast given me to wife is a Rakshasi"

المرأة التي أعطيتني زوجة هي راكشاسي

"Last night I was lying in bed with her"

لقد كنت مستلقيا في السرير معها الليلة الماضية

"By the river I heard the howl of a jackal"

عند النهر سمعت عواء ابن آوى

"My wife too, heard the howl of the jackal"

زوجتي أيضًا سمعت عواء ابن آوى

"Thinking I was asleep; she went towards the howl"

ظنت أنني كنت نائمًا، فذهبت نحو العواء

"I was surprised to see her go out of bed alone"

لقد فوجئت برؤيتها تخرج من السرير بمفردها

"Suspecting some sort of evil, I followed her outside"

اشتبهت في وجود نوع من الشر، فتبعتها إلى الخارج

"But she could not see that I had followed her"

لكنها لم تستطع أن ترى أنني كنت أتبعها

"What did she do, do you think? O horror of horrors!"

ماذا فعلت، برأيك؟ يا للرعب

"From the stream she dragged a dead body out"

سحبت جثة من النهر

"And what do you think she did with the dead body?"

وماذا تعتقد أنها فعلت بالجثة؟

"She wasted no time devouring the dead man!"

لم تضيع أي وقت في التهام الرجل الميت

"All this I had the misfortune to see with my own eyes"

كل هذا كان من سوء حظي أن أرى بأم عيني

"While she feasted on the carcass I went back to bed"

بينما كانت تتغذى على الجثة عدت إلى السرير

"In a few minutes she also returned to bed"

بعد دقائق قليلة عادت أيضًا إلى السرير

"She bolted the door shut, and lay beside me"

أغلقت الباب، واستلقت بجانبي

"Oh my father, how can I live with a Rakshasi?"

يا أبي، كيف يمكنني أن أعيش مع راكشاسي؟

"She will certainly kill me and eat me up one night"

من المؤكد أنها ستقتلني وتأكلني ليلة واحدة

You can imagine the shock of the old goldsmith.

يمكنك أن تتخيل صدمة الصائغ العجوز.

Both father and son agreed about what should be done.

اتفق الأب والابن على ما يجب فعله.

The woman should be taken deep into the forest.

ينبغي أن تؤخذ المرأة إلى عمق الغابة.

And she should be left for wild beasts to devoured.

ويجب أن تتركها لتأكلها الوحوش البرية.

Accordingly, the young goldsmith spoke to his wife.

وبناءً على ذلك، تحدث الصائغ الشاب إلى زوجته.

"My dear love," he said to his wife.

حبيبتي العزيزة قال لزوجته.

"You had better not cook much this morning"

من الأفضل ألا تطبخ كثيرًا هذا الصباح

"Boil a little rice and burn a brinjal"

اسلقي القليل من الأرز وأحرقي الباذنجان

"Because today we are going to see your parents"

لأننا اليوم سنذهب لرؤية والديك

"Your mother and father are dying to see you"

والدتك وأبوك يتوقان لرؤيتك

The woman was full of joy at the unexpected news.

لقد كانت المرأة مليئة بالفرح عند سماعها هذا الخبر غير المتوقع.

She loved returning to her father's house.

لقد أحبت العودة إلى بيت أبيها.

And she finished the cooking in no time.

وانتهت من الطبخ في وقت قصير.

The husband and wife snatched a hasty breakfast.

تناول الزوج والزوجة وجبة إفطار سريعة.

And soon after breakfast they started their journey.

وبعد الإفطار بقليل بدأوا رحلتهم.

The way to her father's house was through dense jungle.

كان الطريق إلى منزل والدها عبر غابة كثيفة.

It was the perfect place to abandon his wife.

لقد كان المكان المثالي للتخلي عن زوجته۔

She was bound to be eaten up by wild beasts there.

كان من المفترض أن تأكلها الوحوش البرية هناك۔

But while they were walking the woman heard a snake.

ولكن بينما كانوا يمشون سمعت المرأة صوت ثعبان۔

"Oh passer-by, in yonder hole there is a frog"

يا عابر سبيل، في تلك الحفرة ضفدع

"How thankful I would be if you caught the frog"

كم سأكون شاكرًا لو تمكنت من اصطياد الضفدع

"And the hole is full of gold and precious stones"

والحفرة مليئة بالذهب والأحجار الكريمة

"Give me the frog, and take the treasure for yourself"

أعطني الضفدع، وخذ الكنز لنفسك

The woman forthwith went to the frog's hole.

ذهبت المرأة على الفور إلى جحر الضفدع۔

And she began digging the hole with a stick.

وبدأت بحفر الحفرة بالعصا۔

The young goldsmith was now quaking with fear.

وكان الصائغ الشاب يرتجف الآن من الخوف۔

He thought his Rakshasi-wife was about to kill him.

كان يعتقد أن زوجته الراكشاشية على وشك قتله۔

And then his wife called for him to help her.

ثم طلبت منه زوجته أن يساعدها۔

"Take all this gold and these precious stones"

خذ كل هذا الذهب وهذه الأحجار الكريمة

The goldsmith did not understand her request.

لم يفهم الصائغ طلبها۔

Timidly he went to where she had dug the hole.

ذهب بخجل إلى المكان الذي حفرت فيه الحفرة۔

But he was infinitely surprised by what he saw.

ولكنه فوجئ إلى حد كبير بما رأى۔

The hole was full of gold and precious stones.

وكان الحفرة مليئة بالذهب والأحجار الكريمة۔

"How did you know there was a treasure here?"

كيف عرفت أن هناك كنز هنا؟

And finally his wife told him of her gift.

وأخيراً أخبرته زوجته بهديتها.

"I can understand all the beasts in the forest"

أستطيع أن أفهم كل الوحوش في الغابة

"Just over there, there is a snake coiled up"

هناك، هناك ثعبان ملفوف

"She had told me there was a treasure here"

لقد أخبرتني أن هناك كنزًا هنا

The husband now felt very blessed with his wife.

الآن أصبح الزوج يشعر بأنه محظوظ جدًا مع زوجته.

"My love, it has gotten very late today"

حبيبتي، لقد تأخر الوقت اليوم كثيرًا

"I don't think we will reach your father's house"

لا أعتقد أننا سنصل إلى منزل والدك

"Nightfall will catch us before we get there"

سوف يفاجئنا الليل قبل أن نصل إلى هناك

"If we stay we might be devoured by wild beasts"

إذا بقينا فقد يلتهمنا الوحوش البرية

"I propose therefore that we both return home"

لذلك أقترح أن نعود إلى المنزل

You can imagine the wife's disappointment.

يمكنك أن تتخيل خيبة أمل الزوجة.

But she agreed with her husband's assessment.

لكنها وافقت على تقييم زوجها.

It took them a long time to reach home.

لقد استغرق الأمر وقتًا طويلاً للوصول إلى المنزل.

They were laden with a large quantity of gold.

لقد كانوا محملين بكمية كبيرة من الذهب.

And they were carrying many precious stones.

وكانوا يحملون أحجاراً كريمة كثيرة.

But eventually the got close to their home.

لكن في النهاية اقتربوا من منزلهم.

"My dear, go by the back door," said the goldsmith.

عزيزتي، اذهبي من الباب الخلفي، قال الصائغ.

"I will go by the front door and see my father"

سأذهب إلى الباب الأمامي وأرى والدي

"And I will show him all this treasure"

وسأريه كل هذا الكنز

So she entered the house by the back door.

فـدخلت إلى البيت من الباب الخلفي.

But the old goldsmith had reason to be there too.

ولكن كان لدى الصائغ العجوز سبب للتواجد هناك أيضًا.

He had gone there to collect a hammer.

لـقد ذهب إلى هناك ليجمع المطرقة.

The old goldsmith saw his Rakshasi daughter-in-law.

رأى الصائغ العجوز زوجة ابنه الراكشاسية.

He concluded she had swallowed up his son.

وخلص إلى أنها ابتلعت ابنه.

And he therefore struck her with the hammer.

فـضربها بالمطرقة.

The blow immediately killed his daughter-in-law.

وأدت الضربة إلى مقتل زوجة ابنه على الفور.

At that moment the son came into the house.

وفي تلك اللحظة دخل الابن إلى البيت.

But it was too late for him to explain.

ولكن كان الوقت قد فات بالنسبة له ليشرح.

And so the eldest prince's story concluded.

وهكذا انتهت قصة الأمير الأكبر.

"You might have to cut a man's head off"

قد تضطر إلى قطع رأس رجل

"But first you should establish the facts"

ولكن عليك أولاً التأكد من الحقائق

"You must see whether the man is really faithless"

يجب أن ترى ما إذا كان الرجل غير مؤمن حقًا

The king then called his second son to him.

ثـم دعا الملك ابنه الثاني إليه.

"I entrust my life and my honor to men"

أسلم حياتي وشرفي للرجال

"But what if one of these men prove faithless?

ولكن ماذا لو ثبت أن أحد هؤلاء الرجال غير مؤمن؟

"How should such a man be punished?"

كيف يُعاقب رجلٌ كهذا؟

The second prince replied to his father, the king.

فـأجاب الأمير الثاني أبيه الملك.

"Doubtless such a man's head should be cut off"

لا شك أن رأس مثل هذا الرجل يجب أن يُقطع

"But first you should establish the facts"

ولكن عليك أولاً التأكد من الحقائق

"What do you mean?" inquired the king.

ماذا تقصد؟ سأل الملك.

"Let your majesty be pleased to listen"

فليكن جلالتكم مسرورًا بالاستماع

Once upon a time there reigned a king.

ذات مرة كان هناك ملك يحكم.

This king was very fond of going out hunting.

كـان هذا الملك يحب الخروج للصيد كثيراً.

One day his horse took him into a dense forest.

ذات يوم أخذه حصانه إلى غابة كثيفة.

He went far from his followers, deep into the woods.

لـقد ابتعد عن أتباعه، وذهب عميقًا في الغابة.

He rode on and on through the endless, quiet forest.

ركب واستمر في السير عبر الغابة الهادئة التي لا نهاية لها.

He saw neither villages nor towns, only trees.

لـم يرى قرى ولا مدنًا، فقط أشجارًا.

On the long, lonely journey he became very thirsty.

فـي رحلته الطويلة الوحيدة، أصبح عطشانًا جدًا.

He could see no pond, nor lake, nor stream.

لـم يتمكن من رؤية بركة، ولا بحيرة، ولا مجرى مائي.

But then he saw something dripping from a tree.

ولكن بعد ذلك رأى شيئًا يتساقط من شجرة.

He concluded it was rainwater resting in a cavity.

وخلص إلى أن هذه مياه الأمطار كانت متجمعة في تجويف.

He stood on horseback beneath the tree, cup in hand.

كـان واقفًا على ظهر حصانه تحت الشجرة، وكأس في يده.

He caught the drops slowly dripping into the small cup.

لـقد التقط القطرات وهي تتساقط ببطء في الكوب الصغير.

The water, however, was not rain from the sky.

ولكن الماء لم يكن مطراً من السماء.

A huge cobra sat on top of the tall tree.

كان هناك كوبرا ضخم يجلس على قمة الشجرة الطويلة.

The snake had struck the tree in rage with its sharp fangs.

لقد ضربت الثعبانة الشجرة بغضب بأنيابها الحادة.

The snake's poison came out and fell downward in heavy drops.

خرج السم من الثعبان وسقط إلى الأسفل على شكل قطرات ثقيلة.

The king thought the falling liquid was simple rainwater.

ظن الملك أن السائل المتساقط كان مجرد مياه مطر.

The horse sensed the danger and tried to warn him.

أحس الحصان بالخطر وحاول تحذيره.

The cup was nearly filled with the deadly snake-poison.

كان الكأس ممتلئًا تقريبًا بسم الثعبان القاتل.

The king raised the cup and prepared to drink.

رفع الملك الكأس واستعد للشرب.

But the horse moved wildly, with the king on its back.

لكن الحصان تحرك بعنف، والملك على ظهره.

The cup fell from his hand, and the poison spilled.

سقط الكأس من يده، وانسكب السم.

The king became angry and struck the horse's neck.

فغضب الملك وضرب عنق الحصان.

The blow from the sword immediately killed his horse.

ضربة السيف قتلت حصانه على الفور.

And so the second prince's story concluded.

وهكذا انتهت قصة الأمير الثاني.

"You might have to cut a man's head off"

قد تضطر إلى قطع رأس رجل

"But first you should establish the facts"

ولكن عليك أولاً التأكد من الحقائق

"You must see whether the man is really faithless"

يجب أن ترى ما إذا كان الرجل غير مؤمن حقًا

The king then called to him his third youngest son.

ثم دعا الملك ابنه الثالث الأصغر.

"I entrust my life and my honor to men"

أسلم حياتي وشرفي للرجال

"But what if one of these men prove faithless?

ولكن ماذا لو ثبت أن أحد هؤلاء الرجال غير مؤمن؟

"How should such a man be punished?"

كيف يُعاقب رجلٌ كهذا؟

"Doubtless such a man's head should be cut off"

لا شك أن رأس مثل هذا الرجل يجب أن يُقطع

"But first you should establish the facts"

ولكن عليك أولاً التأكد من الحقائق

"What do you mean?" inquired the king.

ماذا تقصد؟ سأل الملك.

"Let your majesty be pleased to listen"

فليكن جلالتكم مسرورًا بالاستماع

Once long ago there reigned a wise and noble king.

كان هناك في قديم الزمان ملك حكيم ونبيل.

In his palace he kept a bird of Suka species.

كان يحتفظ في قصره بطائر من نوع سوكا.

One day the bird went out flying into the fields.

في أحد الأيام خرج الطائر ليطير نحو الحقول.

There he saw his father and mother calling from above.

وهناك رأى أباه وأمه يناديان من فوق.

They asked him to come visit them in their nest.

طلبوا منه أن يأتي لزيارتهم في عشهم.

The nest was far away in a distant hidden land.

وكان العش بعيدًا في أرض بعيدة مخفية.

The Suka said, "I'll come if I get king's leave"

قال السوكا سأأتي إذا حصلت على إذن الملك

"I'll speak to the king today and return tomorrow"

سأتحدث مع الملك اليوم وأعود غدًا

"Please wait at this same spot in the morning"

الرجاء الانتظار في نفس المكان في الصباح

That very day, Suka spoke with the gentle, kind king.

في ذلك اليوم، تحدثت سوكا مع الملك اللطيف والطيب.

The king gave permission for the bird to leave.

أعطى الملك الإذن للطائر بالمغادرة.

Although he was sad to part with his bird.

على الرغم من أنه كان حزينًا لفراق طائره.

The next morning, Suka met his parents again.

وفي صباح اليوم التالي، التقى سوكا بوالديه مرة أخرى.

He flew with them to their nest on a tall tree.

طار معهم إلى عشهم على شجرة عالية.

The three birds lived together happily in peaceful joy.

عاشت الطيور الثلاثة معًا بسعادة وفرح وسلام.

They stayed like this for a fortnight of lovely days.

لقد ظلوا على هذا الحال لمدة أسبوعين من الأيام الجميلة.

But even those quiet and pleasant days had to end.

ولكن حتى تلك الأيام الهادئة والممتعة كان لا بد أن تنتهي.

Suka said, "Beloved parents, the king gave me two weeks"

قال سوكا، أيها الآباء الأعزاء، أعطاني الملك أسبوعين

"That time is now over, so I must return tomorrow"

لقد انتهى ذلك الوقت الآن، لذلك يجب أن أعود غدًا

His father and mother agreed and blessed his decision.

وافق والده ووالدته على قراره وباركوه.

They told him to carry a gift for the king.

فأخبروه أن يحمل هدية للملك.

After some talk, they chose some fruit as a gift.

وبعد بعض الحديث، اختاروا بعض الفاكهة كهدية.

The fruit had grown from the Immortality Tree.

لقد نمت الفاكهة من شجرة الخلود.

Early the next morning, Suka went to the tree.

وفي الصباح الباكر التالي، ذهبت سوكا إلى الشجرة.

And he plucked a magical glowing fruit.

وقطف ثمرة سحرية متوهجة.

He held the fruit gently in his beak, full of care.

كان يحمل الفاكهة بلطف في منقاره، مليئًا بالعناية.

The fruit was heavy and slowed his swift flying pace.

كانت الفاكهة ثقيلة وأبطأت من وتيرة طيرانه السريعة.

He could not reach the city before night arrived.

لم يتمكن من الوصول إلى المدينة قبل حلول الليل.

Suka stopped to rest in a tree along the way.

توقفت سوكا للراحة على شجرة على طول الطريق.

He feared the fruit might drop while he slept.

كان يخشى أن تسقط الفاكهة أثناء نومه.

If he kept the fruit in his beak, it could fall.

لو احتفظ بالفاكهة في منقاره، فمن الممكن أن تسقط

But he saw a hole in the trunk of the tree.

ولكنه رأى ثقبًا في جذع الشجرة.

He placed the fruit safely inside the dark tree.

وضع الفاكهة بأمان داخل الشجرة المظلمة.

But inside the hole, there lived a poisonous black snake.

ولكن داخل الحفرة، كان يعيش ثعبان أسود سام.

In the night, the snake bit the fruit with venom.

في الليل، لدغت الثعبان الثمرة بالسم.

And the fruit became smeared with deadly poison.

وأصبحت الثمرة ملطخة بالسم القاتل.

At dawn Suka took the fruit back in his beak.

عند الفجر أخذ سوكا الفاكهة مرة أخرى بمنقاره.

He flew again on his journey to the king's palace.

ثم طار مرة أخرى في رحلته إلى قصر الملك.

As he reached the palace the king was sitting with ministers.

وعندما وصل إلى القصر كان الملك جالساً مع الوزراء.

The king was overjoyed to see Suka return once more.

لقد كان الملك سعيدًا للغاية لرؤية سوكا تعود مرة أخرى.

He greatly admired the beautiful, shining fruit gift.

لقد أعجب كثيرا بهدية الفاكهة الجميلة والمشرقة.

The fruit was lovely to look at and admire.

كانت الفاكهة جميلة للنظر والإعجاب.

It was the finest fruit found across the earth.

لقد كانت أجود الفاكهة التي وجدت على وجه الأرض.

And anyone who ate the fruit was granted immortality.

ومن أكل من الثمرة نال الخلود.

The king was about to eat the beautiful fruit.

وكان الملك على وشك أن يأكل الفاكهة الجميلة.

But his ministers warned him the fruit might be poisoned"

لكن وزراءه حذروه من أن الفاكهة قد تكون مسمومة

"It would be better to test the fruit before you eat it"

من الأفضل تجربة الفاكهة قبل تناولها

He threw the fruit to a crow sitting on the wall.

ألقى الفاكهة إلى الغراب الذي كان يجلس على الحائط

The crow ate from the fruit, and dropped dead instantly.

أكل الغراب من الثمرة فسقط ميتا في الحال.

The king, thinking Suka tried to kill him, grew furious.

لقد غضب الملك بشدة عندما اعتقد أن سوكا يحاول قتله.

He seized the bird and killed him with his bare hands.

فأمسك بالطائر وقتله بيديه العاريتين.

He ordered the seed to be planted outside the city.

وأمر بزرع البذرة خارج المدينة.

The seed became a tree with the same glowing fruit.

أصبحت البذرة شجرة تحمل نفس الثمار المتوهجة.

The king feared the fruit would bring more death.

كان الملك يخشى أن تجلب الفاكهة المزيد من الموت.

So he had the tree fenced off and guarded.

لذلك قام بتسييج الشجرة وحراستها.

There lived in that city an old, poor Brahman man.

كان يعيش في تلك المدينة رجل براهماني عجوز فقير.

He and his wife survived only on the town's charity.

لقد عاش هو وزوجته على المساعدات الخيرية التي تقدمها المدينة فقط

One day the Brahman mourned his long, miserable, life.

ذات يوم حزن البراهمي على حياته الطويلة البائسة.

He said, "Instead of begging, I will eat poison fruit."

قال «ال» :بدلاً من التوسل، سأأكل فاكهة مسمومة.

"I'll end my life beneath that deadly tree in silence."

سأنهي حياتي تحت تلك الشجرة القاتلة في صمت.

That very night, he rose quietly and left his home.

وفي تلك الليلة استيقظ بهدوء وخرج من منزله.

His wife suspected and followed behind in silence.

اشتبهت به زوجته وتبعته في صمت.

She had decided to die too, alongside her sad husband.

لقد قررت أن تموت أيضًا، إلى جانب زوجها الحزين.

She loved him deeply and didn't wish to stay behind.

لقد أحبته بشدة ولم ترغب في البقاء خلفه.

The palace guard was asleep that night, unaware of visitors.

وكان حرس القصر نائما تلك الليلة، ولم يكن على علم بالزوار.

The Brahman reached the garden and plucked a hanging fruit.

وصل البراهمان إلى الحديقة وقطف ثمرة معلقة.

He looked at it once and ate the entire fruit.

نظر إليها مرة واحدة وأكل الثمرة كاملة.

His wife cried, "If you die, my life becomes nothing"

صرخت زوجته قائلة :إذا مت، تصبح حياتي لا شيء.

"I will also eat and die here with you now"

سأأكل وأموت هنا معك الآن أيضًا

So saying she plucked a fruit and ate it.

فـقالت ذلك وهي تقطف ثمرة وتأكلها.

They thought the poison would act slowly through the night.

ظنوا أن السم سيعمل ببطء طوال الليل.

So they both went home and quietly lay down in bed.

فـذهبا كلاهما إلى المنزل واستلقيا بهدوء على السرير.

They believed they would never again rise from sleep.

لـقد اعتقدوا أنهم لن يستيقظوا من النوم مرة أخرى.

To their surprise, they woke up feeling full of life.

وإلى دهشتهم، استيقظوا وهم يشعرون بالحياة.

Not only were they alive, but they were young again.

ولم يكونوا على قيد الحياة فحسب، بل أصبحوا شبابًا مرة أخرى.

And they were strong and had new found energy.

وكانوا أقوياء واكتسبوا طاقة جديدة.

Neighbors hardly recognized them, so changed they looked.

لـم يتمكن الجيران من التعرف عليهم بسهولة، فقد بدوا مختلفين للغاية.

The old Brahman was now handsome and full of youth.

لـقد أصبح البراهمان العجوز الآن وسيمًا ومليئًا بالشباب.

His grey hair vanished, and had colour again.

لـقد اختفى شعره الرمادي، وأصبح له لون مرة أخرى.

His wrinkled cheeks turned smooth, and his skin shone.

أصبحت خدوده المتجعدة ناعمة، وبشرته تتألق.

And as for his wife, she became extremely beautiful.

وأما امرأته فأصبحت جميلة جداً.

She looked as beautiful as any lady of the kingdom.

لـقد بدت جميلة مثل أي سيدة في المملكة.

The king heard of their miraculous transformation.

سمع الملك عن تحولهم العجيب.

He asked his guards to send the Brahman to him.

وطلب من حراسه أن يرسلوا إليه البراهمان.

And he asked the Brahman the source of his youth.

وسأل البراهمان عن مصدر شبابه.

The Brahman told the king every detail of the story.

أخبر البراهمي الملك بكل تفاصيل القصة.

The king then wept for his poor, loyal pet bird.

فبكى الملك على طائره الأليف المخلص والمسكين.

He deeply regretted killing his faithful bird.

لقد ندم بشدة على قتل طائره الوفي.

And he wished he had known the bird's loyalty.

وتمنى لو أنه عرف وفاء الطائر.

And so the second prince's story concluded.

وهكذا انتهت قصة الأمير الثاني.

"You might have to cut a man's head off"

قد تضطر إلى قطع رأس رجل

"But first you should establish the facts"

ولكن عليك أولاً التأكد من الحقائق

"You must see whether the man is really faithless"

يجب أن ترى ما إذا كان الرجل غير مؤمن حقًا

"I know Your Majesty suspects me of evil last night"

أعلم أن جلالتك تشك في شري الليلة الماضية

"Please allow me to explain myself before punishing me"

أرجو أن تسمحوا لي أن أشرح نفسي قبل معاقبتي

"While making rounds I saw a woman leave the palace"

أثناء تجولي رأيت امرأة تغادر القصر

"I stopped her, and she said her name was Rajlakshmi"

أوقفتها، وقالت إن اسمها راجلاكشمي

"She claimed to be the guardian deity of the palace"

ادعت أنها الإلهة الحارسة للقصر

"She said she was leaving because death was near"

قالت إنها ستغادر لأن الموت كان قريبًا

"The king," she said, "would be killed later that night"

قالت»: «سيُقتل الملك في وقت لاحق من تلك الليلة.

"I begged her to go back into the palace"

توسلت إليها أن تعود إلى القصر

"And I promised to do my best to protect you."

ووعدتك بأن أبذل قصارى جهدي لحمايتك.

"I ran quickly into Your Majesty's chamber without delay."

ركضت بسرعة إلى غرفة جلالتك دون تأخير.

"There I saw a cobra circling your golden bedstead."

هناك رأيت كوبرا يحوم حول سريرك الذهبي.

"I fought the snake and killed it with my blade."

حاربت الثعبان وقتلته بشفرتي.

"I chopped the body into many exactly one hundred pieces."

لقد قمت بتقطيع الجسد إلى مائة قطعة بالضبط

"I placed those pieces inside the pan for proof."

وضعت تلك القطع داخل المقلاة كدليل.

"But something occurred as I was cutting up the snake."

ولكن حدث شيء ما بينما كنت أقوم بتقطيع الثعبان.

"A drop of blood fell onto the breast of your wife."

سقطت قطرة دم على صدر زوجتك ـ

"I feared I had saved my father, but killed my stepmother."

خشيت أن أكون قد أنقذت والدي، ولكنني قتلت زوجة أبي.

"I wrapped my tongue tightly with cloth seven times."

لففت لساني بقطعة قماش سبع مرات.

"Then I licked up the drop of venomous blood."

ثم لعقت قطرة الدم السامة.

"While I was licking the blood, my stepmother awoke."

بينما كنت ألعق الدم، استيقظت زوجة أبي.

"She saw me and opened her eyes with confusion."

لقد رأتني وفتحت عينيها في حيرة.

"This is the truth of what I did last night."

هذه هي حقيقة ما فعلته الليلة الماضية.

"If Your Majesty commands, then cut off my head now."

إذا أمر جلالتك، فاقطع رأسي الآن.

The king, full of love and joy, embraced his son.

احتضن الملك ابنه بكل حب وفرح.

From that moment, he loved him more than ever before.

ومنذ تلك اللحظة أحبه أكثر من أي وقت مضى.

www.ingramcontent.com/pod-product-compliance
Lightning Source LLC
Chambersburg PA
CBHW010429170726
48283CB00011B/3122